Cathy Kelly lives in Dublin. She is a feature writer and film critic for the *Sunday World* newspaper in Ireland, where she also writes the *Dear Cathy* agony column. Her first novel, *Woman to Woman*, became an instant bestseller, spending eight weeks at Number One on the *Irish Times* bestseller list and eight weeks in the *Sunday Times* Top Ten.

Praise for *Woman to Woman*:

'A compulsive read'   *Woman's Weekly*

'An unprecedented success story for a debut novel' *Sun*

'All the ingredients of the blockbuster are here ... a page turner'   *Sunday Independent*

'A *tour-de-force* of the Jilly Cooper genre'   *Lifetimes*

'Funny and clever'   *Sunday World*

'Move over Maeve Binchy – Ireland could have a new writing queen ...'   *Star*

SHE'S THE ONE

CATHY KELLY

headline

ISBN 0 7472 6057 5

Typeset by
Letterpart Limited, Reigate, Surrey

Printed and bound in Great Britain by
Mackays of Chatham PLC, Chatham, Kent

HEADLINE BOOK PUBLISHING
A division of Hodder Headline PLC
338 Euston Road
London NW1 3BH

To John, with all my love, always,
and to Kate, I'll never forget you.

Writing acknowledgements is almost harder than the book because I know I'll leave somebody out! But here goes: my heartfelt thanks to my darling John for everything; to my dear family for their help and support, especially my ever supportive Mum, Dad, Lucy, Fran, Anne, Laura and Naomi. And of course to my beloved Tamsin.

Thanks to my dear friend Sarah Hamilton and my favourite nephew Jamie; thanks to Ros Edwards and Helenka Fuglewicz for being marvellous agents; thanks to my girl friends Lisa, Esther, Liz, Joanne, Mairead, Annie and Moira for constant encouragement and thanks to all my colleagues and friends at *Sunday World* – you know who you are; also thanks to Patricia Scanlan for wonderful phone calls and Sally Hamwee for legal expertise.

Special thanks to my wonderful publishing families at Headline and Poolbeg. It's a pleasure working with all of you.

Thanks to dear Clare Foss who is the most marvellously kind editor. Special thanks to Amanda Ridout, Frances, Rebecca, James, Sarah, Ros and all the other people I just know I'm leaving out at Headline who have been so welcoming.

Thanks to Paula, Gaye, Elaine, Emer, Conor, Sarah, Nicole, Phillip, Connor, Kieran and everybody at Poolbeg who have been so marvellous to me and thanks to Margaret Daly for publicity.

Thank you to all the journalists and reviewers who said such lovely things the last time; I really appreciated it all. And thanks to the lovely booksellers I've met throughout Ireland and the UK who were so helpful and kind to me during my first terrifying tour.

Thanks to family friends John and Mary Kelly, John and Joan Gourley and Liz, Arthur and everyone at Kilmurray for their support during Dad's illness, and thanks to Professor Brian Lawlor, all the amazing staff at the Delaney Ward, St Patrick's Hospital, the staff at the Kylemore Clinic and the Alzheimer Society of Ireland.

Thank you so much to the people who liked *Woman to Woman* and to those who sent me fantastic letters telling me so. I hope you like this.

Finally, thanks to Kate Cruise O'Brien who tragically died earlier this year. A wonderful editor and an incredible person, she was a huge loss to everybody. Like everyone who knew Kate, I miss her and I will never forget her.

CHAPTER ONE

Dear Annie,

I hope you can help me. I've been married two months and my marriage is already a disaster. We didn't live together before we got married so I never dreamed it could be like this. I have a demanding job and so does my husband, but he still leaves all the housework to me. It doesn't matter what time I get home, I'm supposed to get dinner and I end up spending all my weekends trying to sort out the house, wash the clothes and iron his shirts. He always leaves the shopping to me, even when he has a day off. He says his mother always did that sort of thing. I can't believe that I didn't know he was like this before we got married.

What can I do? I'm going mad about this and I can't talk to anyone because everyone thinks we're the perfect couple. Please help before my marriage is ruined.

Depressed

Dee paused, fingers poised over the computer keyboard as she looked at the handwritten letter again. Sometimes it took ages to think up replies to the *Dear Annie* letters, especially those from people who needed a miracle by way of an answer, instead of advice on how to improve their relationship with a child-free weekend away somewhere romantic and a bottle of sensual massage oil.

Dee couldn't always get her brain working properly when it came to composing her replies, so she frequently took refuge in the biscuit tin. Today wasn't one of those days. Today she didn't have to think twice because, ironic though it was, she knew exactly how to answer this one.

Dear Depressed,
    You've no idea how common your problem is and my postbag is full of pleas for help from women who thought they were marrying Mr Right and found out too late that they'd inadvertently got hitched to Mr-My-Mother-Always-Did-It-That-Way-And-Reared-10-Kids, Four-Goats-And-Still-Made-Her-Own-Bread.
    You've got to take action or you may as well buy an apron with the word 'Slave' on it.
    First, stop doing all the shopping, hoovering, washing, ironing – and wait until he notices. Believe me, he will . . .

Dee stopped typing. She leant back and massaged her neck with one hand. She was completely exhausted after spending the whole week in the Central Criminal Court reporting on a murder trial and really didn't feel up to spending Saturday, her first day off in ten days, working on her agony column.

She wanted to laze in a bath filled with relaxing aromatherapy stuff, with a thirst-quenching Bacardi and Coke, and a fat, juicy novel by her side. If she felt up to it, she might even shave her legs before they started looking as if they belonged to a Greek taxi driver. Then again, maybe she'd stick to relaxing. Who the hell was going to see her legs? Not Gary, that was for sure. The only legs he noticed these days were incredibly hairy, wore shorts topped with sports jerseys and their owners answered to the name of Manchester United Football Club.

She sighed. The bath would have to wait until she'd finished her column. *Dear Annie* ran in the *Sentinel* on Mondays and Wednesdays and, short of phoning the women's editor from an ambulance bearing her to hospital with a bout of pleurisy, Dee had to produce a column by eleven on Sunday. It would take at least three hours to write. Maybe Gold Blend and a digestive or three would loosen the knot in her neck. Or maybe she'd have one of those Weight Watcher mini cheesecakes she'd hidden at the back of the bottom shelf in the freezer.

They were practically calorie-free. Well, they *had* to be or they wouldn't be called Weight Watchers. One cheesecake wouldn't be too bad. And she'd had Special K and anaemic skimmed milk for breakfast, so she was due a treat.

Dee left the tiny spare room that doubled as her office and made her way past the overflowing wicker linen basket. She tried to ignore it but she couldn't.

Somebody had to do it, she thought crossly, grabbing an armful of wet towels, Gary's soccer jersey and several of his greying T-shirts.

Arms full of laundry, she negotiated the stairs, ignoring the wisps of marmalade cat-hair which covered the dark mulberry carpet in fetching little balls of fluff. Why did Smudge insist on completing her laborious grooming routine on the stairs instead of doing it in the kitchen on the lino? Dee wondered gloomily. To make matters worse, the hoover was kaput and she didn't have the energy to take it to the electrical shop to get it fixed. She stepped over a dusty pile of Gary's soccer magazines which he'd stacked haphazardly at the bottom of the stairs.

'I'll take them up later!' he'd snapped on Thursday night when she'd tripped over what had to be six months' worth of *Soccer Fanatic* magazines. 'For God's sake, Dee, give me a break! I can't spend my whole bloody life cleaning up, can I?'

Then he'd stomped off into the sitting-room. Dee had barely dropped her bulging black briefcase on the floor beside the coat stand before she heard Sky Sports blaring from the TV.

She was too exhausted to argue. Gary's version of cleaning up meant emptying his ashtrays before they overflowed. *Just* before they overflowed, at that. Whoever said 'If you want to know me, come live with me' was right.

Four years ago, when she'd met Gary Redmond, she'd thought he was the answer to her dreams. After several failed relationships with fellow journalists, Dee had decided that she was never going out with a reporter ever again. Neurotic, obsessed with *their* stories all the time and terminally jealous if she got a better scoop than they did that week, her three failed flings with reporters had put her off male reporters as a species.

She'd dumped her last ex's belongings – the toothbrush he'd left in her flat, the sweater she'd bought him for his birthday and the notebook she'd found with his new girlfriend's phone number scrawled in lipstick – on to his desk in the newsroom a mere month before she met Gary. The lithe, dark-haired man in the expensive-looking grey suit who spilled Guinness over her in the Shelbourne's Horseshoe Bar was so apologetic, so charming and so obviously not a journalist, that she found herself agreeing to have a drink with him, 'to make up for my being so clumsy'.

While Gary did his best to charm her, Dee sipped the champagne cocktail he'd insisted on buying her and thanked her lucky stars that she'd spent the past, boyfriend-less month on a severe diet, had lost ten pounds and was a skinny size fourteen verging on size twelve. Otherwise she wouldn't have felt confident enough to have a drink with such an attractive man. And she certainly wouldn't have fitted into the tight-as-a-tourniquet black dress that showed off her generous cleavage and great legs.

Of course, the combination of control panel sheer tights and Marks & Spencer's vacuum-packed knickers meant she felt like an Egyptian mummy, and two champagne cocktails, complete with lots of fizz, were almost too much for the black dress to bear. Dee felt her stomach groan inside its sexy Lycra casing. But you had to suffer to be beautiful. Well, suffer to be reasonable-looking. Other people – mainly her best friend, Maeve – were always telling Dee that she was pretty, sexy and had marvellously expressive dark eyes. But she'd never been too keen on voluptuous curves, a bosom that needed a government health warning because men were always staring at it, mesmerised, or dark rippling curls that needed a gallon of anti-frizz serum applied every single day. She liked her eyes, of course, but what Dee really wanted to be was a classy Nordic blonde, effortlessly chic and effortlessly skinny, with legs up to her armpits.

After an hour in Gary's company, she was charmed by his intelligence and dark good looks, flattered by his obvious interest in her and, even though accountancy had never been high on her list of desirable occupations in a mate, Gary was nothing like any accountant she'd ever known.

'You remind me of those beautiful pre-Raphaelite women in nineteenth-century paintings,' he'd murmured as he leant over her at the bar. She got a waft of Armani aftershave combined with healthy male pheromones. 'They've got long, rippling auburn or chestnut hair, big dark eyes, and always look like they're waiting to be lured away to some shady meadow to do something nineteenth-century girls weren't supposed to do.'

If one of the lads in the newsroom had said anything like that, Dee would have burst out laughing *before* thumping him. But Gary Redmond's deep voice made the words sound like the sexiest thing she'd ever heard. He had a way of looking at her with those strange almost hazel eyes that melted Dee's insides.

'Really?' she'd said, looking up at him and calculating that, as she was five foot three, he had to be over five nine which made him tall enough but not too tall. She hated really tall men. You got a crick in your neck talking up to them all the time. 'So how do you know so much about art?'

'My mother loves improving herself,' he replied with a wry grin. 'When we were kids she insisted we went on holiday to Italy and France so we could visit the Louvre and just about every chapel in Florence.'

'Sounds marvellous,' Dee said, thinking of the O'Reilly family's annual two weeks in a caravan somewhere on the Irish coast. The only gallery they ever visited was the shooting one in the local amusement arcade. She'd preferred the swing boats herself until she was fifteen and realised that you could fit *two* people into a dodgem – perfect for getting close to boys.

'Do you think it's too late to teach art appreciation to a complete philistine?' Dee inquired silkily, giving him the sultry look she'd perfected after years of practice in front of her bedroom mirror. 'I don't know anything about art.'

'I'm sure you're a quick learner,' he'd answered.

Two hours later, they were giggling over a bottle of wine in the Unicorn. A week later, they were in love. Dee still remembered their third date. She'd been convinced that she loved him by then.

Gary had turned up at her flat with a picnic basket jammed with cold chicken, French bread, potato salad, a six-pack of Budweiser and strawberry ice cream in a cooler bag. After three days eating nothing but grapefruit and consuming endless low-cal chocolate drinks in order to keep those damn' ten pounds off, Dee could have polished off the entire basket herself in ten minutes. She felt faint from lack of food and the scent of French bread was driving her insane with hunger.

'We're going on a picnic,' Gary said, grabbing her in a bear hug as soon as she opened her front door.

'Picnic? But it's half-eight!' she said in surprise.

'A late-night picnic, Dee.' Gary kissed her passionately. 'Now bring your fleece jacket. It might be cold.'

They sat cuddled together in his red Mazda at Dollymount with the roof down and soft music on the car stereo. It had been freezing at first. But the beer warmed their blood and when Gary unzipped her blue fleece jacket in an exploratory way, Dee began to feel very hot.

'Who said accountants aren't romantic?' she whispered into his ear as he slid a hand under her jumper.

But romance had certainly gone out of the window the last few months, she reflected. In fact, she couldn't remember the last time Gary had done anything even vaguely caring. He'd nearly forgotten Valentine's Day, for God's sake. Mind you, she would have given a shopful of red roses if he would occasionally remember to put the toilet seat down.

She stuffed the armful of dirty clothes into the machine, sloshed in some detergent, the last dribble of fabric conditioner, and switched the machine on. Then she took a mug from the pile of unwashed china in the sink, cleared enough room to rinse it under the hot tap and briefly considered giving in and washing up. No, damn it. She wasn't going to. Bloody Gary could do it.

Eventually, he'll get tired of seeing the dishes piled high and he'll do them himself. The secret is not to nag him – let him decide to do the housework off his own bat. He might let the sink reach Everest proportions before he thinks of washing up but, give him a week of unironed shirts, no socks and underpants that the Laundry Fairy has somehow missed, and he'll start doing housework. Wait and see.

Giving advice and actually acting on it were two very different things, Dee thought. She knew what the depressed letter writer *should* do about her housework-shy chauvinist. But since Dee still hadn't managed to get her own lazy fiancé to wash up so much as a single plate, she felt a complete hypocrite telling *Depressed* what to do.

She'd been operating the let-the-dishes-pile-up policy for the last week and the only fact that was becoming apparent was that Gary would rather buy a new shirt than wash a dirty one and that he was completely oblivious to a mountain of dirty dishes in the sink, green mould in the fridge and no clean underpants in his drawer.

It was all his bloody mother's fault. She'd ruined him, never let him lift a finger around the house so that he was now convinced that only women knew the secret to cleaning the toilet and hoovering the sitting-room. Or at least, he *pretended* he didn't know the secret. As she constantly moaned to her best friend, Maeve, Dee should have known exactly what she was getting into when she met Gary's mother for the first time. They'd been going out for three months and he was practically living in Dee's flat on the South Circular Road when he'd asked her home to meet his mother.

'She's nothing like your mum,' said Gary who'd been introduced to Dee's parents and younger brothers at a traditional music night in the Submarine pub. The O'Reillys had welcomed Gary into the fold and had done their best to make him feel comfortable. By closing time, he and her dad were best pals and Gary had been invited to Sunday lunch that weekend.

By way of contrast, his mother had invited Dee to afternoon tea which she served in dainty cups after asking her guest to be careful because it was 'my best china'.

Convinced that the snub hadn't been intentional, Dee smiled and said how lovely the royal blue three-piece suite was.

She *should* have noticed that Gary sat comfortably in an armchair and let his mother hurry in and out of the kitchen bearing china cups, scones, sponge cakes and his favourite gingerbread without once offering to help.

And she should also have wondered why her charming, attentive lover turned into an eager-to-please mummy's boy in his mother's presence.

But she was too busy trying to smile sweetly – and, later, too irritated by Margaret's unsubtle probing – to notice.

'How long have you worked on the . . . er . . . the paper, Deirdre?'

'Six years.'

'I see. And you work in news, Gary tells me. That must be interesting. Have you thought about moving on to another publication perhaps?'

'No.'

'Oh. More cake, darling?' Margaret said to Gary, her voice warming up about a hundred degrees. She handed another lump of cake to her son and turned back to the inquisition. 'What does your father do, Deirdre? Is he in journalism as well?'

'He's a mechanic,' Dee answered, toying with the idea of saying that he played piano in a brothel in between acting as the getaway driver during an occasional armed robbery.

'He *runs* a garage, does he?'

'No. He's a mechanic. Specialises in exhausts.'

'Oh.'

It hadn't taken Dee long to realise that Margaret Redmond was one of those Irish mammies who thought nobody, *absolutely nobody*, was good enough for her youngest boy.

An expert cook, skilled seamstress and the first person in the queue for Communion at daily Mass, Gary's mother was a much-admired member of the Clontarf community and was desperately religious. She didn't drink, smoke or swear and never sat down to watch mindless television – unless it was an educational documentary – when she could be baking a lemon sponge for the church fête or painstakingly rubbing Vanish into the boys' shirt collars. She went to art appreciation classes although Dee was convinced she only did it to show off, and once a week played pitch and putt with a ladies' group.

She'd reared five boys, married four of them off to suitable girls, buried her accountant husband and was now biding her time waiting for the first daughter-in-law to get pregnant so she could crochet endless pram blankets and baby-sit religiously.

Short, rounded – from too many lemon sponges – and boasting a tight grey perm and bi-focals, Margaret Redmond was a million miles away from Dee's mother and a very tough cookie underneath it all.

If Dee had realised that going out with Gary meant getting lumbered with his horrible, social-climbing mother on a regular basis, she wasn't sure that she'd ever have fallen for him – despite his sexy eyes, great body and the charm that he could switch on like a light bulb.

He could switch it off just as easily. She sighed. The only spoon left in the cutlery drawer was the ancient soup spoon she'd used to mix the terracotta and mustard paint together when she'd attempted to colour-wash the bathroom walls. The paint was hard. It couldn't be poisonous, could it?

Who cared anyway? Instant coffee and emulsion might taste nice. The last frozen cheesecake had mysteriously vanished. Dee took the Argos catalogue, six plain biscuits – the twenty-five per cent less fat ones that everyone in work was raving about – and sat down at the pine table that wobbled madly when the piece of cardboard under one leg was dislodged.

Outside the patio doors, a pale May sun broke through the clouds, making the raindrops on the whirly clothesline glitter like crystals. The grass in the tiny back garden was at least six inches high. Last year's nasturtiums had greedily outflanked a couple of stunted heathers to take over the entire flower bed by the patio. Dee knew she had to do something with the garden, soon, but she didn't have the time. Next weekend, she'd cut the front grass and pull up a few dandelions. Nobody but the engineering students next door could see the back garden and since *their* garden looked as if it needed to be nuked, they had no right to complain about hers.

When the phone rang a few minutes later, she was gazing at the catalogue's kitchen utensils, wondering whether a gleaming green plastic vegetable rack would look nice in one corner of the kitchen. A rack would also put an end to the problem of the potatoes sprouting shoots in the damp part at the bottom of the fridge. Must do that, she promised herself.

'Dee,' barked Ian Mahon, the *Sentinel*'s news editor. His bad-tempered, forty-Marlboro-a-day voice never failed to make her stand up straighter, even when he was just on the phone. In person, he was much worse. Very tall, stooped and mean-eyed, Mahon was universally loathed by the reporters, who called him Stalin in their kinder moments.

He was very good at his job, but Dee was convinced he'd be better at it if he didn't terrify the younger reporters with his habit of appearing beside their desks and reading their stories over their shoulders before screeching at them for doing something wrong. After six years in the newsroom at the mercy of Stalin's rages, Dee was used to him. More or less.

'There's a story breaking,' he growled now. 'That young Australian pop star, Chazz . . . we've got a tip-off that he's trashed a room in the Conrad Hotel. We've got a snapper down there now but he hasn't got any pictures. We want you to blag your way in. You've a contact there, haven't you?'

'Yes,' sighed Dee. So much for her day off. Typically, Stalin hadn't asked her if she was busy. No. He'd just assumed she'd jump to attention.

'Who's down there?' she asked, professionalism taking over. She grabbed a biro and scribbled down the details on the reporter's notebook she kept by the phone.

'Kevin Mills. I gave him your mobile number and he's going to ring you.'

Dee brightened up. Kevin Mills was a great photographer, who never lost his cool and always got the shot. Plus, he was extremely good-looking in a dark, gypsyish way.

A freelance photographer with his own agency, Kevin specialised in staking out celebrities. As Dee usually covered straight news stories, she'd rarely worked with him. But he had a reputation for being totally committed to the job and was certainly better-looking than Seanie Keane, the *Sentinel* staff photographer she usually worked with.

Kevin was unlikely to bore her to tears the way Seanie did when he wittered on about the painfully slow progress he was making on the crumbling nineteenth-century house he was renovating himself.

'If you can't get any pictures of Chazz, at least try and get into a similar room or suite for pics. Ring me in an hour,' Stalin commanded before hanging up abruptly.

Dee stuck out her tongue at the receiver. Pig!

Upstairs, she changed her comfy grey sweat pants and her favourite blue tie-dye T-shirt for something suitable for mingling with the rich and famous in the Conrad, one of Dublin's plushest hotels.

The severe black trouser suit looked best with her brown corkscrew curls loose but, as she hadn't washed her hair that morning, she'd have to tie it back. The trousers were too tight so she had to leave the top button open. Damn. There was no avoiding the issue by refusing to weigh herself or by wearing her black baggy trousers and sloppy overshirts – she was putting on weight again.

It was all Gary's fault. When Dee was upset, she turned to food for solace, and she was always upset these days. Yesterday she'd eaten three Mars Bars before lunchtime, and had still managed to consume a huge plate of *tagliatelle carbonara* for lunch. Why couldn't she be like her friend Maeve? A beanpole who ate like a horse, Maeve had eaten the *carbonara* and apple crumble afterwards and *she* never needed to leave her waistband buttons open.

In the bathroom, Dee stared at her reflection gloomily. As usual, she didn't notice her pretty, rounded face with its creamy pale skin, dark, expressive eyes and curly chestnut hair that framed her face beautifully.

Instead, she saw a short, plump woman squeezed into a pair of size 14 trousers when she really needed size 16. Dee turned sideways to see how far her stomach stuck out.

'Oh, God,' she groaned in misery.

She was *huge*. How could she even leave the house looking like she did? Her boobs bulged out of the bra under her clean pale pink T-shirt and her waist was almost non-existent. She looked like a pig, Dee thought. A short, dark-haired pig.

She hadn't time to put on the Number 7 foundation that covered up her freckles but she couldn't go out without lavishing a heavy coat of dark brown mascara on her eyelashes.

After a good spray of Opium, she grabbed her shoulder bag, snagged her mobile phone from the charger, and hopped into her white Corolla a mere ten minutes after Stalin's call.

Wait till he got the expenses, she promised herself grimly as she reversed out of the drive. That would teach him to drag her out on her day off. The extra money might be useful for buying the sort of tent of a dress she was going to have to wear soon.

'I'll meet you on Hatch Street at half-twelve,' Kevin said in a low voice over his mobile phone, the line crackling with static. 'I can't talk now.'

The traffic was very heavy. She'd never make it in time. Damn it, Dee thought, adjusting the rearview mirror so she could put on her lipstick at the Sundrive Road lights. Then the rush hit her, that amazing adrenaline rush she got when she was on to something good. It never failed. The buzz of working on a hot story even pushed her misery over her weight problem to the back of her mind, which was saying something.

She hoped another reporter hadn't got there before her. That was the problem with these anonymous tip-offs: people didn't just ring one paper, they rang them all. And nobody was more annoyed than the reporters who arrived to catch their scoop only to discover a representative of every other major paper there.

Kevin was waiting on Hatch Street, smoking a cigarette as he leant up against the silver Porsche he'd bought with the proceeds of selling last year's sunbathing shots of Liz Hurley on holiday in West Cork. His dark green waxed jacket concealed the two cameras which hung around his neck, the tell-tale telephoto lenses pointing downwards. He was gazing at the side of the hotel, eyes narrowed in contemplation.

'What's the story?' Dee asked as she eyed the photographer. Around six two – you had to be tall to reach over everyone's heads to get good pictures – with a rangy frame, dark eyes and a permanent five o'clock shadow on his square jaw, Kevin could have made as much money in front of the camera as behind it.

Even if he knew how gorgeous he was, and Dee reckoned he *had* to because office gossip insisted that there was always a queue of women lining up to date him, Kevin never behaved as if he was the best thing since George Clooney. Dee hated men with big egos.

She tried to arrange her jacket in a flattering way so she'd look as thin as possible. Sucking in her stomach, she stood up straight in the manner magazines were always advising. 'Lose five pounds instantly' the head-lines screamed, advocating the imagine-you've-got-a-string-pulling-your-head-up method. Dee craned her neck and did her best to look as if she'd lost ten.

Kevin took a long drag on his cigarette before he dropped it to the ground and stubbed it out with his Timberland boot.

'He's in there and the cops were called, according to my source. But she's not saying anything else. She was supposed to meet me outside half an hour ago and she never showed. Mahon said you knew someone on the staff.'

Dee gave him an apologetic look. 'I don't. I don't know why he thinks I have a source in there but I wasn't going to correct him. You know what he's like.'

'Fair enough. Let's take a walk round the front,' Kevin said.

As luck would have it, they didn't have to do anything else to get their story. They were walking around the front of the hotel when a dark blue car sped up the ramp from the hotel's underground car park.

The two men in the front were unmistakably detectives. It didn't take a telephoto lens to establish that the man in the back seat, flanked by two more burly cops, was Chazz.

The rock star looked the other way as the car hit the street, which gave Kevin the chance he needed. He ran towards it, his Canon clicking madly, and rolled off twenty shots in as many seconds.

The singer bent his head to escape being photographed but it was too late. Kevin had nailed him!

'Fantastic!' Dee caught up with him as the blue car sped out of sight. 'That was great. Let's hope nobody else gets it before Monday.'

'They won't have those shots anyway,' he replied with a big grin. 'I'm going down to the hotel bar to see if I can arrange to get pictures of the room he trashed. Want to come?'

It was the best invitation Dee had had all day. Gary was away for the weekend, ensconced in Old Trafford, probably pissed as a newt already. The only thing waiting for her at home was his laundry, which he was never going to do no matter how long she left it, and her agony column. The thought of a drink with an attractive man who wouldn't talk for hours about the Premier League was very inviting.

But she had to say no. If Kevin got the pictures of the hotel room, she could describe it from his shots. And the most urgent task was to talk to the cops about the arrest of Chazz, aka Charlie Leonard, lead singer of Panic Zone. Since she was feeling more than a little fed up with Gary, Lord knew what a few stiff drinks with Kevin Mills could lead to. The last time she'd been this angry with her fiancé, the time he'd forgotten the dinner they always had to celebrate the anniversary of their first meeting, she'd been so cross that she'd gone drinking with the crowd from work and ended up flirting drunkenly with the happily married chief sub-editor, Bill. What a mistake that had been.

The next morning at work had been hell. Ribald jokes about her behaviour kept everyone in stitches until lunchtime, never mind the pain of her murderous hangover. Dee shuddered at the memory.

'Can't, sorry. Some other time?'

Kevin grinned down at her.

''Bye.' He touched her hand. 'Some other time. I'll hold you to that.'

Dee couldn't help smiling to herself as she walked back to her car and rang Harcourt Street cop shop on her mobile. Even though her legs were positively furry and her hair was a mess, Kevin Mills had asked her for a drink. Well, it *was* work, she amended. But he'd still asked her.

Dear Annie,

I've been going out with my fiancé for six years. We got engaged two years ago and we live together, but the other day a male colleague asked me out for a drink and I really wanted to go with him. What's wrong with me? I love my fiancé and feel so guilty about wanting to go for a drink with this other man.

I didn't go, of course, but now I can't stop

thinking that there must be something wrong between me and my boyfriend for me to have felt this way. I'm devastated by this.

Confused

Dear Confused,

This is more than likely just a phase you're going through. Now that you're engaged to be married, you probably think that you're 100 per cent 'safe', that you'll never fancy anyone else again. That's not necessarily the case.

Plenty of happily married people occasionally fancy someone else and the test of the relationship is whether they actually do anything about this momentary feeling or not. Don't feel guilty for merely being attracted to someone else. You haven't done anything wrong, you're a perfectly normal woman.

If your relationship is going through a rocky stage, that could contribute to your feelings of confusion. All relationships have bad patches, you've just got to make more of an effort to make your relationship work at these times. It's so easy to get bored with someone but think of all the reasons why you fell for your fiancé in the first place . . .

It was late afternoon by the time Dee got home. She'd finally got her story confirmed by a police contact and Kevin had rung while she was parking the car outside the supermarket to say he'd got the pictures of the room Chazz had ruined.

'He hadn't done very much, actually, but my source says the management called the police when he tried to hit one of the room-service guys. The hotel won't stand for that sort of thing. They don't know I was even in there, so don't phone them for a comment until tomorrow in case they give the story to someone else.'

'Of course.' Dee knew the rules of the game. If you told them what you were going to do, then somebody in the hotel might tip off another journalist they were friendly with, thereby ruining the *Sentinel*'s scoop.

'I'll have the pictures on your desk first thing tomorrow morning, OK?' Kevin's voice was brusque with none of its earlier warmth.

'OK,' answered Dee brightly. ''Bye.' She must have imagined that he was interested in her. She carried the grocery shopping into the hall, the six heavy Superquinn bags dragging her down like a pack pony.

At least she had something nice for dinner, she thought, as she stowed the chicken stir-fry ingredients in the fridge. She jammed two packs of mini strawberry cheesecakes in the freezer. The kettle had nearly boiled but Dee changed her mind about having a cup of coffee and poured herself a glass of white wine to take upstairs while she worked on her column. It was a bit early for a drink but she felt she deserved one. Gary would be phoning later and she'd tell him she was sorry they'd rowed and that she loved him.

At ten o'clock on a Sunday morning, the offices of the *Sentinel* were usually very quiet. Even though there was a full staff working on Monday's edition, people still came in slightly later than on other days. On Sundays they wanted to lie in bed longer, eating toast, drinking coffee and reading the papers from cover to cover, especially when it was raining so hard that the raindrops bounced off the pavement.

Dee hated working on Sundays. Today, she was tired,

she'd got a spot on her chin and knew she was heading into her PMT danger zone. She was also utterly depressed to discover that she now weighed eleven stone four pounds, most of it on her stomach. She'd just made a pot of percolated coffee and was searching for milk in the fridge in the tiny kitchen when her best friend, Maeve Lynch, hurried past, clutching her bulging briefcase with one hand and dragging a drenched black PVC raincoat with the other. Tall, thin and with short hair that she was always dyeing a variety of wildly unnatural burgundy colours, Maeve was one of the paper's sub-editors, responsible for laying out pages and coming up with headlines.

'Coffee. Thank God,' she breathed, like an addict in need of a fix. 'You're an angel, Dee.'

'At least *somebody* thinks so,' Dee muttered gloomily. Gary hadn't rung the night before and she'd gone to bed fuming. She'd spent the restless night hours planning exactly what she'd tell him when he got home. Most of it involved swear words and copious amounts of shouting.

'What's wrong?' asked Maeve sympathetically. 'Gary?'

'When is it ever *not* Gary?'

'What happened?' Maeve put three spoons of sugar in her coffee. Dee could never understand how her friend could consume so much sugar and still remain positively anorexic-looking. 'I thought he was away for the weekend, anyway?'

'He is. Hasn't even bothered to phone me.'

'Oh. Well, you know what men are like,' Maeve said sagely.

'No, but I know what Gary's like.'

They took their coffee into the newsroom, a large and untidy open-plan office with computer terminals on every desk, fax machines in one corner and four TVs high on the walls.

There were none of the potted plants and tasteful prints you saw in other offices: the *Sentinel*'s newsroom was a no-go area for horticulture. Once six o'clock came, everyone who smoked got out their fags and lit up eagerly.

By then, the editor's executive secretary, a hard-nosed anti-smoker who was a born-again tyrant, was gone and they could do what they liked. No plant had ever lasted more than six weeks in this atmosphere, even the gossip columnist's trailing ivy that she'd religiously fed with Bio-Gro.

Dee had never smoked, apart from the odd one when she was in the pub with Maeve and wanted something to do with her hands. But sometimes she wished she did – nicotine was supposed to suppress your appetite. She had visions of herself as a very thin, very soignée woman with ribs like a greyhound's and an elegant cigarette holder constantly held aloft in one slender hand. Then she realised that cigarettes or no cigarettes, she loved food. That was her problem.

Dee plonked the coffee down on her desk which was still covered with the previous week's newspapers. She made a space by pushing all the junk to one side, opened a reporter's notebook and wrote the date on the top of a fresh page. She'd always done that. Her first news editor had said it was the best way to keep track of what you were doing – to write *everything* in one notebook so you never lost valuable phone numbers on bits of paper.

'Here.' Maeve handed her a brown paper bag with three sugary ring doughnuts inside and dragged a chair over to Dee's desk.

Dee did her best to ignore the doughnuts. She felt fat enough.

'We won't talk about your crappy weekend if you don't want to,' Maeve said. 'I'll bore you senseless telling you about mine.'

Dee sat back in her chair, put her feet up on the desk and sipped her coffee mournfully. 'I have to talk about it to *someone*, Maeve,' she said. 'Otherwise I'll go mad. Contradiction – madder.'

'What's he done now?' mumbled Maeve, her mouth still full of doughnut.

'It's what he *hasn't* done that's driving me mad. We had a huge row on Friday morning about the housework. And he said he was sick to the teeth of me nagging him about it. I mean, honestly, he barely washes a cup these days. The sink has been full for nearly a week, we're completely out of cutlery and he still won't touch it . . .'

'So you've cleaned up?' interrupted Maeve.

'I haven't!' said Dee firmly. 'But I'm going to,' she added. 'I can't face the house looking like a tip for one more day. But what's made it worse is that he hasn't even rung me once since he left. He's so thoughtless!'

Maeve reached into the paper bag, took out another doughnut and offered it to Dee, who looked longingly at it for a millisecond and then took it.

'Well, if it's any consolation, my weekend was a complete disaster too. That charming TV producer, the one who asked me last week where I'd been all his life, never phoned to arrange our evening out.'

'Oh, that's awful. What did you do?'

'Went out with the girls from the flat downstairs. They're mad, that pair. Every time I go out with them we end up standing outside some nightclub at four in the morning trying to remember where we live so we can tell the taxi driver.'

Dee couldn't help feeling mildly jealous. Maeve had been having a whale of a time knocking back tequila slammers while she'd been stuck at home waiting for bloody Gary to ring. It hit her once again that she'd made the classic female mistake. She'd lost touch with her girlfriends when she became seriously involved with a man.

But Gary continued to go out with his pals as though he were still young, free and single.

It wasn't as if he stopped her going out with her friends; Dee just felt that they should do things together because they were a couple. She fancied meandering round Habitat at the weekend looking for nice pieces of bedroom furniture or buying books and then spending hours in quaint Dublin pubs, drinking Irish coffees and reading. But Gary preferred to go boozing with his pals.

'Let's forget about men,' Maeve said suddenly. 'I'm taking you out for a drink after work and we aren't going even to *talk* about the weaker sex. But first, I've got some great gossip for you.'

Dee perked up. Like all reporters, she loved gossip. 'What?'

Maeve grinned wickedly. 'Antonia's leaving! Hubbie has got a job with a London pharmaceutical company. An offer he couldn't resist, apparently. He was going to commute every weekend but he's been offered so much money that Antonia feels they can survive on his salary, no problem, so she's going with him and plans to freelance for a couple of the British women's magazines. The kids are grown up so she doesn't have to worry about them any more.'

Dee was stunned. 'I can't believe it!' she said. 'When I

think how hard she fought to get the women's editor's job, I can't believe she's giving it up this easily. How did you find out? She didn't tell you, did she?'

Dee knew that Antonia and Maeve weren't the best of friends. But then nobody had ever managed to hit it off with the highly strung Antonia who made every crisis into a grand-scale drama and who never let anyone forget that she came from a wealthy Anglo-Irish family with a duchess for a cousin.

'One of the sports guys told me. I met him last night when the girls and I were in Slattery's. He heard it from the temp in advertising, who overheard her boss on the phone to Antonia's husband – they play golf together – talking about buying property in London. But you're not to tell anyone yet,' Maeve warned. 'The temp was pissed when she told Tom. Nobody else knows about it yet.'

'I see,' said Dee slowly. With Antonia out of the running, the way was clear for her to escape from the newsdesk into the challenging world of the women's pages. She was sick to the teeth of hard news and longed for the chance to prove that she was a natural features writer. She'd only worked as a news reporter in the beginning because it was much easier to get a job there than in features.

But she was eager to get away from brutal murder trials and stories about drug barons and pushers. And it wasn't as if Nigel Burke, the editor, didn't know that she was a good features writer. She'd worked in features all over Christmas when half the staff had been laid up in bed with a brutal 'flu virus. Everyone had raved about her *Unsung Heroes: People Who Save Lives Over Christmas* series which had run for a week. This was the chance she'd been waiting for. Antonia, who had no interest in harder-edged stories, had only ever written about the next season's fashions or what sort of lipgloss lasted longest on your lips without transferring to either a wineglass or your boyfriend. Dee was keen to transform the women's pages from eight pages of beauty hints into a part of the paper which dealt with serious women's issues.

'I know what you're thinking. And you'd be perfect for Antonia's job,' Maeve said. 'You could do it in your sleep and probably make the women's pages a thousand times better.'

'I could hardly make them any worse,' Dee remarked.

'You said it,' Maeve added fervently. 'I can't begin to tell you the times I've wanted to strangle that bloody woman when she'd insist on changing her fashion pieces after I'd already laid them out because she'd found this "fabulous new designer we must write about, darling". And as for the arguments we'd have when I'd rewrite some of her stuff because she went off on tangents that made no sense whatsoever . . .'

'Now, Maeve, don't sit on the fence about this one,' joked Dee. 'Tell me what you *really* think about Antonia?'

'She thought she was far too good for this paper. We're well shot of her.'

'I know. Would you like to work with me?' Dee inquired, her mind racing. This was it, her big chance.

'I'd love to work with you,' Maeve said, before adding more cautiously, 'but don't forget, Dee, you won't be the only one after Antonia's job.'

'The only person who's got a chance is Phil Walsh and she loves being features ed. She wouldn't even go for women's editor,' Dee said dismissively.

Maeve scrunched up the paper bag the doughnuts

had come in and pushed back her chair. 'There'll be plenty of people outside who'd kill for the job,' she pointed out. 'I mean, who wouldn't?'

'Nigel would never bring in anyone from outside,' Dee answered, lowering her voice as she saw the editor unlock the door to his office. 'You know he wouldn't.' She got up and clutched her friend's arm excitedly. 'This is fantastic news. I can't wait to tell Gary!'

CHAPTER TWO

Isabel pulled the clothes out of the washing-machine and groaned. One of the girls had left a tissue in a pocket and the entire load was covered in bits of shredded tissue paper.

'Shit!' she muttered crossly. The moment she'd ripped a giant ladder in her last pair of new ten deniers that morning, Isabel had known it wasn't going to be her day. She'd been right.

She'd stopped to get petrol on the Stillorgan dual carriageway which meant it took ten minutes to nose the car back into the early-morning traffic. So she'd been late for the editorial meeting.

As a result, her new boss, Richie Devine, who was clearly in a bad temper, icily demanded to know why she thought she could waltz in fifteen minutes later than everyone else, especially since she was only temporary. Meaning 'temporary, never to be made permanent', Isabel knew. She'd flashed him the winning smile her husband had once told her lit up her face like a hundred-watt bulb, but it had no effect.

Winning smiles worked quite well when you were a twenty-something student with pert boobs, zero experience of life's tragedies and no crow's feet. But not when you were thirty-nine and the combined stresses of marital separation and moving house meant that you'd lost so much weight your cheekbones were hollow and your collar bones more prominent than your cleavage. At that stage, no amount of smiling had the slightest effect.

'At *Motor 2000*, we have deadlines and we expect all our staff to adhere to them,' Richie Devine said bossily, before he went on to discuss the 'high concept of an advertising supplement on jeeps'. Isabel couldn't think of anything more boring than designing the pages for the jeep edition but she smiled brightly at Richie and tried to remember that she really, really needed this sub-editing job even if the pay was dreadful and the work about as thrilling as watching an extended version of *Prisoner Cell Block H*.

Designing the layout of pages and writing headlines was interesting when you worked as a sub-editor on a women's magazine, which was what Isabel had done for ten enjoyable years. But doing the same thing on a third-rate car magazine, where any evidence of originality was treated with suspicion by a mercurial boss, was utterly draining and very depressing. To put the icing on the cake, the bank had just rung her about her overdraft, which was 'way over your agreed limit, Mrs Farrell'.

My life is way over my limit, Isabel thought gloomily as she poked around all the wet pockets trying to find the culprit responsible for messing up her washing.

'Mum, where are my Levis?' yelled a shrill voice from upstairs.

'Wet and covered in the tissue you left in your bloody pocket,' she yelled back as she found the sodden remains in the Levis in question.

Her elder daughter didn't reply, but Isabel could hear

Robin stomp into her bedroom and slam the door loudly. This was standard behaviour for her fifteen-year-old daughter. Well, standard behaviour nowadays.

Isabel could still remember when Robin had been her best friend, closest ally and biggest admirer. That had been a mere three months ago, before they'd left the leafy suburbs of Oxford to move to Isabel's parents' home in Wicklow. She knew it hadn't been easy for the girls to leave their comfy home, private school and lots of friends, but she'd had no choice.

David had left them with no choice, she thought darkly, as she picked bits of tissue off everything. It hadn't been easy for *her* either. She'd left a home she'd lovingly renovated from a shell and a job she really enjoyed. And all because her damned husband had lost every penny they owned trying to drag his stupid advertising agency out of trouble. That had been the final nail in the coffin of their marriage.

Broke and with the building society on the verge of repossessing their home, Isabel had felt she'd no option but to leave both David and Oxford and start again. And she'd never forgive him for it.

They'd weathered so many storms together that she had actually thought there was nothing about David Farrell she didn't know. After sixteen years of marriage, she was convinced there wasn't anything else he could do to shock her. And she'd always hoped the love would eventually come back into their marriage. Somehow. She should have known better.

They'd recovered from his affairs – three of them – his two years of unemployment, and even his disastrous flirtation with the stock market. But when Isabel found out that he had gambled, and lost, their home on a business that was shaky to start with, she knew she had

31

to leave him. It wasn't just for her sake, it was for the girls'.

If David could gamble *their* home and threaten the security of their young lives, without even thinking about it, then Isabel couldn't stay with him though she had known that Robin and twelve-year-old Naomi would be devastated by the break-up.

David had stopped loving her a long time ago, round about the time she'd lost the baby. Isabel hadn't known which was worse: losing the baby boy she'd longed for, or enduring the months of depression afterwards when her husband hadn't been able to communicate with her and didn't seem to want to anyway.

It had been August, nearly five years ago, a gloriously sunny month when Isabel had spent her days off sitting in the garden, sipping iced water and trying to read while eight-year-old Naomi and ten-year-old Robin waged war on each other. She didn't have the energy to shout at them, so they rampaged through the garden, into the kitchen and up the stairs, screaming blue murder while Isabel lolled in her deckchair with a magazine on her lap and thought up babies' names. She was fourteen weeks pregnant and convinced she was having a boy. After much consideration, the girls in the office agreed. Isabel had been thrilled. After two girls, she wanted a boy and knew that David secretly longed for someone with whom he could discuss football and carburettors in the future.

She'd never forget the pain of losing that baby, her precious little boy. It had all happened so quickly. One minute, she was washing a lettuce in the cracked old Belfast sink: the next, she was doubled up in pain, the sort of pain that meant only one thing.

David brought flowers to the hospital when he got

back from London the next day. He couldn't meet her eyes. All she wanted was to be held, to be told that it would be all right. And to be allowed to grieve for the baby she'd lost; not told that they could 'have another one soon, to make up for it', as one thoughtless doctor had said the day before. You couldn't make up for a baby you'd loved, Isabel had thought, and howled with pain.

David would understand, she told herself. Yet, when he came to see her, it was as if they were separated by a thousand miles of icy water. He held her hand for ages but couldn't speak, except in platitudes.

'They say you can come home tomorrow,' he'd said in a low voice. 'The girls will be thrilled. I bought Robin this fantastic doll in Regent Street. You can do her hair and put make-up on her. I bought a painting-by-numbers set for Naomi.'

'Great.' Isabel sat back against her pillows, feeling hollow. There was a gaping hole inside her, a part of her missing. And David was talking about dolls and paints as if she was in hospital after spraining her ankle!

He never did talk about the baby. At first, she wondered if he didn't care. Or if he felt guilty for not being there when she'd had the miscarriage. By the time she realised that he was distraught at the loss of his son, it was too late. She was crippled by depression and unable to mother him to recovery. For God's sake, she was only able to mother Naomi and Robin on autopilot. Her grown-up husband could deal with his own pain while she tried to survive hers. Their marriage had limped along like a lifeboat with a hole in it. They shared the same house, the same bed and the same dinner table. And that was it.

Maybe she should have left him then, when she was

thirty-four and had an energy for life she certainly didn't have now. Then, Robin had been a malleable ten year old who might have coped with her parents' separation better than she did now. But then, Isabel was worn out with grief and didn't have the energy for the hassle. And who the hell knew the right time to split up anyway? Isabel didn't feel that she knew anything any more.

She slammed the washing-machine door shut, stood up wearily and leaned against the gleaming white formica worktop that her mother spent hours scrubbing with Dettox. The whole kitchen gleamed, from the cooker top to the spotless white windowsill where a single geranium sat in splendour, without a brown leaf in sight.

Isabel hated her mother's kitchen, hated its cold, clinical feel, the way it looked as if nobody ever left toast crumbs on the table or as if little hands never left jammy handprints on the fridge.

The sterile environment of 23 Sycamore Avenue was in direct contrast to Isabel's Oxford kitchen.

That had been warm and cosy with distressed wooden cupboards and worn terracotta tiles on the floor. An entire oasis of plants on the window trailed leaves untidily over the draining-board. Unhygienic, her mother would have said. The cork notice board had been jammed with school photos of Robin and Naomi, shopping lists and cartoons the girls had cut out from comics.

The worktops were cluttered, the iron permanently upright beside the kettle from Isabel's usual early-morning ironing session. It was a family kitchen, but they weren't a family any more.

She'd told David she was leaving him in that kitchen,

during a last, dreadful row. He'd been sitting in the den watching soccer with a can of beer in one hand and the remote control in the other when she'd come downstairs with the letter from the building society.

It was brusque and terrifying. The recently extended mortgage on the house hadn't been paid in six months and, unless funds were forthcoming shortly, they would take legal proceedings. Reading those threatening words had made Isabel sick to her stomach. She'd felt weak, exhausted, stunned. And then, she'd felt angry.

'How could you do this to us?' she'd yelled at David. 'How could you? And why the hell didn't you tell me? Did you really think I wouldn't be interested in knowing we haven't a penny to our name?'

'Relax, Izzy,' he'd said, in the laid-back tone he always used when she was angry with him. It simply made her even more angry.

'Relax!' she yelled. 'How can I relax? The building society is going to repossess the house! I know there isn't enough money in the current account to pay those kind of arrears. Have you any idea what that means?'

'Yes, of course I do.' David stood up slowly, unfurling his long, lean body with the languid grace that Isabel had once loved. Now, it merely irritated her.

His height and his handsome, smiling face had drawn her to him all those years ago. She'd been the tallest girl in her class at college, a willowy five foot eight with long blonde hair and hippie-ish clothes. She'd never been sure whether it was her height or her faintly distant air – to disguise a crippling shyness – that had put men off. But something had. So when the six-foot rugby winger asked her to partner him at the end-of-term dance, she'd accepted his offer joyfully and had never looked back.

Eighteen years later, while she watched him asleep beside her, his girlishly long lashes resting on remarkably unlined cheeks, she'd wondered how she had ever fallen in love with him.

Why hadn't she seen past the good looks and the charm that masked a habitual liar? David had had more pie-in-the-sky dreams than a sixteen-year-old would-be rock star with an air guitar.

She could see past the mask now and she could see that if she stayed with David Farrell, one-time insurance salesman and currently broke advertising agency boss, she and the girls would live to regret it.

He'd walked past her into the kitchen and took another Budweiser from the fridge, brushing back a curl of the dark hair that reached his blue polo shirt collar.

'Why didn't you show me the letter?' Isabel had demanded. 'When were you planning to tell me? When the bailiffs arrived? Or when the estate agent stuck a For Sale sign up outside?' She waited for his answer, waited for some shred of hope that this wasn't really happening.

But as David sipped his beer slowly, before turning to look at her with those pale blue eyes, she'd known that it *was* happening. He had lost everything.

'Izzy, honey,' he'd said softly. He'd put down his can and tried to hug her. Isabel pushed him away angrily.

'Don't lie to me, David. Don't butter me up. Just tell me the truth, will you?'

'Izzy,' he'd said again, in hurt tones, 'it's not as bad as it looks . . .'

'Don't lie!'

'OK, OK,' he'd replied quickly. 'It's still not as bad as it looks. I've got a contingency plan. Freddie says we should declare ourselves bankrupt and start again. Maybe in London this time . . .' He'd stared into space, as if his mind was already on the new business.

Isabel knew what he was thinking of – a new agency, called Farrell Ellis instead of Ellis Farrell. Well, they'd have to have a new name if they went bankrupt.

So they'd put Freddie's name last, instead of the other way around. New premises in a smart area of London, expensively decorated in muted tones, with chrome and glass coffee tables strewn with copies of *Time* and *Campaign*, and a sexy receptionist with a silly name and legs up to her armpits for the clients – and the boss – to fancy.

Bay trees in expensive containers outside the front door. A genuine oil painting or two in reception to show that the agency men knew what 'real' art was even if they prostituted their talent for £100,000 accounts and new BMWs. Leather armchairs scattered around reception, of course, those intricately designed ones that were uncomfortable but chic. And fresh flowers every second day.

All paid for with cash from another mortgaged house. A house that Isabel, Robin and Naomi would never feel really safe in because the carpet was always in danger of being swept from under their feet. If the VAT man blinked, they'd be homeless. If the agency lost a big account, they'd be homeless. Well, not any more, Isabel had thought fiercely. She'd never again wager their future on a man who couldn't keep a tenner in his pocket for five minutes without an overwhelming urge to spend it.

From now on, Naomi and Robin would be financially secure if Isabel had to work her fingers to the bone to make sure of it.

She'd looked around the room slowly, her eyes lingering on the bits and pieces she and David had bought over the years when they'd had the money to go abroad on holiday. She especially loved the two large painted plates they'd brought home from Portugal one year. She'd adored those plates – a riot of blue and pink flowers handpainted on gleaming white china – the day she saw them in a street market in Lisbon. David had insisted on buying them for her.

Naturally, when it was time to bring them home, Isabel had ended up dragging them with her in a huge plastic bag, while she held on to Naomi's small hand and her own bulging suitcase at the same time. David was carrying six bottles of sparkling rosé. He was convinced he could make a fortune by importing that particular brand to the UK. All he needed was the go-ahead from a pal of his who was a big name in the import/export business and they could have their own villa on the Algarve this time next year! Six bottles ought to convince him, surely . . .

Isabel also loved the Russian dolls he'd brought back from a trip to Russia. They'd sat on top of the freezer, bright crimson touched with gilt. They were totally gaudy but so sweet, five little figures each smaller than the one before. Naomi had loved playing with them when she was little and, more than once, Isabel had rescued the smallest one from being stuck up her daughter's nose. From the age of three onwards, she'd tried to push *everything* up her nose, from pasta shapes to peas. After the second trip to the doctor's surgery, Isabel had thought of buying her own nasal forceps.

'I'm leaving you, David,' she'd said, tearing her eyes away from the Russian dolls. 'I can't take this any more.'

'Don't be stupid,' he'd replied scathingly, as if this was the latest in a series of idiotic ideas. 'Where will you go?'

'Home. To Ireland. Anywhere but here.'

'Izzy, don't be ridiculous. Why do you want to leave?' he'd demanded.

'Because we don't *have* a marriage and, since you've just lost our home, I've suddenly realised I can't stand the uncertainty of life with you, David. That's why.'

She was suddenly utterly sure that she was doing the right thing. It was a bizarre, liberating experience. As if she'd finally tidied out a room she'd been meaning to dejunk for years and found that, without the clutter, she felt like a new woman.

Amazingly, she didn't even feel like crying. She felt strong and brave. She should have done this a long time ago, six months ago to be exact. Maybe then they'd actually have had some property to sell in order to split their assets. Now, all they had were the furnishings she'd painstakingly restored because they'd never had the money to buy new stuff.

As if he'd suddenly sensed a sea change, David crossed the room to touch her.

'Don't do this, Isabel,' he'd urged. He'd tried to wrap her in his embrace, fitting her body close to his in the old familiar way. Isabel couldn't remember a time when they hadn't been together, a time when his body scent hadn't been as familiar to her as her own. That was the problem.

Gently and without speaking, she'd moved out of his arms. She'd leant against the scrubbed pine kitchen table and looked at her husband who hadn't moved. Head bent sorrowfully, hair falling forward and obscuring his face. It was his James Dean pose. But however well it had worked eighteen years ago, it certainly wasn't working now.

'There's no need to make this difficult, David. We

both know it's been over for years, since the baby . . .'

He didn't even flinch. Isabel thought of the times she'd sobbed into the night thinking about the lost child.

She remembered what it had been like to look at the unneeded baby clothes and to realise that no tiny baby would wear them, that no downy head would nestle against her breast wrapped in this soft white cardigan or that fluffy old blanket with the rabbits on it.

It was a tragedy that they'd never been able to talk about it, and a double tragedy that David had seemed to stop caring about everything else afterwards. But Isabel had no intention of spending the rest of her life living with the aftermath of that tragedy. Especially with a man she realised she no longer really loved, a man who'd forgotten about the most important people in his life – his daughters.

'I'm going back to Dublin with the girls,' she said quietly. 'We can't pay the school fees for next term and I'm not putting them through the torture of staying in Oxford and watching all their friends go back to school, when they suddenly can't. We might even get a refund for the months they'll miss.'

It was simpler to talk about practical matters. Simpler to reduce their relationship to a series of financial transactions and travel plans instead of talking about the emotional side of things.

'You should go to London and do your own thing – it's what you've always wanted.' She couldn't resist saying it. 'I'll get a job in Ireland. I want to go back, I've always wanted to. You didn't.'

David didn't say anything. Isabel wondered whether he was trying to think of something clever, something to get him out of all the trouble he was in. Or whether he was relieved and thought it unwise to say anything in case she changed her mind.

Then he got angry.

'What the hell are you talking about, for Christ's sake? You can't leave me. What about the girls? What about them?'

'You should have thought of that when you and Freddie were spending money like it was going out of fashion,' Isabel had said contemptuously. 'You didn't worry about the girls then, did you? How many trips abroad with important clients was the house worth, anyway? Three or four? I'd love to know how much of my hard-earned cash went into impressing people who didn't spend enough with the agency to cover their bloody trips to the Monte Carlo Grand Prix, despite all the champagne you poured down their throats!'

David had started yelling at her then.

'What gives you the right to be so high and mighty, Isabel? Did you work your butt off to make this family a fortune? Well, I did, *I did*, and I wanted it to work. And it will! But you, you stupid bitch, you just can't wait. We *had* to put money into entertaining. That's the way business is done. It takes time, we were nearly there . . .'

She'd walked out of the kitchen, picked up her car keys and got into the car. She had to pick up the girls from friends' houses later on but couldn't bear to wait in the house with David until then. Her battered Volkswagen was going to have to last a bit longer, she'd realised grimly as she reversed out of the drive after the usual fiddling with the gear stick to find reverse.

The moss that had spread through the lawn in the front garden wasn't going to irritate her the way it had for the past few months, she remembered thinking idly as the car shuddered backwards.

She'd be gone soon and another woman would look out of the front window past the lavender bush and promise herself she'd apply moss killer. That was one thing fewer for Isabel to worry about.

Those last few days before they'd left Oxford had been dreadful, with constant recriminations from David and crying fits from the girls.

'Why are you doing this?' screeched Robin when she heard. 'You can't break up our family, Mum, you can't!'

Even though Isabel felt she really hadn't any choice but to go back to Ireland, she couldn't explain to Robin, the teenager who adored her feckless, charming father, that it was go home or stay in Oxford and endure the painful process of bankruptcy. Isabel knew she couldn't bear to watch strangers march through the house, complaining about the damp in the downstairs loo and trying to knock a couple of thousand off what was already a knock-down price.

She'd thought about what would happen if they stayed in the UK. The indignity of relying on charity from friends and renting some squalid flat, which would be all she could afford as she certainly didn't have the deposit for a new home. The girls would have hated it, she knew.

'You can stay with us. Please stay,' begged her friend Anna, whose family published *Today's Woman*, the magazine for which Isabel worked. They'd sat in Anna's kitchen and made inroads into a bottle of wine. Neither of them bothered with the cheese and salad sandwiches Anna had made. 'We've lots of room, you and the girls can stay in the granny flat. And you'll soon be back on your feet.'

Isabel had tried to explain why she had to leave. It

wasn't running away, she'd said. But she needed to be as far away from David as she could in case she ran back to him when she got afraid or lonely. She'd read about other women who did that and didn't want to be one of them. She couldn't afford to be, for the girls' sake.

'What about *your* sake, Isabel?' Anna asked quietly.

Isabel had shrugged helplessly. She didn't know what to say. 'I've lived so much of my life here but I need to go somewhere different,' she'd said finally. 'All my married life, I've gone where David wanted to go. Belfast when he wanted to, London, and then Oxford. He picked where he wanted to work or where the next big business opportunities were happening. I think I finally need to go somewhere *I've* picked. And the only place I can go right now is Ireland. We can stay with my parents – not that I'm looking forward to that because my mother and I don't get on,' Isabel added wryly. 'But it's somewhere I can go to think about things. And, when I get a job, I'll be able to save some money for a deposit on a house or apartment. I think it'll be good for the girls. You know, a new country and a new school. It might take their minds off the separation.'

But her plan had backfired. Robin had barely spoken to her mother for a week before the move. And when she did speak, it was to demand that she be allowed to stay and live with David. Isabel couldn't explain that his plans didn't include having his daughter to live with him.

He was already checking out flats in London – bachelor flats, perfect for a man setting up a new business. His earlier rage had gone, to be replaced by enthusiasm for a fresh start. Freddie knew just the man they needed to see, apparently.

'You know, I can make this work, Izzy,' David had

said. 'Maybe it's best if I'm on my own for a while – it'll keep the bills down. I can live very cheaply. I can't imagine you in the sort of crappy flat I'll get. You'd hate it.' He was still trying to charm her, trying to get round her.

Isabel watched his face grow animated as he talked about setting up again on his own and wondered again why she'd stayed with him so long. It wasn't as if his reckless behaviour was a surprise to her. She'd realised exactly what sort of man she'd married by the time Robin was born. He'd just lost money on a 'surefire' deal. The computer software systems he'd bought in bulk through a 'friend' had proved impossible to shift.

It was a miracle he'd had any money to buy the expensive champagne he'd insisted on to toast their first child. That was typical of David. No matter how broke they were, he always insisted on buying the best of everything – like gold earrings from Tiffany's for Isabel on her thirty-third birthday, the same year they'd abandoned their plans to replace the oil-fired central heating in the house because they didn't have the spare cash. As they all shivered through a bad winter, she knew she'd have preferred cheap earrings, a bit of scrimping and saving – and heating that worked.

'The only problem is the girls . . .' David stroked her hand as he talked. It was one of his ploys and it worked, but only with women who didn't know him. Isabel had had enough hand-stroking to last her a lifetime.

'I doubt if I'll get anywhere nice enough for them to stay. Me, I don't care what sort of hovel I live in. It'll work out, Izzy,' he said again. 'Freddie has a pal who's interested in investing in us. When I've got the business going, you'll come back, won't you?'

She'd never asked him why this mysterious investor

hadn't bailed out the existing firm instead of waiting for two bankrupts to start their second ad agency before arriving with lorry loads of cash. What was the point? David would have had some excuse for that too.

So she'd said nothing and instead packed up everything she could afford to transport back to Ireland. And, somewhere in the laborious moving process, around the same time as the packing case containing all her saucepans and pots went missing, Robin had changed from caring daughter into the teenager from hell. After two weeks at her new school, St Clodagh's, all the clothes she'd previously liked suddenly became 'crap'. She wanted highlights in her hair because 'everyone has them' and her language had deteriorated at a frightening rate.

Isabel found it exhausting and infuriating coping with a girl who was bolshy, difficult and moodier than a roomful of hormonally challenged women. Dealing with Robin was almost worse than working with Richie Devine.

Robin had an excuse – she was a teenager – while Richie was the grown-up editor of a car magazine, even though he behaved more like an adolescent than any spotty fifteen year old Isabel had ever met. At least twelve-year-old Naomi was still the same – funny, sweet and accident-prone. The last time Isabel had laughed had been on Tuesday when Naomi had broken into giggles after tripping over her schoolbag in the hall.

Naomi was a funny child with such an off-beat sense of humour that you had to laugh with her. And, if Isabel hadn't found something to laugh at, life at her parents' home would have been completely unbearable. The anti-depressants helped, too, of course. Not that anyone knew she was taking them. She'd gone to the doctor after the first week at home, when she'd cried at least twice each day.

Two months later, she wasn't crying much at all and, apart from the fact that she was so sleepy in the morning, nobody would have a clue she was taking anything.

Isabel had picked up the clothes basket and opened the back door when the phone rang loudly. She dropped the basket quickly but before she had time to reach the phone in the hall, she could hear Robin pound across the landing to answer it in her grandparents' bedroom.

Pound, pound, pound, went Robin again.

'It's for you,' she roared down the stairs.

Wonders will never cease, thought Isabel, astonished that it wasn't another of Robin's new best friends, the ones who'd told her all about the correct, horrendously expensive trainers to buy, the right place to have her highlights done and what sort of utterly cool top she 'just had to have' before next Saturday's disco.

'Hello.'

'Isabel – I've got the most amazing job for you.'

Suzanne sounded as breathless as ever. But then her cousin had always sounded out of breath whenever she had news to impart, be it about her latest – dull – boyfriend or how well she'd done in the French exam – always better than Isabel.

'What sort of job?' asked Isabel, convinced it would be something daft, like running a community paper for a pittance. Suzanne hadn't grasped the fact that Isabel and David would not get back together, that she was broke because David's firm had gone belly-up, and that Isabel therefore needed a proper, full-time job so she could buy a house and move out of her mother's.

'Tim heard about it in the office.'

Isabel perked up slightly. Suzanne's husband was an estate agent and, even if Isabel couldn't figure out how he'd heard about a sub-editing job for her, she knew that Tim was about ten times more practical than her scatty cousin and would not mention jobs unless they were at least vaguely suitable.

'What sort of job?' she asked.

'It's because of the house in Sydney Parade. A mansion, Tim says. They want a quick sale, you see, that's why he got it instead of Anthony, because Anthony is up to his eyes with the Ailesbury Road auction . . .'

'Suzanne,' said Isabel with more patience than she felt, 'what the hell are you talking about?'

'The FitzSimonses! They're selling up to move to London and you know what she does, don't you?'

'*She? Who's she?*'

'Antonia FitzSimons! She's the women's editor of the *Sentinel*!'

The penny dropped. Clanged, in fact. A job vacancy! The position of women's editor on a paper like the *Sentinel* was the stuff of which dreams were made. The *Sentinel* was an upmarket tabloid with a huge readership. Before Robin was born, Isabel had wanted to work on a publication like that.

But it was a top job and she'd been out of the country for ten years, which meant she now knew nobody on the *Sentinel*.

Experience in journalism had shown her that complete strangers rarely walked into the best jobs – those generally went to people on the staff or who'd freelanced for the paper for years.

Isabel knew she had the experience for the job but it mightn't count as she'd worked abroad for so long. She'd worked as deputy editor of a top – well, medium

– UK women's magazine and before that had spent five years as chief sub-editor on a local Oxford paper. She'd still be working for *Today's Woman* if bloody David hadn't forced her to run home to Mother and Father. Getting Antonia FitzSimons's job would transform her life. But did she have a hope in hell?

'When did all this happen?'

Isabel dragged one of her mother's spotless white kitchen chairs across the black and white lino so she could sit and talk at the same time.

'They rang the agency yesterday and Anthony – that's Tim's boss – only put him on to it today. Anthony's raging he can't handle it himself but he really can't because he's up to his eyeballs with Ailesbury Road. Tim says the commission on Ailesbury will nearly pay for Anthony's conservatory . . .'

'Suzanne,' interrupted Isabel, utterly confused, 'just tell me about the FitzSimonses.'

'He rang yesterday, said he wanted the house sold ASAP because they're moving to London next week and want everything sorted because they need the cash to buy a new house. Holland Park, he said, apparently. Tim says the house prices there are astronomical,' Suzanne rambled on. 'It sounds wonderful. Six bedrooms, three en suite, a conservatory and granny flat . . .'

'In their house in Sydney Parade? Wow, that'll make a bomb!'

'No,' said Suzanne. 'The house they want in Holland Park. He told Tim all about it. Boasting, really.'

Isabel gave up. 'I've got to go, Suz. Can I ring Tim at work now or will he be out?'

'Ring him,' urged Suzanne. 'He'll tell you everything.'

After she'd talked to Tim, Isabel rang a friend on

Style, one of Ireland's top fashion magazines. Rhona McNamara was the only person from her college days whom she'd contacted since she'd come home. It was embarrassing to have to explain to everyone why she'd left Oxford, and why David wasn't with her. So Isabel decided not to bother.

Their old friends would find out eventually so she'd be spared the pain of telling them about the bankruptcy and all the other miserable details of her marital break-up. Rhona was different. She could be relied upon not to pry, nor to lord it over Isabel although she had a husband, three adorable kids *and* a career.

'Wouldn't mind Antonia's job myself,' said Rhona now. 'The *Sentinel* crowd get paid buckets, have expense accounts better than an MEP's *and* they all get company cars. You'd better get your oar in quickly, Isabel. That job will go like a shot.'

'I know, Rhona. But do you think I've a chance?'

Isabel absently fiddled with the fraying cuff of her faded grey sweatshirt. She'd only unpacked about a quarter of the black plastic sacks in which she'd transported her clothes. So far, she was getting most use out of the ancient casual stuff that was too worn or too wrecked to wear outside the front door. What was the point of unpacking her elegant work clothes when nobody but *Motor 2000*'s deeply demoralised staff would get to see them? Anyway, her hair needed highlighting badly as the mousy roots were showing through and she was too broke to get them redone. Getting all dressed up and still having two inches of mouse showing would be too depressing.

Rhona's voice broke into her thoughts. 'The downside of the job is that you haven't worked for the paper before and most newspapers like to employ people they already know. But,' she added, gleefully, 'I hear there are huge problems at the *Sentinel*. Circulation figures are going down and the editor, Nigel Burke – who's been there for ten years and is either burnt out or verging on insane, according to gossip – is keen on the idea of bringing in outsiders to shake up the staff.

'You never know, being a complete outsider who's worked abroad for ten years could swing it in your favour. Send in your CV today and ring tomorrow.'

'Oh, God, I don't know,' said Isabel slowly. 'Everything's been so awful for the past few months, I'm totally messed up. Robin's barely talking to me, I'm on the verge of being fired by piggy Richie Devine, and I can't even stop my own mother from telling me where I've gone wrong and how to run my life. Am I insane to think of applying for a job like women's editor of a national paper?'

'Don't be silly, Isabel. You'd be perfect for the job,' Rhona said briskly. 'Anyway, a chaotic personal life is a necessity for a women's editor today. How else would you write all those "juggling your life" editorials if you weren't juggling yourself?'

'I'm not even juggling, I've dropped everything,' protested Isabel, half-serious.

'So? You'll be able to empathise with your readers, won't you?'

Afterwards, Isabel went upstairs, found her old portable typewriter and spent an hour working on a CV.

Painfully putting all the details on paper made her feel even more unsure about applying for the job. How had she done all those things – run magazines and papers and actually enjoyed it? Now she felt tired all the time; tired and lacking in confidence. Could she really do a job like the one on the *Sentinel*?

The old Isabel could have. The pre-break up Isabel who was used to getting compliments about her style, her wonderful taste in clothes and her ability to stay calm in the face of any office catastrophe.

'How do you do it?' Penny Southark, Isabel's old editor on *Today's Woman*, had demanded when a new and inexperienced sub-editor managed to wipe out half the magazine on her computer hard disc and only Isabel had remained composed enough to sort things out.

She'd just smiled. 'Simple. My mother is such an organised person that my entire childhood was spent listening to her telling me how to do things right. In my mother's book, panicking about anything meant you were definitely doing it wrong. Calm was her favourite word – she should have been a Buddhist.'

Isabel didn't add that growing up with such a perfectionist was very, very difficult, especially when the perfectionist in question lost all her much-vaunted calmness when her daughter did things wrong.

Lately, Isabel felt that she'd lost her ability to be calm in the face of disaster. She'd also lost a lot of her hard-won confidence, as if the gradual erosion of the important parts of her life had somehow eroded part of her spirit at the same time. She felt sad, weary and more unsure of herself than she'd been for years.

Always quite slim, she'd lost weight over the past few months and it didn't suit her. Her face was pale, emphasising a fine bone structure a little too near the surface for comfort. The large blue eyes looked haunted, and without make-up – she hadn't really bothered wearing any for months now – her shoulder-length dark blonde hair combined with darker roots made her face look even more wan.

She could always unearth that fake tan, Isabel

thought, as she examined herself critically in the bedroom mirror. She had to do something. Nobody would hire her looking the way she did now. And she just *had* to get a decent job. Maybe Rhona was right – maybe she was well able to work for the *Sentinel*.

Pamela Mulhearn thought it was a shade ambitious when her daughter Isabel mentioned applying for the job on the *Sentinel* that night. Just back from her bridge club, Pamela walked into the kitchen and took off her cream linen jacket, eyeing herself in the mirror to check that her short, frosted curls were perfectly in place.

Tall, slim and still able to fit into the clothes she'd worn when she was twenty – a fact of which she was very proud – Pamela's posture was ramrod straight. She still climbed in and out of cars with the ladylike precision her own strict mother had drummed into her nearly sixty years ago.

'It's a good paper, Isabel, but are you sure you're ready for such a demanding job right now?' Pamela said doubtfully, wrinkling up the elegant nose that was so like her daughter's. She sat down and crossed slim legs, smoothing down the cream plaid skirt she'd bought in Harrods thirty years ago. 'Surely you'd be better off staying at the car magazine? Being women's editor would be very difficult and you're getting on all right where you are now. I doubt if you're ready for it.'

You doubt if I'm able for anything, Mother, Isabel thought with irritation. Why the hell couldn't her mother be supportive? Just for once. But that would be breaking the habit of a lifetime. No matter what Isabel did, it wouldn't be enough. It wouldn't measure up to anything Luke had done.

Lucky old brother Luke, living thousands of miles

away from Ireland and still the apple of his mother's eye and the yardstick by which everyone's achievements – mainly Isabel's – were measured. If he'd lived round the corner, perhaps Pamela would have realised that even her precious surgeon son made mistakes. Not as big as the mistakes her daughter had made, like going off with David, but mistakes nevertheless. Anyway, for all they knew, he could be busking on Hollywood Boulevard instead of working in a plush private clinic as an ophthalmic surgeon. Who knew what he was really up to since he phoned about twice a year and they'd only visited him a couple of times in the last decade?

If only her mother had had a career, something to occupy that rapier mind, life at home would have been so much better, Isabel thought. But a lifetime of watching other people struggle with tasks that Pamela Mulhearn could have done in her sleep, had made her bitter, frustrated – and always ready to leap down Isabel's throat.

Totally unaware of the bitter thoughts rattling through her daughter's head, Pamela flicked open her handbag with tapering, pearly pink-tipped fingers, took out a tiny silver pill box and extracted two of her migraine tablets.

'Be a dear, Harry, and get me some water, will you?'

Even though Pamela phrased the sentence as a question, she wasn't actually *asking* her husband to get her some water – she was ordering him. As she ordered everyone from him right down to the packer at the supermarket, who would be pointedly told to unpack the shopping if he'd inadvertently stuck a tin of consommé on top of the asparagus tips. Her mother was so good at ordering that she should have been in the army, Isabel thought privately. She even had a driver. Harry didn't play bridge but he faithfully drove his wife to her friends' houses three times a week and was content to return four hours later and pick her up.

He handed her some water and looked briefly towards the garden. Isabel knew her father desperately wanted to slip out to his shed, put on his ancient gardening clothes and leave the women to it while he tended his vegetables.

'What do you think, Harry?' asked Pamela. 'I think Isabel has been through too much lately, what with David,' she hissed his name, 'and having to move jobs and sell that beautiful house. A new job is too much to take on as well.'

'I agree with you, love,' Harry said, as he always did. Harry Mulhearn would have said that the moon was made of blue cheese if his wife asked him to. It was easier that way, as he'd learned after forty-five years of living with her. Isabel had never been able to stop herself from arguing.

Duty done, Harry went out of the back door to look round his beloved garden, the pride and joy of his life. Isabel loved gardening too, probably because she'd spent so many enjoyable hours with her father in the sun-filled back garden when she was young, watching him prune, plant, dig – and stay out of his wife's way.

The garden was a credit to his effort and skill, a curving lawn with three separate areas: the rose garden, the vegetable patch, and Isabel's favourite, the wild flower garden, a mass of cowslips, bluebells and dog roses, which her mother disliked.

'Mother,' Isabel argued now, 'it's a fantastic job and it would be wonderful if I got it. Of course it'll be demanding, but that's what I want right now. Something to take my mind off David and the separation.'

'Separation?' erupted her mother. 'I do hope you mean divorce? That's the only way to get rid of that weasel.'

Isabel ignored the interruption. 'As I was saying, the only problem is that there'll be incredible competition for the job.'

Her mother shrugged coolly, angry because Isabel had ignored what she'd said about getting divorced. 'You don't have to take my advice, Isabel. You never have before,' she said sharply.

Isabel dug her nails into her palms. She was sorry she'd ever mentioned the job.

'But when you have a nervous breakdown, *I'll* be the one picking up the pieces. I'm not the sort to say "don't come running to me" when that happens, Isabel, but that's how I feel.'

Isabel sat grinding her teeth. After three difficult months, she was desperate to get away from her parents' house. Please God, or whoever was up there, let her get a decent job so she could buy a three-bedroomed house or flat and then the girls wouldn't have to share a room. And *she* wouldn't have to listen to her mother's endless litany of Isabel's mistakes.

Her errors included getting into journalism in the first place: 'I wish you'd done medicine, Isabel, like your brother. It's not as if you didn't have the brains. You just didn't try hard enough.' Marrying David: 'I knew he was a wastrel the moment I set eyes on him.' And leaving the country when David got a job in sales with a large computer firm in the UK: 'Very stupid.'

'Well, if you *are* going for an interview, you'd better get your hair cut,' her mother said disapprovingly. Pamela Mulhearn felt that women over thirty should have short hair. At thirty-nine, Isabel was far too old to have hair past her ears. A nice sleek short style would be more suitable, more mature. 'Gordon would love to do your hair, Isabel,' Pamela added.

'Thanks, Mother. But I like my hair the way it is.'

Isabel couldn't afford to get her hair highlighted, which it badly needed, so she wasn't going to bother coughing up £25 for Gordon to butcher it into a frosted helmet like her mother's. She was convinced he could only cut hair one way, the way he secretly wanted his own to look.

'Have it your own way,' Pamela said. 'But I think you could do with a more suitable cut. Claudia's is so nice.'

Claudia was Luke's wife, a paragon of elegance and the sort of woman who wouldn't dream of leaving the house without wearing the entire Estée Lauder range, French-manicured nails and at least half a can of hairspray welding her gamine haircut in place.

'We haven't seen her *or* Luke,' Isabel emphasised, 'for so long that she could have Rapunzel-length hair by now, Mother.'

'Don't forget, Isabel, your brother invited your father and me over to Los Angeles last year. It wasn't his fault we couldn't manage to go the only week he was free.'

Isabel grabbed the kettle, shoved it under the tap and filled it up. There was no point in arguing that it seemed odd that a successful man like her brother could only take *one week* off during the entire summer. Dear God, please, please let me get the job so I can move out of home, she prayed.

Anything, anything, would be better than grinding her teeth every five minutes. No wonder she'd jumped at the chance to leave Ireland when David had suggested moving to London ten years ago.

Robin slouched into the kitchen wearing no bra and a

skin-tight black T-shirt – which Isabel had never seen before – with her black jeans. Her hair, the same dark blonde as her mother's, hung straight around her face and the heavy, over-long fringe almost obscured blue eyes that were sooty with Isabel's mascara. The combination of her height – she was nearly as tall as her mother now – and the sort of slender body that a supermodel would envy, meant Robin looked a lot older than fifteen. With make-up, she could have passed for nineteen or twenty, a fact that worried Isabel more and more.

The sweet, conscientious Robin of old wouldn't have given her mother a moment's worry about her whereabouts or her friends. But this sullen stranger was a different proposition altogether. Visions of her heavily made-up daughter hitting nightclubs with a dangerous, older crowd haunted Isabel.

She wanted to ask Robin where the T-shirt had come from, but knew that if she said anything her mother would go into outraged overdrive. Family rows were magnified tenfold when Pamela was involved. Robin pulled open the fridge, poked around until she found a yoghurt, and started eating it, completely unconcerned about the effect she was having on her grandmother.

'See ya,' she said once she'd finished her yoghurt. She dumped the spoon in the sink and tossed the pot blithely into the bin.

'Where are you going at this time of night?' asked Pamela.

'Out.' Robin stared at her grandmother insolently.

'It's half-eight on a school night! You've got homework to do,' Pamela said tartly. 'I don't think that's a very good idea, young lady . . .'

'You're not my mother!' retorted Robin.

'Don't you talk to me like that!' shrieked Pamela.

'Robin! Mother! Stop it!' Isabel intervened. 'Mother, this is between Robin and me. And, Robin, don't talk to your grandmother like that.'

'She can't tell me what to do, she's not my bloody mother! Or my father,' yelled Robin. 'I hate her, I hate you, I hate this place. I want to go home to Dad!'

Eyes blazing and tears running down her cheeks, taking plenty of mascara with them, Robin ran from the kitchen, sobbing loudly. They heard the door to her bedroom slam shut.

Pamela turned on Isabel. 'I didn't take you in to be treated like that,' she hissed. 'You know what these arguments do to my nerves. And it makes me wonder how you've brought that girl up when she speaks to me in that tone of voice.'

Isabel didn't point out that her mother started a fair percentage of the said fights. But she knew that didn't excuse Robin's appalling behaviour for one moment.

'I know, Mother. I'm sorry,' she said wearily. 'All this has been so hard on Robin.'

'It certainly hasn't been easy on the rest of us,' snapped her mother. 'I'm going to lie down. My migraine is getting worse.'

Pamela marched out of the kitchen and upstairs while Isabel leant against the sink. Her legs felt like jelly and she could feel the beginnings of a brutal headache throbbing at the base of her own skull. She hated arguments of any kind, always had. And unless she and the girls found somewhere else to live, there were going to be plenty more.

CHAPTER THREE

The office was like an oven. A great gust of hot air greeted Dee when she walked into the newsroom. The windows were open and the editor's secretary had positioned a huge electric fan right beside her desk, blowing papers and wafts of Chanel No. 5 towards the sub-editors' desks in the middle of the room.

'The air conditioning's bust,' muttered one of the sports reporters as he hurried past Dee. 'I'm going to a match,' he yelled to the sports editor who was just coming out of the editor's office, his face pale, no doubt after one of Nigel Burke's legendary tellings-off.

'He's probably going home to sit in front of the box and watch Sky Sports,' grumbled Maeve at the reporter's departing back. Dee pulled up a spare chair and sat beside her.

'Lucky sod. The heat's killing me and the smell of that damn' perfume is making me sick,' Maeve whispered. Nobody ever complained too loudly about the editor's secretary, Sheila Smyth, because she had ears like a rabbit, heard everything and reported it straight back to Nigel.

Dee cast a quick glance at Sheila and caught her staring beadily in Maeve's direction.

'Drill Sergeant Smyth is looking this way,' she said

under her breath. 'I'd better let you go back to work or she'll send her thugs round to nail your kneecaps to the floor.'

Dee got up. Maeve put a hand on her arm.

'Hold on,' she whispered. 'Since you couldn't make it, I had lunch with Phil Walsh and she's got the latest on Antonia's resignation. Come to the kitchen and I'll tell you – I need a break anyway.'

In the tiny kitchen, Maeve made a speedy cup of instant coffee.

'Antonia told Nigel first thing this morning. That's why he's going round like a bear with a sore head. He's already bawled out all the photographers for not getting pictures of Johnny Depp in the Clarence last night. And he was brutal to that poor trainee reporter from Cork. She's hiding in Advertising, sobbing her heart out.'

'God, he's such a bastard!' Dee said. 'But I can't believe Antonia didn't tell him immediately. You know how cross he gets if he doesn't hear everything straight away.'

'Well, you know how dense she can be. It probably never occurred to her that the editor would like to be one of the first to know she was going to resign. Or that her eighteen-carat golden handshake could very quickly turn into a gilt one if she left him in the lurch. Anyway, according to Phil, she ended up in floods because he called her every name in the book and then she went home – without finishing her bloody column, I might add. It's only half-written so I'll have to stick loads of bloody pictures in . . .'

'What did Nigel say to her?' demanded Dee. 'Did he say anything about a replacement?'

Maeve raised one eyebrow. 'From what Phil told me, I

don't think Antonia took in much of what he said apart from, "You stupid cow!" '

'Sorry I missed it,' said Dee regretfully. 'Should I go in and ask for the job today? I spent all last night working on my ideas for the women's section. All I need to do is print them out and I'm ready.'

The sports editor came into the kitchen with a cup in one hand and a mournful expression on his face. Normally an incorrigible flirt, he didn't even smile at the two of them. Nigel Burke's tirades did that to people.

As editor of the *Sentinel*, Nigel was the man in charge and had six people directly below him in the paper's hierarchy – his deputy editor and the women's, sports, news, features and pictures editors. Of those six, only one was just as bad-tempered and aggressive as Nigel, and that was the news editor, Ian Mahon.

Between them, they made more noise and had more rows than the rest of the staff put together, and their fights meant that sparks, and occasionally ashtrays, were always flying in the office.

'I've been thinking, Dee,' Maeve whispered, 'you'd better not go in and say you want the job yet. Give him a day to settle down. Because if you go in with your ideas today, it'll be obvious that you heard about Antonia leaving before he did, and he's quite likely to consider you the worst kind of traitor for not telling him.'

'Good point. I'll go in tomorrow.'

They were walking past Nigel Burke's office as they made their way back into the newsroom when his door burst open and he emerged, red-faced.

'Mahon!' he shouted in the direction of the news editor's office, which was right at the back of the newsroom, behind thirty or so reporters' desks. 'I want to know who's responsible for all these libel writs that have just landed on my desk!' he yelled, brandishing a sheaf of faxes in one hand.

'We're being sued by every bloody solicitor in the country. *You're* supposed to make sure we don't libel anyone, so *you're* not doing your bloody job right! And it's costing this newspaper a fortune!'

Nigel pounded past the subs' desks like a bull in a china shop.

Dee followed him into the newsroom, where all the reporters who'd been making personal phone calls and flicking idly through the papers while waiting for stories to break, hastily attacked their keyboards like people possessed.

The gossip columnist, whose desk was nearest Stalin's office, dropped the Yves St Laurent powder compact she'd been using to touch up her make-up, snatched up her phone and started talking at length to the engaged tone. 'Really, how interesting. And which member of the Royal family is coming to the ball? Ooooh, Princess Anne! Lovely!'

Nigel Burke didn't notice. He strode through the newsroom, marched into Stalin's office and slammed the glass door so hard the panels shook.

Unfortunately for the news editor, the glass front that let him watch every move the reporters made from the comfort of his own office wasn't soundproofed. The entire newsroom could hear everything Nigel yelled at him and the sports department listened in delight, thrilled to see another department in trouble.

'You stupid bastard . . .' Nigel screeched.

The news reporters kept their heads down and prayed *they* wouldn't be called in to explain exactly why a story of theirs had resulted in the paper's being sued for libel.

'*More* libel cases?' Dee asked Gerry, the political correspondent.

'That's the third today,' he replied, never taking his eyes off his computer screen. 'Nigel is going out of his mind about them. He's only just recovered from shelling out fifty grand to that bloke who was wrongly named as a drug pusher last year.'

'Did you hear about Antonia?' Dee inquired, as she switched on her computer.

'Heard last week. Just as well she's going. She'd never stick the next six months.'

Dee was surprised. 'But Nigel's always adored her – apart from today, of course – no matter how dreadful her column was. Why do you say that? Do you know something I don't, Gerry?' she added suspiciously.

He typed another sentence before answering. 'Let's just say that the powers-that-be aren't too pleased with our beloved Nigel. If the circulation figures keep dropping the way they've been for the past year, the paper's going to start losing money.'

'Wow!' Dee was stunned. 'I didn't know it was that bad.' She blanched as she thought of the massive mortgage she and Gary were saddled with, the holiday to Florida they'd been discussing for months and the expense of their wedding the following year. Well, she *hoped* it would be the following year.

'Nigel had better get his finger out if he wants to keep his job,' Gerry remarked, turning back to his story. 'So, you're thinking of going for Antonia's job, are you?'

'Do you know *everything*, Gerry?' Dee asked, startled out of her nightmare over finances.

He grinned at his screen. 'Most things.'

The first thing that struck Dee as she opened the front

door was the delicious scent of garlic and lamb wafting out of the kitchen. Fantastic. Gary had decided to cook after all. So he *had* listened last night when she'd complained about having to do all the washing, cooking and cleaning.

'I'm home, Gary. That smells fantastic. Is it really my favourite garlic and rosemary lamb?'

'Deirdre, you're home at last,' her future mother-in-law said sweetly from the kitchen. 'Dinner's nearly ready. I've sent Gary out for some milk as you didn't have any in the fridge except that dreadful skimmed sort which really isn't good for you at all. Oh, and some proper coffee. I do hate instant.'

Shit! When the hell had Gary's bloody mother decided to come over? And why hadn't he warned her? Dee dropped her briefcase on the floor and marched upstairs. No way was she going into the kitchen to say hello to Margaret Redmond wearing this outfit. Margaret always said that she hated women who wore 'vulgar, tight clothes' and Dee's clingy top was both. Not that Margaret could talk. Her clothes might all have been expensive stuff bought from chi-chi little suburban boutiques, but she still looked like a Sherman tank in every single one of them. Mumsy didn't just enjoy baking lorryloads of cakes and meringues – she loved eating them too.

'I'll be down in a minute, Margaret,' Dee said loudly, taking the stairs two at a time. Give you a chance to hide your broomstick, you old battleaxe.

'Take your time, Deirdre. I've everything under control. Where do you keep the napkins I gave you for your engagement? I can't find them anywhere.'

'That's because they've been at the bottom of the linen basket for the last three months with red wine stains on them,' Dee muttered to herself. *Bloody bitch is just checking up on me.*

'They're dirty, Margaret,' she yelled down the stairs. 'We'll have to use the tissue ones in the third drawer down.'

Another black mark. Dee didn't measure up to her future mother-in-law's exacting criteria. The daughter of a wealthy butcher, Margaret Redmond considered herself to be upper middle class and Dee, with her working-class roots and propensity for speaking her mind, didn't conform with Margaret's idea of the sort of woman her beloved younger son should marry.

Dee could see it all: the social-climbing Mrs Redmond hadn't been grooming her son with trips to art galleries and expensive violin lessons for him to go out with a mechanic's daughter. Only a huntin', shootin', fishin' gel with a lineage like a racehorse's and at least one parent with a posh accent would do for Mumsy.

'Interfering old cow,' Dee muttered as she changed clothes.

She pulled her comfy old black ski pants out of the wardrobe and had one foot in before she realised that her usual evening outfit – ski pants and a huge jumper which covered her bum – wouldn't be suitable for dinner with this particular guest.

Damn Gary! He could be so bloody insensitive. If he'd known his mother was planning to come round, he could at least have phoned the *Sentinel* to warn her.

The front door slammed.

'I got Rombouts filtered coffee. Is that OK?' Gary was clearly talking to darling Mumsy and not to Dee. *Whose bloody house was this? Hers or theirs? And what was wrong with instant coffee?*

Dee gritted her teeth and pulled a silky yellow

polo-neck jumper from a drawer and dragged it over her head before adding a voluminous black shirt. The last thing she wanted this evening was a forced conversation over dinner while her future mother-in-law bitched about everything from her missing linen napkins to the lack of decent food in the fridge.

'Hi, Dee. Did you have a good day?' Gary called up the stairs in a slightly tense voice. He had every right to be tense, Dee thought crossly as she ran a comb through her hair.

'Lovely, *dear*,' she replied.

She flounced into the bathroom to slap on some more make-up. As she reached for a bit of loo roll to remove a smudge of mascara, she realised there was none left.

She opened the cabinet under the sink to look for more loo roll and the box of strawberry condoms she'd bought Gary as a joke a few months earlier fell out. They'd used one but that was it. Dee stuffed them hastily at the back of the cabinet and was about to close the door when she changed her mind.

She took the box out and left it on the windowsill where Mumsy was sure to see it. About time she realised her son wasn't a saint, Dee thought with a wicked grin.

Dinner was hell. Gary avoided looking Dee in the eye and she noticed that he'd changed into the white cotton sweater his mother had bought him for his birthday the year before. He normally slobbed around in ancient T-shirts and threadbare jeans, but he had to dress up for his mother. It suited him, the pure white showed up the tan he'd got from playing lots of soccer in the evening sun. But Dee wasn't in a mood to appreciate her fiancé's finer points when he'd let his mother come over unannounced. *And* was sucking up to her like mad.

The cardboard that stopped the dining-room table from rocking was still missing, so Gary spent ages wedging bits of the cornflake box under the wonky leg. A lengthy grace was said and then Margaret dished out the vegetables like some Biblical princess distributing shekels to the poor.

'Some potatoes, Deirdre?' she said coolly. Then, in a much warmer tone, 'I've made your favourite cheesy ones, Gary.'

Margaret could certainly cook and the smell of succulent lamb was enough to make Dee drool with anticipation. But it was hard to enjoy the meal when her future mother-in-law was at the same table, ostentatiously holding up her knife to the light before breathing on it and polishing it with her napkin. Tissue napkin. To Margaret, paper napkins were on a par with having tea served in mugs and sticking the milk carton on the table instead of using a jug.

'Is your dinner all right, love?' Margaret asked her son anxiously.

'Beautiful. There's nothing like home cooking.' Gary smiled warmly at his mother and shovelled another forkful of lamb into his mouth.

Traitor, thought Dee. She stabbed a pea with her fork and a splash of gravy sailed on to the red place mat. I could make bloody lamb and cheesy potatoes every night if I didn't have a job. Or if I didn't spend so much of my time at home doing extra work or hoovering because your bloody son doesn't.

'He loves his lamb,' Margaret said fondly, her mean little eyes softening. 'All my boys love my cooking. I've got a great cookbook at home I could lend you, Deirdre,' she added with saccharine sweetness. 'It's got some of

Gary's favourite meals in it. He loves shepherd's pie, you know. Only with good mince.'

Dee simmered. This woman had marched into *her* house, stuck her nose up at the contents of Dee's fridge and the state of the place, and now she was insinuating that Dee couldn't – or wouldn't – cook! She clenched her jaw and imagined what she'd *like* to say . . .

'*You do spoil your boys, Margaret. In fact, you've spoiled poor Gary so much, he doesn't know how to boil an egg for himself and hasn't a clue how to do anything more complicated than phone the pizza delivery people, do you, darling?*' Dee smiled to herself, imagining the look of shock on her future mother-in-law's face. '*But he's marvellous in bed, of course. He nearly broke the chandelier the other night swinging from it on to the mattress!*'

She could visualise Margaret spluttering into her half glass of mineral water. What a howl it would be. Dee wouldn't let her get a word in edgeways.

'*In a modern relationship, people work together. Last night we decided to split all the housework and the cooking, didn't we, Gary?*'

'More wine, Dee?' his voice broke into her little daydream. He was holding up the bottle with a self-satisfied smile on his face. Of course he was pleased, she thought crossly. He'd made Mumsy happy and that was what counted. Who cared what Dee felt?

She barely spoke during the rest of the meal and left when Margaret started to dish up the rice pudding, pleading that she had to work on her agony column. Dee hated rice pudding with a vengeance; it was nearly as bad as tapioca, another nursery food staple that Gary unaccountably loved. Margaret probably had a cook-book full of recipes on thrilling things to do with tapioca and sago. Yeuch! If the stupid woman stopped fussing about her boys and had the odd glass of wine, she might be slightly more human. Then again, it'd take more than a glass of Chianti to turn Margaret Redmond into anything approaching a human being.

Upstairs, Dee turned on her computer but couldn't bring herself to write a word. She felt so angry. Angry and hurt. Gary *could* have told her Margaret was coming over. To add insult to injury, he'd never made it so plain that he'd hop to his mother's bidding when he wouldn't lift a finger for Dee. When was the last time he had gone anywhere near a shop unless he wanted to visit the off-licence or drop a video back to the shop? But once Mumsy clicked her fat little fingers, he hopped to it like a soldier on parade. So much for a relaxing evening at home watching the Tuesday movie. It was Woody Allen's *Hannah And Her Sisters* too.

Dee got the detective novel she was reading from her bedside table, sat in her tiny office, feet propped up on the desk, and ate an entire packet of butterscotch sweets. That was two big meals, five chocolate digestives in the office, four glasses of wine *and* a pack of sweets. Damn and blast. Nothing but black coffee and fruit tomorrow, she vowed.

The waistband of her size fourteen jeans was getting painfully tight. That was the problem with living with someone who could eat what he liked and still stay whippet-thin. Gary regularly brought home chocolate bars and giant tins of Pringles and left them lying around where Dee couldn't resist them. And then he had the temerity to say *she* had better watch her figure!

Dear Annie,

I've been big all my life. Not fat exactly, just plump. I could lose a stone and a half. Well, two stone. I've also spent most of my thirty-two years on a diet. My problem is my boyfriend.

When I met him, I was somewhat thinner. He said he loved the way I looked, but he hated women who dieted. He says you should eat what you want and you won't put on weight because that's what he does and he's slim.

So I eat what I want and I've put on weight, which he hates. I have to hide the dieting books and my low-calorie stuff at the back of the saucepan cupboard because he says I should throw out 'that rubbish'. He also says I look better slimmer and now our love life is non-existent. I know it's because he doesn't find me attractive any more. I can't look at the bathroom scales and I'm eating more than ever. I'm beginning to hate myself. What should I do?

When Dee heard the front door slam at half-ten, she switched off the computer and marched downstairs. Gary was stacking clean plates in the cupboard. The sink was empty, a tea towel was draped over the mixer taps and the worktops were spotless.

If Gary had done it, Dee would have been thrilled, but since his bloody mother had tidied up – no doubt, muttering that the whole place could do with a proper spring clean – Dee was irritated by the gleaming surfaces and cutlery-free dish rack.

Totally ignoring Gary, she filled the kettle and angrily got a cup from the mug tree. She didn't trust herself to speak even though she had a million things to say.

'I'm sorry, Dee, I should have told you she was coming. But she sounded so down when she rang today, I had to ask her over,' Gary said in a pleading voice. 'You know how cut up she is over its being Dad's anniversary. She's all alone in that big house . . .'

I wonder why? thought Dee savagely. She wrenched the lid off the coffee jar with some force. The old cow has completely alienated most of her neighbours, *all* of her daughters-in-law, and the only people who bother talking to her are her besotted little boys, five chauvinists who blindly worship the ground she marches on.

'She's lonely,' Gary repeated.

Dee turned around angrily to face him.

'I don't mind having your mother here if she's really lonely and miserable, but I *do* mind that she spends every moment of her time here criticising me! I don't cook proper food for you, I don't have decent food in the fridge, I use skimmed milk, instant coffee and, perish the thought, I even expect you to get your lily-white hands dirty doing a bit of housework! *That's* what I object to,' Dee hissed. 'Her constant harping.'

'She's not like that,' protested Gary.

'But the worst thing is the way you back her up. *Don't worry Mumsy, dopey Dee will never be able to cook like you, so why don't you come over every week and inject a little home cooking into our humdrum lives!* How the hell do you think that makes me feel? You won't even back me up in front of your bloody mother!'

'Oh, for God's sake, Dee, give it a rest,' he said wearily. 'I don't know what your problem is with my mother. God knows, she doesn't have much pleasure in her life these days and if cooking my dinner makes her happy, then I'm happy.'

'But I'm not!' shrieked Dee. 'Are you deaf or something? Don't you hear the way she puts me down constantly? And doesn't it occur to you that she has no right to march into my kitchen and start slagging off the way I run this house? Because,' Dee paused for breath, '*I* run this house. *You* certainly don't.'

He put a calming hand on her arm but Dee shrugged it off.

'Don't try and placate me, Gary. This isn't a joke, it's serious. I'm sick of you treating me like a skivvy. I work just as many hours, and sometimes more, than you do, I earn as much money and yet you still expect me to tidy up after you and wash your clothes. Well it's not on. I'm not doing it any more.'

'OK, OK, I'll help. But I don't see the need to tidy up as often as you want to,' he said mildly.

Dee clenched her teeth to stop herself from thumping him. He was so bloody stupid sometimes. He'd missed the whole point.

If Gary limited his tidying-up duties to the times he felt it was necessary, they'd live in squalor. Because he *never* saw the need to tidy up. They'd be back to square one in a week, with her screaming at him to wash the bloody dishes.

'There's no point talking to you, Gary. If you can't respect me enough to do your share of the housework, how can I expect your mother to? *She* puts me down because you put me down, and she knows she can say whatever nasty things she likes and you'll never stop her.'

'Don't be ridiculous,' he said. 'We're only talking about the washing up, not the future of the civilised world!'

'You just don't get it, do you?' Dee said tiredly. What was the point of talking about it all? Gary was never going to see her point of view.

'By the way,' he said in a calmer voice, 'Mum asked me could we take her to Simon's wedding because she doesn't want to drive her car.'

Dee raised her eyes to heaven. It was bad enough that Gary had accepted his cousin's wedding invitation without mentioning it to her until the previous week. But the idea of carting bloody Margaret all the way to Ashford in Wicklow was worse. At least an hour each way of bitching and smart comments. Dee groaned inwardly.

'Yeah, fine,' she snapped.

Simon was the son of Margaret's sister – another sharp-tongued, bossy harridan. His wedding to a wealthy solicitor's only daughter was 'the society wedding of the year' according to his doting Auntie Margaret. Dee was dreading it. She'd heard quite enough of how the Delahuntys were having the reception in the four-acre grounds of their stately Georgian pile in Ashford. Grounds that contained a rose garden bordered by a box hedge, several statues, a fountain and a tennis court.

'Yvonne's parents are charming. I think it's a wonderful idea to hold the reception in their grounds. They've even got an indoor swimming pool,' Margaret had explained.

God only knew what she was going to wear, Dee thought morosely. She'd have to buy something new or she'd look quite out of place among all the identikit pastel pink, blue and yellow £500 suits from Brown Thomas that all the other female guests would doubtless be wearing with the family pearls. More expense. Well, Gary could buy the wedding present. It was the least he could do.

'Tell you what,' he said, sitting down behind her at the table and massaging her bare neck, 'let's go out to dinner on Friday night, just the two of us to somewhere romantic. What do you think?'

She turned to face him. 'OK. That would be lovely.'

'I *do* love you, Dee,' he said gently, tracing the contours of her cheek with one hand.

He looked tired, she realised with a jolt. There were shadows under his eyes and he'd been stifling yawns all evening.

'I know it's difficult having Mum to dinner, but I feel so guilty when she rings and I say she can't come over,' he said. 'You'd want to do the same if your mother was in the same position, wouldn't you?'

'Yes,' Dee said, relenting. Maybe she *was* being a bit of a cow. Work was getting to her lately. Although all that would change if she got Antonia's job. Who knew? On Friday she could be celebrating her new appointment as women's editor. Now that *would* be a celebration!

CHAPTER FOUR

Nigel Burke slammed the door of the MD's office shut behind him.

'Would you like a cup of tea?' asked Ted Holt's secretary, a frosty-faced, fortyish brunette, seated behind an imposing desk.

Isabel sat down on a large black leather armchair and immediately slid uncomfortably into its depths.

'Sorry, er, no.' She tried to pull herself up in the chair. Why did so many offices have waiting-room chairs that you sank into without a trace? It was hard to look dignified when you were struggling to get out of a chair, your tights and knickers on view, your knee-length skirt hoicked up.

Isabel's feet touched the ground once more and she tried to smile at the woman opposite her, a confident, I'm-not-fazed-by-sliding-into-chairs look. The secretary stared determinedly at her word processor. A yellow mug with steam rising out of it stood on the desk beside her and Isabel wished she'd said 'yes' to that tea.

She'd have killed for a cup after her fifty-minute interview with the *Sentinel*'s managing director, Ted Holt, and Nigel.

They'd certainly grilled her thoroughly. Every aspect of her previous career was discussed, from 'Why did you leave Ireland in the first place?' to why she'd decided to leave her job in the British women's magazine. They'd wanted to know how she'd develop the women's pages if she was appointed. Isabel had been prepared for all these questions and had spent two hours the night before running through every possible answer, as calmly and professionally as possible, with Naomi standing in for Nigel.

As she sat on a hard chair in front of Nigel and Ted, Isabel had been very grateful for the previous night's practice run. Of course, she hadn't told Naomi that she'd come home to Ireland because she had split up from her husband and was thinking of getting a divorce.

Nigel's eyes had warmed momentarily at the words 'divorce'. *He* might have been impressed by her on-the-knee black skirt, her slim, seven-denier-clad legs and the elegant red jacket she wore. But it was impossible to tell if Ted Holt liked her as a person or, more importantly, as a job candidate. His sharp little eyes gave nothing away. He sat back in his chair, arms folded across a vast blue-striped chest, another question on his thin lips as soon as she'd finished answering the last one. The way he'd looked at her, Isabel didn't feel she'd a hope in hell of getting the job.

The secretary's phone rang. Isabel jumped in her seat nervously.

'Mr Holt's office,' the secretary said, winding a stray strand of hair behind her ear. 'No, he's not to be disturbed. He'll ring you back in half an hour.'

Half an hour? marvelled Isabel. Was that how long she'd have to wait outside the MD's office while they considered her for the job? It was already eleven-forty-five and she was due in at work by twelve.

She'd got the morning off by pleading a dental

emergency. Her *Motor 2000* boss, Richie, would be furious if she arrived any later, especially if she didn't look as if she'd spent the morning having a filling replaced. Maybe she could suck a big boiled sweet for the first hour back at work so her mouth would look swollen.

Isabel grinned to herself. But if she got the women's editor job, it wouldn't matter how cross Richie was. She wouldn't need his crummy job any more. Still, it was a big 'if'.

She tugged her skirt down towards her knees and wondered if she'd made the right choice in wearing something shortish instead of a skirt down to her ankles. Could a short skirt be construed as too sexy or flirtatious? It felt like a million years since she'd last gone for a proper job interview. The job in the car magazine hadn't counted because they'd only been looking for a freelance sub-editor and any sub with half a brain would have got it.

The *Sentinel* wanted a woman with fashion experience, so she could hardly have turned up looking drab, could she?

Forget about the skirt. The interview is over, it's immaterial what they think of your bloody outfit at this point, she told herself. She sighed and cast a desultory look at the daily papers which were spread over the table in front of her. The waiting was agonising – she might as well have been in the dentist's having a major bit of drilling done. At least he gave you an injection before he hit a nerve.

Suddenly, the inner office door swung open and Ted Holt appeared. He didn't waste time on pleasantries like nodding at Isabel or addressing his secretary by name – he just barked out orders.

'Get my car sent round and phone the restaurant and tell them we'll be late. I've got to call into the lawyers' on my way.'

The secretary was obviously used to his brusque manner and didn't bat an eyelid. 'Right. Do you want your messages now, Ted, or will I give them to you later?' she asked.

'Later.' He turned to Isabel. 'Come in,' he said, his voice warming.

Isabel did her best to smile and followed him back into the office where she'd been interviewed. Her heart was thumping so loud she was sure he could hear it and her mouth was as dry as the Sahara. Ted looked friendly for the first time. But was he lulling her into a false sense of security before telling her she hadn't got the job – or were they going to offer it to her? Who knew? And if he treated his staff the way he'd treated his secretary – with a bluntness that was verging on rude – then did she really want to work for him?

Isabel sat in the same hard chair she'd taken before and forced herself to clasp her hands gently in her lap instead of squeezing them tightly. That's what all the self-help articles told you to do when you were nervous. It didn't work.

Both men smiled expansively.

Ted leant against the front of his vast mahogany desk, opened a polished wooden box and extracted a cigar as fat as a frankfurter.

'We want to offer you the position of women's editor,' he said, 'and I think that calls for a celebration!'

'Hear, hear.' Nigel leant over to proffer a lighter.

Isabel didn't know what to say. She couldn't believe it. They'd offered her the job! *She* was the new women's editor of the *Sentinel*!

'Thank you. I accept, of course.' She beamed at the two men. 'You won't regret it, I promise you,' she added fervently.

'Nigel and I never regret anything, isn't that right, eh?' Ted winked at his editor. 'Now, can you join us for a spot of lunch, Isabel? We've got some important details to discuss, such as your salary, naturally, and I enjoy doing business over a glass of wine, especially when the company is so attractive!'

She flushed at the remark and thought of *Motor 2000* and the three-page article waiting on her desk to be transformed into a thrilling feature on buying the correct van for a small business. Much as she disliked Richie Devine, she hated to let anyone down.

Still, she reckoned, it would be a mistake to say no to her new bosses on day one, even if it did seem a little presumptuous to expect she'd be free for lunch at a moment's notice.

Isabel liked to be able to pencil in a date in her diary at least a week before the event. David used to drive her mad when he asked friends over for dinner at one day's notice. It was one of the many things they'd argued about.

'How the hell am I supposed to knock up dinner for six tomorrow evening when I'll be working late? I won't have time to get any groceries at lunchtime and the house is a disaster area,' she'd yelled the last time this had happened.

Maybe Ted Holt was just another man who did everything on the spur of the moment, particularly as he'd called her in for an interview a mere two days after she'd applied for the job.

'I'd love to,' Isabel said, giving her new boss the benefit of the ultra-confident smile she'd practised in front of the bathroom mirror the night before, 'but I must make a phone call first.'

'Sure, sure. Use the phone outside.' Ted waved one hand in the direction of the door. 'We'll be leaving in ten minutes.'

'Ted said I could use your phone,' she said to his secretary by way of explanation. 'We were never introduced. I'm Isabel Farrell,' she added.

'I'm Marion,' the other woman replied. 'Dial nine for an outside line. Would you like a cup of tea or coffee this time? Ted won't be leaving for a while and I've got a pot of coffee brewed.'

'I'd kill for a cup of coffee,' Isabel said gratefully. 'Thanks.'

Marion left the room with two cups and Isabel quickly dialled the office. Thankfully, Richie wasn't there.

'Tell him I'm really sorry and I'll be in extra early tomorrow morning to finish the pages I'm working on,' she told the other sub-editor. 'Yes, I *know* he's going to go berserk but I can't help it. I'll see you tomorrow.'

She hung up.

Marion came back with a small tray containing coffee, sugar, milk and some chocolate digestives.

'Welcome to the *Sentinel*.' She put the tray on the coffee table.

'Thanks.' Isabel had no idea how Marion knew she'd got the job, but then how had the secretary known she was going to lunch with Ted and Nigel? Perhaps she was psychic.

'They never leave on time for lunch,' Marion added. She took a couple of chocolate biscuits over to her desk with her coffee, sat back in her chair and prepared to chat.

'This really is a great place to work. I've been here ten years – I worked for the previous MD before Ted – and I'm telling you, I wouldn't leave here for anything. This office has a buzz about it. Not like some places I've worked in.' She took a bite of digestive and went on talking with her mouth full. 'It's lovely to have new people coming on board, a bit of excitement is good for all of us!' She smiled matily. 'Antonia was very nice, but a bit posh, if you know what I mean.'

Isabel didn't but was too interested in the gossip to say so. She nodded encouragingly.

'Everybody liked her – well, most people,' Marion continued. 'She'd been here since the paper started and she'd got great fashion sense. Always perfectly turned out. Have you always worked in fashion yourself?'

'No, not really. I've worked in women's magazines in the UK for a long time, but I've never really covered women's issues for a newspaper before,' Isabel explained.

'Really? And why did you leave your other job?' Marian inquired, leaning forward intently.

'It's a long story . . .' Isabel hesitated. Should she be going into this with the MD's secretary?

'Oh, go on, Ted won't be out for ages.' Marion glanced at her phone. A red light indicated that her boss's line was busy. 'I love a good chat.'

When Nigel and Ted emerged from the office fifteen minutes later, Isabel had drunk a second cup of coffee and was left with the feeling that Marion now knew an awful lot about her, while she knew next to nothing about Marion. Except that she was fond of both gossip and chocolate digestives, which probably explained why she wore a vast patterned overshirt that could have doubled as a maternity smock any day. Isabel cursed the nervousness that had made her chat away to the secretary.

'Sorry to keep you waiting, Isabel.' Ted buttoned up his jacket and headed for reception. 'I won't be back this afternoon,' he said over his shoulder to Marion. 'I'll be on the mobile if you need me.'

In the restaurant, they started with glasses of white wine – 'To keep us going while we order,' said Nigel, taking a deep sip – and moved on to two bottles of wine – red, to go with Ted's *filet mignon*. Determined to look cool and collected no matter what, Isabel barely touched her wine during the meal. The last thing she wanted was to get drunk at lunchtime, but it was obvious that Ted and Nigel had no such reservations.

They drank like it was going out of fashion, in between eating enough to stuff a small mattress. While Isabel enjoyed her grilled sole with salad, Nigel and Ted tucked into the sort of cholesterol-laden meal that had heart attack written all over it.

'I hate all that fancy French cooking – one bit of meat and two tiny bloody potatoes on a huge plate,' Ted said unnecessarily, as he speared a large piece of rare steak with his fork. 'Good Irish cooking, that's what I like.'

And lots of it, Isabel noted. Finally, Ted ordered horrendously expensive port to go with the selection of Irish cheeses.

Nigel and he were certainly entertaining company, and the editor's stories of the people he'd worked with were genuinely hilarious. But it was clear to Isabel that no matter how jovial or friendly he was today, Nigel wasn't a good man to have as an enemy.

'It was the story of the year, the decade, maybe,' he explained to Isabel, his face animated as he spoke. 'The bishop with two young grandchildren nobody knew about. We all knew he'd a daughter in her twenties but he'd managed to live that one down. "A youthful indiscretion", he said. Nobody had ever managed to track down the daughter, and not a soul knew she was living in Canada with twin sons.' He took a deep slug of port.

'Those kids were the image of the bishop. I'd been working on the story for six months and just before we were going public with it, that bastard Dick Morgan scooped it from under my nose and ran it on the front page of *Ireland Today*. I said I'd get him back and I did.'

Nigel's face lit up with glee. 'His wife had a fling with an old crony of mine and I made sure Morgan, and every reporter in Dublin, heard about it. It nearly killed him!'

'What goes around, comes around,' Ted said solemnly.

'I'll drink to that,' Nigel said with satisfaction.

There wasn't anything they *wouldn't* drink to, Isabel thought as she grinned and raised her glass with theirs.

The meal was over before Ted began talking about her new job.

'We've had a lot of interest in the position, I can tell you,' he said, lighting another cigar. 'Antonia had barely left when we got six letters of application for the job.'

'Really?' said Isabel, gratified to know how many people she'd beaten.

'It's a hell of a job and it's very important for the paper,' Ted added, which is why we needed a replacement immediately. Tell me, I've been wondering how you knew about Antonia going? It wasn't common knowledge. I was very impressed that you knew about the vacancy so quickly, especially since you've been out of the Irish journalistic scene for so long. You must have some great contacts.' He smiled at her eagerly, obviously dying to know exactly which *Sentinel* staffer had been feeding her information.

Isabel thought for a moment before replying. If they believed she was a red-hot journalist with her finger on the pulse, so much the better. They were never going to hear she'd discovered the job was up for grabs thanks to her cousin's estate agent husband. Or that her gossiping skills were so non-existent the MD's secretary now knew her life history while she knew nothing about the other woman.

Isabel smiled archly at them and tapped the side of her nose with her forefinger. 'Trade secret, gentlemen,' she said.

Ted burst out laughing. 'You'll be well able for them all on Tuesday,' he said confidently.

Isabel kept smiling, the sort of fixed grin that would hurt if she kept it up much longer. Able for whom? It sounded ominous.

'You see,' Ted drained his port and looked impatiently around for the waiter, 'there were six applications for the job – and you were the only outsider, or non-*Sentinel* person, to apply. Nigel and I both feel that the paper needs new blood, someone to shake things up a bit. We don't want people getting too comfortable, you know,' he added.

'It's bad for a paper when the staff get complacent and that's what's been happening recently. Another couple of these,' he said loudly to the waiter, holding up his empty glass. 'So, in getting the job, Isabel, you've pulled the rug out from under quite a few people. But I expect you already know that?

'I can't wait to see their faces on Tuesday morning when we introduce you at the editorial conference!' He smiled maliciously. 'You'll put the cat among the pigeons, I can tell you, Isabel.'

He and Nigel laughed, sharing the same joke. Isabel didn't know exactly what was amusing them so much, but she was beginning to get an inkling. Five *Sentinel* journalists had applied for the job and she'd got it – an outsider. What was worse, Nigel wasn't going to give the people who had applied unsuccessfully the chance to get over their disappointment in private. In fact, it was quite possible he wasn't even going to tell them they'd *been* unsuccessful. Oh no, he was going to introduce Isabel as the new women's editor in a blaze of glory on Tuesday morning and then stand back and watch jaws drop.

To the staff, she would look like Ted and Nigel's hired hand, their stooge, someone to keep an eye on a staff they clearly mistrusted. What the hell had she let herself in for?

'I've changed my mind,' Isabel said to the waiter who'd just brought over two more glasses of port. 'Can I have another too?'

'Mum, you're brill!' shouted Naomi when she heard. A slight, freckle-faced girl with her father's cool blue eyes and hair the same rich brown colour as his, Naomi had inherited David's sunny disposition – without his reckless, devil-may-care attitude.

She danced into the kitchen singing her favourite All Saints' song until she reached the cooker and slid her arms around her mother's waist. Isabel hugged her younger daughter warmly.

Thank God for Naomi, she thought for the thousandth time since the break-up.

'I'm glad *somebody* thinks so. Your sister barely spoke to me this morning. She's still sulking about being told she can't go to that overnight party on Friday. And your grandmother's in a mood because I told her not to interfere.'

'Don't mind them, Mum,' Naomi said indignantly. 'They're so childish.'

Isabel grinned wryly. Naomi was right – the other pair were far more trouble than this wise and kind young girl who wouldn't be a teenager for another two months.

'Robin will get over it. She wants to be angry with *someone*, that's all.'

'Oh, I know.' Isabel sighed. 'I just wish she didn't always have to be angry with *me*.'

She turned to stir the onions and chopped garlic she was sautéeing on the cooker. She was making real *Provençale* sauce for her special chicken dish to celebrate getting the job. If she let the onions and garlic burn, it would ruin the sauce. It was half-five and she was enjoying a few minutes alone with Naomi before her parents got back from their shopping trip into the city.

That was one of the things Isabel hated about living in this house: she never had any time alone with the girls. Not that Robin seemed to care these days. She spent hours with her friends, supposedly studying in their houses, although Isabel suspected that schoolwork was way down her elder daughter's list of priorities.

But it was lovely to be on her own with Naomi so they could chat the way they had at home in Oxford.

'When do you start?' asked her daughter, shrugging off the faded denim jacket she'd inherited from Robin. She perched on one of the kitchen chairs, long skinny legs folded under her.

'On Tuesday. I haven't actually seen the office I'll be working in because the editor didn't have time to show me. The managing director's office, where I was interviewed, is on a different floor from the newsroom.'

Isabel didn't mention that showing her the office would have ruined Nigel's malicious plan to shock the other journalists by introducing her for the first time on Tuesday morning.

'Will you have your own office?' Naomi inquired.

'No. Well, I don't think so. Nobody mentioned it.'

Isabel added the tomatoes she'd chopped up and the mixture sizzled.

'Did you meet any of the other journalists?'

'No, I didn't, but . . .'

Isabel broke off as she heard the front door open. Her mother's carrying tones could be heard even in the kitchen.

'Thank the Lord we're home! I can't stand travelling on the DART. All that pushing and shoving, and horrible people with those Walkmans turned up so loud I get a headache from the hissing noises. And they won't give up a seat for anyone . . . I don't know what the world's coming to.'

Isabel and Naomi exchanged knowing looks. Their 'quiet time' was over. Naomi raced out of the kitchen.

'Hello, Granny. Did you have a nice time shopping?' she asked in an innocent voice as if she hadn't just heard her grandmother moaning a moment earlier. Isabel smiled as she bent over the steaming saucepan. The little minx!

'It wasn't too bad, pet.' Pamela, like most people, couldn't resist Naomi's cheery good nature. 'Where's your mother?'

'Cooking, Granny. She's been dying for you to come home so she's got someone to talk to. She gets bored talking to me.'

When her mother marched into the kitchen, Isabel was conveniently facing the other way, trying not to snigger out loud.

'Hello, Isabel. What *are* you cooking?' Her mother sniffed the air.

She felt her hackles rise.

There was something about the way her mother spoke to her that constantly reminded Isabel of her childhood. Even now, it was as if Pamela was speaking to a wayward twelve year old instead of a thirty-nine-year-old separated mother-of-two. Her mother was just so *bossy*. Isabel sometimes half-expected Pamela to order her to tidy her room and not to leave the house wearing make-up.

As the head of a high-powered corporation, she would have reigned supreme and won countless Businesswoman of the Year accolades. As a woman bored both with her family's company and running a home, she was positively shrewish.

Isabel stuck a forced smile on her face for what felt like the tenth time that day and turned around.

'Mother,' she acknowledged, 'buy anything nice?'

Her mother sighed heavily. She put her navy leather handbag on the table and went straight to the kettle, patting a few non-existent stray hairs into place.

'There's nothing but rubbish in the shops. I don't know why I bother. And your father couldn't keep up with me, kept saying he was out of breath and needed to sit down.' She sniffed. 'That's why we're so late. What is that you're cooking? It smells strange. I've some bacon and cabbage for tonight.'

Which nobody likes but you, Isabel muttered to herself.

'It's a French dish, Mother. Robin and Naomi love it

and, as we're celebrating tonight, I thought I'd cook it for them.'

'I hate to see good food going to waste,' her mother said crossly. 'You should have told me you were going to cook something else, Isabel. You just don't think, do you?'

Isabel ignored her and tasted the sauce from the wooden spoon, trying not to burn her mouth. It needed more basil, just a pinch. But it was still gorgeous. As the rich, garlicky aroma filled her nostrils, she could remember the last time she'd cooked it: Robin's birthday in February. David had given her a £50 voucher for Miss Selfridge and she'd been over the moon.

The four of them had eaten together, but Robin had finished quickly so she could phone her best friend and tell her that the wispy purple chiffon dress she'd admired for so long in Miss Selfridge window was no longer a daydream.

'I won't be long on the phone, I know you've got a birthday cake ready, Mum,' Robin had said, giving her mother a quick hug before she'd danced out of the room.

Isabel could barely remember the last time Robin had been so affectionate. That was what hurt the most about their relationship these days – the fact that Robin had always been a loving daughter before, the most affectionate kid you could imagine.

And now she was permanently sullen, never gave or looked for a hug, and was only even vaguely animated when she was angry. Which was often enough.

Isabel sighed. So much had changed.

'What are we celebrating?' demanded her mother. She refolded the tea towel Isabel had left scrunched up by the sink.

'I got the job on the *Sentinel*, Mother.'

'*Really?*'

'Yes, don't sound so shocked.' Isabel wrenched open the oven and took out the browned chicken pieces.

'I'm not shocked. I'm merely surprised you found out so soon. Didn't they have any other applicants?'

Don't lose your temper, Isabel. Stay calm.

'Of course they did but they've seen everyone else, Mother, and I was the one they wanted. I start on Tuesday and I'm thrilled.'

'Well done,' her father said abruptly.

Isabel hadn't even noticed him come into the kitchen. He usually stayed out of it, regarding it as his wife's territory and, therefore, giving it a wide berth.

'Thanks, Dad,' Isabel said warmly. Why couldn't her mother have said that?

'Here are your tablets, Pamela,' he said, handing his wife a pharmacist's bottle, 'for your headache.'

'I got a bottle of wine, Dad,' Isabel said. 'It's on the windowsill. Maybe you could open it and we could have a glass before dinner.' Or before I murder my bloody mother.

'I'll have a sherry, Harry,' her mother said with a meaningful sniff. 'You know I can't drink wine when I've got a headache. It makes migraine worse, as you know, Isabel,' she added pointedly.

All the more for me, she thought, and didn't mention the second bottle she'd bought. It might come in useful if the Mulhearn family dinner proved as tense as usual.

Her mother wasn't to be deflected by a glass of sherry, though.

'I hope it's not one of those contracts where they can fire you after six months? You should get a lawyer to look at it for you, Isabel, you're hopeless with things like that. You could ask that nice lawyer friend of Luke's, he's got his own firm now,' Pamela advised. 'I'm sure he wouldn't charge you too much under the circumstances. And I hope they're paying you a decent wage? After all, you're a deserted wife with two children . . .'

'Mother, I'm not a deserted wife. I'm separated. David didn't desert me, we split up. There's a difference, a *big* difference. And I'm not *hopeless with contracts*. How the hell do you think I held down two decent jobs in the UK? Because they all felt sorry for me?'

'Don't get on your high horse, Isabel.'

'I'm not.' But her hand shook as she slopped the tomato sauce over the chicken pieces. Calm down, she told herself. 'They'll be paying me a very good salary but it's nothing to do with my circumstances. Salaries don't work like that, Mother. Otherwise, there wouldn't be any *poor* people in the world.'

'Well, I don't know, Isabel. It's a pity you've got to support the children on your own now. Not that David was ever much of a breadwinner but at least he was a father and contributed *something*.' Pamela paused to sip her sherry. 'And it's not as if you're going to meet anyone else at your age, is it? I was talking to your Aunt Janet this morning and she said that Annette had split up with her latest man, which is no surprise to me. If you haven't got married by the time you're thirty-five, there's no hope for you.'

'Here.'

Her father shoved a very full glass of wine under Isabel's nose.

'Thanks, Dad.'

'Have a sip.' His eyes were warm with understanding.

To hell with a sip. Isabel took a good gulp and winced slightly. It wasn't the best wine she'd ever tasted. But she was on such a tight budget that anything over a fiver was too expensive. David knew enough about wine to pick something good no matter what the price – a skill she'd never had. Well, she'd learn. She didn't need him any more.

'This will be ready in another half an hour,' she announced, determined not to be goaded into losing her temper. 'Mother, you have a rest this evening. Put your feet up and I'll lay the table. Naomi can help me.'

Pamela smiled for the first time. 'I *am* tired,' she said. 'I think I'll have a lie down then.'

'Great.'

As soon as she was alone, Isabel picked up the newspaper her father had left on the kitchen table and riffled through it until she found the property section. Big, small, indifferent, infested with vampire bats or painted acid yellow all over – she didn't care what sort of place she bought so long as she could get out of her mother's house.

Dinner was not a roaring success. For a start, Robin was half an hour late. The chicken was practically cremated by half-six, so Isabel had served it, mentally cursing her daughter for not turning up in time.

'I told you I'd netball practice this evening,' Robin said when she marched into the kitchen and met her mother's angry glare. Robin's ponytail still looked as silky and fresh as it had that morning after she'd hogged the hairdryer for thirty minutes. She didn't look as though she'd just spent an hour running around on the netball court. But Isabel decided not to say anything. She couldn't face another row.

Pamela was too busy pushing her chicken around her plate to comment. The look on her face said dried up chicken *Provençale* was not her idea of a proper meal. Certainly not in the bacon and cabbage league.

'Robin, it's your favourite,' Naomi said helpfully, pulling the chair beside her out for her sister.

Robin sank moodily on to it.

'I'm not hungry,' she announced.

'Mum got the job,' Naomi added.

'I was hoping you'd be pleased for me,' Isabel said drily.

Robin had the grace to look ashamed.

'That's great, Mum,' she said. 'Well done.'

Isabel smiled, got up and put a small portion of chicken and baked potatoes on a plate for Robin. Robin gave the chicken the same sort of glance her grandmother had given it.

'I made chicken *Provençale*, specially for you, love,' Isabel said. 'Not that it resembles anything *Provençale* any more, it's so dried up.'

'I can't believe you did this,' said Robin in a strange, high voice. 'This is Daddy's favourite. You *know* the last time we had this – on my birthday. How *could* you?'

She pushed the plate away from her, scraping her chair on the floor in her haste, and ran out of the kitchen sobbing.

'Don't mind her.' Isabel felt her father's hand on her sleeve as the tears threatened to fall. 'You know what young girls are like. I remember you at that age.' He patted his daughter's sleeve. 'You were an awful handful.'

'Disgraceful, that's what it is,' Pamela snorted, and took the opportunity to push her untouched dinner away from her. 'You've ruined that girl. Mark my words, you'll have nothing but trouble with her. Wayward, that's what she is . . .'

'Give it a rest, Pamela!'

The sound of Harry Mulhearn's raised voice gave them all a shock. Isabel couldn't remember the last time she'd heard her father speak angrily.

'She's just a confused young girl. She can do without your interference, Pamela. Leave Isabel to rear her family on her own.'

Enraged, Isabel's mother launched another attack. 'I won't have that kind of behaviour here. I open my home to Isabel and the girls and look what I have to put up with. That child is a disruptive influence. She's rude, she's inconsiderate, and I don't know why I put up with it.'

Isabel remained standing and put her head in her hands. She wanted to block out all the shouting and yelling forever. She wanted to climb into bed, pull the duvet over her head and wake up to find it had all been a horrible dream, a nightmare.

She'd come to in her comfortable bed in The Gables, with the light streaming in through the pale green-sprigged curtains and the scent of her rambling rose drifting in from the open window. Robin would be singing along to the radio in her bedroom as she carefully applied the little bit of eye-shadow allowed in school, Naomi would be trying to stay in bed for a few minutes longer, and David would have just come into the bedroom with a steaming cup of tea for Isabel . . .

No, that wasn't a dream – that was a fantasy. David had never got up to make her a cup of tea in their entire married life. *She* had to make the tea for him, never the other way round.

Her mother was still muttering, but she was doing it quietly.

'Mum, are you OK?' Naomi stood beside Isabel, her eyes wet.

'I'm fine. Fine, darling.' Isabel put an arm around the trembling child. This wasn't fair on poor Naomi. Whatever happened, she just had to get out of this house.

It was bad enough coping with Robin on neutral ground, but in the explosive atmosphere of her parents' house, it was impossible.

'Everything's going to be fine, Naomi,' she said, resting her cheek on the top of her daughter's head. 'I promise. This weekend, we'll go house hunting,' she whispered. 'It'll be our secret, yours and mine. All right?'

CHAPTER FIVE

Dee swung into the *Sentinel* car park at high speed and drove to the parking spot near the front door which she usually occupied if she was in early enough. A rather battered, British-registered green Volkswagen she didn't recognise was parked there. Blast! It was raining heavily. The only other spot left was the one in front of the security hut which was as far away from the entrance as you could get. She'd be drowned in the torrential downpour before she reached cover. And, naturally, she didn't have an umbrella or a raincoat with her.

'The wet look really suits you,' said one of the photographers moments later as Dee stood in reception and shook the rain off her hair.

'Ha, bloody ha,' she retorted as she ducked into the ladies to see how frizzy her hair was. It didn't matter how much non-frizz serum she sloshed on – all it took was a bit of rain and her carefully styled hair was like a pile of dirty brown straw.

She was rummaging through her bulging handbag for a brush and her small can of hairspray when a loo flushed and a tall slim blonde came out of one of the cubicles. Taller than Dee and around three stone thinner, the woman was very pretty with a delicate, fine-boned face, large blue eyes and a cupid's bow mouth that was curved into a shy smile.

'Hello,' she said. She turned nervously towards the mirror and carefully washed her hands. Married, Dee observed, noticing the slim gold wedding band and antique diamond ring. And definitely well-off. That beige trouser suit hadn't cost less than £300 and the cream suede handbag and matching pumps were hardly chain store stuff either. What's more, *her* hair hadn't been ruined in the rain. Dee fluffed her own mop resentfully as she eyed the other woman's blonde wavy hair – not a strand out of place.

'Awful weather, isn't it?' the stranger said hesitantly with another shy smile.

'Yeah,' Dee agreed. And wondered why anyone stylish, elegant-looking and so *slim* could be lacking in confidence.

'Trust me to forget my bloody umbrella,' she said, to put the other woman at her ease. Maybe she was one of the interviewees for the advertising secretary's job, Dee thought. Poor dear, she looked far too reserved and quiet to cope with the banter and ribald jokes in that department. The blonde woman took out a lipliner and shakily outlined her lips with a pale pink the same colour as her nails. God, she was nervous.

Dee decided to do her good deed for the day. 'That's a lovely suit,' she said kindly. 'Where did you get it?'

'Thanks.' When she smiled, the blonde woman's face lit up. 'I got it in a sale in this little boutique in Oxford about two years ago. It's my favourite shop . . . well, it *was*. I moved home a couple of months ago and I doubt if I'll be going back,' she added sadly.

'Oh,' Dee said, aware that she'd somehow said the wrong thing. 'Well, it's lovely. I'm always on the look out for nice suits for work but I keep buying boring black ones, like this.' She laughed, indicating the fitted black velvet jacket and matching mini skirt she wore with a cream lacy T-shirt. She'd felt so enormous when she'd looked in the mirror that morning that she'd decided to dress so outrageously over the top that nobody would notice how fat she was. Her make-up was expertly applied, she'd worn her favourite dangly jet earrings and, with spindly suede mules accentuating her black-clad legs in the mini skirt, she hoped she'd achieved the desired effect.

'Black suits you,' the other woman protested. 'Your hair is so vibrant you can get away with it. It just makes me look washed-out.'

'Thanks,' said Dee, thrilled at the compliment. Vibrant, huh? Gary had been too grumpy and too interested in the paper over breakfast to notice what she'd been wearing or what she'd looked like, which was nothing new.

She sighed. Maybe they needed a weekend away, somewhere secluded and romantic. That was it. She'd get some holiday brochures later and they could pick where to go tonight.

''Bye.' The blonde woman smiled shyly.

'See you,' Dee replied. 'Oh, and good luck.'

Isabel was still smiling when she walked along the corridor to Ted Holt's office. What was she worrying about? That woman in the loo had been so kind and friendly, exactly the opposite of what she'd been expecting.

Isabel was almost certain she was Dee O'Reilly because she'd seen Dee's picture byline in the paper the day before. The photograph didn't do her justice. Dee was much better-looking in real life, no black and white picture could do justice to her stunning colouring. She was incredibly attractive with creamy pale skin, a smattering of tawny freckles and big, dark eyes. And she had the most amazing hair. Isabel would have killed for those lustrous, chestnut corkscrew curls. Dee was certainly a big girl but she could carry it off. She had a wonderful sense of style, was very sexy and obviously bursting with self-confidence. What a pity all bigger women weren't as assured, Isabel thought. *Of course!* What a great idea for her first fashion spread – clothes for women over size sixteen.

Pleased that she'd added another idea to her list, Isabel stopped for a moment before going into Ted's secretary's office. With a look around to make sure nobody could see her, she hoisted up her bra straps and boobs with one quick movement. There. She was never going to be Dolly Parton, but a padded, plunge bra certainly helped in that department.

She hoped the bronzing powder she'd brushed on liberally didn't come off on her jacket.

Ted and Nigel were waiting for her. Nigel had abandoned the smart suit and tie he'd worn at the interview for an open-necked shirt in a bilious green, and black, slightly shiny trousers.

At least Ted was well dressed in a grey pinstripe suit even if he was openly eyeing her up through his piggy little eyes.

'Ready?' asked Nigel. He reached into his shirt pocket, took out a cigarette and lit it in one practised movement.

'Yes,' Isabel answered. 'I'm ready.' Almost. It was a long time since she'd been in a daily newspaper office. The noise and bustle hit her as soon as Nigel pushed open the big door and showed her into a massive room that took up an entire floor of the building. It was buzzing with activity. People were talking on phones, sitting at desks scanning the day's newspapers and writing furiously on screens.

Two televisions droned in the background, one turned to the teletext service, the other to CNN, while raucous laughter came from a little group at the far end of the room. From the door, Isabel could barely make them out.

A couple of people turned and looked at the three of them, staring curiously at Isabel for a moment. But no one else took any notice. They were too busy following up stories or talking animatedly on the phone. She could feel her legs trembling. It had been so long since she'd worked in a daily newspaper, so long since she'd been a part of that frantic world where everyone's lives depended on getting the story before the deadline.

To judge by the number of desks, at least sixty people worked in this office alone. No, probably more. God knew how many worked in the rest of the place. It didn't look like the sort of office where you'd make firm friends for the rest of your life. Unlike her last permanent job, where, in the tiny magazine office, they'd all lived in each other's pockets.

'The newsroom is the hub of the place,' Nigel explained. 'We don't have lots of different journalistic departments on different floors here. I like to keep an eye on things, so everyone is based here – the sports department, features, you name it, it's all here, right in front of me. Apart from the photographic department, which is in the basement. This is my office,' he added, as he opened a door into a very untidy room, dominated by a big desk. The walls were stained brown with nicotine and the air was stale with the smell of old cigarette smoke. Newspapers were stacked higgledy-piggledy on the floor, on a coffee table and on the low, grey couch against one wall.

Yellow post-its with phone numbers scrawled on them littered the desk, along with curled up sheets of fax paper and several uncapped biros.

'Have a seat.' Nigel sank into the chair behind his desk.

Isabel cleared a section of the couch and sat down nervously. Be calm, she told herself fiercely. You've just earned yourself a great job, don't panic now. Think of Robin and Naomi – you're doing it for them, too. You've got to get a place of your own for the girls.

Nigel riffled through the heap of paper beside the phone. His face darkened.

'Jesus, look at this,' he said angrily, holding up a sheet of fax paper. 'The lawyers say we haven't a hope in hell of getting away with an apology for a fraud story where we named the wrong effing person. I'm going to kill that stupid reporter for putting an extra initial in the man's name. Smyth P. Mitchell became Smyth P.J. Mitchell,' he explained to Isabel, 'and Smyth P.J. wasn't very pleased to see his name wrongly splashed over our front page last week.

'The lawyers say we're going to have our asses sued,' he added to Ted.

Ted sat down heavily. 'I thought you'd talked about this to Mahon?'

'The news editor,' interjected Nigel for Isabel's benefit.

'The soon-to-be-*ex* news editor if he keeps this up,' snarled Ted. 'Next time we get sued, he can bloody well pay the damages himself. That might make him a bit more careful about checking stories for libel. We can't afford another big case, not now.'

'Nigel,' said a female voice on the editor's phone intercom, 'I've got a call for you on line one.'

'Can't you take a number? I'm busy,' he snapped.

'It's Simon Walsh. He says it's urgent.'

'I'm in a meeting.'

'He wants an answer now, Nigel.'

'I'll call him back at twelve, right?'

'Fine.'

'Stupid bitch never knows when to interrupt me and when not to,' he said testily.

What a charmer. Isabel fought to keep a neutral expression on her face.

She'd only been on the premises ten minutes and the editor and managing director had already slagged off two members of staff in her presence. Nigel handed both Ted and Isabel a stapled sheaf of pages.

'This is a list of the subjects we'll be covering at the editorial meeting,' he said. 'I'll get everyone into the conference room. You two can make your grand entrance in half an hour when we're nearly finished.' He grinned maliciously. 'Let's ruffle some feathers!'

Isabel didn't even bother to smile as he left. She flicked through her pages but she couldn't read them, could barely focus at all. This was going to be a nightmare, she knew it. A meeting that would include the five furious journalists who'd wanted the job she'd just got.

She could have coped with that but she was beginning to think that the *only* reason she'd been brought in was to do just what Nigel had said – to ruffle their feathers. Or, worse, to completely undermine them.

'I'm going to talk to Nigel today. Antonia's only doing

the rest of this week as women's editor and we need a replacement, which, hopefully, will be me. What do you think?' Dee perched on the edge of Maeve's desk and looked at her friend anxiously. 'I'm going berserk wondering what he's thinking. If he hasn't mentioned the job to me so far, do you think that's a bad sign?'

Maeve keyed in another command on her word processor before swivelling her chair around.

Today, she wore a sloppy deep red jumper and matching lipstick, neither of which did a hell of a lot for her pale skin and short, dyed burgundy hair. Sometimes Dee longed to take her friend aside and give her a complete makeover, starting with throwing out all of Maeve's rather eccentric wardrobe. But she wouldn't have hurt Maeve for the world and to point out that her dress and colour sense were non-existent would have been very hurtful indeed. She'd just have to keep buying Maeve jumpers and shirts in the pale, subtle colours that suited her for Christmas and birthdays and hope that she might suddenly realise what looked good on her.

'With Nigel, *everything* is a bad sign, whether he's mentioned the job to you or not,' Maeve remarked. 'He loves to play games, Dee, you know that. Making you wait while he figures out who to give Antonia's job is just another of his little tricks.'

She reached into a drawer for a packet of Silk Cut and a lighter. 'Right now, I bet you a tenner he's working out exactly *who* he can give the job to in order to irritate the maximum number of people.'

Dee sighed. Maeve was probably right. Nigel made Machiavelli look like a boy scout leader. Stabbing people in the back was his forte.

Maeve got up. 'C'mon, I need a cigarette before the editorial meeting.'

Smoking was banned in the building but the diehard smokers like Maeve still smoked in the loos and, if they could get away with it, in the long corridor outside the conference room.

They stood there beside an open window while Maeve smoked and Dee fretted. Blast Nigel. Why the hell couldn't he tell her whether he was considering her for Antonia's job? All this waiting would give her an ulcer. It was *days* since she'd sent in her application. How long did it take to compile a list of suitable candidates – a month?

Nigel sauntered down the corridor whistling, a folder under his arm. He looked positively jaunty. 'Hello, girls,' he said with a nod, before going into the conference room.

Girls! Dee hated it when he said that. They were women. Not girls. What bloody age did he think girls became women – fifty?

'He looks very pleased with himself,' muttered Maeve out of the side of her mouth.

She was right. Nigel did look happy. And what did he have to be happy about? Dee wondered. She was still wondering five minutes later when the editor finished lacerating both Mahon and Henry, the unfortunate reporter who'd added an extra initial to the defendant's name in the fraud story.

Dee shifted in her chair and for the second time rearranged her notebook and pen on top of the conference table. She resisted the impulse to doodle on her notebook because Nigel took a particularly dim view of people not paying one hundred percent attention to what he was saying – or shouting, as the case may be.

Doodling was a sure sign of not paying attention and

could get you sent off to do some horrible rats-in-the-neighbourhood story which would involve hanging around a housing estate all day while each and every resident complained about the rat invasion and the lack of council help in getting rid of them. Photographers who got on the wrong side of Nigel also got rat duty but they had to hang around and try to get a *picture* of a rat, which was even worse. One reporter insisted he knew a photographer who kept a dead rat in his freezer for that sole purpose.

The editor finished bawling out poor Henry and smiled slowly. Dee shifted uneasily in her seat. Expenses – that had to be it. Everyone's expenses claims were too high and they were all going to get a telling off. Nigel loved telling people off.

But he didn't say anything about expenses. He worked his way down the news list, in his usual bullying way. Everyone and their granny was told they were incompetent, useless and destined for the high jump if they didn't get some decent stories that could be printed without libelling too many people. In other words, it was business as usual.

The only strange thing was that neither Nigel, nor the news editor, assigned Dee any stories. She couldn't figure out why. And then a glimmer of hope came to her.

Maybe Nigel was going to appoint her women's editor after all! That's why he hasn't given me anything new to work on, she thought joyfully. They've finally recognised what I can do, after six years!

She desperately wanted to blurt it out to Maeve but thought she'd better wait. She could be wrong after all. Nevertheless Dee sat through the rest of the meeting in a state of complete and utter joy.

She could see herself telling Gary. He'd always hated her working in news because the hours could be so anti-social. Now he'd be thrilled. And to think of telling her parents that the first member of the O'Reilly family to go to college, had been given a top job at the age of thirty-two! Dee remembered how delighted mum and dad had been when she'd got her first full-time job in journalism. They'd been so happy and proud. Wait till they heard she was women's editor.

When the meeting ended, Nigel didn't dismiss the assembled journalists with his usual: 'Scram! You won't get stories sitting on your backsides.' Instead, he left his place at the top of the table and opened the conference-room door to usher in the managing director and the tall blonde woman Dee had met in the ladies a little earlier.

The woman smiled uneasily at the thirty people who sat around the polished table and quickly sat down in the chair beside Nigel's.

'He's either going to tell us that circulation is up – which is why Holt is here – or he'll explain that they've got to economise by reneging on the last pay scale deal and the blonde is the accountant with the figures to back it up,' Maeve whispered.

Belinda, the gossip columnist, who'd just bought an horrendously expensive new house, groaned at the remark.

'Doesn't look like an accountant to me,' said the sports editor, Tony, appreciatively. 'If she *is* an account-ant, I think I definitely need to hire one!'

'Me too,' added one of the news team.

'I bet she's a time-and-motion spy sent to see how long it takes us to write stories in between making cups of coffee. And you boys don't need accountants,' whis-pered Dee, who was so happy she couldn't care less what bad news the accountant or time-and-motion woman was ready to impart.

'Anyway, *I* can do your accounts, boys,' she added with a laugh. 'I'll show you: you spend all your money in the pub. QED. That'll be two hundred quid and I expect the cheque in the next post.'

'Hilarious, Dee. Can you do mine too . . .'

'Shush!' hissed someone.

Everyone shushed. The news editor, sitting near the top of the table, fiddled with his tie and looked anxious. So he bloody should, Dee thought. If he wasn't pushing all the reporters to track down six or seven news stories every day, Henry wouldn't have made such a stupid mistake in the fraud story. He was simply overworked, like everyone else on the news team. That was how costly errors were made.

'Good morning,' said Ted Holt loudly. He gazed smugly around the table like Solomon about to impart a pearl of wisdom. 'I'm sorry to barge in on your editorial meeting but there's someone I'd like you to meet.'

Maeve and Dee exchanged brief glances.

'Accountant,' mouthed Maeve.

'Time-and-motion expert,' whispered Dee.

'As you all know . . .' intoned Ted gravely.

Dee raised her eyes to heaven. They'd be here all day if Holt started one of his sermons.

'. . . a valued member of staff is leaving the *Sentinel* for pastures new and she'll be sorely missed.'

Dee stared at the managing director in shock. What was this? Ted was hardly about to arrange a party for Antonia. In his mind, once a member of staff left the paper, they were useless to him and, therefore, not worth the time or the money a leaving party demanded. No, that wasn't it.

The only other possibility was that he was announcing Antonia's replacement. He couldn't be doing that, could he?

'But we're not the sort of paper to let the grass grow under our feet, so today I'm introducing you to . . .'

Omigod, he *was*!

'Isabel Farrell, our new women's editor.' He gestured to the woman sitting beside him. 'Stand up and say hello, Isabel.'

Isabel rose to her feet slowly. This wasn't the time for nervousness, not any more. She had the job and that was that. There was no going back and definitely no hope of the earth swallowing her before the five disgruntled would-be women's editors got their talons into her. It was up to her to make the first move.

As she stared at the curious faces who must be wondering where she'd come from and whether she was a management stooge or not, Isabel felt a surge of courage.

She could do the job, she was sure of it. She was a damn' good sub, a good writer and had always enjoyed great relationships with the people who worked under her. Her head was buzzing with ideas to freshen up the women's section. All she needed was the self-confidence to do it. She took a deep breath and told herself to keep it simple.

'I'm delighted to meet you all,' she said, pitching her voice a fraction lower to hide her nervousness. 'I'm sure you're wondering where I've come from and why you don't know me, but I've been living in the UK for the past ten years where I've worked almost exclusively in women's magazines, always at management level. I was deputy editor of *Today's Woman* for five years.'

She paused and, out of the corner of her eye, saw a

flash of chestnut curls that made her notice Dee O'Reilly. A very thin woman with almost purple hair sitting beside Dee was speaking softly to her. Neither woman was looking at Isabel.

Dee was a dedicated news reporter, Isabel knew. The appointment of the new women's editor was probably of no interest to her. Lots of news reporters thought that their part of the paper was by far the most important; the features and women's sections trailed behind miserably in their opinion. Isabel pushed on with the little speech she'd been rehearsing all weekend.

'I've come back to Ireland for good and I can't tell you how pleased I am to be joining such an excellent paper and such a great team of journalists. It may take me some time to get to know you all.' She smiled warmly around the table. 'But I'm confident that I'll settle in pretty quickly and I'm sure we're going to work very well together.'

She gave them another smile and sat down, her heart belting along like a racehorse heading for Becher's Brook. Thank God that was over. The job would be a cinch compared to addressing a crowd of people she didn't know.

'Well done!' cried Nigel. He got up and patted her on the back. 'As you can see, folks, Isabel is going to be a great addition to our team. I'll bring her around and introduce her to you all later. But first, a toast to our new women's editor!'

Dee sat stunned as Nigel's secretary, Sheila, unceremoniously plonked a tower of plastic cups and four bottles of sparkling wine on the table.

'We won't get drunk on that,' muttered a voice. 'Four lousy bottles! What cheapskates.'

When everyone had at least half an inch of wine sloshing around in the bottom of their plastic cup, Nigel shouted 'Cheers!' enthusiastically.

'Bastard,' Dee said fiercely to Maeve. 'He's such a bastard. He could at least have told us. He could have shown us that courtesy. I mean,' she added, her face pink with rage, 'I spoke to that bloody woman in the loo earlier. I was *nice* to her, for Christ's sake! And I guarantee she knew exactly who I was.'

Dee pushed back her chair savagely and stood up, flinging back a strand of hair that had swung over her face. 'I bet Nigel told her exactly who applied for the job, so she knows who she's swiped it from. Well, if she thinks she's going to lord it over me, she's deeply mistaken. I'll never ever talk to that bitch!'

'Dee,' cautioned Maeve, 'calm down, will you?' She grabbed her friend's arm. 'Don't give him the satisfaction of seeing you're angry. That's what he wants.'

'Well, if that's going to please him, I'm going to make him very bloody happy today,' Dee hissed. She grabbed her notebook and marched out of the room, hair swinging behind her.

All she wanted was to sit quietly somewhere before she broke down and sobbed.

Dear Annie,
    I've been passed over for a job I was sure I'd get and now I'm devastated and hurt. I don't know how I can face anyone in my office, or the person who got the job. I was convinced I'd get it and, now that I haven't, I feel like a balloon that's had all the air let out. What do you advise me to do?

Surrounded by people at the top of the conference

table, Isabel didn't notice Dee's rapid departure. People were being really nice to her, she realised, after ten minutes of being introduced to various reporters, subs and photographers. Even the sports editor seemed pleased to see her.

'Tony Winston,' he said in a suave voice. He stretched out one tanned hand and held hers for longer than was strictly necessary as he gazed down her cleavage.

Latin-looking and dressed in a bright pink polo shirt to show off his tan, he was incredibly handsome and knew it. 'We must go out to lunch,' he added, giving her the benefit of a salacious grin.

'Hello, I'm Maeve Lynch.' Isabel looked up to see that the woman who'd been sitting beside Dee O'Reilly was staring at her intently. *She* didn't look too pleased. Maybe she'd applied for the job.

'Nice to meet you, Maeve,' said Isabel.

'Maeve's the sub-editor who works on Antonia's . . . well, *your* pages,' explained Nigel's secretary who had taken a shine to Isabel and was introducing people to her. Yes, if Maeve had worked on Antonia's pages she had almost certainly applied for the job.

'Oh, I'm looking forward to working with you,' Isabel said with a smile. Maeve must hate my guts, she thought silently. That's all I need – a sub-editor who absolutely loathes me. She'd better try the friendly approach. Maeve was friends with Dee, she'd try that angle.

Isabel looked over Maeve's shoulder inquiringly. 'I saw Dee O'Reilly with you – I spoke to her earlier in the loo. Is she still here?'

'Er . . . no, she had to leave in a hurry,' Maeve improvised.

'Pity. I'd really like to meet her properly,' Isabel said earnestly.

'You will, Isabel,' interrupted Nigel smoothly. 'Come on, I'll show you your desk. Sheila, will you find Dee and tell her I want to talk to her in my office in,' he looked at his watch, 'fifteen minutes?'

Maeve checked the newsroom, saw that Dee wasn't at her desk and then ran down the back stairs as fast as she could. She found her friend around the back of the printing works, smoking a cigarette as she paced up and down miserably.

'I can't believe you're smoking!' exclaimed Maeve.

Dee turned reddened eyes towards her friend. 'At times like this, I wonder why I never started,' she murmured. 'Although Camel are too strong. I got this from the security guard. They're supposed to relax you.' She took another deep drag and then tossed the cigarette away. 'Gimme one of yours. They're milder.'

'I'll give you one and then never ask me again. Only yesterday you were giving out stink to me for not stopping smoking,' Maeve remarked as she proferred a Silk Cut.

'Yesterday was different,' snuffled Dee. 'Yesterday I thought I had a great job and a chance of promotion. Today, I'm a has-been.'

'Don't be daft,' said Maeve, lighting up. 'Think of this as a minor glitch in your plans. You can still get promotion.'

'Not to the job I really want, though,' protested Dee angrily. 'I want to be women's editor or features editor, and unless that Isabel bitch or poor Phil Walsh drops dead tomorrow, there's no hope of me getting *their* jobs, is there?' She paced some more.

'No,' admitted Maeve. 'Come on in, Dee, it's starting to rain and you're going to get drenched.'

Dee could feel tears in her eyes again. Damn. Why

the hell was she so emotional? Why couldn't she be one of those women who never cried, no matter what happened? She sobbed at everything from *Gone With The Wind* to TV shows where abandoned guinea pigs were given loving new homes. And now she'd have red eyes. Everyone in the office would know she'd been upset and would also know why. How horribly humiliating.

She gingerly wiped away the tears under her eyelashes, hoping not to smudge her mascara.

'Do I look awful?' she asked Maeve. 'I do, don't I?' she answered without giving her friend a chance to reply. 'Will you do me a favour? I can't go back looking like this, so will you discreetly grab my handbag and I'll go to the pub for a coffee until I look normal, which could take some time.'

She'd love a big gin and tonic to calm her nerves, but that would be fatal. There was no such thing as one drink in Magee's Lounge. One led to two, then three, and before you knew it, it was closing time and one of your less drunk colleagues was grinning at you smugly, making you wonder exactly whom you'd insulted or, worse still, what dark secret you'd inadvertently revealed.

'Bad news, kiddo,' Maeve said. 'Nigel's looking for you. He wants you in his office pronto. That's why I came looking for you – I didn't want Drill Sergeant Smyth to find you first.'

'Shit! Give me another fag.'

'What are you like?' demanded Maeve. 'One minute you're Ms-Anti-Smoking, the next you're Dennis Leary. Are you sure you don't want a cigar?'

It worked. Dee couldn't resist laughing.

'If Demi Moore and Sharon Stone can smoke cigars, I

can too. Maybe piggy Ted Holt will graciously give me one of his Romeo y Julietas to make up for not giving me the job.'

'Somehow I doubt it,' said Maeve. 'You only get one of those if you do some serious sucking up, which is why Nigel always has one stuffed in his mouth.'

'Maybe I *should* have done a bit of sucking up.' Dee took a long drag of her cigarette. 'At least then I'd have got the job I wanted. And I bet that's why Ms Prim, Butter-Wouldn't-Melt women's editor got it. She's probably an expert sycophant.

'You wait, Maeve,' Dee said bitterly, 'she won't be in the place five minutes before she's going up and down, to and from Holt's office like a bloody yo-yo spilling the beans on all of us. She *could* be having a fling with him. They're probably having a torrid groping session in Nigel's office right now. I can see it all – Nigel standing outside like a good little yes-man, telling them when someone's coming . . .'

At that precise moment, Isabel was admiring her new desk which was opposite the features editor's. Sheila explained that Antonia had moved her stuff out of the office and was working from home during her last week with the *Sentinel*. But she was coming in on Wednesday to fill Isabel in on who did what on the women's pages, apparently. She'd also give her a list of contact numbers for everyone from fashion PRs to battered wives' shelters. As Isabel hadn't worked in journalism in Ireland for ten years, her Irish contacts were nil, so she really needed Antonia's help.

'Nice to meet you,' said Phil Walsh, the phone clamped between her jaw and shoulder. 'Welcome to the mad house.'

'It doesn't look too mad to me,' Isabel said with a grin.

'Oh, don't mind me,' said Phil, 'I've been here years and I'm jaundiced. Ten years of Nigel Burke would drive anyone insane. Yes,' she said into the phone, 'I've been holding for five minutes and I'm sick of "Greensleeves".'

Isabel examined her surroundings with pleasure. The people in the middle of the room had to make do with an open-plan office, but she and Phil had a mini 'office' by the windows all to themselves, neatly separated from the rest of the room by grey partitions. Their little dogbox was totally private and very cosy. Phil was clearly into horses and children in a big way. Half of her section of the office was decorated with pictures of a huge brown horse with various rosettes pinned to its bridle. The other half was crowded with pictures of four smiling teenagers, nearly all in jodhpurs, clinging to one horse or another.

Antonia's side was bare. Isabel thought it looked nicer without too much clutter. Pictures of Naomi and Robin on her desk and a calendar on the wall, she decided. That was all she needed.

The view from the second-floor window wasn't exactly inspiring, it looked out on to the car park. But Isabel didn't care. She loved being able to see out of a window, even if the view was only of rows of dusty cars, a couple of motorbikes and a skip.

She had brought a few things from home – the large yellow spotted ceramic mug she'd always used as a pen holder, the Rolodex with all her now-useless phone numbers on it, and the cactus Naomi and Robin had given her that morning.

'Is this a not-so-subtle hint that I'm prickly these days?' she'd joked when she'd opened the carefully wrapped parcel.

'No,' giggled Naomi. 'You got it because it was the only thing we could buy yesterday. The big flower pots were too dear and Robin said you'd like this.'

'Thank you both so much.' Isabel had hugged her daughters, happier with her odd-shaped little present than she would have been with a diamond necklace. The fact that Robin had bothered to buy her anything at all for her first day at work had meant a lot. She tried the cactus on each side of her computer to see which way looked better. On the left.

At least she knew how to work the computer. It was the same as the ones in *Motor 2000*. Poor Richie Devine, she thought, remembering her previous boss.

'I was going to make you permanent,' he'd raged when she'd told him she was leaving.

'Really?' Isabel said mildly. 'Then you should have told me, Richie, and I wouldn't have bothered applying for other jobs.' She still felt a bit mean about leaving him in the lurch but he'd get over it.

'I thought I'd bring you some stationery,' said Sheila. She struggled into Isabel's little cubbyhole with a load of notebooks, A4 pads, boxes of pens and a stapler.

'I'll order you some business cards once you've decided which ones you want. You and Phil share a secretary but she's out this week. I'll do any typing you need.'

'Thanks,' Isabel said, bemused by the other woman's attentiveness.

Phil hung up the phone. 'I don't know what you've done to deserve that,' she said as Sheila left, having made Isabel promise to call her if she needed *anything*. 'She rarely bothers with the rest of us.'

'What's her name again?' asked Isabel.

'Sheila Smyth, or Drill Sergeant Smyth, depending on how well she treats you. And I should point out that she's Drill Sergeant Smyth to everyone else except her boss and Ted Holt. Which means you are privileged to have her being nice to you.'

'Is it good or bad having her like you?'

'Scary. She only likes you if you're flavour of the month. So if they're going to fire you, you'll have advance warning. Sheila will start treating you like dirt as soon as she finds out. Which will be before you, I might add.' Phil grinned.

'Charming.' Isabel liked Phil who was straightforward at least.

She obviously wasn't interested in making a fashion statement. She was around fifty, rotund, and wore a man's grey cotton cardigan over a navy T-shirt and jeans so old and worn they were almost white. She wore her long, dark hair tied back in a neat ponytail and obviously never bothered with make-up.

Shrewd grey eyes examined Isabel from behind wire-rimmed glasses.

Isabel wondered if she dare ask Phil which of the other members of staff had applied to be women's editor. But she wasn't sure if it was too soon to ask. After all, Phil hardly knew her.

Her phone rang. It was Nigel, all charm and politeness.

'Isabel, dear, could you pop up to my office for a few minutes? There's someone I want you to meet.'

'Of course.' Did he call all the women 'dear'? she wondered.

Nigel didn't want to talk about Isabel's ideas for the paper, even though she'd brought the carefully typed up sheets she'd been working on all weekend. He wasn't interested in new ideas. He wanted to talk about appointing a deputy women's editor.

'We've never had a deputy women's ed before,' he said, twiddling a biro in one hand. 'But I think we need one now. The paper's getting bigger and there are more freelances than ever working for us, so it's a good idea to have someone else to help you with the day-to-day running of your section.'

Isabel nodded, wondering where all this was leading. He was the boss and she was the new employee. If Nigel wanted to appoint a lobotomised gorilla to the position of deputy women's editor, there wasn't a damn' thing she could do about it.

'You and features share a lot of the same writers and you'll have to liaise with Phil Walsh to make sure you don't overlap. Another helping hand would be useful. Don't you think that's a good idea?' he asked.

'Sure,' Isabel replied. 'I'd appreciate some help, especially until I settle in. Who were you thinking of appointing?'

A sharp rap at the door stopped Nigel from answering.

'Come in,' he yelled.

Dee stepped into the room. She didn't see Isabel seated on the couch nearest the door.

'You wanted to talk to me, Nigel,' she said shortly.

'Yes, Dee.' He smiled. 'I want you to meet Isabel Farrell, the new women's editor.'

Dee wheeled around rapidly.

'Hello.' Isabel stood up and reached out her hand.

'Hello,' Dee said coolly. There was no 'Welcome to the *Sentinel*' or anything like that.

'I wanted you girls to meet because you'll be working

very closely with each other in future,' Nigel said. 'Dee has been interested in moving out of hard news and into features for a long time, and I know she really wants to work in the women's section. That's why I've come up with a plan that should please both of you – I'm appointing her as deputy women's ed.'

Silence. Isabel watched Dee's pale face flare into a vivid pink. Oh, God, what the hell was going on here?

'Don't you think that's a good idea, Isabel?' asked Nigel silkily. 'Dee is a very experienced news reporter and a good writer.'

'It's a great idea if she wants the job,' Isabel said evenly. She couldn't think why the other woman looked so angry unless Nigel was pushing her out of news reporting for some reason.

'Dee *is* very interested in this area of the paper, and in fact she's wanted to get out of news for some time now.' Nigel paused to take a sip of coffee. 'I know you'd set your sights somewhat higher, Dee, but I think we need someone with Isabel's experience in the top job and as there are no openings in features, I figured you'd like working with her . . .'

So *that* was it, Isabel realised. Dee *had* applied for her job and now Nigel was offering her second prize as a sop. How awful. And what a pig he was.

Couldn't he see how insulting this was to Dee, to offer her a lesser job in front of the very woman who'd won what she wanted?

Dee still hadn't said anything.

Isabel got up.

'I'll leave you two to talk,' she said. 'I'd love to have you as my deputy, Dee,' she added, 'if you're interested?'

Outside the editor's office, Isabel leant against the wall tiredly. She'd won the job of her dreams but she'd jumped out of the frying pan and right into the fire. A fire hot enough to melt gold, at that.

Still, there was no point brooding. She had a lot of work to do and there was nobody to rely on but herself. The usual story, Isabel though wryly.

CHAPTER SIX

Maeve had just poured the last drop of slimline tonic into Dee's glass when she grabbed it. She took a couple of huge gulps and coughed as the power of a double gin hit the back of her throat.

'You all right?' asked Maeve.

'Fine.' Dee settled back into her seat at the bar. 'Can I have two bags of cheese and onion crisps, please?' she asked the barman.

It was just after five and the roomy, mock-rustic bar in Magee's was empty. The after-work rush wouldn't happen for another hour when the second shift at the *Sentinel* – Magee's best customers – left work. The barman was taking what he felt was a well-deserved rest before the thirsty hordes arrived, demanding beer and whiskey chasers, toasted cheese sandwiches and the odd bottle of champagne if a major story had worked out.

Dee handed Maeve one of the bags, ripped open the other morosely and ate as if she hadn't had anything for a month. She had – but lunch didn't count. She'd been too shocked to eat more than a few bites of her tuna fish sandwich.

She hadn't gone to the kitchen for her daily half a dozen cups of coffee because she couldn't face passing Nigel's office in case she either screamed at him or started crying. The rat! Thankfully Maeve had been able to skive off work early to have a drink with her, otherwise Dee would have gone mad. Her phone hadn't stopped ringing all day, so she'd finally told the switchboard operator to say she wasn't in to any callers. She particularly wanted to avoid personal calls.

No matter how successfully she could put on a cheerful act to business contacts, there was no way she'd have been able to do it if a friend had rung. One kindly 'How are you, Dee?' would have sent her into floods.

She ate another handful of crisps and took a sip of gin to wash them down.

'I still can't believe he did that to me, I just can't believe it,' she said blankly, gazing at the bottles lined up behind the bar. The overhead lights glinted off whiskey and scotch, lighting them up like polished amber.

'I can,' Maeve replied. 'Nigel is a Grade A bastard and his idea of fun is making everyone else's life a misery, you should know that.'

'But why me?' wailed Dee.

Maeve patted her friend's arm. 'Remember what someone said about why they climbed Mount Everest? The answer was "because it was there". Well, that's Nigel Burke for you. He shafted you because he *could* and probably because he wanted to teach us all a little lesson along the lines of "I can do what I want because this is my empire".'

Dee finished her crisps. 'I can't believe he had the audacity to offer me the job with Isabel Farrell sitting there. That was practically the worst thing. It was as if they'd planned it together.'

'At least she left the office,' Maeve pointed out.

'Only because she could tell I wasn't going to say

anything until she did. I'd love to have told Nigel I wouldn't touch the deputy editorship with a barge pole. I should have . . .'

'No, you shouldn't.' Maeve waved at the barman for two more drinks. 'If you'd done that, you'd be spending the rest of your days covering beauty contests and school board elections. At least being made a deputy editor is promotion.'

Dee nodded gloomily.

'A springboard to other things,' insisted her friend. 'You never know what this could lead to.'

'Possibly me getting life imprisonment for murder. I just haven't figured out exactly *how* to kill Nigel. Which would be more painful – that "death by a thousand cuts" thing I've read about or just stabbing him with my blood transfusion service pencil?'

Maeve laughed. 'I know you're getting better when you can joke like that, O'Reilly.'

Dee looked at her mournfully. 'I wasn't joking. Well, maybe a little.' She drained her drink and picked up the next one. 'More crisps,' she announced. 'That's what we need.'

Three-quarters of an hour, two more bags of crisps and three more drinks each later, Dee felt a lot more cheerful.

She'd taken off her jacket and hung it over the back of her seat, no longer bothered about the fact that the lacy T-shirt showed her bra plainly and was only wearable with a jacket over it. Her mascara had run so much that Maeve had given her a tissue to wipe it off and her hair was a mess.

But as she peered woozily at her reflection in the mirror behind the bar, Dee thought she looked pretty good. Big, yes, but good. Sexy, almost. Definitely not fat.

And the amazing thing was, she reflected, ripping open the packet of dry roasted peanuts Maeve had kindly bought her, she didn't feel at all drunk. Not a bit. She was quite sober, really, considering.

'How long have you been here?' Gerry Deegan, pulled up a bar stool beside the two women.

'Not long.' Dee smiled hazily at the political correspondent. 'We've only had three drinks.'

'Four,' said Maeve. 'Or was it five?'

'Could we have had five?' Dee asked in surprise.

'We could. And your first two were doubles.'

'Ooops!' Dee giggled.

'What are we celebrating?' Gerry asked, one eye on the barman who was slowly pouring him a pint of Guinness.

'I'm leaving journalism to become a nun,' announced Dee. She twirled a ringlet around one finger and smiled dreamily at Gerry. 'I'm thinking of one of those enclosed orders where you don't have to talk to people. I don't feel up to talking to people at the moment.'

'That'll be the day,' said a voice. It was Tony Winston with one of his sports freelances in tow. 'What would we do without gorgeous creatures like you, Dee, to brighten up the office?' He gave her a peck on the cheek. 'I can't see you in a nun's habit, unless you wear stockings and stilettos under it and are on your way to a fancy dress party.'

'Get out of here, you walking hormone,' said Maeve loudly, hitting him across the arm with Gerry's evening paper.

'You didn't waste any time chatting up our new women's editor, did you?' said Dee sharply, who'd heard all about Tony's attempts at charming Isabel.

'I believe you were on the verge of asking her round

to your place to show her your World Cup mementoes there and then.'

'Ah.' He nodded sagely. 'So that's it.'

'That's what?' asked Dee.

'That's why the two of you are over here getting plastered. You wanted that job, didn't you, Dee?'

She ignored him.

'Tell your Uncle Tony,' he coaxed, putting his dark head close to hers. Dee could smell his aftershave. It was cloying, horrible stuff although he obviously thought it rendered him irresistible.

'Bugger off, Tony.' She gave him an almighty push that sent him cannoning into Gerry and his barely touched pint of Guinness. Beer went everywhere – all over Tony's prized pink Lacoste shirt and Gerry's shoes.

'Sorry, Gerry,' Dee apologised.

'What about me?' demanded Tony, holding his dripping shirt away from his body in disgust.

Dee gave him a scornful look.

'I think we should get out of here before Tony gets really pissed off,' Maeve whispered.

He stalked off to the men's room, cursing as he went.

'C'mon.' Maeve grabbed her rucksack, Dee's enormous handbag, and her friend by the arm.

'Sorry, Gerry,' Dee said again. 'I didn't mean to get you.'

'It's OK. My shoes got most of it. I'm fine. I'm sorry about you not getting Antonia's job,' he said surprisingly. 'I had an idea Nigel would pull a trick like that. He's made you deputy, hasn't he?'

Dee nodded. The office gossip machine was obviously working as efficiently as ever.

'A word of advice from someone who's been round the block more than once, Dee. Get back there and do it, and remember to do it well. Don't give Nigel Burke the satisfaction of thinking he's won. He loves that. Do your best and you'll get a hell of a lot more out of the job than if you do it half-heartedly.

'Besides,' Gerry added with a wicked smirk, 'I don't know if Nigel will be around that much longer anyway. Think of the party we'll have when he goes!'

'Thanks, Gerry.' Dee smiled.

Maeve dragged her off. 'Ring Gary and tell him to pick you up as you can't possibly drive home,' she instructed once they were outside Magee's.

Dee clumsily dialled her home number on her mobile phone. The answering machine kicked in after three rings.

'He's not home,' she said forlornly. Suddenly, she desperately wanted to see Gary, to let him hug her and tell her it was going to be all right. That he loved her even if she wasn't appreciated by her boss. And now he wasn't there. He'd rejected her too. Dee felt tearful all over again.

'Was he going out tonight?' Maeve asked.

'Can't remember,' she muttered.

Maeve slid an arm around her. 'Let's get a taxi to your place. I'll cook us something and we can watch *Thelma and Louise*. How does that sound?'

'Wonderful. Thanks, Maeve. What would I do without you?'

'Don't thank me,' her friend replied briskly, and stuck out her arm at an approaching taxi. 'Just wait till you get my bill!'

Maeve was a good cook. Given a few withered mushrooms, an elderly onion, tomatoes, surprisingly fresh cheese and some eggs, she could make a Spanish omelette any chef would be proud of.

'I *was* going to make a salad to go with the omelette,' she said, poking around in the salad crisper part of the fridge, 'but everything's gone off somewhat.' She threw the dripping remains of an iceberg lettuce into the bin.

'It's Gary's week for cleaning and shopping,' muttered Dee from the depths of the settee.

'Surprise, surprise!'

Dee got up, put knives and forks on the coffee table, added napkins – paper ones – and inexpertly uncorked a bottle of red wine.

'I don't know if I could drink anything else,' said Maeve when she brought the plates into the sitting-room to find Dee filling two huge wineglasses. 'I've got to be in early tomorrow and I couldn't face another hangover.'

'That's OK.' Dee smiled crookedly. 'All the more for me.'

The film was one of her favourites and she'd often watched it when she was depressed. They sat side by side on the settee, ate Maeve's succulent omelette and empathised.

'That's it, Maeve,' Dee mumbled. 'Thelma has crossed over, she can't go back. That's just like me. I can't go back into work and do that stupid job with that horrible woman.' She gazed at her friend through bleary eyes. 'I just can't.'

At half-ten, Maeve called a taxi.

'Please go to bed, Dee. You'll feel better in the morning.'

'My head won't,' she said darkly.

'True.' Maeve hugged her. 'Now go to bed. I'm going to turn the TV off and I want you up those stairs before I leave.'

'Right, officer,' Dee clumsily climbed up them.

'Thanks, Maeve. You're a great friend,' she mumbled when she reached the top. 'I'm going to bed now. Very tired. I'll think in the morning.'

Isabel sank down on to her mother's uncomfortable Chesterfield, leant back and closed her eyes. What a day! She felt as if she'd run a marathon. And she would never wear those bloody cream Roland Cartier sling-backs ever again. They looked good but they hurt like hell. That was what you got for buying sale shoes which were too tight.

She levered them off her feet, struggled out of her jacket and allowed herself to imagine what it would be like to be able to sit there all evening, watching soaps and stupid game shows until it was time for bed. She wouldn't have to talk to anyone, other than Naomi and Robin. She wouldn't have to make forced conversation with her mother.

'Hiya, Mum.' Naomi raced into the room. She jumped on to the settee beside her mother.

'So, how was it?'

'Great, darling. Everyone was very nice to me. I've got a lovely desk beside the features editor, Phil Walsh, and she's very friendly.'

'You don't have your own office?' Naomi sounded disappointed.

Isabel smiled and smoothed her daughter's unruly hair.

'Nobody has an office, darling. Except for the editor. We all work in a very big room with lots of desks in the middle. I'm one of the lucky ones because I sit beside the window and I've got a big partition which stops everyone from seeing what I'm doing.'

'When can I come and see it?'

Naomi had been a frequent visitor to Isabel's other offices, apart from *Motor 2000*, but somehow she didn't think the *Sentinel* was the sort of place where the staff's children would be made welcome.

'I don't know, maybe during the summer.'

Naomi's face fell.

'Or I suppose I could take you in on Saturday,' Isabel relented. Nobody would be at work then because there wasn't a Sunday edition of the paper.

'Cool! Robin told Granny she was going to make dinner this evening,' Naomi announced. Isabel's eyebrows shot up. 'She made a casserole thingy in home economics and we're having that with rice.'

Isabel hoped that Robin was more talented in the rice department than she was. It always ended up either too hard or a slushy mess, no matter how she weighed rice, water, whatever. Hopefully, Robin would be a better cook. She certainly seemed to like home economics and had concocted a delicious vegetable lasagne in her class a couple of weeks previously.

'I'm making dessert,' Naomi added proudly. 'It's a surprise. You don't have to do anything, Mum. It's chocolate mousse,' she whispered, 'but you're not supposed to know.'

'My lips are sealed. It all sounds delicious, Naomi, and so long as I don't have to do anything, I'm happy.'

'Do you want a drink, Mum? I told Granny you'd need wine because you like some at dinner and because it was your first day at work.'

Isabel groaned inwardly. That was all she needed. Her mother would think she was on the verge of becoming an alcoholic.

One sherry per evening and brandy after disasters – that was Pamela's idea of drinking. There was no use in trying to explain that Isabel and David had always enjoyed wine in the evenings. Or that she'd quite enjoyed those evenings when he wasn't around for dinner, so she could decide whether she wanted red or white and drink a couple of glasses in blissful solitude with her feet up.

'How did Granny look when you mentioned the wine?' she asked Naomi. 'What did she say?'

Her daughter shrugged. 'Nothing. Why, Mum?'

Isabel smiled at her. 'No reason. Now tell me, what was school like today? Did you get your English essay back?'

Naomi pulled a face. 'Yeah. I got a D. I always got Bs at home, Mum.'

'I know, love. It's very difficult to get used to a new school, new teachers and a new syllabus. It's going to take time before you settle in.' She gave her daughter's hand a squeeze. 'I already know you're going to be a world-class journalist, Naomi.'

Her portable typewriter was her most prized possession and she longed to be in the same business as her mum. Isabel hoped to buy a decent computer for the girls before the end of the year as David had kept his Mac when they'd moved away. She was still broke, though.

'But it may take St Clodagh's some time before they realise it too. Now go and see if you can persuade your big sister to make me a cup of tea, would you?'

Naomi grinned and jumped off the settee. Isabel made a mental note to ring St Clodagh's the next morning and talk to the headmistress.

When she'd enrolled Naomi there a couple of months previously, she'd told the headmistress that her shy twelve-year-old daughter was going to need some gentle treatment before she found her feet in a new country and school. Mrs Robinson, the headmistress, had claimed to understand that.

Isabel knew that no matter how long it took Naomi to settle into her other classes, she was always instantly at home in English, her favourite subject. She was an avid reader and devoured everything from Enid Blyton to the Brontës. Which was why the news that Naomi had got a D for an essay she'd worked hard on made Isabel realise that not everybody in St Clodagh's had listened to her.

You didn't understand at all, Mrs Robinson, Isabel thought angrily. But you will by the time I've finished with you.

Still, ringing the school would give her the opportunity to find out how Robin had been getting on too. Her elder daughter had to cope with a totally new syllabus for exams in June, which she was dreading.

If only Robin would talk to her! Isabel despaired of ever having a conversation with her daughter that didn't involve phrases like: 'You *never* let me do anything' and 'If Dad were here, it would be different'.

And, as if all that wasn't bad enough, Isabel knew she'd have to face Dee O'Reilly in the morning, who, if her enraged expression when she'd finally left the editor's office was anything to go by, loathed Nigel and Isabel equally.

Not for the first time, she sent up a silent word of thanks to the good people who made anti-depressants. Without a little chemical back-up, she'd have gone to pieces by now, she was sure of it.

'Tea.' Robin came into the room with a china cup and saucer, and a bourbon biscuit on a tray. Isabel was thrilled. Not because of the tea, but because Robin had made an effort for her. She beamed at her daughter.

'Thank you, Robin, you're a pet.'

She took a sip, then nibbled her biscuit.

'How was work?' Robin perched on the edge of an armchair. She was still in her school uniform – grey skirt and jumper, white blouse and royal blue and grey striped tie. Robin looked like a schoolgirl again and not the minxy madam she could pass for in her clingy tops and figure-hugging hipsters.

'Hard going,' Isabel answered honestly. 'My deputy wanted the job I got. So I don't think we're going to be bosom buddies. Everyone else was nice, but it's going to be a demanding job, that's for sure.' She stretched her arms and yawned. 'I have to say, I *am* tired.'

'Well, you don't have to do anything this evening, Mum, I've made dinner.'

'So Naomi was saying. What is it? Something certainly smells delicious.'

Robin smiled with pleasure. 'Lamb with tomato and haricot beans.'

'Gorgeous! I'm famished.'

'It won't be finished for another twenty minutes because I just put the rice on,' Robin explained. 'Gran is having a rest – she's got another of her migraines. She wanted me to cook boiled potatoes but I hate them so I did rice. I'll call you when it's ready.'

Isabel sank back into the settee, turned on the TV and relaxed. She might as well enjoy this evening of blissful peace because, as Scarlett O'Hara once said, tomorrow was going to be another day.

As she drove into work the following morning in the late-May sunshine, Isabel felt ready to tackle anything. It didn't take long for her good humour to disappear. After five minutes in the office and just one call, she slammed down the phone angrily. Antonia FitzSimons had promised to help her in her new job but now she'd backed out. She wasn't pleased with the far-from-golden handshake Ted Holt had offered her.

'Obviously I feel under less of an obligation now,' she'd said when Isabel rang to find out what time Antonia would meet her in the office.

'Antonia, this is only my second day here. I need some back-up,' Isabel insisted, doing her best to ignore the feeling of panic rising in her chest.

'I'm afraid that's out of the question,' she snorted. 'Talk to Nigel and tell him how upset I am about all this, that's all I can suggest.'

Isabel stared at the phone grimly. What she wouldn't do to that lazy, spoilt cow if she ever got hold of her! Just because Antonia could afford to give up a full-time job, thanks to her husband's fat salary, didn't mean that everyone else was so privileged.

Isabel glanced anxiously at the big clock on the wall beside the nearest TV screen.

It was half-nine on Wednesday morning, she was due in an editorial meeting at two, and without any contact numbers or helpful information from Antonia, her hands were not just tied, they were virtually handcuffed.

Shit, shit, shit!

Antonia had even managed to sabotage her further by taking home all the fashion transparencies and press releases sent in by fashion companies. So there was damn-all to write about.

None of the freelances had rung to say hello or that they were sending in articles. Isabel had to get moving on tomorrow's women's pages or there'd be a very big gap in the paper. Hardly the ideal way to start her new job.

And, to add insult to injury, Dee O'Reilly, her supposed deputy, was nowhere in sight. Even Phil Walsh, who would probably help if she could, was out.

'It's Phil's day off,' muttered Jackie, the assistant Isabel shared with her. Jackie was not the sort of assistant to inspire confidence. She was around twenty, with coal-black dyed hair, a Band Aid-sized mini skirt, Doc Marten's, and an air of complete apathy.

'D'ya want coffee?' she asked when she came back from the loo with newly applied thick black eyeliner that made her look like an ancient Egyptian.

'Yes. Black, no sugar, please,' Isabel said.

Jackie ambled off and Isabel watched her dispiritedly. She needed at least one energetic, enthusiastic person on her side. It didn't look as if Jackie was going to measure up.

Ten minutes later, she returned with a cup of milky white coffee and a batch of post for the women's editor.

Ignoring the coffee, Isabel fell on the post with delight. Several of the large envelopes carried personalised mailing stamps from the large retail chains and designers' studios, so she knew that these were press releases and, hopefully, pictures, of the latest ranges of summer clothes.

She didn't give a damn whether they were actually meant for Antonia who had shown that she couldn't care less what happened to Isabel and the women's pages. Isabel was bloody well going to open the post that had been sent to the *Sentinel*'s women's editor because that was now her job, and stuff Antonia.

Anything private would be sent on to her, but Isabel needed to fill six empty pages for Thursday's paper.

'Wonderful!' she cried as she ripped open an envelope and found pictures of a range of bikinis, a new line of summer knitwear being launched the following day, and some elegant suits from Paul Costelloe's collection. That was the fashion pages covered for a few days at least.

The post also yielded a feature about infertility from one of the paper's regular contributors, Jane Wood, as well as ideas for a couple of other articles.

Thank you, Jane! Isabel grinned and put the extremely well-written piece into her 'in' tray. She wrote down Jane's number in her diary before rummaging through the rest of the post. That was four pages pretty well covered.

'Sorry, I gave you the wrong coffee,' said Jackie, swopping Isabel's cup for another one. 'I'm never very awake until I get my first cup,' she added apologetically.

Isabel smiled at her. Perhaps Jackie was nervous about working for a new boss and that was why she'd made the mistake. Maybe things were going to work out after all.

'Get up, Dee, get up! You're going to be late.'

What was wrong with Gary? she wondered numbly. He sounded as if he was at the bottom of a tunnel. What was going on? It was the middle of the night, surely?

The duvet was rudely ripped off the bed. Dee opened her eyes gingerly to stare blearily at her fiancé. He was already dressed in a blue suit and white shirt and looked very, very cross.

'This is the last time I'm calling you, Dee. I've called you five times already and you're going to be late for work if you don't get up now!' he snapped.

'Whaddya mean, you called me before?' Dee muttered. 'I'd have remembered if you'd called me.'

She sat up in bed and immediately felt horrendously sick.

'Ohmigod,' she sighed, lying down again. She felt as if she'd vomit if she sat up. Maybe lying down and breathing gently would do the trick. 'Omigod, what happened?'

'That's what I'd like to know,' hissed Gary. He looked incredibly angry. His hair, still wet from his shower, was slicked back from his face and he'd cut himself shaving. A little bit of loo roll was stuck to his cheek where he'd nicked it. 'I came home last night to find you pissed out of your brain, screaming at the top of your voice about Nigel Burke and some woman called Farrell. When I tried to calm you down, you slapped me and said you weren't taking orders from anyone ever again!'

'Oh, I'm so sorry.' Dee burned with shame and remorse. 'I'm so sorry, Gary. I just got drunk with Maeve . . .'

'I knew it would be Maeve,' he interrupted triumphantly. 'She's bad news, that woman. Can't get herself a man so she wants you out drinking with her till the middle of the night. It's just not on, Dee!'

She did her best to protest. 'Gary, you've got it wrong. It wasn't Maeve's fault. It was mine.'

'And that's supposed to make it better?' he yelled. 'It's a quarter to nine and I didn't sleep for hours, what with your drunken rambling, so I overslept and now I'm late for work. I'll see you tonight.'

And he was gone, leaving Dee miserable, exhausted, and very, very hungover. She dragged the duvet back over her head and stifled a sob. All she'd wanted was a little comfort and Gary hadn't been there. If he knew why she'd got so drunk, surely he'd have understood?

She felt so sick, so awfully ready to puke at any moment, she'd just lie in bed for a little while longer and then she'd feel better.

Ten minutes later the phone rang, making Dee jump in her duvet cocoon.

'Hello,' she said miserably, after inadvertently pushing a couple of books and her hand cream off the bedside locker in her attempts to pick up the receiver.

'You're not still in bed, are you?' demanded Maeve.

'Don't shout,' said Dee weakly. 'I've got an awful headache.'

'I'm not surprised. You got through a lorryload of booze last night.'

'I remember. I didn't say anything awful, did I?' Dee asked, pulling the phone back under the duvet with her.

'Not at all, you were hilariously funny until the very end when I thought you were either going to pass out or head off into the night to give Nigel a do-it-yourself vasectomy with a sharp kitchen implement.'

'So long as I was amusing.'

'Are you up yet? Maeve asked. 'Stupid question. You sound like you're speaking from a coal mine so I presume you're still in bed. It's nearly nine and you've got to get in for your first day of deputy editing along with the bitch from hell.'

Dee groaned. 'Don't remind me! I just don't feel up to it. You'll never guess what I did last night?'

'What?'

'I slapped Gary. I don't even remember it but he's very cross. I think he wants to divorce me.'

'He can't. You're not even married yet. Now, are you getting up? Last night, you vowed to show everyone what a brilliant women's editor you'd have made so that

Nigel and Ted would be desperately sorry for appointing Isabel. Come on,' Maeve cajoled, 'get up. I'll book a taxi for you for nine-forty-five, right?'

Dee groaned again. 'All right. I don't know if I can stand up though.'

'That's no excuse. See you in work later.'

Every bump the taxi went over made Dee feel even more nauseous. She prayed she'd feel a bit better when she got a dose of percolated coffee inside her at the office. And a Twix might help. Or perhaps it wouldn't.

She hadn't been able to face breakfast and anyway, she'd needed the time to shower and put on enough make-up to look even halfway decent. Despite wearing full war paint and lots of blusher, she was still very pale.

Clutching a polystyrene cup of coffee, she walked delicately up to her desk before remembering that Nigel had given her a new one – in the features department – only a few feet away from Isabel's.

Her old desk was still cluttered with her filing trays, papers, notebooks, small scraps of phone messages lying everywhere and little black marks where the after-six smokers had kindly left their butts filter-first on the desk until they burned down. She'd move properly tomorrow. There was no way she could face it now.

Dee plonked a few things down on her new desk and grabbed that day's copy of the *Sentinel*. The office was still quiet and, thankfully, there was no sign of bloody Isabel.

Dee was flicking through the paper and drinking her coffee when she heard a voice address her.

'Morning, Dee.'

Isabel stood in front of her, sickeningly cheerful, incredibly slim and beautifully dressed in a navy linen trouser suit. Her blonde hair was silky and fell perfectly to her shoulders, her large blue eyes were expertly made up. *She* didn't look as if she was dying of a hangover. Smug bitch.

'Good morning,' Dee replied, although she couldn't see what was so good about it.

'Dee, Phil's away so maybe you could sit at her desk while we talk about this week's pages and what we need to do?' Isabel said. 'Antonia hasn't left me any information about who does what or which articles are being written for the women's section. Maybe you could help me sort through that.'

'OK,' she mumbled.

'Great. Jackie's getting me some phone numbers and each of us can phone half of them, just to make sure we've enough stuff to fill the next few editions. Then we can talk about how we're going to work together. And you can tell me what you're interested in doing,' Isabel added.

'Right,' Dee said warily. She wasn't sure she trusted all this '*we'll* talk about it' stuff. She suspected it was a ploy to catch her off guard before Isabel started laying down the law about exactly who was boss.

She reluctantly got out a pen and notebook and sat down on Phil Walsh's chair. Isabel's phone rang almost immediately and, while she answered it, Dee surveyed Isabel's side of the cubbyhole.

She obviously had children because she'd a photo of herself and two girls on the far side of her computer. One was a very pretty teenager and the other was a few years younger. You wouldn't think she'd had kids judging by Isabel's figure. She was slim, verging on too thin. Not that Dee ever thought anyone could be too thin, but Isabel was practically model-girl underweight. Dee could see her collarbones jutting out above her simple white camisole top and her wrists and ankles were very skinny. Still, she looked good, classy.

The only thing that revealed she wasn't a wealthy lady of leisure were her nails. Cut short and filed straight across, they weren't even polished. Which was odd because, from the look of her, Dee would have guessed that Isabel Farrell had both the money and the time to spend in beauty salons. She probably had a filthy rich husband who paid all the bills, while her salary was spent as 'pin money', buying little designer numbers.

Dee glanced at her own nails. The chocolate brown varnish was a bit chipped, which was how she felt herself. Compared to Isabel's elegant ensemble, Dee felt that in her straight brown skirt and slinky coffee-coloured blouse – worn loose to hide her bulges – she looked drab and cheap. And fat. No, *the outfit* didn't make her look fat, *she* was fat, end of story. She sighed miserably.

'Dee, you look a little tired. Do you want a coffee or something?' Isabel asked kindly, as she hung up.

Startled, Dee nodded. She was probably just going to yell at Jackie to get the coffee, Dee figured. Isabel would hardly get it herself. But she stood up.

'Black, white, sugar?' she asked.

'Er, white with two sugars,' Dee replied. 'Thank you.'

Isabel came back a few minutes later with coffee for both of them and a Danish pastry in a paper bag for Dee.

'One of the runners got it for me in the shop across the road. I thought you looked as if you needed an energy lift. You don't have to eat it if you don't want to,' she added hesitantly.

'Thanks,' said Dee, amazed. 'I don't really know if I could eat it. I'm feeling a little off-colour today.' She didn't want to say that she was dying from a hangover as a result of a misery drinking session because Isabel had got the job she wanted.

'Oh. Are you up to doing any work?'

'Of course,' said Dee, stung by the implication that she'd run home on her first day as Isabel's deputy. 'Right, where'll we start?'

As Isabel talked about the article she'd received in the post and when they should use it, Dee drank her coffee but didn't touch the pastry. She could smell its sweet, buttery scent through the bag and her stomach began to feel better and very empty all of a sudden.

But she hated eating in front of people she didn't know. She hated eating in front of people full stop. If Maeve wasn't around to have lunch with, Dee nibbled fruit at her desk and ate a yoghurt virtuously. She saved her lasagne-and-chips binges for lunch with her friend.

There was no way she was going to eat that Danish in front of Isabel, even if it was screaming 'eat me' at her. Isabel probably thought Dee lived on cream buns and tubs of ice cream. If she saw Dee shovelling down a calorie-laden Danish, Isabel would think, 'That's why she's enormous – she can't stop eating.'

Dee shoved the bag away from her and started to work.

With Jackie's help, Isabel and Dee tracked down all the freelances whom Antonia used for her pages, and at twelve o'clock two of the staff journalists who worked between features and the women's pages arrived.

The only problem was that neither Carol-Anne nor Emily appeared to have been given anything to do by Antonia for weeks.

'I've got an article on famous divorces that I started doing for Phil but I can give it a women's pages slant, if you like?' offered Emily, a sweet-looking twenty-something brunette with almond-shaped green eyes.

'Great. We can use that on Saturday,' Isabel said, pleased at Emily's enthusiasm. 'Don't forget to get plenty of famous, attractive movie-star couples in there so the subs can use glamorous photos.'

'No problem.' Emily sat down at her desk and started rummaging through a pile of brown folders.

Isabel turned to the other woman. 'Carol-Anne, do you have anything you can write quickly for Friday's paper?'

'No. Not really.' Carol-Anne stared at her blankly. A thin, taut-faced woman with a swathe of ash-blonde curls and bags under her eyes from incessant partying, Carol-Anne prided herself on being the ultimate in glamour – red nails, red lips and a sporty car – and believed that, as a longstanding member of staff, she didn't have to take orders from anyone.

Dee watched with interest. In her opinion, Carol-Anne was as lazy as sin and Dee had once heard a rumour that she had actually been fired from her last job for writing a review of a play that had been cancelled at the last minute. But she and Antonia had been best pals since college and Antonia had always given Carol-Anne cushy jobs like writing the beauty notes from press releases. Dee knew for a fact that Carol-Anne had applied for Antonia's job too, and you didn't need to be a Mensa member to figure out that she'd got it in for Isabel.

'Nothing?' asked Isabel, surprised.

'No,' said Carol-Anne. The crimson lips curved smugly and turned back to her desk and her morning paper. Dee wondered for the millionth time why the other woman didn't get out of journalism when she daily made it clear to the world that she hated her job and did her best to do as little work as possible. Unlike Antonia, however, Carol-Anne didn't have a husband to support her, so it was either the *Sentinel* or the dole queue.

Dee glanced at Isabel. The other woman stared at Carol-Anne's back and seemed to be thinking.

'Carol-Anne,' she said suddenly, 'as you've nothing to do, I've a great idea for you. I'm sure there's a file somewhere on this sexual harassment case in America. Do a feature on it, updating the story with current Irish legislation. Give me a thousand words.'

Oooh, Dee thought, with a grin, that was a killer article to write. She had to hand it to Isabel. She had the measure of Carol-Anne and was obviously determined to get her to do some work.

Carol-Anne looked up, eyes narrowed as she stared at the woman who thought she could order her around.

Round one to Isabel, thought Dee. But she doesn't know Carol-Anne. If she gets that feature by next Wednesday, she'll be lucky.

'And, Carol-Anne,' Isabel said in a louder voice, so that everyone nearby could hear, 'I want it by tomorrow at ten.'

Game, set and match to Isabel! Carol-Anne wasn't going to be in for such an easy ride with *this* boss.

'You should have seen Carol-Anne's face, Maeve, she was *livid*!' laughed Dee. 'It was priceless.'

They were sitting in the coffee shop across the road from the office. Dee was eating chips because she needed carbohydrates for her hangover. Maeve had chosen lasagne because she was always ravenous at lunch.

'I have to hand it to Isabel, she's well able for Carol-Anne.'

'This is the same woman you were never going to speak to again last night?' inquired Maeve, as she dug into her lasagne.

'I know, I know,' Dee said irritably. 'I can hate her guts and still see her good points. And she *was* tough with Carol-Anne.'

'I wouldn't be too sure her methods will work,' Maeve cautioned. 'Wait and see. Tomorrow morning at around nine-thirty Jackie will most probably get a call from Carol-Anne to say she's very sick, the doctor wants her to lie down for at least a week, poor dear, and she can't *possibly* come into work. She won't phone Isabel, of course. She'll phone a naive assistant who'd swallow a brick and readily believe she's at death's door.'

'You're right. I forgot about the hypochondriac defence. "Poor me, my leg/stomach/head/big toe hurts so much I can't come in for a month." Delete where applicable.' Dee grinned.

'So are you going to tell Isabel how Carol-Anne's mind works, or are you going to let her figure it out for herself?' Maeve asked.

'I'm not going to tell her anything! She stole my job.'

'Two minutes ago you were saying "fair play to her". Now she's back to being a bitch again. Come on, Dee at least be consistent.'

She looked hurt. 'I thought you were on my side?'

Maeve put down her fork. 'I am. But I don't want to see you start a big fight that's going to last years. Isabel has been fair with you . . .'

'So far,' interrupted Dee.

'So far. But perhaps this is a little test, like Carol-Anne's. And if you end up fighting her, it could last as long as she's women's editor. And that could be a long time. Do you want that?'

'No. But I don't trust her, either.'

'Fair enough. Just give her a chance, Dee. That's all I'm saying.'

'But what about the Danish pastry?' she demanded. 'I've been thinking about it all morning. Maybe she bought it to suck up to me, because she thinks I'm a great big tank of a thing that she can wrap round her little finger by giving her cakes.'

'*Dee!*' said Maeve. 'Sometimes a Danish pastry is just a Danish pastry, right? Stop being paranoid and analysing things so much. I bet she'd have got one for me if I'd looked bad.'

'Maybe.' Dee wasn't so sure. 'She's so thin, Maeve. She makes me feel like a giant hippo beside her. I wonder, does she diet? If she does, I'd love to know what diet she's on.'

'She might be like me and not need to,' Maeve said as she started on her apple crumble.

'Oh, great,' Dee grumbled. '*Two* women in the office who can eat what they want and never put on an ounce. I swear I'm going on a diet tomorrow. The F-Plan always works well for me.'

'I don't know how you can eat all that horrible bran for breakfast,' Maeve pointed out. 'It tastes like cardboard.'

'That's the whole point. It's so tasteless you don't want to eat anything else and it fills you up like cardboard too. Tomorrow, definitely,' she said firmly. 'This is the diet that's going to change my life.'

★ ★ ★

After lunch Dee and Isabel spent two hours going over new ideas for the women's pages. When Isabel talked of having a serious interview piece every week, Dee couldn't hide her enthusiasm. That was exactly the sort of thing she'd wanted to do for years.

'It's a brilliant idea,' she said, eyes shining.

'Would you like to do the first one?' Isabel asked. 'We'll run it this week, so you've got until Monday evening to write it.'

'I'd love to do it.'

'That's settled then.'

Around four-fifteen, Dee's hangover went into the exhaustion phase. She suddenly felt dog-tired and barely had the energy to write. She'd love to go home early, but could hardly do that two days in a row.

Isabel passed her desk with a bundle of old copies of the paper and gave Dee a broad smile. Maybe she should go home early . . . She wasn't going to be much good for the rest of the day and at least Isabel knew she'd been working like a slave since morning.

Hell, she'd go home. A couple of hours in bed before Gary came back was just what she needed. She'd cook him a lovely dinner to apologise. There was nothing to eat in the house, so she'd nip into the Superquinn and buy something. Shepherd's pie, that was it. He loved it. She'd never made it before but it couldn't be that difficult, could it?

Dee quickly tidied her desk and switched off her computer. At that precise moment Nigel Burke appeared beside her, grinning like a Cheshire cat who'd just been lapping double cream.

'How's it going, Dee?' he asked. 'Settling in under your new boss?'

'Er, yes,' she muttered.

Nigel looked pointedly at his watch. 'Going a bit early, aren't you?'

'I told her to,' said a calm voice. Isabel held his gaze. 'Dee will be working late tomorrow night doing an interview and we've already got through an incredible amount of stuff today.'

There was nothing he could say to that.

'So long as you girls are getting on all right, that's all that matters,' he said quickly. 'I want to have a meeting with you both tomorrow.' He walked away briskly.

'Thanks,' Dee said to Isabel in amazement.

'You really have done so much today, Dee, and I've never believed in clocking in. Flexi-time works much better in a job like this,' Isabel replied. 'See you tomorrow morning.'

Dee got into her car slowly. Nothing was going as planned. Instead of being hostile, caustic and ready to argue with Isabel about everything, she'd actually worked hard for her all day. And had ended up looking so wrecked that the new women's editor had actually stood up for her!

On the surface at least Isabel Farrell was nothing like Dee had expected her to be. Still, it was early days yet.

CHAPTER SEVEN

Dee twisted round to see herself from every angle in the changing-room mirror. There was no doubt about it – the dress looked hideous on her. The forest green silk had looked like the answer to all her prayers when it was hanging up. It was obviously expensive and had 'class' written all over it, which she'd thought would make it perfect for the Delahunty/Thomas nuptials in Wicklow the following day.

But on Dee's now size sixteen body, it appeared to have shrunk several sizes. It made her bum look like a bean bag, not to mention what it did to her stomach. There was only so much those control top tights could do, let alone the fact that the middle seam would be visible under the sliver-thin silk.

Dee managed to undo the zip, thankful she'd come to one of Dublin's poshest shops. Because even though a lot of the clothes cost more than an average worker earned in a week, at least the changing rooms were private and for one person only.

Nothing put Dee off clothes shops more than having to wriggle in and out of things in communal changing rooms. In her experience they were always jammed with stick-thin girls who demanded to know if they looked fat in little bits of Lycra. People like Dee were doomed to look on in misery then try to struggle out of clothes without exposing any flesh so nobody could see their fat stomachs.

In Brown Thomas, the sales assistant hovered discreetly outside the cubicle. She asked if Dee needed anything instead of sticking her head around the curtain at inopportune moments.

'How does it look?' the sales lady inquired tactfully.

Like I've been sprayed with green cling-film, thought Dee gloomily. 'Er, it's not very me.'

She couldn't face the thought of pulling her clothes back on and going outside to hunt desperately through rails and rails of garments. She loved the luxury of buying clothes, normally, but never when she had to buy something for a specific event. Then, all the lovely, ultra-slimming things she'd drooled over but hadn't bought because she was broke mysteriously disappeared and she was left struggling to find anything even vaguely decent.

That was exactly what seemed to have happened today. What was even worse, Dee knew she was getting so enormous that she hadn't a hope in hell of buying anything that wouldn't look like a marquee. She stuck her head out of the cubicle.

'Could *you* take a look and see if you've anything that would suit me?'

The assistant's face lit up at the challenge. 'I have a couple of dresses you might try, but what I'd really suggest is a suit.'

'I don't want one of those on-the-knee, pastel suits you can only wear for a wedding,' Dee said firmly, with visions of herself fading into a sea of such outfits the following day.

'Don't worry, it's nothing like that,' the sales lady assured her.

Half an hour later, Dee marched up Grafton Street to the Stephen's Green car park, holding a large Brown Thomas bag triumphantly in one hand. The suit was beautiful and looked marvellous on her. All she needed now was a bit of fake tan to give her that just-back-from-Marbella colour.

The suit was a rich terracotta, its perfectly cut long jacket flattering her curves. The skirt showed off her great legs and the white camisole – which she'd picked because of Isabel's – was cut low enough to be seriously sexy when she took off the jacket. *If* she felt thin enough to take it off.

Of course, it had been horrifically expensive – all the best over-size-fourteen clothes were. But it hung so well, and made her look slimmer than she felt, that it was worth it.

Even crabby Margaret Redmond couldn't complain about her future daughter-in-law's taste this time. And Dee would be able to talk about her promotion to deputy women's editor and how she was the youngest person ever to get the job. Wonderful!

Well, she *was* the youngest person ever to get the job. Margaret didn't need to know that Dee was also the *only* person ever to get it.

Dee would have whistled if she'd been able to. What a great day it was turning out to be! She'd spent two hours that morning interviewing one of Ireland's female business tycoons and the interview had gone really well.

Donna Fratelli was friendly but as tough as old boots – she'd needed to be to bring her family's ailing pasta business out of the doldrums and into the Irish food business as a major player. But she was also very down-to-earth, very clever, and possessed the sort of sense of humour that would come across really well on paper.

When Dee had asked whether there was a man in her life or not, she wasn't too forthcoming but did point out that many men were frightened off by successful, independent women.

'Listen, if I had a penny for the number of guys who proudly tell me how successful they are, and then take a big step backwards when I tell them exactly how prosperous *my* business is, then I'd have a much bigger house and a Ferrari to boot,' Donna had told her drily.

Despite all her money and success, Dee felt sorry for Donna. She was nearly forty, very good-looking with dark Italian skin and eyes, very rich – and, evidently desperately lonely.

'Believe me,' she had said at the end, 'a woman's success manages to neuter men quicker than a surgeon performing a vasectomy.'

It was a brilliant quote and the perfect way to finish off Dee's article. But it was also a sad and telling comment.

Dear Annie,

All my friends think I have everything – money, success, good looks, you name it. But I'm so lonely. All the men I meet are either married or scared of commitment and, when they discover how successful I am, they run away. Am I really an 'ice maiden', as one guy called me?

Career Lady

Dear Career Lady,

You're no ice maiden. That's a sign of this particular man's inadequacies – not yours. He's wary of women who are independent and in control of their own lives. That's what he's afraid of – so he does the only thing he can and belittles you.

The real problem is that you are rich and successful. You are moving away from Mr Average's picture of the sort of woman he can cope with. You need to meet a man who isn't threatened by your success and power. Unfortunately, this will probably have to be a guy who is successful and powerful in his own right. But there is a man like that out there, somewhere . . .

'You're engaged, I see.' Donna had noticed Dee's engagement ring.

'Yes,' she'd said with a wry smile. It was incredible, really. Donna wore beautiful jewellery, including several platinum rings on her long, tapering fingers, yet she'd looked longingly at Dee's simple solitaire.

'And your fiancé is happy that you've got such a great job and your own independence?'

'Absolutely,' Dee said.

It was true, she mused now, as she paid her parking fee and drove out of the city centre to the office. Gary had been thrilled that she'd been promoted. He'd forgiven her drunken escapade – even the fact she'd hit him – and immediately went to the off-licence to buy a bottle of champagne to go with the shepherd's pie she'd attempted to make for dinner.

'Think of it – we'll be the success story of the year,' he'd said, one arm around Dee, a glass in his other hand. 'I reckon I'll make partner in the firm next January and you're at executive level on the paper. What a team, eh?'

Dee had snuggled up to him happily. He'd forgiven

her and was thrilled about the job.

His enthusiasm was infectious. They'd ended up making love in the sitting-room with half their clothes on. It had been months since they'd done anything so spontaneous. The memory of that passionate session made Dee feel sexy just thinking about it.

The one blip in their improved relationship was her weight. Gary had added that they really ought to join a gym, possibly one of the trendy and ultra-expensive ones in the city centre.

'It would do us good,' he'd said, giving Dee a gentle poke in the ribs. 'And if you're going to be the rising young executive, you'd better get rid of that extra weight you're always talking about. I can just picture you in one of those clingy chiffon dresses at my firm's Christmas party, all slim and sexy. All the other guys will be mad for you.' As he nuzzled into her neck, Dee had frozen in misery.

'Aw, come on, Dee,' he'd protested, feeling the tension in her body. 'I love you the way you are, you know that. I've always adored your Rubensesque figure. But *you're* the one who's always saying you want to lose weight – I'm just backing you up. Don't you understand that, darling?'

When Gary stared at her beseechingly, those hazel eyes in that handsome face just begging her to agree with him, Dee couldn't resist. He was only trying to help, she knew that. And she *was* always going on about her figure – he was right about that, too.

'I know,' she said slowly.

'You could do step aerobics? All the girls at the office are obsessed with step classes,' Gary said. 'I'll phone around tomorrow and check out a few gyms.'

Dee *was* lucky and it was about time she appreciated

it. She resolved to stop bitching about how Gary never did any cleaning. Her constant nagging hadn't worked. In fact, all it had done was create an icy atmosphere at home. From today on, she vowed, she'd be different – cool, calm and most definitely not the sort of woman to fly into a fury when she found the toilet seat up or the laundry basket full of dirty soccer kit. Yes, that was it. There was going to be a new Dee O'Reilly, a new woman who wouldn't get stressed out when office politics upset her and who would be able to speak to Margaret Redmond without immediately being overcome with an urge to hit the other woman with her handbag.

She was just too emotional, too fiery, Dee decided. It was the red O'Reilly hair that did it, her father had always joked. Dee was the only member of the family to have the rippling, chestnut curls of her paternal grandfather, a Corkman with an explosive temper.

Grandad O'Reilly had died a very unhappy man. None of his family had been on speaking terms with him. She didn't want to end up like that. So what if Gary was useless around the house? Her father didn't know one end of a tea towel from another and her mother coped. It was just a matter of how you handled things.

CHAPTER EIGHT

Dee smiled as she watched the smallest flower girl carefully pull a pink satin hairband off her head and fling it carelessly into the rose bushes before sitting down to take off her tiny pink ballet shoes. The operation complete, the four year old raced off into the garden, screeching with delight. The Delahuntys' pedigree Dalmatian ran after her.

It was about the only natural thing that had happened at the wedding so far. The whole event was an exercise in pretension. Dee wondered if Yvonne Thomas, *née* Delahunty, had asked a professional events organiser to copy *Bride's Magazine*'s version of the perfect wedding.

She could just picture it: Yvonne, brushing a skein of long, perfectly bleached hair back from her face with one plump manicured hand, saying: 'I don't care what it costs – I want it to be *the* society wedding of the year. I want it to be a work of art.'

But it wasn't so much a work of art as very artful, Dee thought sourly. The ceremony had been directed like an opera, with the choir all dolled up in flowing robes, Simon and his brothers in morning suits and three priests in front of the altar. As if Yvonne had wanted to be triply sure that she was married.

The church had been a riot of pale pink roses with

posies at the end of each pew. Yvonne's dress had a train so long it took six bridesmaids clad in pink silk meringue dresses to carry it, with three adorable flower girls and one outraged-looking page boy wearing velvet knickerbockers to help.

When the wedding party arrived at the Delahuntys' substantial country house, a string quartet was energetically working its way through Vivaldi's *Four Seasons*. Black-suited waiters brought around an endless supply of champagne – in real crystal glasses, Dee noticed. Smoked salmon niblets were provided for the two hundred or so guests. It would be at least an hour before lunch because two photographers were taking endless society pictures in the garden.

Dee just hoped they had plenty of Vaseline for the camera lenses to give the pictures that smudgy look. For Yvonne, despite all the tennis lessons, membership of an exclusive gym, endless sessions at the beautician, and a dress that probably cost as much as a small car, was definitely no raving beauty.

Nor had she succumbed to the usual pre-wedding nerves which made most brides lose half a stone. In her voluminous Brussels lace gown, she looked as if she'd put *on* weight since Dee had last seen her.

If she'd had one ounce of modesty, or wasn't so desperately spoiled, Yvonne could have been much more attractive. Dee would have sympathised with her about hips that spread when she just *looked* at cheesecake, because Dee understood that feeling very well. But Yvonne was so smug and self-satisfied, convinced she really was the greatest thing since sliced bread, that it gave Dee a perverse pleasure to criticise her.

Especially as she was still smarting over a remark Yvonne had made about 'that awful newspaper Deirdre works for'. Gary couldn't stand her and insisted that his cousin was only marrying her because Yvonne's father was a senior partner of Simon's legal firm.

'She's such a snob,' Gary said under his breath as he handed Dee another glass of champagne. He was the most handsome man in the room, she thought proudly. His wavy hair was brushed back from his strong face, winged eyebrows arched over eyes that glittered as he looked at Dee in her beautiful and very expensive new suit.

'Well, if Yvonne is a snob, so's Simon,' Dee countered. She refrained from adding, 'And so's your mother.'

'He's not that bad,' Gary demurred. 'But she's the limit. Apparently she went ballistic last night when she realised the caterers were serving Möet instead of Cristal.'

Dee stared at him in amazement. 'What a spoilt brat! She's just unbelievable. Doesn't she have a clue about the real world?'

He shook his head. 'I doubt it. But Simon will be well able for her. He's quite tough and she'll have to understand that once Daddy's not picking up the tab any more, she'd better economise.'

'*Economise*!' Dee exclaimed. 'Yvonne thinks she's slumming it if she spends less than a hundred and fifty quid on a skirt. She probably thinks "the real world" is the name of some cute boutique in London where they won't let you in unless you wave an American Express gold card at them and say you're a close personal friend of Nicole Kidman.'

Gary laughed. 'You're priceless, Dee, you know that?' He leant over and kissed her gently. 'And you look stunning in that outfit. Good enough to eat.'

Dee gave him an arch look. 'Maybe we could sneak

upstairs and find a spare bedroom?' she suggested. 'Your mother keeps telling me this house has ten, so we may as well use one of them.'

'Don't tempt me,' he murmured. One hand slid surreptitiously under her jacket and reached inside her camisole. Dee leant against him, feeling a wave of desire sweep over her. The combination of champagne, no lunch and the warm sun made her feel languorous and sexy.

What's more, she knew she looked great in her elegant terracotta suit, and looking good was one of the most powerful of aphrodisiacs.

'Gary and Deirdre . . .' Margaret Redmond appeared with a horsey-looking woman in tow. Gary whipped his hand out from under Dee's jacket.

'. . . have you met Mrs de Vere-Smyth? Her son is doing a degree at the London School of Economics. You've a couple of pals there, don't you, Gary?' Margaret lowered her voice a fraction and said meaningfully, 'And her husband is in banking, a merchant bank.'

'Really?' said Dee, cross at having been interrupted when she and Gary were sharing the only private moment they'd had all day. 'How interesting. You'll have to excuse me for a moment, I see someone I must talk to.'

She left Margaret open-mouthed and hurried towards Millie, a lovely Donegal girl who was married to Gary's older brother, Dan.

Millie was sitting alone on a white-painted iron bench, with a plate of smoked salmon parcels and tiny cheese nibbles on her lap. Dan was one of Simon's groomsmen and was off having endless photographs taken with the happy couple.

'I saw you escape,' Millie said indistinctly, her mouth full.

'I had to,' sighed Dee as she sat down. 'An hour and a half with that woman in the car this morning as we drove down was torture enough. I don't want to spend the entire reception listening to her boasting about her marvellous boys, her marvellous house, all the marvellous things she does for charity and the last art exhibition she went to. Horrible woman wouldn't recognise a decent painting if it bit her. She's such a pseud.' Dee took a cheesy thing off Millie's plate.

'I thought you were on a major diet for your holiday in Portugal next month,' she added. 'Wow, these are yummy.'

Millie grinned. 'Don't say anything – especially to Mother-in-law – but I'm eating for two.' She looked down at her stomach.

'Wonderful!' cried Dee. 'Congratulations, Millie. How far gone are you? You can't see anything.'

Millie looked her normal sturdy self in a gauzy cream jacket worn over a matching long dress. The pale colour suited her pale complexion and strawberry blonde bob.

She smiled ruefully. 'I'm three months gone and I've already put on eight pounds. You wouldn't notice in this outfit but I do look pregnant in my work clothes.

'We didn't want to say anything until at least three months. I knew Margaret would drive me insane if we told her before today. Can't you just imagine it? Everything I put in my mouth would be bad for the baby, everything I did would be wrong, and as for carrying on working while I was pregnant . . . forget it!'

The two women laughed in mutual understanding. Millie had been married to Dan for five years and worked in a bank. Dee had become good friends with the merry Donegal girl. They'd both had their fair share of snide remarks from Margaret who felt neither of them was good enough for her beloved boys. But Millie had a tougher hide than Dee, and rarely let her mother-in-law's barbs strike home. Dee, on the other hand, was often deeply hurt by Margaret's cutting remarks, although she tried to hide it.

'I'm due at the end of November so I'm going to work till around the beginning of the month,' Millie explained. 'Margaret will freak when she finds out that I'm not giving up work to sit at home with my feet up awaiting the birth of the first Redmond grandchild. But I'd go mad at home and it's not as if I'm delicate or anything.'

She took another salmon parcel and swallowed it whole. 'I think she likes to imagine all her daughters-in-law are little fragile things. Thinks we sound posher that way. She's never quite got over the fact that I'm from such a big, country family.' Millie was the youngest of eleven children. 'Apparently large families are provincial.'

'At least your family have a big farm and *some standing in the local community*,' Dee mimicked Margaret's marble-in-the-mouth accent. 'I'm never going to be forgiven for having a mechanic as a father and a mother who cleans the local school.' She didn't mean to sound bitter, but she did. Dee was actually very proud of her family.

'All the O'Reillys work damn' hard, we always have,' she said. 'None of us has ever sponged off the State, and just because my mother doesn't have bloody pastry forks and my dad goes down the local to watch football matches instead of listening to recitals in the Concert Hall, doesn't mean stuck-up Margaret Redmond can look down her crabby nose at us!' She finished abruptly, aware she'd suddenly become too emotional.

Millie patted her knee kindly. 'Don't let her upset you. She's not worth it. And, I promise you, when I tell her I'm going to keep working in the bank until a few weeks before the baby's born, I'll make sure you're there to see the look on her face. She'll go bananas! It'll be priceless. But Dan won't let her get a word in edgewise.'

That was the difference between the brothers, Dee reflected. Dan stood up to his mother and wouldn't let her pick on Millie. But Gary wanted to be his mother's pet, the youngest, the most devoted. Which meant he wilfully blinded himself to her faults – even when she was a cast-iron bitch towards Dee.

The musicians had done Vivaldi to death by now and had moved on to a rather kitsch version of 'Here Comes the Bride' to greet a beaming Yvonne who'd arrived from the rose garden with her entourage of bridesmaids.

'How many million photos have they taken?' Millie asked. 'I'm starving. Pregnancy does that to you,' she added with a grin.

Dan loped towards them with a champagne flute in one hand. His long legs looked even longer in stripey morning suit trousers. He wasn't nearly as good-looking as Gary and was slowly losing his hair. But he was very kind, a total gentleman and obviously adored his wife.

'How are you, Millie?' he asked, planting a kiss on the top of her head. 'Did you save me anything to eat?'

'I'm sorry, Dan, I've been a greedy pig and nearly polished off the lot. But it must be time for lunch soon.' Millie popped the last salmon parcel in her husband's mouth. 'I'm ravenous. I've told Dee the good news. We'd better tell your mother tonight, so she can start knitting.'

'Congratulations.' Dee gave him a kiss on the cheek. Dan beamed down at her.

'If you will all move into the marquee, lunch is served,' announced a waiter grandly.

'Will my two favourite ladies let me accompany them?' Dan held out both hands.

'We'd better hold on for a moment or we'll be squashed in the rush,' said Dee, as the wedding guests, ravenous after waiting so long for lunch, made for the striped marquee like starved piglets bustling towards the trough.

'There's no hurry, anyway,' Dan said. 'There are place names.'

'Written in copperplate on ivory parchment and held by silver place-name holders, I presume?' inquired Millie wickedly.

'Of course,' Dee said. 'What sort of wedding do you think this is, Millicent? Something common, or what?'

They all burst out laughing.

'I expect the same sort of thing from you and Gary,' Millie joked. 'Champers, string quartets and lots of gorgeous nibbles, plus seventeen bridesmaids who'll shower you with rose petals as you walk up the aisle.'

'Don't hold your breath,' Dee answered. 'My family wouldn't be into this type of party.'

'But Margaret would,' whispered a grinning Millie as the three of them walked into the marquee.

Robin ran one finger along a window ledge and then scrutinised the finger with distaste.

'This place is filthy,' she announced.

Isabel closed the airing cupboard door and looked tiredly at her daughter.

'Robin, it's only dirt. We can clean up. You've got to look beyond a bit of grime to see what you think of the house.'

'Only grime?' said Robin crossly as she marched across the room in her patent platform mules. 'I'm not sleeping in a house this filthy.'

To stop herself from saying something she'd regret, Isabel left the small kitchen and went back into the sitting-room. Robin was right about one thing – 12 Eagle Terrace was filthy. A small three-bedroomed terraced house in Bray, it could have been very pretty if the previous owner had ever bothered to paint or clean any part of it.

The peeling window frames outside and dirty grey façade gave the house a run-down look and inside it wasn't much better. The kitchen was 1960s, complete with swirling purple wallpaper which reminded Isabel of the once-cool Pucci designs that looked so good on leggings and shirts, and so bad on walls.

The sitting-room was painted a dark crimson colour and matching carpets gave it the look of a dilapidated brothel. The upstairs bedrooms were all painted off-white and had carpets that could only be called dirty brown. The small bathroom was a hideous pink.

All in all, you'd need to wear sunglasses to walk around the house, and even then you'd still get a headache, Isabel thought.

She struggled with the sitting-room window, trying to open it so she could see what the back garden looked like from a different angle. From the kitchen door, it was a long, narrow wasteland with a horrible clump of red hot pokers bang in the middle, spreading out like some giant, ugly spider. The window flew up suddenly and Isabel was able to see that the view wasn't any better from the sitting-room. Dispiritedly, she pulled the window shut.

The house was pretty awful and needed to be totally redecorated. But it was cheap and didn't seem to have any structural problems. It had gas central heating and on-street parking. The small terraced street it was situated in was quiet and in a nice area, so she wouldn't have to worry about the girls walking home in the dark winter evenings. And, because the house was in Bray, they could stay with her parents if Isabel had to work late.

Robin flounced downstairs. 'The bedrooms are tiny,' she pointed out.

'They're not,' Isabel sighed

'Well, they're not as big as the ones at home,' Robin said sulkily.

And whose fault is that? Isabel wanted to snap. Your bloody father's, that's who. If he hadn't mortgaged our lovely house against his business, we wouldn't have had to sell The Gables or leave Oxford.

And I wouldn't have to take a loan from my parents to put down even the tiniest deposit on a house, and I wouldn't be putting myself to the pin of my collar trying to get a mortgage because I'm a single woman now with no husband to share the bills.

She said nothing for a moment and let her blood cool.

Poor Robin, it wasn't fair on her at all. Naomi was her mother's girl and happy to be with Isabel, no matter how much she missed David. But Robin idolised her father.

She was deeply upset about the separation and wanted to lash out at someone. Isabel was that someone.

At that moment the estate agent walked back in after seeing out other prospective buyers.

'What do you think?' he asked urbanely, as though he'd just shown them a penthouse flat in Dalkey instead of a house that was so dirty it was a health hazard.

'We'll think about it,' Isabel replied coolly.

'Well, I should point out that it's not often a property comes on the market at this price,' the estate agent said smoothly. 'It's only because the new owners want a quick sale, and because the place needs a bit of work, that they're asking such a low price.'

Isabel hoped that Robin didn't pick up the words 'new owners'. If she knew that the previous inhabitant of 12 Eagle Terrace had died in his sleep in the sitting-room in front of the fire, she'd have run out of the place.

The estate agent shrugged. 'Those other people are pretty keen, I feel I ought to tell you.'

'Thank you,' Isabel said again. 'I'll be in touch. Come on, Robin.

'Let's go and have a cup of coffee and a sticky bun,' she suggested once they were outside.

'Yeah!' Robin's face lit up. She was still a child, even if she tried so hard to be grown-up, Isabel thought fondly. It was just as well that Naomi was in bed with 'flu. Being alone with Robin meant Isabel could talk to her on a different, 'us adults' basis that just might work.

Over a coffee slice, an éclair and two cappuccinos, Isabel explained the way she was thinking.

'Robin, we need a place of our own, you can understand that. Your dad isn't here and I'm looking to borrow money from the building society on my own, so it's very difficult. Normally they loan couples money by working out what both of them earn but they're only prepared to loan me money based on what *I* earn, so it's less. Do you understand?'

Robin's face was pale and taut. 'Yes.'

'That's why I'm looking at cheaper houses than the one we had in Oxford. I can't afford anything else.'

'What about Dad?' protested her daughter. 'Isn't he coming here?'

Isabel took another sip of coffee.

'Robin, your father and I have separated. You know that. I can't say what will happen in the future. I love him and I know you do too,' she began.

Tears glistened in her daughter's eyes.

'But he lost all our money. And that's not the worst thing,' Isabel hastened to add. 'The worst is that he lost the home we'd made for you and Naomi. That's what I can't accept, that's why we split up. He gambled with your security and safety.'

'You didn't have to leave him,' said Robin shakily. 'He would have worked it out.'

'There was no way to work it out, Robin. We were bankrupt. If I'd stayed, we'd have been completely broke. I couldn't do that to you and Naomi. Coming back to Ireland was the only choice. Please understand that,' begged Isabel.

Robin shoved her éclair away and stared at her mother mutinously. Isabel gave up. Robin was just like her father. There was no talking to her in this mood.

Isabel was doing the ironing when the phone rang at seven that evening. Robin had gone to see her friend, Karen, with strict instructions that she was to be back by half-eight, while Naomi was cuddled up in her duvet in the sitting-room watching TV. Isabel's parents were visiting a friend in hospital.

As there was nobody to yell, 'I'll get it,' Isabel answered the phone herself. It wasn't one of Robin's monosyllabic girlfriends as she'd expected. It was David.

'Hello, Izzy,' he said. 'How are you? And how are the girls?'

'Fine, we're all fine. I got a new job.'

'The one Robin told me about?'

'Yes. In the *Sentinel*. I'm the new women's editor,' she said flatly.

'Sounds like fun.'

'*Fun?*' She couldn't believe he'd said that. 'Working my fingers to the bone in a tough new job because it's your fault I had to leave the last one is hardly my idea of fun,' she snapped.

David ignored her outburst. 'Good money, I hope?'

'Enough for me to afford to pay a mortgage,' Isabel answered, bitterness in every syllable.

'Unlike me, is that it, Izzy?' he asked.

'Since you ask, yes, totally unlike you,' she said bitterly. 'It's going to be a couple of weeks before I can get the mortgage sorted out on the house I want but, when I do, that money's going to be in the building society every month without fail. No "Oh, dear, I'm overdrawn at the bank, darling Izzy, so let's skip a month's mortgage and get the building society to stick it on at the end of the mortgage. They don't mind doing that".'

'That only happened a couple of times,' he protested.

'*Couple of times?*' Isabel said incredulously. 'Oh, please, David. You may be able to fool other people but you can't fool me. Well,' she amended, 'you can't fool me *now*. There was a time when I believed your bullshit about our finances. But not any more. I learnt the hard way. The we-can't-get-the-heating-fixed-because-I've-blown-the-money hard way.' Even after a few months away from David, Isabel was stunned by how bitter she still was. Just one phone call and she wanted to kill him; wanted to choke him for all his empty promises and denuded bank accounts.

'Don't be like that, Izzy,' he said in that infuriatingly relaxed way of his. 'Please calm down. Your mother's getting to you, huh? She always got on your nerves.'

Isabel fought for control and lost.

'It's not my *mother* that's the problem, David. It's you,' she hissed. 'And, by the way, I haven't heard from you for over two weeks, and while *I* can certainly spend the rest of my life without ever needing to set eyes on you again, your daughters, unaccountably, don't feel the same way. They love you and miss you. And *you* can't even be bothered to ring . . .'

'I've been busy setting up the new business. I had to go to Germany, I'm just back. You know how it is,' he protested.

'Oh, I know. What's her name? Heidi? Bettina?'

'Jesus!' David said in exasperation. 'You always shift the conversation around to that, don't you?'

'And why do you think that is, David? I know exactly what you're like when there's something, or *someone*, new on the horizon. I know the signs. And no new business ever keeps you that enthralled.' Isabel suddenly felt very tired. Why did she even bother to go through all this with him. She'd left him; it was over. He could do what he wanted to, whether it involved Heidi, Bettina or both at the same time. He could have a *ménage à gang* for all she cared.

What was important now, was how he treated the girls. It would be great if he'd occasionally remember the only two people in the world who genuinely loved him. He hadn't seen them for over a month, since he'd visited Dublin on a flying twenty-four-hour visit.

Typically, he'd arranged it as a sort of teenage sensory overload that included ten-pin bowling, lunch in McDonald's, a blockbuster movie in the Savoy in the afternoon and dinner at Planet Hollywood. No wonder Robin had been wretched when he'd gone. In a day spent with her beloved father, they hadn't had one single unoccupied moment in which to talk. A typical David day. He hated to talk.

'I'm not a kid, Mum,' Robin had told Isabel tearfully afterwards. 'I wanted to speak to Dad. I don't want to spend a day playing.'

Yeah, but your father does, Isabel had thought wryly. And a day jam-packed with activities had the added advantage of making deep, meaningful conversations completely impossible. Deep, meaningful conversations are his idea of hell, as you'll find out soon enough.

'Listen, David,' she said briskly. 'Let's stop arguing. I want to talk about the girls. You're going to have to be in touch more frequently, and you've got to come to visit them soon,' she added firmly. 'Robin is taking the separation very badly and needs to see you.'

'They can come to London next weekend,' he said.

'They bloody well won't,' Isabel said immediately. 'I can't afford the plane fare for both of them and, even if I could, I don't want them travelling on their own. Naomi's too young. Be realistic, will you?'

'OK, OK. I'll come the weekend after next. The good news is I've managed to get enough money together to pay off the mortgage arrears and the building society isn't going to repossess The Gables. Isn't that great?'

Isabel was stunned. They still owned the house after all? That was fantastic. They'd make some money selling it. She'd be able to put a deposit down on a house with her half. David might even be able to start paying maintenance for the girls. But where had he got the money from?

'I know what you're going to ask me, Izzy, and it's legal, I promise. It's a long story . . .'

'Tell me,' she ordered.

'I'll tell you when I see you.'

'Tell me now!' Isabel said sharply. 'What do you mean "it's legal"?'

'Izzy, I can't talk now, I'm in a rush. I'll phone next week with details of my flight. Now, are the girls there so I can say hello and give them the good news?'

'Robin is out but I'll get Naomi for you,' she said resignedly. She knew that when David didn't want to tell her something, nothing could induce him to do so. 'Naomi has 'flu, poor thing, and hasn't been getting on too well in school, so cheer her up, will you?'

'I wouldn't need to cheer her up over the phone if you hadn't walked out on me,' David said softly. 'She was getting on very well in her old school.'

'Don't start that,' Isabel groaned.

'Do you miss me, Izzy? I miss you. A lot. And there's no Bettina or Heidi, I promise.'

'Sure. 'Bye, David,' Isabel put down the receiver and called Naomi to the phone. She went back to her ironing but couldn't concentrate.

There's no Heidi or Bettina. I promise.

Since when had any of David's promises actually meant anything?

I promise you, Izzy. She didn't mean anything to me. It just happened. We were drunk and the shoot had gone so well. The crew were celebrating. It only happened once, I'd never do anything to hurt you. You're the one I love . . .

Next year will be better, I promise. Business is great.

You'll probably be able to give up work in a couple of years, we'll be doing so well. Imagine it – we could buy a house in Portugal. What do you think?

The iron hissed over one of Robin's school blouses as Isabel ironed vigorously. Damn David. Damn him and all his stupid, money-making schemes that had gone wrong. And he never seemed to learn from his mistakes.

But then neither had she.

Isabel hung the blouse on a hanger and started on another one. She was as bad as David, she reflected angrily.

After eighteen years, you'd think she'd have been smart enough to figure out that he'd never change, that he'd be a dreamer all his life. But no. She'd spent years convincing herself that one day it would all work out. Or that one day David might actually grow up and settle down to some boring nine-to-five job that would give her and the girls the security they desperately craved.

She was the stupid one. He wasn't going to change. And she'd never been strong enough to walk away. Until this time. She was broke and things were tough, but at least she'd actually done the right thing. She hoped.

CHAPTER NINE

'This was a brilliant idea, Gary,' said Dee. 'I love Wexford. I love drinking wine in the sun. And,' she leaned over and gave him a gentle kiss, 'I love you.'

She sat lazily back in her chair and stretched out her legs to give them a better chance of getting a sun tan. It was incredibly hot. The August sun was beating down on the verandah of the Ferrycarraig Hotel, toasting everyone who sat outside on the wooden deck as they gazed over the tiny bay and enjoyed their lunch. Seagulls swooped and dived over the water. A small boat slowly made its way out to sea, laughter coming from on deck.

Dressed in shorts and T-shirts, Dee and Gary relaxed facing the sun, letting the blissful warmth sink into their limbs.

The remains of two crab salads lay on the table in front of them and they'd got half way through a bottle of deliciously cool white wine.

Soft music drifted out from the bar, mingling with the conversation of people enjoying their lunch in the sun. Only a couple of marauding toddlers threatened the peace and even they were getting sleepy, if a little fractious, in the heat.

'We should do this every weekend,' Dee said happily.

'I agree. Now that you've got normal working hours, we can go away more often,' Gary pointed out. 'What do you think about going to Amsterdam in October? One of the guys from work went there for a weekend with his wife and they had a fantastic time.'

'Yes, I'd love it,' Dee said enthusiastically. 'But can we afford it? We're supposed to be saving for the wedding. If we can ever pick a date, that is,' she added.

'No, I've had a better idea,' Gary said seriously. 'We're going to go to Vegas to get married by an Elvis impersonator in a drive-by chapel of lurve. It'd be cheaper.' He leaned over and poked her gently in the ribs. 'Only kidding. I know you want the full works.'

Dee sat up. 'I don't,' she protested.

'You do, you know you do. I've seen all those copies of *Bride's Magazine* under the bed. I know you fancy yourself in one of those enormous lacy dresses with half a dozen bridesmaids and a veil with a tiara.'

'Perish the thought,' Dee said, poking him back. 'If you think I'm wearing one of those meringue dresses, you're mad. I'd look like a tank done up in net curtains.'

'Stop that, Dee. You wouldn't. You haven't got much weight to lose.' Gary sounded annoyed. 'You've got such a hang-up about your figure. Stop going on about it, for God's sake, right?'

Chastened, she nodded. She knew Gary hated it when she went on about her body. But he didn't understand what it was like to be an overweight woman, constantly tormented by the feeling that you'd look much better three stone lighter and with a washboard stomach. Gary could eat as much as an entire rugby team and never put on an ounce. Dee only had to look crossways at a chocolate biscuit to gain two pounds. She surreptitiously slid a hand under her T-shirt and pinched a bit of her stomach.

What did the diet cereal commercial say? *If you can pinch more than an inch . . . blah, blah, blah*. She could pinch more than an inch. She could pinch several inches in fact, she thought ruefully. God knew how many years she'd have to be eating Special K and skimmed milk for breakfast before she looked like one of the women in their adverts.

It was so unfair. She'd been so good all week in preparation for the weekend. She'd cut down on the sugars in her coffee and had only eaten salad sandwiches for lunch, despite the fact that she normally ate with Maeve who had a two-course meal twice a day and retained the physique of a long-distance runner. Dee had even given up ordering Mars Bars when the office runner went around at eleven asking everyone what they wanted for coffee break. But she couldn't resist the odd chocolate ice cream. Cornettos were her downfall.

Gary poured more wine into her glass.

'D'you fancy dessert?' he asked. 'They've got cheesecake.'

Dee's mouth watered. Cheesecake. She adored it. But they were going out to dinner later and she couldn't have two big meals in one day. Her favourite black trousers were now very tight around the waist and she hadn't bothered to pack the black velvet dress Gary loved her to wear because she looked three months pregnant in it.

'No, I'm full,' she lied. 'You have some. And get two forks.'

'Oh, yeah,' Gary said with a grin, 'so you can eat all mine? I'll just get two cheesecakes.'

What the heck? thought Dee. I'm on holiday. 'Yeah, I'd love some cheesecake.'

After lunch, she suggested a meander down by the bay to walk off the eight billion calories she'd just consumed. They held hands as they walked, happy, relaxed and totally contented. A family were a little ahead of them, three children and a bouncy Red Setter running around energetically.

'This is wonderful,' Dee said again. 'It's so relaxing.'

Gary picked a poppy from a drift of red flowers and handed it to her. 'Mademoiselle, a leetle present for you to tell you how much I luv you.'

'I think we should move down here,' Dee said dreamily. 'Wouldn't it be wonderful to have a walk like this every day, away from the hustle and bustle of the city?'

'This from the woman who gets withdrawal symptoms if she's away from the office for more than two weeks?' Gary asked incredulously.

'I don't,' Dee insisted. 'Not any more.'

He put an arm around her shoulders. 'I apologise. Now it's *three* weeks before you get withdrawal symptoms.'

He ducked as Dee swatted him with her flower. 'All right, I admit it – you're about a hundred and fifty times more relaxed since you got the new job,' he said.

'Do you think so?' she asked, surprised.

'Of course. When you worked in news, you were like one of those drumming bunnies they use to advertise batteries. "Use our batteries and the bunny never stops drumming, ever." You never stopped, Dee. Now you're much more laid-back. I think working with Isabel Farrell is good for you.'

'I suppose,' she conceded. She still hadn't quite forgiven Isabel for taking her job, even though the two of them got along very well.

Dee had taken the big interview slot as her own and

loved picking subjects for it and interviewing them. She also had more time to work on her agony column which meant she wasn't always under so much pressure at work.

Isabel was a surprisingly good boss, calm, considerate and always ready to give praise where it was due. She had slowly changed the whole look of the women's pages, with Maeve, Emily and Dee's help. After years of Antonia's tantrums and mental block when it came to grammar, working with Isabel was a welcome change. Maeve said she enjoyed it.

So did Dee, if she could have brought herself to admit it. Since their first frost moments in Nigel's office, both women had been ultra-polite to each other. Isabel always inquired after Gary, whom she'd never met but had spoken to on the phone, while Dee tried to be equally polite by asking after Isabel's daughters.

Thanks to Ted Holt's gossipy secretary, Marion, Dee knew that Isabel was either separated or divorced and that her ex still lived in the UK. But that was all she knew. Isabel was reserved and never volunteered any information about her life. Dee had no idea where Isabel lived or if she was involved with anyone else. And for someone as curious as Dee, that was very annoying indeed.

All in all, the new women's editor was quite mysterious. The only time Dee had extracted anything personal from her was a few weeks previously when she came back from lunch early to find Isabel at her desk, studying her bank statement with a worried expression on her face.

'I hate that job,' remarked Dee as she took off her jacket and sat down at her desk. 'I always overspend, particularly on clothes.'

Isabel looked up. 'It's a long time since I had the chance to overspend on clothes,' she said wryly. 'Two teenage daughters can spend your salary faster than the speed of light. Not to mention how quickly the bills mount up when you buy a house.'

'Oh, you've just bought a house. Where?' asked Dee, interested.

'Bray. Well, when I say house, I mean terraced hovel,' Isabel explained. 'It needs a lot of work. Work I can't afford, I might add.'

'I'm supposed to be saving for our wedding,' Dee said. 'But I'm not very good at saving.'

'Have you decided on a date?'

'No,' admitted Dee. 'I know we should have but we haven't got round to it yet.'

She didn't want to say that Gary had proved to be noticeably reluctant to settle on a date, apart from saying 'September sounds good', which he'd said the previous year as well. Dee wanted to know *which* September.

'I got married in a rush and it was a very small affair,' Isabel recalled. 'My dress was hideous, now that I think about it. I bought it in a hurry. It was all frills and ribbons, neither of which suit me.' She looked down at her classy white chinos, white linen blouse and cotton cricket jumper with a smile. 'That's why I stick to such simple clothes these days. My wedding photos put me off frills for good.'

Dee gazed at Isabel's figure enviously. There was no way in hell *she'd* ever be able to wear a pair of white trousers. Her bum would look like an elephant's and, with a matching sweater, she'd be a dead ringer for the Michelin Man.

It was very difficult working alongside someone with

Isabel's figure and dress sense. Always flawlessly turned out, she made Dee feel like a fat, frumpy matron. Apart from that, Isabel was really quite nice, though.

Not that *everyone* liked her. Carol-Anne still loathed her and took every opportunity to make smart remarks behind the women's editor's back.

Dee had been fascinated to see how Isabel would deal with someone of Carol-Anne's calibre, someone for whom bitching wasn't so much a habit, as a way of life.

'Wait till Madam has to deal with Nigel in one of his tempers,' Carol-Anne said when she saw how incredibly, and uncharacteristically, polite the editor was to Isabel. 'That'll wipe the smile off her self-satisfied face!'

If Isabel ever heard Carol-Anne's repeated vicious comments – and she must have – she never said a thing. Instead, she treated the other woman politely but firmly. And she made her work. Carol-Anne was doing three times the amount she'd done pre-Isabel.

And I'm doing less but I'm much happier, Dee reflected. She'd only acknowledge it to herself but she *did* like working for Isabel.

The sun went behind a patch of cloud and a soft breeze wafted across the bay. Dee shivered in her light T-shirt.

'Let's turn back,' she said, as she peered up at the sky. 'There's a huge patch of cloud and the sun won't be out for ages.'

'Spoilsport,' Gary said. 'I thought you said you'd like a walk? Come on, it'll do you good to get a bit of exercise.' He playfully swiped her on the behind. 'You might shift a couple of pounds off your rear end.'

'What do you mean by that?' demanded Dee, stung by his remark. 'Ten minutes ago you were telling me I was too hung-up about my figure. Now I'm heap of the week who needs a brisk walk to shift the fat off her behind!'

Gary threw his hands into the air in exasperation. 'This is why we can never talk about your weight problem. You just fly off the handle immediately.'

'*My weight problem?*' shrieked Dee.

'Come off it, Dee,' Gary said irritably. 'You know you have a weight problem. When I met you, you were miles slimmer. You were *thin*, for God's sake. Now look at you! You've just let yourself go and I hate it. But,' he looked at her coldly, 'I daren't say anything about it.'

'You're talking now,' Dee hissed.

He ignored her as he got into his stride. 'You wouldn't believe the number of times I've thought of buying you a piece of sexy lingerie or a nice dress when I'm away with the lads from the football club, but I can't. And why not? Because you'd have a fit if I came home with something that had a size sixteen label on it, that's why.'

Dee stared at him, dumbstruck.

'*You* know you're a size sixteen, *I* know you're a size sixteen, but we can't possibly mention it. Oh, no.'

He was enjoying this, she thought. He really was enjoying it, getting stuff off his chest that he'd been harbouring for months, years maybe.

And how did he know what size she was? She'd been hiding it from herself for weeks now, determined not to push all her size fourteen stuff to the back of the wardrobe in favour of her emergency tent-like clothes. If she did that, it'd be giving in to the fat instead of convincing herself she'd lose it.

'Oh, no, we have to pretend that the extra weight you've put on is just an unfortunate phase you're going through. When in reality, it's nothing of the sort. You're fat, Dee, have been for at least three years. How do you think that makes me feel, huh?' Gary demanded.

'How do you think I feel at my office party when everyone else's wife or girlfriend is done up in slinky little dresses and you're in some shapeless jacket with a ton of make-up on so you have something to hide behind? When you're not hiding behind ten vodka and oranges, that is. I mean,' he continued hotly, 'I thought you'd cop on when you got promoted. I thought you'd realise that a deputy women's editor should look elegant, well-groomed and slim. But no. You just started using more bloody make-up.'

He stopped suddenly and took a deep breath. Dee wanted to say lots of things. Like, 'Run out of steam, darling?' But she couldn't. Her mouth was frozen, like her heart.

People had called her fat before. Kids in school. She'd been Ten Ton Deirdre or Mars Bar O'Reilly. She'd hated games in secondary school, loathed putting on the deeply unflattering gym skirt to trundle heavily up and down the netball court, sweating profusely and missing the ball all the time. There was always someone ready to tease her, to call her names, to humiliate her.

Only this time it wasn't some spotty fourteen-year-old girl being venomous because the fat O'Reilly girl was clever and got better marks in the English exam. No, this was her boyfriend, her *fiancé*, who was saying all these nasty things to her. Dee simply couldn't believe it.

'Well, aren't you going to say anything?' Gary asked. 'Or are you just going to stare at me and blub?'

Dee felt like bawling her eyes out but she wouldn't crumble in front of him, not after what he'd just said.

'What can I say?' she asked simply. 'You've said it all – I'm nothing but a fat, stupid bitch you're ashamed of. I can't think of any answer to that.'

She turned on her heel and walked away as swiftly as she could. She wanted to go back to the hotel, collect her stuff and go home. She couldn't spend another minute with Gary, not after this.

He caught up with her and stood on the path in front of her, blocking her way. He looked mildly repentant.

'Dee, I'm sorry. I shouldn't have been so blunt, so brutal. But I *had* to say it, you know that. It's because I love you.'

The tears came then. '*Because you love me?*' she said shakily. 'All that was done for love? Because it certainly didn't feel like it from this angle.'

'Dee . . .' He grabbed her and wrapped his arms around her.

She stiffened. 'Don't touch me. I can't bear it, not after what you've said.'

He held on firmly. 'I love you, Dee, you know that. But I have to be honest with you. I've wanted to say all that to you for so long. Wouldn't you prefer me to be honest?'

Dee couldn't answer – she was sobbing into his shoulder.

'I want the best for you and that includes making you look your best. *Helping* you look your best,' he amended. 'Please don't cry, Dee.'

He took her hand and led her back up the winding, grassy path to the hotel and into the bar.

'I can't go in, I look a mess,' she mumbled, head down and hair obscuring her tear-stained face.

'There's nobody in here, everyone's sitting outside in the sun,' Gary pointed out. 'Two brandies. Doubles,' he said to the barman.

'I don't want it,' said Dee tearfully when the barman

put the balloon glass in front of her.

'Drink it,' Gary said firmly.

She took a sip of the amber liquid and then a gulp.

Refusing to look at Gary, she stared out at the beautiful bay, a scene that had delighted her such a short time ago. Before Gary had completely decimated her world.

How had that happened? How had they gone from utter happiness to utter misery in a few short minutes? It had been such a wonderful weekend away, she'd been having such a lovely time, thinking about how she was enjoying work and about how fantastic it would be to have a mini-holiday in Amsterdam in a couple of months. And now this – total annihilation. Gary hadn't simply destroyed her confidence, he'd destroyed *her*.

He'd picked on the one subject that was guaranteed to tear her apart – her weight. Her horrible, fat, lumbering body that couldn't fit into half of her clothes any more; the body that had betrayed her all her life. It was still betraying her. And so had Gary.

She felt his hand on her knee.

'Don't be angry with me, Dee,' he said softly. 'I only wanted to help. Somebody had to say it.'

But why did it have to be you? You traitor, the one I loved the most. She bit her lip.

'Finish your drink, darling.' He pushed the glass towards her.

Dee turned to face him, her eyes dark and glassy. 'A moment ago, I was the woman who got plastered at office parties to give herself Dutch courage,' she said bitterly. 'Now, you want me to down a double brandy in two minutes because you've just insulted me, you haven't got any smelling salts handy and you hate people seeing me cry in public. You couldn't bear them

187

to think you'd been so nasty you'd made me cry, isn't that it?' she said harshly.

'It's not like that, Dee. You've . . . you've . . . had a shock,' Gary said. 'I'm sorry about that, but we can get over this, I know we can.'

Yeah, right, thought Dee. There'll be snowballs in hell first. Well, if he wants me to finish my drink, I bloody well will. She grabbed her glass and drained it. The pain stayed in her heart but the brandy numbed it ever so slightly. She felt lightheaded suddenly. It was better than feeling totally devastated.

'Order me another. I'm going to the loo to fix my make-up – and put another ton on,' she added caustically. She pushed past him, shoving a spare bar stool out of the way with her knee. As she strode out of the bar, Dee was conscious of every single stone she weighed. She felt enormous, like a 747 manoeuvring itself through a small space. Was everybody in the hotel looking at her? Were the guests and the staff wondering why such a fat lump of a woman didn't simply stay at home with the fridge for company instead of coming out into the open along with 'normal' thin people?

All the old, hateful remarks flooded into her mind.

The last time I saw something that big, the ISPCA were trying to push it back into the water. Ha, ha, ha.

What's the similarity between a 50cc moped and a fat girl? They're both fun to ride until somebody sees you. Ha, ha, ha.

In the toilets, Dee stared at her red-rimmed eyes and red nose with disgust. She looked dreadful when she cried. She rummaged in her make-up bag for her foundation and was just about to open the tube when she changed her mind. Why bother? Gary was the only person who was going to be looking at her and he'd already made it plain he wasn't impressed. Why waste make-up on him? Anyway, he'd accused her of hiding behind her pancake foundation. She wouldn't do that again.

Instead, she slicked on some lipstick and scrubbed away her smudged mascara. She didn't bother putting any more on. Fat women could wear all the mascara in the world and they'd still be fat.

A fresh brandy was waiting for her.

'Are you all right?' Gary asked.

'Wonderful,' Dee said tightly. 'There's nothing I enjoy more than being savagely criticised by my own boy-friend. I could do this all day. Let's sit outside. You might get some inspiration for more insults because I'm sure there's a ferry due along in a minute. You could work out how much more weight I have to gain before I'm ferry-sized.'

She grabbed her glass and headed for the open door. 'Can we have two more of these?' she called to the barman as she passed him.

'We don't want to get pissed or we'll never be able to drive into Wexford this evening for dinner,' Gary said.

'You can drive where you bloody like, *darling*,' she said. 'I'm going to sit out in the sun and get drunk.'

After three more doubles, consumed in total silence, they were both quite drunk. Dee felt sleepy, light-headed. But she could still remember every word Gary had said.

The sun had gone in by four o'clock and Dee decided she wanted to go back to their hotel bedroom and put on something warmer.

'I'll come too,' Gary said, getting off his seat.

'Suit yourself.'

He turned on the TV in the room, slumped down on

an armchair and watched football. Bloody typical. Dee sat on the bed, wrapped a cardigan around herself and picked up her latest novel. A murder story was exactly what she needed to keep her mind off what Gary had said.

And it might contain a few hints on how to kill someone without getting caught, she thought darkly.

She woke at half-seven, her head muzzy from a mixture of sleep and brandy. Gary sat beside her, gently kissing her face.

'How do you feel, my love?' he asked tenderly.

'Dreadful,' she muttered.

He kissed her cheek, her forehead, her nose, and then her mouth. His tongue slid inside, questing and passionate. 'I love you, Dee, you know that,' he murmured as he moved one hand under her T-shirt to caress her breasts through her bra.

'I've got a headache,' she said rudely. He wasn't getting away that easily. A quick grope and she'll be eating out of my hand? No way. How could she let him touch her or see her body after all he'd said? Every caress would feel like torture, as if he were measuring how huge she was.

'OK. Let's have dinner. I'm starving,' he said. 'I've booked a table here since neither of us is in a fit state to drive.'

'Fine,' Dee said shortly.

She didn't bother dolling herself up. Her black trousers and silvery grey velvet overshirt would do. She gave her hair a desultory comb and put on more lipstick and a dab of eye-shadow. She was having dinner with Gary because she was hungry and because there was no way she could get back to Dublin tonight. That was all.

They sat silently in the restaurant, both staring at the

menu. Dee was ravenous but wasn't about to order a huge meal. She'd have salad and more salad. That'd show him. She'd just decided on avocado salad for a starter and seafood salad for main course when a waiter arrived with an ice bucket containing a bottle of champagne along with a single, long-stemmed red rose.

'To say sorry,' Gary said softly.

Dee had always been a sucker for a romantic gesture. Roses and champagne! He must have arranged it all while she was asleep. He *did* love her, she knew that. And she loved him, madly and desperately. But could she ever forgive him for what he'd said? Or forget, for that matter. She didn't know if she could. Those hateful words spun in her head, every syllable as crisp and clear as if he'd just spoken.

Dee stared at the champagne bottle. The waiter opened it with a flourish and the people at a nearby table clapped, obviously thinking Gary and Dee were celebrating something. An engagement, perhaps. How bloody ironic.

How she'd love to have been able to talk to Maeve, to ask her if she agreed with all the things Gary had said. Maeve was a very truthful person, she wouldn't lie. She'd say if she thought Dee was a fat pig, if Dee really had let the side down with her loud clothes and too much make-up.

But then, Dee knew she'd never be able to tell Maeve about this. She'd be too ashamed to tell her. Too ashamed to admit that her loving fiancé had insulted her viciously.

It was odd to think she'd felt slightly sorry for Maeve recently, sorry for her beloved single friend who never seemed to be able to keep a man for longer than a weekend, while Dee was effortlessly happy with a handsome fiancé, a lovely town house and a wedding looming somewhere in the future. Hilarious. Now *she* was facing a ruined life thanks to the same handsome fiancé, while Maeve was probably spending a riotous Saturday night with her girlfriends, drinking pints of Guinness and drunkenly discussing why they didn't need men anyway.

'Dee?' Gary was looking at her. So was the waiter who'd just filled her glass with bubbles.

She was expected to drink it, Dee realised blankly. So she did.

Gary smiled warmly at her. Dee smiled back. She curled up her mouth at the edges and crinkled up her eyes the way she always did when she smiled. It had never been a mechanical effort before, it had always reached her eyes. But not this time.

'What are you ordering?' Gary asked sweetly. It was business as usual for him. Everything was back to normal. No, it isn't, Dee wanted to yell. She didn't. She gathered all the pain and the hurt back inside her heart where she could hide it, only to emerge when she could cope with it.

'I'll have the avocado and then the seafood salad for main course,' she told the waiter.

'Good girl,' said Gary encouragingly when the waiter was gone. 'Let's enjoy our weekend as if today never happened.'

'Yeah, let's.' Dee practised her mechanical smile again.

They clinked glasses.

Gary was asleep, snoring loudly as usual. Careful not to wake him, Dee turned in the bed and squinted at the small alarm clock she always brought with her on holidays. It was quite dark but she could see the luminous numbers: ten to two in the morning. She'd had a lot to drink, so had Gary, but she couldn't sleep.

She'd pretended to the moment her head hit the pillow. It was easier to feign sleep than to get into an argument with an amorous Gary who wanted to be forgiven.

She turned and lay on her back, staring at the outline of the pretty watercolour print on the far wall of the bedroom.

'Deirdre, you can't stay at home today. You missed a day last week and there's no way the principal is going to believe it if you have another day off sick.' Elizabeth O'Reilly tried to look severe and failed. It was hard to be angry with her fourteen-year-old daughter when she was such a sweet-natured, responsible and very kind girl. Normally, she didn't give her parents a moment's bother. She had only one problem – she was too heavy for a five-foot teenager.

'I'm not overweight, I'm under-tall,' Deirdre used to joke bravely.

But Elizabeth knew that no matter how hard her daughter attempted to make fun of her size, she was, in fact, utterly depressed about it. You could hear her at night when she sobbed miserably into her pillow. There was no point trying to comfort her – Dee would immediately rub her eyes and claim that nothing was wrong.

Elizabeth didn't know why Deirdre was heavy. None of the others was overweight. Her younger brother Shane, was a rail-thin, lanky ten year old, her father was positively thin, and Elizabeth herself had always kept her figure.

'Please, Mum, it's sports day and I just can't face it. Please let me take the day off,' begged Deirdre.

She knew exactly what sort of day she'd have if she went. The sports teacher would insist on getting every single third year on the pitch for the relay race or the five-a-side-soccer, and Deirdre dreaded it.

She couldn't run for more than a minute without going puce in the face and having to rest. That cow Julia Myers would run alongside her, taunting her.

'What's wrong, Ten Ton Deirdre? Eaten too many cream buns to run?'

Dee gazed unseeing at the hotel bedroom wall. *Ten Ton Deirdre.* No wonder she'd shortened her name when she started in journalism college. She'd told her family it was because she wanted to reinvent herself with a snappy new name suitable for newspaper by-lines. But it was really to stop her remembering all those horrific nicknames. Not that everyone in school had been horrible. She'd had lots of friends, pals who'd told bitches like Julia where to stick it when they called Dee names. But she remembered Julia and her vicious gang of four acolytes far better than she remembered all the friendly people. She felt the burning sensation in her eyes, the sting of hot, angry tears. Dee thought she'd spent enough of her life sobbing into pillows when she was a fat teenager. Obviously, she'd been wrong.

CHAPTER TEN

'Any messages, Jackie?' asked Isabel as she walked briskly past her assistant. She slung her handbag on to the desk and picked up the empty mug that sat beside her computer. She was dying for a cup of tea, something hot, liquid and comforting. Her throat felt raw and she was sure she was getting 'flu. Two hours in a stuffy, windowless room jammed with fashion journalists, who all seemed to smoke like troopers, hadn't helped.

Isabel was sorry she hadn't simply left in protest at having to wait until half-eleven before the fashion show, which was actually scheduled for half-ten, started. She couldn't stand being late and loathed bad time-keeping in others.

The clothes had all been dreadful too, lots of flimsy baby doll dresses that made skinny eighteen-year-old models look like jail bait and would make anyone else look completely ridiculous.

Jackie still hadn't answered.

'No messages then?' Isabel inquired again, looking at her for the first time. Jackie looked more like a rock chick than the features/women's department assistant. She wore her customary black mini, her long hair was done up in a thick plait and a heavy silver cross hung from her neck on a black satin ribbon. Usually, she was alert and ready for work. Once she'd had her first blast of caffeine, of course. But today her heavily kohled eyes were doleful and red.

'What's happened, Jackie?' asked Isabel, shocked at the girl's expression. She crouched down beside Jackie's chair. 'Are you all right, love?'

'We've been bought. Ted Holt's gone, Nigel's gone, and there are going to be huge staff cutbacks, I'm sure of it. And since I've only been here since January, I'll be fired.' Jackie started to cry.

Astonished, Isabel stared at her. 'What do you mean, "we've been bought"?'

'The *Sentinel* has been sold,' Phil Walsh said as she put a cup of very strong tea on the desk in front of Jackie. 'It's been sold to Roark International. We now belong to one of the biggest publishing companies in the world.'

'Oh,' said Isabel blankly. 'But that doesn't mean you're going to lose your job, Jackie. Does it?' she asked Phil.

The features editor shot her a glance over Jackie's head.

'Of course not,' said Phil with a bright smile. 'You're great at your job, Jackie, and Isabel and I won't let anyone fire you, we promise.'

'Absolutely,' added Isabel. She put her arm around Jackie. 'Nobody's going to fire you with us around. You're the best assistant I've ever had and I'll make them fire me before I let them fire you, right?'

Jackie nodded and gave her a tearful smile. 'Thank you,' she said in muffled tones.

Phil produced a tissue for her.

'I'd better go to the loo,' Jackie mumbled. 'I must look awful.'

'No, you don't,' Isabel and Phil assured her at the same time.

'Take your time,' said Isabel kindly, giving Jackie a quick hug. 'I'll answer the phones.'

When Jackie had gone, Isabel turned to Phil anxiously. 'No bullshitting. Tell me exactly what all this means. Do you think they'll fire us?'

'Who knows?' said Phil honestly. 'But we've got the National Union of Journalists behind us. People like Jackie aren't so lucky.'

'Are you serious?' Isabel was shocked. 'I mean, Roark International own the *Irish Telegraph* and *Ireland Today*, and I've never heard anything about mass firings.'

'Pity you weren't in Ireland two years ago, then. They gutted *Ireland Today* within a week of taking it over. Not that it didn't need a bit of pruning staff-wise,' Phil added reflectively. 'They had enough staff to run a couple of Cunard liners as well as bring out a daily paper. But the sackings were pretty brutal. They called it Night Of the Long Knives in Mulligan's. When they sobered up, that is. Which was two days later.'

'Oh, God,' said Isabel weakly. She sat down in Jackie's chair. 'Phil, what if they *do* fire people on the basis of "last in, first out"? I've just bought a house I can barely afford, I've the girls to think of and it was hard enough getting this job, never mind another one. What the hell am I going to do?'

She was panic-stricken. However the new bosses got rid of staff, however the sackings were dressed up, she could easily be out of a job in a week. She still owed the solicitor half of his conveyancing fee and the second month's mortgage was due.

To make matters worse, Robin insisted that she needed expensive new trainers and Isabel had just bought a washing-machine on the electricity bill. God only knew how she was ever going to pay any of it back.

Phil sat on the edge of the desk and folded her arms. That was a lovely pale blue cardigan she was wearing, Isabel thought idly, her mind desperate to think of something other than impending doom. It was a woman's cardi at that. Phil normally wore huge men's ones because she liked roomy clothes.

Stop it! she raged at herself. Why the hell am I thinking about cardigans at a time like this?

'Look, nobody knows what's going to happen,' Phil was saying. 'It depends on who Roark puts in here as managing director. Jack Carter – he's the chairman of Roark's Irish division – has a few guys he's groomed for this type of job and we could get a nice one, someone who wants to build the paper up and increase the staff. Or,' she paused, 'we could get a real hatchet man.'

'What are the chances of us getting a hatchet man?' Isabel asked.

Phil grinned. 'Don't panic, Isabel. You're doing a great job. They'd need to be crazy to fire you, surely you can see that?'

Isabel stared at her helplessly. 'Phil, if there's one thing I've learnt over the past year, it's that what you *see* and what is *really* going on are often two very different things. Just because you and I think I'm doing OK as women's editor doesn't mean diddly squat if the powers that be have someone they want to appoint instead.'

'On that basis, no job is safe,' Phil interrupted. 'They could get rid of us all but it would cost them a fortune in redundancies and they're not going to rush into anything, I'm telling you. Relax.'

If only I could, thought Isabel wryly.

'What's Jack Carter like? Is he a ruthless corporate

raider – or a sweet little pussycat of a man?' Isabel asked with a dash of sarcasm.

'I've never met him,' Phil said. 'He's one of those "left school at fifteen and started working as a post boy before crawling up the ranks" sort of guys. He's late-forties, very well off, and married to this real high society queen, Elizabeth Carter. There's no charity ball in this country she isn't at, fundraising for everything from one-eared donkeys to bewildered chimpanzees.'

'I met her once,' interrupted Jackie, back from the loo with red eyes but a brave smile on her face. 'It was at that TV telethon thing. She was lovely. Really beautiful, sort of like Cindy Crawford but older.'

'A lot older,' put in Phil. 'She's pushing fifty though she doesn't look it. Must be either good breeding – her uncle was Lord something or other – or a quick nip and tuck job. She's the high-profile member of the family. You never see Jack at the charity balls and premières.'

'Maybe he'll feel charitable towards us,' Isabel said hopefully.

'I've never heard anything bad about him,' Phil said. 'Although I did hear that she's partial to the odd recreational pharmaceutical – cocaine, in other words. He's supposed to be OK, one of the tough-but-fair school.

'Listen, ladies, I don't know about you but I've got some work to finish. If we can't produce a decent paper tomorrow, we might all be for the high jump.'

By three that afternoon, the rumours were flying. One common theory was that Eugene 'Slasher' Flynn would be leaving his post as MD of Roark International's flagship paper *Ireland Today*, in order to rip the *Sentinel* to pieces before rebuilding it as a very different sort of paper.

'Let's go to the pub, lads,' muttered the deputy sports

editor glumly when he heard this. Slasher hated both sports and sports reporters, having been the smallest and least athletic guy in his class at school, which had led to constant bullying he'd never forgotten.

The other rumour flying around was that Jack Carter would import some young blood from the company's Australian papers to give the *Sentinel* the benefit of some antipodean expertise. This was a much better prospect.

'Brilliant!' said the picture editor, a native of Sydney.

'Brilliant and then some!' smiled Maeve, her mind already picturing a few hunky Mel Gibson-lookalike executives brightening up the office – and her life.

There was very little work done that afternoon. Stalin bellowed loudly as usual but nobody paid much attention to the news editor's rantings. They were in deep enough shit without worrying about an irate boss. And anyway, as Phil remarked, the new bosses would undoubtedly change the pecking order so the management from the old regime could easily end up sweeping floors under the new one. The idea of Stalin on his hands and knees, scrubbing the canteen floor, cheered up quite a few people.

Isabel was so uptight about the whole takeover that she stared blankly at her computer and tried not to listen to all the rumours.

She was writing a piece about the latest skin cancer statistics but, no matter how many times she read and re-read the report from the Department of Health, she kept thinking about all the bills she had to pay and about the chance that she'd be made redundant a mere three months after getting the job.

By six o'clock, half the office had gone to Magee's to discuss the latest rumours, while the other half were pretending to work while mournfully discussing the chances of some descendant of Atilla the Hun's arriving to manage the paper.

Isabel couldn't take any more of it. She grabbed her briefcase and left, trying to remember if she'd defrosted the pork chops she'd planned to cook that night or if she'd have to go to the supermarket on the way home. Blast it, she thought wearily as she drove out of the office gates, she might as well go to the supermarket and get something anyway. She wasn't in the mood for cooking and could pick up some more tonic for the remains of the gin while she was there. An enormous drink was probably the wrong thing to have in this moment of crisis, but that's just what she felt like. A huge, huge gin to blot out all the terrifying fears in her head.

The late-night supermarket was jammed with after-work shoppers in a rage after being bossed around all day in the office and therefore determined to reassert themselves with some aggressive trolley manoeuvring. Isabel's trolley was crashed into three times before she reached the safety of the checkout.

It was then she realised she'd forgotten the tonic. She felt like crying. The queue had quickly built up behind her and the checkout guy had just started on her groceries. There was no way she could make a dash for the drinks section without being screeched at by the shoppers behind her. After her awful day, Isabel felt like sitting down in the middle of the supermarket and sobbing. Why couldn't things ever go well for her? What the hell had she done wrong for her life to be permanently screwed up?

'Are you paying by credit card or cash?' asked the assistant for the second time.

Isabel's mind focused.

'Cash,' she said, hoping she had enough in her purse. She smiled at the assistant. There, she'd done it again. Smiled as though everything was going perfectly when inside she was in despair.

That's my problem, Isabel thought grimly, stuffing her groceries into plastic bags. I smile when my heart is breaking and never let anyone know what's really going on. My brave smile never lets me down. She chuckled mirthlessly. At least *something* never lets me down.

At home, Robin was on the phone, perched on the bottom step of the stairs.

'Hiya,' she mouthed as her mother staggered in, weighed down with shopping bags, her briefcase and the pile of papers and articles she hadn't got round to reading in the office.

Still clutching all the bags, Isabel leant down awkwardly to kiss Robin on the cheek and went into the tiny kitchen where Naomi was curled up on the brown squashy settee. She was watching *Neighbours* on the portable TV which sat on the breakfast bar. A half-empty bowl of Rice Krispies was in her lap.

'Hiya, Mum,' she said cheerfully. 'I was too hungry to wait for dinner.'

'Sorry I'm late, Naomi,' Isabel said, as she unloaded her cargo with relief. She flexed the hand that she'd been carrying the plastic bags with, to get the circulation back. 'Has Robin eaten?'

'She had toast.'

'And is that all you've had to eat?' Isabel asked, indicating the cereal Naomi was eating.

She nodded.

'That's not enough, love. I'll fix up something light for us all. Robin can't exist on toast alone any more than you can live on Rice Krispies. How was your day? Did you both walk home from Granny's or did Grandad drive you?'

They talked as Isabel unpacked the shopping. Naomi put everything away and laid the breakfast bar neatly with plates and cutlery.

Isabel washed lettuce, tomatoes, mushrooms and cucumber and quickly assembled a salad. With the French crusty bread she'd bought, some Cheddar cheese and the remains of the salami in the fridge, they'd have a nice meal.

'Call your sister, will you?'

Robin took one look at the salad and turned up her nose. 'I'm not hungry. I've eaten,' she said, taking a Diet Coke from the fridge. She pulled the evening paper out of the pile on top of Isabel's briefcase, sat down on the settee and flicked through it aimlessly.

'Toast isn't enough for dinner,' Isabel said evenly. She could tell that Robin was ripe for an argument, which was the permanent state of affairs these days. Her perfectly shaped cupid's bow mouth was set in a pout, and her brows were heavy under the curtain of blonde hair which hid most of her face.

'Have a little bit of salad, Robin,' coaxed Isabel. 'There aren't any nutrients in toast.'

'I don't want anything else,' she said stubbornly, refusing to lift her head out of the paper.

Isabel took a deep breath. 'What did you have for lunch?'

'Oh, please. What is this, the Spanish Inquisition?' demanded Robin angrily. She threw the paper on the floor and stared at her mother defiantly. Naomi kept her eyes on her plate and nibbled a bit of cucumber.

'There's no inquisition. I simply want to make sure you eat properly, Robin. That's all. If you don't want to eat, I can't make you. And after the sort of day I've had, I don't want a fight, got it?' Isabel stared hard at her elder daughter. If Robin made just one more provocative remark, she'd explode.

For once, Robin seemed to realise that her mother was not in the mood to be crossed.

'Fine,' she mumbled. She left without slamming the door and ran upstairs. Isabel and Naomi heard her bedroom door bang shut and almost immediately the sound of Oasis could be heard from Robin's portable CD player.

At least she didn't have the music turned up to eardrum-splitting level.

Isabel shoved her fork into a bit of mushroom, not feeling very hungry any more.

'This is lovely, Mum,' said Naomi, trying to be helpful.

Isabel relaxed. 'Thanks, Naomi,' she said. 'What would I do without you?'

After dinner, Naomi washed up while Isabel reluctantly went into the sitting-room to tackle the wallpaper stripping. Since they'd moved into 12 Eagle Terrace a month ago, she'd been taking it room by room, stripping off the disgusting wallpaper and painting at the weekends. She'd taken four days off work to make the girls' rooms habitable. Robin had found a picture in *Homes & Gardens* of the sort of bedroom she wanted, so Isabel had done the basics, painting it the cool apple green her daughter wanted, and had left the rest to her.

With the magazine as her guide, Robin had then carefully painted her old chest of drawers, dressing-table and bedside table in a rich forest green before stencilling a fleur-de-lys design in gold paint all over her handiwork.

With the addition of a plain cream carpet and heavy cream curtains sprigged with an apple green leaf design, the room looked very pretty.

Robin had stencilled the same gold pattern as a frieze around the walls, just below ceiling height, and she'd even found some bronze brocade cushions in a local charity shop. Isabel had to hand it to her – she was very inventive and artistic.

'You've done such a beautiful job of your bedroom, you should pick what we'll do with the sitting-room,' Isabel had said, wanting to encourage Robin in her interior decorating skills. Unfortunately, she had been so grouchy for the past fortnight that Isabel hadn't been able to bring the subject up again.

With her father's help, Isabel had papered Naomi's small bedroom with a pretty and romantic floral paper in rose and peach shades. She'd spent some of her meagre budget on a brass bedhead and, with the addition of a ruinously expensive white broderie anglaise duvet cover and pillowcases, the effect was just as feminine and girlish as Naomi could want. She still needed a better bedside lamp than the old wooden one. Isabel was determined to get her a brass one and had decided to save until she could afford it.

She hadn't done anything with her own bedroom, apart from painting the walls with cheap magnolia paint and giving the woodwork a couple of quick coats of white gloss.

Old yellow curtains from The Gables, which didn't fit properly, covered the windows and she'd put down a couple of large burgundy cotton rugs to hide the horrible dirty-brown carpet until she could afford to replace it. Carpeting, papering and painting the girls' rooms had cost more than she'd intended.

It took hours, but she'd painstakingly stripped and painted the kitchen and replaced the ancient lino until it was the only room downstairs that was fit to sit in, which was why she and the girls watched TV there instead of in the horrible sitting-room.

Tonight, Isabel had planned to tackle the wallpaper over the fireplace in the sitting-room. But when she'd changed into her ancient leggings and an old T-shirt, she simply didn't feel up to it.

She sighed and pulled on the ancient Marigolds she'd been trying to remember to use for the wall-stripping. She was exhausted from double jobbing – working by day and decorating by night. Naomi wanted to help but Isabel refused point blank.

'You can help me tidy up, but I don't want you wearing yourself out. It's far too tiring for you. Besides,' she added, putting an arm around her slender daughter, 'who else is going to make me endless cups of tea if you're stuck in the middle of a difficult patch of wallpaper?'

Robin hadn't offered to help for ages, not since they'd first moved and she'd been struggling with maths homework she didn't feel like doing. Isabel remembered the last time the knotty subject of maths had come up in the Farrell household. It had been an astonishing conversation.

'I don't see the point of maths,' Robin had moaned. She was studying for her summer exams. 'It's not as if I'm ever going to want to work out the equation of a line in normal life, now am I? Yeah, knowing that's really going to come in handy if I'm travelling round the world working.'

Isabel had blanched. 'What do you mean, "travelling round the world working"?'

'That's what Susie's older sister is doing. She started off in India, now she's in Thailand and she's going to Australia next.' Robin's eyes lit up as she described the traditional back-packer's itinerary. 'She sent Susie a brilliant Gucci watch – fake, of course, but it looks real. And she's only nineteen,' she added.

'Is that what you'd like to do, Robin?' asked Isabel weakly. 'What about college and getting some qualifications when you leave school?'

Her daughter's expression was dismissive.

'That's what *everybody's* parents say. Taking a year off is *like* going to college, only you're learning things by going round the world. It's experience. You can go to college when you get back.'

'Well, you've a few years of school to get through first,' Isabel pointed out. 'You might have changed your mind about what you want to do a dozen times by then.'

'I won't.'

Robin was growing up so fast. It was hard to believe that only a couple of years ago, her biggest ambition had been to have a pony. Robin would be eighteen in three years, Naomi would be fifteen and Isabel would be nearly forty-three. *Forty-three!* It seemed so old. She was beginning to feel old too. Her fortieth birthday loomed ahead of her next month, like a huge stone wall she couldn't climb over.

Being thirty hadn't bothered her the way it had some people. David had practically gone into a decline on his thirtieth. He'd announced he was out of his wild twenties and it was all downhill from now on. Isabel had just laughed and told him she quite fancied older blokes.

She'd never been scared of aging. No cosmetics

company had ever seduced her into buying their 'use this and look like a seventeen year old forever' moisturisers because she knew it was all bunkum. People got old, that was that.

Women who stayed thirty-nine for years had always amused her. But now that she herself was on the verge of entering her fortieth year, she felt sick at the very idea. A divorcée in her thirties didn't sound quite so scary as the notion of one in her forties.

She went into the hall and peered at herself in the mirror. There were definitely more lines around her eyes. She'd always been proud of them – a pale aquamarine the colour of the sea on white sands, as David had once poetically said. He was an expert at that sort of rubbish – all talk and nothing to back it up. Well, her eyes didn't look particularly aquamarine now, she thought glumly. They just looked tired, surrounded by wrinkles, smudged mascara and coffee-coloured eyeshadow that had worn off. She looked tired, full stop.

'Who's looking at me, anyway?' she said out loud to the mirror. 'Nobody.' The last person to give her a flirtatious smile had been the security man on the office gate, and he looked young enough to be going out with Robin. He was probably flirting with her for a bet: 'See if you can chat up that blonde forty-something, the tall one with all the wrinkles and no boobs.'

There was no point moping about it. Isabel was going to be forty in September whether she liked it or not. Armed with a scraper and a bottle of water and washing-up liquid, Isabel went back into the sitting-room and started to spray the paper over the chimney flue. The fireplace had obviously been there since the house was built in the thirties and probably hadn't been swept since, if the dirt was anything to go by.

Sadly, it wasn't one of those fabulous Art Deco ones that thrilled do-it-yourself-TV-show presenters were always finding in architectural salvage yards. It was a horrible beige tiled affair that Isabel simply hated. Whatever happened, she thought, gazing at it with dislike, she had to get a new fireplace. Of course, getting a new one depended on whether she actually had a job or not by the next day. Shit! She'd almost managed to forget about the takeover. Who the hell knew what was going to happen?

But worrying wouldn't help. Isabel checked her watch. It was a quarter to eight. She'd work till half-nine and then have a drink and a bath.

The thought of sinking into a steaming bath filled with bubbles and that relaxing neroli oil she'd got in the Body Shop would keep her going. If she *had* to be a forty-year-old divorcée with more wrinkles than a linen shirt, at least she could be a beautifully relaxed, very clean, and – if she could ferret out some orange juice for the gin to make up for having no tonic – a slightly tipsy one.

By half-nine the following morning, the newsroom was packed to capacity. Everyone, from staff reporters to columnists who worked from home and rarely ventured into the office, had turned up, all awaiting the death knell or the celebratory news, as the case might be.

'I didn't get a wink's sleep,' confessed Belinda, the gossip columnist, nervously. '*Today* doesn't have a social column so they mightn't want one here either. I don't know what else I'd do – I mean, I've been writing a diary page for the past ten years. I'm hopeless at news.'

Dee would have liked to have consoled her, but she couldn't. She felt pretty inconsolable herself. Since

CATHY KELLY

Maeve had rung her with the news that Roark International had bought the *Sentinel*, Dee had been feeling terribly anxious. She'd desperately wanted to go to Magee's that evening where everyone would discuss and rediscuss the takeover endlessly, and where there was a possibility that the odd pertinent piece of gossip would be dragged out of someone.

Instead, she'd spent the evening at a terminally boring surprise fortieth birthday party for one of Gary's colleagues. She'd smiled lots of hard, bright smiles at the people who'd tactlessly asked about her position on the paper now that the legendary Roark had bought it.

'I was amazed when I heard it on the news this evening. Will you all keep your jobs?' inquired one of the accountants' wives nastily. She'd had it in for Dee ever since her husband had drunkenly chatted Dee up at the last Christmas party.

Knowing this, Dee had given her what she hoped was a smug smile and tapped her nose enigmatically. 'I'm afraid I can't talk about it now, but you'll know soon enough.

'Cow!' she'd raged to Gary on the drive home, quite plastered from all the screwdrivers she'd drunk to cheer herself up. 'Honestly, if her bloody company had been taken over, I wouldn't be pleased as hell and practically asking her if she was going to be fired, now would I?'

''Course you wouldn't,' Gary replied, keeping his eyes on the road. 'She's just green with envy because you're gorgeous and sexy, and she's an anorexic crone with no personality.'

Dee stiffened. *Anorexic crone*? Was it possible that he'd finally realised how devastated she was after the Wexford incident? She'd tried to be normal on the outside, even though her insides felt as frozen as a Lean

210

Cuisine. But then, Gary had been at the back of the queue when God had been handing out intuition. He put one hand on her knee, edging up under her wrap-over skirt to stroke her thigh. The crash diet that had made her lose five pounds in a week had had a good effect, she thought wryly. Suddenly she was irresistible again.

'Anyway, Dee, they aren't stupid enough to get rid of someone with your talent and enthusiasm.'

'You never know,' she fretted.

Perched on the edge of her desk with a barely touched mug of extra strong Rombouts in one hand as she listened to the latest hypothesis on the takeover, she was still fretting.

'Can I have a cigarette?' she begged Maeve.

'All right.' Maeve gave her a Silk Cut and they stood outside in the corridor, along with a group of other nervous smokers.

'I can't tell if my hand is shaking from nerves or from a hangover,' said a green-faced news reporter, sucking on a Marlboro.

'Hangover,' Dee pronounced. 'Nobody would fire you, Noel. You'd sell your granny for a good story, so you're way too valuable to lose.'

Noel grinned with pleasure.

The newsroom door swung open.

'They're on their way up,' yelled someone.

'Who's on their way up?' demanded Maeve.

'Several blokes in suits.'

'Anyone we know?'

'Yeah, Slasher Flynn.'

'You're kidding?'

'I'm not.'

211

Eugene Flynn cleared his throat and looked at the assembled staff from behind thick glasses. Short, skinny and bald, he looked quite harmless. His suit, which had to be expensive, was a fraction too big and at first glance he appeared to be the sort of man whom women loved to mother.

Then he started to speak.

'I'm delighted to announce that I'm taking over the running of the *Sentinel* as managing director from today.' His voice was smug as he looked around for a reaction. Everyone was too shocked to give one. 'I can understand that you're all worried about your jobs but I want to reassure you, Roark International will not be purging the company. All the staff will be staying on and there'll be no redundancies. Certainly for the next year,' he added swiftly.

'Naturally, we can't speak for the future, but I want to point out that we will honour the job security agreements you had with the past management.'

The ripple of relief that went through the newsroom was palpable. Dee felt herself relax in her chair for the first time all morning.

'There will be changes, of course, and one vital change is the appointment of a new editor. Malley McDonnell from the group's Melbourne office will be taking over.'

Malley who? wondered Dee. She'd never heard of any journalist of that name before.

Everyone craned their necks to see which of the five suit-clad men behind Eugene Flynn was the new editor. The only woman in the group, a tall striking brunette in a mannish grey trouser suit, strode forward to stand beside Flynn. She dwarfed him, in height and build. The lines on her broad, strong face meant she had to be in her mid-forties, but she had a lean athletic body that belied her age.

'Hello, I'm Malley McDonnell,' she said, in a husky voice with just a touch of an Australian accent. 'I know this is all a bit of a shock to you – one day you're working for one group, the next another. It's pretty scary. But,' she looked searchingly around the room, 'this takeover is for the good of the paper. Once you get to know Roark International, and especially me, you'll see we have your interests at heart. We want to bring the *Sentinel* up-to-date, make it a newspaper for the twenty-first century. It's been losing circulation and all you guys could have been out of a job in a couple of years. But not any more,' she said passionately.

'I'm proud of the work I've done with the group's titles in Philadelphia and Hong Kong. Now I want you all to work with me to make us proud of the *Sentinel*, and to strengthen the paper's position so you're all sure of your jobs in ten years' time.'

When Eugene Flynn started clapping, everybody joined in enthusiastically, if a tad manically.

Malley stood back with her arms crossed and smiled.

'Either that's the most genuine "one for all and all for one" speech I've ever heard or we've just been given a dose of grade-A bullshit from a real expert,' Maeve whispered in Dee's ear.

'I hope it's the first,' she replied fervently. 'I'm not able for this takeover stuff. If I didn't have an ulcer over the whole women's editor job shenanigans, I've got one now.'

After half an hour of speeches from both Malley and Slasher, a clearer picture was forming. No changes were to be made until the new management had had a chance to inspect the paper closely.

Malley and Flynn would hold a series of meetings with the different section editors over the coming days. Their opinions would be sought.

And just to let people see that Roark International believed in the future of the paper – and, more importantly, had faith in the existing staff – the editors and deputy editors were invited to a charity bash at Jack Carter's home in Dalkey the following Saturday night where details of the new management would be formally announced.

'We want you to see that we're not here to rip the organisation to pieces, but to build it up to the very successful paper we think it can become,' Eugene Flynn added in sincere tones. 'I know that Mr Carter wants to meet you all personally to assure you we value your help and expertise, and that we want to safeguard your jobs.'

'Why does it sound more convincing when Malley McDonnell says it?' asked Phil Walsh cynically.

'Because he's so crooked that if he ate a six-inch nail, it'd come out a corkscrew, that's why,' Dee replied. 'But we haven't any option but to trust him. I just hate it when he talks about the paper *becoming* very successful. What the hell did he think we were already? A disaster?'

'I think he means to turn the *Sentinel* into something three times as successful as it already is,' interrupted Gerry Deegan.

They rounded on him. 'Where have you been for the last two days?' demanded Maeve. 'I bet you knew all about the takeover last week, you crafty pig. Why didn't you tell us what was going on?'

Gerry shrugged. 'I knew something but I was sworn to secrecy.'

'Well, tell us everything now,' said Dee. 'I can't

believe you let us all suffer yesterday without telling us what was happening. I didn't sleep a wink worrying about it,' she said, untruthfully. In fact, after all the vodka she'd had at the party, she'd been out like a light once her head hit the pillow, which hadn't pleased a lustful, stone-cold-sober Gary.

'Sorry, girls, no can do, I'm afraid,' Gerry said. 'I'm due to meet my old pal Malley McDonnell any minute now, and we'll be closeted together for hours while she asks me whom she should fire.'

Maeve looked at him suspiciously. 'You mean, you know her already?'

'Yes. But I'm kidding about me telling her who to fire. She's a good editor, I worked with her in Philadelphia. There's nothing to be afraid of with Malley, I promise you. She's a real professional and as straight as an arrow.'

'She's not the one we're worrying about,' Maeve snapped. 'It's the thought of Slasher running this place that gives me the creeps.'

'Join the club,' said Gerry. 'I know him from years ago and he's not exactly my favourite person either. I've got to rush, ladies, see you later.' He gave them an apologetic grin and left.

'What next?' demanded Maeve. 'Lord knows who else knew all about this, or who else knows Malley like the back of their hands. Ten to one we'll find half the photographers went to school with her and Tony Winston's slept with her . . .'

'Yeuch! I think she's got better taste than that,' Dee insisted. 'That was a lovely suit she was wearing. Definitely Calvin Klein. Anyone who has such nice clothes isn't going to be taken in by Tony's greasy flirting. And talking of clothes, whatever will we wear to this party on Saturday?'

CHAPTER ELEVEN

As Phil manoeuvered her ancient, dog-hair-covered estate car on to the grass verge between a gleaming black BMW and a silver Lexus, Isabel gazed out of the windscreen at the house in front of them. The moon glittered in a midnight blue sky, burnishing the ornamental pond in front of Jack Carter's house with silver. A graceful Georgian mansion set amidst several acres of trees and shrubs in one of Dublin's most expensive suburbs, Temple Isis had to be worth a small fortune.

'Some place, huh?' Phil remarked. 'He's done well for himself.'

'I daresay you could fit my house into this one about ten times and still have room for a swimming pool,' Isabel remarked, as she extricated her foot from a bit of horse's bridle that was jammed under the passenger seat. 'I wonder if they have a pool?'

Phil climbed out of the car. 'Haven't a clue, but Belinda will know. She's been frantically mugging up on Elizabeth Carter's endless charity committees so she can impress the boss's wife. It's all part of a grand scheme to keep her job.'

'I think it'll take more than a bit of flattery to safeguard any job once Eugene Flynn has made up his mind to axe it,' Isabel remarked. 'If his reputation is anything to go by, we'd better all update our CVs.'

Conscious that she sounded a bit too gloomy for a party, Isabel changed the subject. 'I wonder what Belinda's going to wear? Yesterday, she told me she couldn't figure out whether to go for a long black silk dress that looks great but isn't made by anyone famous, or some second-hand pink silk Yves St Laurent cocktail dress with frills everywhere that sounds hideous.'

'Knowing Belinda, she'll go for the YSL. She can't resist the lure of designer labels. Neither can I,' Phil joked, picking Red Setter hairs off the navy chain-store shirtdress that made her stocky figure look heavier than ever. 'It was either this or the little Chanel number. Decisions, decisions.'

Isabel laughed. 'I had the same problem myself, wondering how many hundreds I should spend on a designer ensemble for this evening,' she said in a put-on posh voice. 'Or whether I should spend the money on the mortgage and the gas bill instead, and just pluck something from the back of the wardrobe.'

'You look lovely,' Phil said, admiring the amber silk palazzo pants and matching evening jacket Isabel wore with a black and amber *devoré* bodice.

'It's ancient,' Isabel protested, shaking her trousers in a vain attempt to loosen the coating of red and golden dog hairs. 'I bought it in the January sales eight or nine years ago for next to nothing and the bodice is Marks & Sparks underwear.'

'You've a real way with clothes,' Phil said. 'I gave up bothering twenty years ago when I got involved with horses and the kids were small. We were always totally broke in those days and preferred to spend any spare cash on upgrading the stables or buying new tack. And it's hard to be fashion conscious when you've got three very hairy dogs,' she added, plucking a wisp of rough collie fluff off Isabel's jacket. 'I normally keep Sellotape in the car for getting the hair off but the roll is empty.'

'We'll do.' Isabel slammed her door shut. 'The guest list is probably so full of the rich and famous that nobody will notice if you and I are wearing dresses made *entirely* from dog hair. And, believe it or not, there actually *is* a woman who makes coats and jumpers from knitted Red Setter hair.'

'She'd love my house, then,' Phil said. 'The dining-room carpet has several coats, a couple of jumpers and a very big bedspread's worth of hair on it. The kids are supposed to hoover but they never do.'

They were still laughing when they entered the vast, ornate hallway and followed the noise past a big, curving mahogany staircase with massive red Chinese urns set to either side of the first step.

The party was spread between a huge Chinese drawing-room and an airy ballroom. Guests spilled out on to the terrace from the French windows. Outside, fairy lights twinkled in the trees. Waiters cruised through the throng noiselessly, bearing hors d'oeuvres and booze.

Inside, the ballroom walls were covered with pink watered silk, and hung with oil paintings in Gothic-style gold frames. Giant flower arrangements on spindly gilt tables made the room look like a hothouse.

'I think Belinda may have made the right choice with the YSL number after all,' Isabel whispered, as they gazed at the plethora of very definitely designer outfits. 'And to think they say designers don't really make that much money any more. It's like having a ramp-side seat at Milan fashion week in here.'

'No dress should cost more than a horse,' Phil said

briskly. 'It's sinful. I don't recognise a single person here,' she added, peering at the crowd of dark-suited men and women in bright jewel colours, real rocks glittering on their necks and fingers. Blondes and brunettes of a certain age, with frosted helmet hairdos, little nipped-in cocktail dresses and spindly heels, stood cheek by jowl with stunning twenty-something models who wore breathtakingly little and sipped champagne.

The whole effect was very elegant, but very formal. Nobody looked as if they were keen to let their hair down or start limbo dancing after too many gins.

'I don't recognise anyone, either,' Isabel said as she looked around for a familiar face. 'Will we stay here until we see someone we know, or will we scout around for people from work?'

'Girls, where have you been, you latecomers? You've missed the Thai dancers.' He might have been the first person they recognised in the entire room but Tony Winston was, as usual, almost instantly annoying. 'Our crowd are all over the far side of the ballroom, beside the kitchen.'

'Surely you mean beside the bar?' said Isabel wickedly.

'No.' Tony brazenly put one arm around her waist as he led them towards the other side of the crowded room. Isabel stiffened at his touch. His dark hair gleamed with some sort of gel and he must have poured at least a pint of Boss over himself. 'The food's so good, nobody is drinking much at all yet.'

'Wonders will never cease,' remarked Phil.

'Lovely perfume you're wearing,' Tony said, his face very close to Isabel's neck as he inhaled. 'What's it called?'

'Piss off,' said Phil sharply.

Isabel moved away from Tony.

'Funny name for perfume,' he drawled, deliberately not taking the hint.

'You think *that's* funny? They're bringing out one soon that's called Come Too Close And You're Dead,' Phil retorted. 'I think it was created with you in mind.'

'Narky tonight, aren't we, Phil?' he said maliciously. 'Is it PMT? I bet Dick was delighted to get you out of his hair for one night.'

'Tony, if that's the only level of conversation you're capable of, please leave,' Isabel said frostily.

'Only if you leave with me, darling,' he purred. 'We could go home to my place . . .' He leant towards her with a suggestive grin.

'I didn't know two people could fit under a rock,' Isabel said smoothly.

Tony's face flushed with anger and he strode off.

'Well done,' Phil said admiringly. 'I've been watching him make cow's eyes at you for months now and I was wondering when you'd crack.'

'I feel like cracking his head open with a bottle,' said Isabel. 'He really is the limit. As if I'd be turned on by him! You've no idea what he's like, Phil.'

'Oh, yes I have.' Phil swiped two glasses of champagne off a passing waiter and handed one to Isabel. 'Prehistoric Man Vulgaris. He was all over one of the freelance sub-editors like a rash earlier this year – until she got vexed, threw a cup of cold tea over him and said she was taking him to court for sexual harassment. She didn't, but he got the message.'

'I suppose I should have said something sooner,' Isabel sighed. 'He's been driving me mad every day for months now, and if I go to the kitchen to make a cup of coffee, he's behind me in a flash saying, "Oh, sorry to bump against you, Isabel, it's such a tight squeeze in here, ha, ha, ha!" He's a creep.'

She took a sip of her drink. 'I'm not very good with men. Well, on a personal level,' she amended. 'If we were working together and disagreed on something, I'd be able to stand my ground and argue my case. But when it comes to somebody like Tony . . .'

'Harassing you?' supplied Phil.

'Yes, I suppose, harassing me, I'm just not very comfortable being rude with them. Although that's the only sort of treatment the Tonys of this world understand.'

'You amaze me, Isabel. You always *look* as if you could handle anything.'

'Looks can be deceptive,' she said dryly. 'Being married for so long means you forget everything you ever knew about men.'

'How come I've been married longer than you and I don't have any problems with lecherous men chatting me up?' joked Phil. 'Only kidding. You're gorgeous, Isabel, and now that you're single, you'd better get used to handling lots of men, lecherous or otherwise.'

'But I'm going to be forty next month,' she protested.

'So what?'

'A forty-year-old single mother, Phil, is hardly every man's dream date. Especially one with a mortgage she won't have paid off until she's sixty-five, which means I won't be able to save up for a face lift until it's too late.'

'Don't be so negative,' Phil said. 'You could always meet some sweet, very lonely, eighty-year-old millionaire with no dependants, a house on every continent, a Zimmer frame and the life expectancy of a mosquito. There are bound to be loads of them here tonight. And you know what they say – "I never met a millionaire I didn't like".'

Isabel laughed out loud. 'If I do meet one, you'll be the first to know. But I don't hold out much hope. And even if I did find one, ten to one he'd have a twenty-year-old "actress/model" welded on to his arm, glaring hands-off at every woman who came within a fifty-foot radius.'

'Come on.' Phil moved through the throng. 'Let's find the rest of the crew and see if Tony has started spreading the rumour that you're a lesbian yet.'

It wasn't hard to find their colleagues. The thirty or so journalists were in full party mode, a startling contrast to the rest of the partygoers who were behaving in a much more restrained manner, sipping their champagne rather than guzzling it.

Stalin, who was still – 'astonishingly', as Phil put it – a member of staff, looked uneasy as he smoked a cheroot standing beside Belinda, wearing his best outfit – a dark blue Western-style suit complete with one of those leather string ties held together at the collar by a turquoise and silver clasp. The suit's shiny patches matched his perspiring face.

'Isabel – Phil!' squeaked Belinda delightedly, quivering with excitement in a fuchsia taffeta confection that reminded Isabel of one of the costumes Naomi's old Barbie doll had come with. 'You'll never guess – I met Elizabeth Carter and *she knew who I was!* Isn't that fantastic?'

'Yeah, Jack Carter was here with Slasher Flynn and he met us all,' put in Fred, the head photographer.

'She's so nice, beautiful but very friendly,' gushed Belinda. 'And Jack was very polite, he shook my hand for *ages* . . .'

'Listen,' interrupted the chief sub, Tom, a stalwart of the union and a professional pessimist to boot, 'don't count your chickens till they're hatched. Just because the management is nice to you tonight, doesn't mean diddly squat. They could be as nice as pie to your face tonight, and *still* fire you on Monday. Although I'd like to see them try.'

For half an hour they stood and talked, eating endless won tons and sesame prawn toasts from the trays of passing waiters and drinking whatever they felt like. Beer, wine, vintage champagne or spirits – they had it all, according to a glassy-eyed Stalin, who'd obviously tried a bit of everything and was now knocking back shots of tequila. There was no sign of Dee O'Reilly, which Isabel thought was odd as she'd seemed quite excited at the idea of the party only yesterday.

Isabel sipped a second glass of champagne and looked around her warily. She was tired after a busy week and felt distinctly uncomfortable. The wealthy guests were obviously of the 'don't have to work ever again, what is a mortgage anyway?' league – a million miles removed from the *Sentinel* staff.

She wondered had any of *them* felt the icy grip of fear at the news that their company had been taken over and their jobs could be on the line? Not in a long time, she reckoned, eyeing the gold chains and diamond necklaces.

What was the point of this party anyway? If Jack Carter wanted to tell the staff about the new management, he could have done it in the office without all this palaver. But no, he wanted to admit them to his mansion and let them take a one-off look at his world of wealth and privilege.

It was as if he *wanted* the journalists to feel like complete outsiders, so he could make them see exactly who was boss. It was an exercise in arrogance, an act of supreme condescension. At that moment, she hated the very idea of Jack Carter. No matter that everyone said he was decent, he'd have to try very hard to impress her after tonight.

Isabel glanced at her watch. It was five to nine. *ER* would be starting soon and she could have been curled up on the couch watching it, with a glass of wine and some of that cheesy popcorn she was addicted to.

Naomi had a friend to stay and they'd be giggling in her room, pretending to get the sleeping bag ready for Joanne and secretly having no intention of sleeping for hours. Robin was keeping an eye on them, in between watching *Good Will Hunting* on video and gazing longingly at Matt Damon, her current hero.

It would have been so nice to be there with them, instead of standing aimlessly in a ballroom listening to fragments of conversations and watching people get drunker.

What was more, it was getting hotter by the minute. There were just too many people crammed together. Isabel had once read that charity hostesses invited at least twenty-five per cent too many people to functions on the grounds that most of them wouldn't be able to make it. If the jammed ballroom at Temple Isis was anything to go by, nobody turned down an invitation from Elizabeth Carter. Though Isabel fervently wished she'd been able to do just that.

She picked up a napkin and fanned herself with it. She could feel her pale skin turn a deep, unbecoming brick red, and knew that it didn't matter how much Ô de Lancôme she'd sprayed down her cleavage, it wouldn't be much good if she started to sweat like a racehorse. She tried to listen to the conversations around her. Phil was in the middle of a long, convoluted story about someone whom she and Belinda both knew – Belinda could be interested in horse stories so long as the people involved were rich enough to have their own stables, their own trainer, and at least one Cheltenham-going racehorse.

Tony was telling blue jokes in between glowering in her direction. Stalin swayed happily, not talking to anybody. He was clearly on the verge of passing out.

'This is getting to me,' Isabel said finally. Nobody was listening. She turned and slipped through the crowd, making for the French windows. People moved to let her through and more than a couple of the male guests stared at her, taking in her tall elegant figure, the fragile, almost sad face and the swathe of dark blonde hair that was swept up into a classic French pleat.

Plenty of people had had the same idea as Isabel and the terrace was nearly as full as the ballroom. She walked down stone steps into the garden, walking carefully so her heels wouldn't sink into the grass. The cool night air was like a balm to her hot skin and she breathed in deeply.

Twenty yards away from the terrace and the party-goers, she came upon a wooden seat framed by a sweet-smelling rambling rose. She sat down gratefully and wondered how soon she could slip away from the party completely without being noticed.

'Enjoying yourself?' inquired a voice. He moved out of the shadows towards her, a tall, powerfully built man. Lights from the terrace lit up tanned, weathered skin and narrow eyes that seemed to bore into her. In a dark, beautifully cut suit with a pale tie, he wasn't handsome but he was certainly striking.

'It's so warm inside, I needed to get some fresh air,' Isabel replied. 'And I had to get away from the party.'

'I know what you mean.' The man crossed the lawn to stand in front of her and a small furry dog of indeterminate breed followed him. It scurried over to Isabel and immediately put wet paws on her knees.

'I'm sorry,' the man said. 'Kerry, down.' He moved as if to grab the dog's collar, but Isabel spoke first.

'It's OK. Leave her,' she said, smiling genuinely for the first time since she and Phil had arrived at the party. 'I love dogs.' She bent forward, ruffling the dog's grey ears, letting its soft shiny black nose burrow into her sleeve inquisitively.

'Good,' he replied, a hint of dry humour in his voice, 'because there's another one on the way.'

As if on cue, a large Golden Retriever belted up the lawn excitedly, tongue hanging out. The dog headed straight for Isabel.

'Duke, steady!' warned the man. 'Sit.'

Duke blithely ignored his master and rushed towards Isabel, burying his nose in her crotch.

'Duke! I warn you, he's very friendly,' the man said apologetically.

'This sort of friendliness is allowed in dogs,' she said, giggling as Duke's insistent nose investigated her. 'Though not in humans,' she quipped.

His laugh was a rich, throaty sound that seemed to come from deep inside his large frame. And when he laughed, the haughty look disappeared and the deep lines around his mouth curved up with good humour. He was very attractive when he smiled.

All male and very predatory, like a wolf. That was it. His hair was the same colour as a wolf's pelt, rich brown shot through with paler shades of burnt umber and gold. She'd bet it was as soft as Duke's fur to the touch . . .

Isabel's eyes widened in shock. She couldn't *believe* she'd just thought that! Talk about thinking like a lovestruck teenager. The readers' stories in Robin's *Just Seventeen* were more mature.

She bent over Duke in embarrassment, running her hands over his rippling honey-coloured fur. Kerry squeaked in abandoned indignation and wriggled closer for more attention.

'I'm not forgetting about you, love,' Isabel crooned, stretching her right hand out to the small dog, her left one rubbing Duke's ear as he almost purred with pleasure.

'You've made two conquests there,' said the man. 'Or maybe three.'

Isabel could feel herself blushing but kept her head down as she talked gently to the dogs.

'They get very restless when there's a party on,' he said, sitting down on the bench beside her. He took up the rest of the seat and stretched out long legs in front of him. He really was a big man, taller even than Isabel. She could smell the tang of Armani, about a zillion times more subtle than Tony Winston's drenched-in-aftershave smell. Duke shuffled his furry rear end over towards his master so they could both pat him at the same time.

'They're beautiful dogs,' Isabel said, still stroking Kerry's ears. 'They're so friendly.'

'Duke is a bit of a rake, he loves everyone, but Kerry's much more discriminating. She's very particular about whom she cuddles up to. You must have a magic touch with dogs.' He turned to face her and Isabel sat up.

Now that he wasn't facing the lights any more, his face was half in shadow and she didn't feel so self-conscious looking at him. He couldn't see her very well

228

either, she reckoned. Well, she hoped he couldn't. Her face was undoubtedly quite pink from a mixture of heat and embarrassment and she probably reeked of over-heated perfume and the remainder of Robin's Impulse deodorant. Not to mention the fact that her unsmudge-able mascara was probably halfway down her cheeks already.

'My mother isn't very keen on dogs, or any animal for that matter,' Isabel explained. She leant back against the seat to keep her face in the shadows. 'My father got me a Cocker Spaniel one Christmas but when he chewed the leg of the dining-room table, she insisted we get rid of him.' Isabel's eyes still filled with tears at the thought of Sasha, the puppy she'd loved with all her ten-year-old heart, until her mother had insisted he was given to another family.

David hadn't been much of a dog person either. He'd bought the girls two goldfish once, although he soon forgot all about Jaws and Flipper, so that Isabel was the one who had to race to the pet shop for a replacement each time one of them died. By Flipper Number Six, both girls were bored with fish and David said he hated rodents and wouldn't have a hamster in the house.

'I'd love a dog,' she said fervently, as Duke and Kerry looked up at her with adoring eyes, 'but I'm out all day and don't have the time to walk one.'

'What about your husband?'

'I'm separated,' she said shortly.

'Sorry,' he said, not sounding it.

'And you?' asked Isabel, determined not to let him get away with all these questions.

'Yes, I'm married.'

'So why are you outside chatting up strange women

in the garden?' she asked with a grin.

He replied instantly, 'I have a better chance of success in the dark. That way, you can't see my hump, my lazy eye and the facial tic. My left eyebrow does forty jumps a minute, you see. I'm in the *Guinness Book of Records*. It puts women off.'

Isabel burst out laughing.

'You're quick, I'll give you that.'

'But it's the truth.' He sounded wounded for a moment. 'Actually,' he added, 'I had to get away from the heat and the crowds myself. I can only take so many charity balls. I couldn't cope with meeting another ambassador or making polite chit-chat with people I really can't stand. Right now, I'd prefer to be sitting back after a decent dinner ready to watch something good on the telly. That would be luxury.'

Isabel nodded. 'Exactly what I was thinking myself. I love *ER* and it's on now.'

'I rather fancy a Western, something forty years old with John Wayne in it. I didn't really come out here to chat up strange women,' he added, his voice very soft. 'I was walking the dogs and saw you . . . and I just had to talk to you. That's my excuse.'

'That's very flattering,' Isabel said quietly. 'But isn't that a bit dangerous at a party? Couldn't your wife appear and wonder what you're up to with some stranger in the garden?'

He laughed. Bitterly, Isabel thought.

'At this precise moment, my wife wouldn't notice if I were out here sandwiched between Kim Basinger and Michelle Pfeiffer.' He glanced at her wryly. 'Although you're more beautiful than both of them.'

Before Isabel even had a chance to turn puce again, he added: 'I'd better introduce myself while I'm at it.

I'm Jack Carter.' He stretched out one large hand and Isabel stared at it, shocked.

Of course he was Jack Carter. The party was in the Carters' home and he was walking dogs in the garden, dogs that got restless when there was a party. Who the hell else would be walking them but the man of the house? What sort of idiot are you Isabel? *And* you said you had to get away! Talk about putting your foot in it.

'Isabel Farrell,' she said, and took his hand tentatively.

He certainly didn't give the sort of limp handshake she loathed, those damp, weak ones with all the backbone of a dead kipper. Jack Carter's handshake was a strong, warm one.

When he let her hand go, she got up quickly, leaving the dogs gazing up at her curiously.

'I'd better go back inside,' she said. Now that she'd met him, talked to him as if they were on the same level, she didn't want to have to tell him who she was. That she wasn't one of the party guests who'd brought a ten-thousand-pound cheque for his wife's favourite charity but one of his employees, one of the 'little people' she was sure he hadn't time for.

''Bye,' she said stiffly. Reaching down to pat Duke and Kerry goodbye, she quickly turned on her heel.

'I'm sorry, I should have told you who I was earlier,' Jack said. 'I hope I didn't embarrass you?'

Isabel didn't turn around. 'Not at all,' she said crisply, her heels getting stuck in the grass in her hurry to get away. Inside, she made her way back to the *Sentinel* crew who were gathered around a stunning dark-haired woman in a figure-hugging red silk dress.

Tall, curvy and with the creamy skin of someone who lived on mineral water and fruit, she was a dead ringer for an older Cindy Crawford, complete with full red lips, dark arched eyebrows and voluminous curls courtesy of at least half an hour with the Carmen rollers. All she needed was the mole, thought Isabel. And then it hit her – this was *his* wife.

'Isabel, this is Elizabeth Carter.' Phil took Isabel's arm and propelled her into the centre of the group alongside Elizabeth, exactly where she didn't want to be.

'De-lighted to meet you,' Elizabeth drawled. Her smoky, upper-class voice made even the shortest word sound at least two syllables long.

'Hello,' said Isabel stiltedly. The word was barely out of her mouth before Elizabeth quickly turned away to address the men in the group, all of whom were clearly very impressed by their hostess's overt sex appeal. 'We're thrilled you could all make it tonight,' she said throatily, gazing at each man in turn.

'The Cancer Ball is usually held in a hotel but we decided to keep costs down and have it here instead. The only problem is space.' She airily gestured around the massive ballroom. 'There simply isn't enough here. Does anyone have a cigarette?'

Immediately every man who smoked, and quite a few who didn't, felt frantically in their pockets for something to offer her.

'Thanks,' Elizabeth purred, after selecting a cigarette from Fred who kept his Dunhills in a silver cigarette case.

After inhaling as if she was underwater sucking on a diving respirator, Elizabeth then took a hefty swig from the crystal tumbler in her left hand.

'So what do you do?' she asked Fred.

'I'm the paper's head photographer,' he said, blossoming under her gaze.

'Fascinating. Could you do some shots of the house

for me sometime? I've been meaning to get someone in . . .'

Phil raised her eyebrows at Isabel and they moved discreetly away. 'She's something else,' Phil remarked. 'She could flirt for Ireland in the Olympics.'

'You can say that again,' Isabel replied. 'It's certainly working. The boys all look like they'd crawl on their hands and knees across the Kalahari Desert to get her a cup of tea. Tony's practically drooling.'

'That's nothing new. But I doubt if she'd want a cup of tea. More like a few lines of finest Colombian cocaine,' Phil remarked. 'Unless I'm mistaken, she's out of her tree.'

'What do you mean?' asked Isabel in amazement. Elizabeth had looked all right to her. She'd looked wonderful, in fact.

'She's stoned, high, whatever,' whispered Phil, looking around her in case anyone was listening. 'Which isn't the sort of behaviour you normally see in society hostesses at their own charity parties.

'My brother-in-law was heavily into drugs – he was a cocaine addict, actually – and I can spot the signs a mile away. Mrs Carter's very good, mind you. She can obviously cope without most people suspecting. I doubt if many of them here could spot that she's high. And the worse she gets, the posher her accent will be too, I guarantee it.'

'Wow!' Isabel was stunned. She craned her neck to look back at Elizabeth Carter. In her eye-catching dress, she looked the epitome of chic. Isabel bet that she wasn't feeling as hot and sweaty as everyone else on the premises.

'I could be wrong, of course,' Phil whispered. 'But she's pretty hyper for this type of party. Normally, the society queens sip the odd glass of champers when they're working the room and save their gimme-a-big-drink-quick mode for when the guests have gone. I reckon our hostess did a couple of lines in the bathroom before anyone arrived and now she's backing it up with booze. Let's hear it for excess, as my poor brother-in-law used to say.'

'Is he still doing coke?' whispered Isabel.

'No. He bankrupted himself and my sister in the process and when the cash ran out, he had to stop. Nearly killed him, of course.'

'Darling!' said Elizabeth, loudly summoning a passing waiter. 'Another vodka martini, no olive and only a little ice.' She carefully placed her glass on his tray and returned to her conversation.

Phil gave Isabel an 'I told you so' look.

Elizabeth's next drink, a full-to-the-brim tumbler, lasted precisely ten minutes. She was ordering a third when Dee O'Reilly arrived, chestnut curls flying and a sheen of perspiration glistening on her face as she reached the group.

Dressed in a clinging black velvet dress that molded every one of her voluptuous curves, she looked stunning, Isabel thought a touch enviously. Big but very sexy. Like Elizabeth Carter, Dee simply exuded sexuality and there was no doubt that men adored them both.

They were so different – one model-girl slim; the other a Rubensesque beauty. But they both had that indefinable *something*. Isabel felt like a dull older sister beside them. A very unsexy, dull older sister. She thought of the man in the garden and how she'd felt about him for the brief moment before she knew who he was. He'd certainly *seemed* to be attracted to her, or maybe she was imagining it.

'Sorry I'm late,' gasped Dee. 'Gary was driving me out here in my car when the bloody thing got a flat tyre. It took him ages to change it because I've misplaced the jack.' She grimaced. 'Still, it was just as well he was there. I'd have spent hours trying to work out how to get the car up without a jack, but he just rang the AA. And I told him that if he hadn't pranged his precious Alfa Romeo, he wouldn't have been driving mine and it would never have happened.'

'Well, you're here now and you haven't missed that much.' Isabel smiled at her. 'Do you want a drink? You look like you could do with one.'

'Oh, please, yes,' Dee said fervently. 'I could murder a drink and I'm ravenous. Who's that?' she asked, gesturing at Elizabeth.

'Our hostess,' said Phil, 'and host.'

Isabel looked up to see a tall figure join the group. Jack Carter's hair looked even more tawny under the lights and she could see that the eyes that had bored into hers so intently were a clear, gun-metal grey.

'How are we doing, everyone?' he asked.

'Marvellous,' said Stalin, raising a glass jerkily.

'I'm glad you're all enjoying yourselves. Have you tried anything from the buffet yet?'

'We love the salmon sautéed in vodka,' said Tony.

Elizabeth giggled. 'Have we got that? I didn't know. A bit of a waste of vodka, don't you think? The only thing I like to be sautéed in vodka is myself. Isn't that right, darling?' she said to her husband, her voice suddenly brittle.

He smiled woodenly at her.

'Ooh, something's going on there, don't you think?' whispered Phil in Isabel's ear.

Isabel didn't hear her. She was looking at Jack, still a

little shell-shocked after their encounter in the garden. Her stomach fluttered. She couldn't understand the feelings he'd aroused in her, couldn't believe that a man could make her feel like this again.

And here he was, standing by his wife in his palatial home with his friends and employees all around him, and she was wondering whether he was interested in *her*. What sort of a fool was she turning into? Did being on the verge of forty turn you into a complete idiot or was it just Isabel?

Dee introduced herself to her host and hostess.

'Sorry I'm late,' she apologised. 'Car trouble.'

'No problem,' Jack said calmly. 'It's nice to meet you, Dee. I've heard a lot about you.'

She went pink.

'All of it complimentary,' he assured her.

She went pinker.

His eyes moved from her face to Isabel's. Wordlessly, he stared at her for an instant. He was waiting for her to say something, she realised with a jolt.

'Isabel Farrell, women's editor,' she said formally, her voice as cold as she could make it.

His gaze never faltered. 'Hello, nice to meet you,' he said before turning away.

So that was the way he wanted to play it, she thought. The I've-never-met-you-before way. Fine. She could do that too.

'Come on, Elizabeth. It's time for your speech,' Jack said crisply. 'I'll see the rest of you in the *Sentinel* offices during the week.'

'God, isn't he gorgeous in the flesh?' Dee remarked as she drained her glass. 'Lucky old Liz.'

'Yeah,' Isabel replied quietly. 'Lucky old Liz.'

CHAPTER TWELVE

Where the hell were they? Dee fumbled through her handbag, clumsy fingers finding lipsticks, a Twix, pens, tissues, a half-unwrapped tampon and scrunched up petrol receipts. But no house keys. She must be drunker than she'd thought. It was all the champagne Tony had poured down her. She should have said no, but she was enjoying herself and it was nice to have an attentive man at her side, even if he was the ever-so-slightly-sleazy sports editor who kept looking down her dress. *He'd* obviously been turned on by her figure, even if she wasn't a Kate Moss clone.

And at least he hadn't tried anything on the drive home. Apart from putting his hand on her thigh and she'd belted him across the chest for that. What sort of a girl did he think she was anyway?

Dee shivered. It was very cold for August. She'd forgotten her coat. It must be in Tony's car. Blast.

Her mobile phone fell out of the bag, making an awful racket when it hit the ground. Double blast. Gary was bound to hear it and wake up. She didn't want to wake him because he'd go ballistic when he saw how drunk she was.

He'd told her he had something very important to discuss with her when he was driving her to Jack

Carter's party. And then the car had got that flat tyre so he hadn't been able to tell her what it was. So she'd promised to be home early and then they'd talk.

Since it was now very late, she was very drunk and definitely not in a state for serious conversation, Gary would undoubtedly be furious if she woke him.

Got them! Dee held up her keys with a triumphant rattle. Now all she had to do was creep in quietly, undress downstairs and sneak into bed without disturbing Gary. Oh, yeah, and bring up a big glass of water for the morning when she just knew she'd wake up dreaming of slurping entire bottles of 7UP to quench her burning hangover thirst.

Her plan didn't work out. When she half-crawled, half-walked up the stairs wearing only her underwear, clutching her dress in one hand and a glass of water in the other, Gary wasn't asleep. He was sitting up in bed reading, with his clock radio facing the door.

According to the clock, it was half-three, around three hours later than Dee had told him she'd be home.

'Did I wake you?' she asked, wide-eyed with assumed innocence. 'I was trying to be quiet.'

'If your idea of "quiet" is spending ten minutes outside the front door dropping things and swearing so loudly the whole street can hear you, then yes, you were quiet,' he snapped. 'Unfortunately, your definition and mine don't correspond.'

'Sorry,' mumbled Dee. Why was he so cross with her? She'd only been at an office party, not living it up at a nightclub or anything. And she'd *had* to go to the Carters' house, it wasn't as if she'd wanted to.

She'd have preferred an evening at home with Gary. Because she still loved him, despite everything he'd said. She'd felt frozen in anguish since their disastrous weekend in Wexford, devastated by what Gary had said. But an evening of constantly flowing champagne and plenty of compliments had defrosted her icy heart. After too much to drink, Dee felt warm, loved and happy again.

She decided to tell Gary all this.

She dropped her dress, banged the glass of water on the bedside table and lurched into bed on top of him, squashing his copy of *Arena*.

'Sorry,' she muttered again. 'But I love you, Gary, I really, really do. I know you were horrible to me, but I'm crazy about you. Can't live without you.'

Gary didn't respond.

Straddling him, she planted a big sloppy kiss on his forehead before moving down to his mouth. She'd make love to him, that would cheer him up. It always did. She nuzzled his neck hopefully.

'Will I take off my bra or will you?' she asked archly, as she sat up and provocatively slid down one of the straps of her black Wonderbra until she was spilling out of it. 'Ooops,' she added, as she nearly fell off the bed. She wasn't *that* drunk. Gary was pushing her off him.

'You're pissed, Dee. Again.' His face was dark as thunder and his mouth was set in a tight line as he dragged his legs from under both the duvet and Dee, and got out of bed.

'I can't believe you went out and got drunk tonight. You knew I wanted to talk to you about something important. "*Don't worry about me, Gary, I'll be home by twelve at the latest, so wait up and we'll talk.*" Does that sound familiar?'

Dee flinched at the sound of Gary angrily repeating her words. She *had* meant to be home earlier but it just hadn't worked out that way. Phil and Isabel could have given her a lift if she'd wanted it, but they went home at around half-ten and she'd only just arrived. It would have been rude to go then. She started to say that but Gary was speaking to her.

He was standing by the bed, looking at her angrily, obviously not even slightly in the mood for sex even though she was sitting on his side of the bed, wearing her sexy undies and the sheer black hold-up stockings he loved.

'I wanted to discuss something important . . .'

'We can still discuss it,' she pleaded.

'No. We won't,' he said tightly. 'The time for discussion is over. In the light of your behaviour, I've made up my mind, Dee. I've been offered a six-month stint in the firm's office in London and I'm going to take it.'

She gazed at him in shock. London. Six months. Away for six months. He couldn't be serious? Her brain couldn't cope with the idea.

'B . . . b . . . but you can't,' she wailed. 'Why? Why and how? How can you leave me? What does it all mean?' Her face crumpled as she began to think about what Gary had just said.

'You're too pissed to think straight,' he said coldly. 'Pass out, why don't you, and I'll talk to you in the morning.'

He left the room and Dee could hear him rummaging in the airing cupboard. Wriggling off the bed, she hurried on to the landing to find Gary dragging the spare duvet downstairs.

'Where are you going?' she bleated.

'To sleep on the couch,' was his reply. He slammed the sitting-room door behind him. Dee was left hanging over the banisters miserably, wondering what had gone wrong. He couldn't mean it, could he? Fighting back the urge to bawl her eyes out, she padded back into the bedroom, climbed into Gary's side of the bed and curled the duvet around her. She could smell his after-shave on his pillows and it comforted her.

He couldn't leave her, surely? He knew she needed a couple of drinks to make her feel relaxed because she was self-conscious at parties. Stone cold sober, she was convinced she was unbearably fat and ugly. She liked a couple of drinks to loosen her up. That was all.

Gary had no idea what it was like to walk into a room crammed with bloody size ten supermodels staring at you superciliously, all with handspan waists and boobs that didn't spill over the top of their bras. Being big in a skinny world was her worst nightmare. Gary just didn't have a clue.

Her hangover wasn't the first thing that hit Dee on Sunday morning so much as the sensation of being alone in the double bed. The foot she sent over to the far side to test for Gary's body didn't hit anything except empty bed. She opened one glued-up eye and looked at the alarm clock. Half-eleven. He'd obviously gone off to play soccer without waking her.

If she wasn't working, Gary usually brought her a cup of coffee on Sunday mornings before he went off with the lads for a couple of hours of footie. Once upon a time, Dee had gone with him to important matches, standing on the sidelines in the freezing cold, cheering his team on and screaming at the other side if they fouled.

But his team didn't play league matches in the summer and she'd got out of the habit of getting up early on Sundays if she didn't absolutely have to.

Hopefully Gary would have cheered up by the time

he got home and would have got over his bad temper about the night before.

And as for moving to London, he couldn't possibly mean it. He was doing far too well in Dublin to risk even six months in another office, surely?

She'd promise never to drink again, she'd promise to stop nagging him about housework and she'd go on a diet. Anything to make everything all right again. Whatever Gary wanted, she'd do it. *Anything*. She'd make him see that they were meant for each other. How could he leave her then?

Dee kicked off the duvet and stretched before getting up. She felt quite OK really, not too hungover but very hungry. There probably wasn't anything in the house to eat. Wait a minute – she had some of those croissants that came in a tin. She could buy eggs when she went out to get the papers, cook the croissants, scramble some eggs and have a lovely brunch waiting for Gary when he got home. That was it. That'd cheer him up.

Delighted with her plan, Dee showered, washed her hair and got dressed, singing along to the radio. Visions of the reinvented Dee O'Reilly came into her mind – a slim, elegant Dee in a sleek size-ten trouser suit, with her hair straightened into a shiny bob, not the usual mess of tumbling, wayward curls. Subtle make-up. She could get made up at the Lancôme counter in Arnotts and learn how to apply eyeliner so she didn't look as if she'd gone four rounds with Mike Tyson.

She'd dump her usual enormous handbag for one of those classy little bags that looked businesslike. And she'd diet like a mad thing, resolve *never* to touch a Mars Bar again, eat fruit and drink eight glasses of water a day, the way you were supposed to, instead of hoping her usual eight cups of coffee covered the daily required liquid intake.

Yes, a new Dee would make Gary fall madly in love with her all over again so he'd forget about going to London.

When she'd dressed, Dee thought she looked the ultimate in cute – fat cute, but cute all the same. She wore blue jeans and a teeny weeny pink velour T-shirt that clung provocatively to her boobs. Her hair was tied on the top of her head like Pebbles from the Flintstones and she'd drenched herself in delicious vanilla Angel perfume. Gary wouldn't be able to resist her, she was convinced of it.

By five o'clock, she'd read all the Sunday papers, eaten both Gary's and her portions of scrambled egg and had polished off most of the croissants into the bargain. Smudge's belly was swollen up like a balloon with all the scrambled egg leftovers and she was fast asleep on one of the armchairs, only moving one paw as she swatted the occasional dream mouse.

Dee threw down the third TV supplement in exasperation. There was still no sign of Gary. He hadn't phoned. His mobile phone was gone but he didn't have it switched on. Dee had discovered his football kit and bag lying under the stairs. He obviously wasn't playing football so where the hell was he? And why hadn't he phoned? He couldn't still be cross with her, surely?

Dear Annie,

My boyfriend and I had a terrible fight, and he stormed off. He wouldn't even listen to my side of the story, which was extremely unfair of him because I had to go to an office party and you can't go to a party without having a drink, now can you?

The problem is, he hasn't come home and I'm not sure whether I'm worried or very, very angry. How dare he do this to me? What do you suggest – screaming at him when he does come in or giving him the silent treatment?

Dee made another cup of coffee and read her horoscope for the fifth time in a different paper. Scorpios in relationships were having a very bad week, whichever way you looked at it.

Prepare to let go of something you've dreamed of for a long time. This Tuesday's planetary movement suggests that you are at a crossroads in your life and what you do next will have extreme significance for your future . . . said one.

Your lucky colour is green, your lucky number is ten and single Scorpios are destined to meet the love of their lives on Tuesday. Scorpios with partners should expect some bad news on the romantic front, said another.

It didn't look good. Dee flicked through the TV channels. Nothing on but news and she was sick to the teeth of news.

At six she was seized by a fit of energy and manically tidied the kitchen, dried up all the dishes in the drainer, industriously cleaned the cooker top and bleached everything in sight.

By seven, she had flopped back on the settee and was looking around miserably. Something was definitely wrong. Gary would never stay out this late usually without at least phoning her.

Maeve answered the phone after about fifteen rings. 'I was in the bath,' she said breathlessly. 'I'm shaving my legs, de-fuzzing my moustache and dyeing my hair.'

'All at the same time? Isn't that dangerous?' asked Dee.

'Probably. But Karl is going to pick me up in an hour, so I've got to do it all at the same time. If I don't dye my hair, he'll discover I'm not a natural redhead. How was the posh party? Did anyone embarrass themselves hideously?'

Dee grimaced. 'Only me.'

'What did you do?' demanded Maeve, agog.

'Well, I didn't do much at the party exactly. It was more a matter of how long I spent at it, how much I drank while I was there and what happened when I got home.'

'Don't tell me.' Maeve sounded scathing. 'Sweet adorable Gary went ballistic because you got plastered and now he's in a major bad mood?'

'Sort of.' Dee was surprised at how quickly Maeve had diagnosed what was wrong. 'He was offered a job in London and wanted to talk to me about it but . . .'

'But you rolled up at half-four in the morning, incapable of intelligent conversation, giggling madly, and with a handbag-full of men's telephone numbers scrawled on bits of paper,' Maeve finished.

'Half-three, actually, and no phone numbers. Although I slapped Tony Winston when he drove me home . . . but no, that's too long a story to go into,' Dee said hurriedly. 'When I got home, Gary said he'd wanted to talk about the job in London and ask me what I thought. It's only for six months. But he said he'd decided to take it anyway because he's so fed up with me. He slept downstairs and I haven't seen him all day,' she added mournfully.

'Oh, you poor thing,' Maeve said sympathetically. 'Don't panic, Dee. You know he's only milking this for all it's worth. He probably wanted to take the job in London anyway and just wanted an excuse.'

'That's worse!' said Dee in a strangulated voice. She started to cry. 'It means he wants to leave me. But I love him, Maeve, you know that. If he wants me to change, I will. I can't bear to be without him.'

'Dee,' Maeve said in measured tones, 'don't do this to yourself. You can't change who you are any more than Gary can. And, let's face it, you'd love him to change. But he won't. Because he's a man and men don't change.'

'But I *don't* want him to change,' Dee wailed. 'I just want him back!'

'You wanted him to change last month. You wanted him to take his turn at the housework and stop being such a lazy slob. And you wanted him occasionally to say nice things to you, not purely when he was horny.'

'That was *last* month. Oh, Maeve, where is he? Why isn't he coming back? What'll I do?'

'His mobile phone is switched off?'

'Yes.'

'Where do you think he might go?'

'I don't know. Maybe to Len's flat. Or to the pub near Len's place, the Bleeding Horse.'

'Well, phone Len's place or phone the pub.'

'I can't.'

Maeve sighed. 'Give me the phone numbers and I'll do it.'

Gary was tracked down in Len's house. 'He sounded smashed out of his mind,' Maeve reported. 'They've been drinking whiskey all afternoon. Len even went so far as to invite me over. They must be desperate. The last time I saw Len, he told me he wouldn't go out with me if I was the last woman on earth. Mind you, that was because I'd told him he obviously has a small willy because he's so obsessed with his Porsche. A ten-year-old Porsche at that . . .'

'What did Gary say?' asked Dee in a small voice.

'He wouldn't talk to me,' Maeve replied. 'I could hear him in the background yelling that he'd "be home when he felt like it". Charming.'

Dee couldn't say anything. She felt crushed, as if all the breath had left her body. She sat down on the bottom step and hugged her knees into her body. This was a nightmare, a complete nightmare. Her life was crumbling apart in front of her and there was nothing she could do about it.

'Are you all right?' Maeve asked.

It wasn't fair to lay all her troubles on her friend. She'd been so utterly thrilled when Karl, an instructor at the gym she'd just joined, asked her out. Dee couldn't ruin Maeve's longed-for date with the first man in months who'd told her he'd phone her and actually *had*.

'I'm fine. Thanks, Maeve, go back to your de-fuzzing. I'm OK, honest.'

'You're not . . .'

'I am,' Dee said firmly. 'Get ready for your big night out. I know how much you've been looking forward to this. After all, I don't want to be the one responsible for Karl finding out that you're not a natural redhead,' she said, attempting to joke.

'I can't leave you like this.'

'Like what? Hell, I'm like this all the time,' Dee said brightly. 'You know Gary and me – always fighting. We never mean it. He'll come home when he's ready.'

She tried to sound flip, composed.

'Are you sure?' Maeve didn't sound terribly convinced. Dee longed to shout 'No!' and to have Maeve spend the evening with her, consoling her with stories about feckless, uncaring men and how they always came home in the end. But she knew she'd have hated herself if she was responsible for Maeve's cancelling her first date with Karl. Apparently good-looking, a vision of rippling muscles *and* solvent – a rarity for Maeve, who always picked the most dreadful, unemployable men – he sounded wonderful.

'Maeve, don't be ridiculous. Now that I know where Gary is, I'm satisfied. Absolutely not worried any more. Actually, I think I'll go out this evening just to spite him. I haven't seen Mum and Dad all week,' she added for authenticity. 'I'll visit them. Mum has the 'flu and could do with cheering up.'

'Good.' Maeve sounded relieved. 'You shouldn't sit in the house on your own all evening. It'd be bad for you.'

'I won't,' said Dee, privately planning to do just that. There was an unopened bottle of Absolut Citron Vodka in the freezer, a container of orange juice in the fridge and an entire pack of mini Mars Bars in one of the cupboards. Dee was going to have a wonderful evening.

'Have a brilliant night out and I want to know all the gory details tomorrow,' she instructed. 'Inside leg measurement, bank balance, job prospects and . . . is there anything I've left out?'

'No. That covers every eventuality.' Maeve laughed. 'Take care, Dee. I'll see you in work tomorrow. Everything will be OK, I'm sure of it. Gary loves you.'

'I know, I know,' she said. ''Bye, and thanks for everything. You're a great friend.' She was glad that Maeve couldn't see her or the fat tears that had started to roll down her face.

''Bye.'

Dee sat on the bottom step with the phone on her lap for a long time. Then she went into the kitchen and took the vodka out of the freezer. If she had to sit up all night until he came home, then she would.

When Gary finally arrived home, Dee had drunk only two small screwdrivers. She'd planned to get absolutely smashed so she wouldn't think about all the things Gary had said the night before. But she didn't feel like drinking. The memory of her own drunken antics were clear in her mind and she was astonished to realise that she didn't want to be that plastered ever again. She'd tried to hide her misery and insecurity in a flood of champagne but all she'd done was create even more problems.

Alcohol was not the answer, Dee thought wryly, remembering all the times in her life when she'd thought it *was*.

Without booze to take her mind off things – and she desperately wanted something to take her mind off things because she couldn't cope with facing the ugly thoughts that lurked in the recesses of her brain – she'd decided to watch some of her collection of *Absolutely Fabulous* videos. They were guaranteed to make her howl with laughter and she wouldn't have time to think while she was laughing.

But memories of Gary telling her he was leaving flickered on and off in her head, along with his taunting voice telling her she was fat – fat, ugly and shameful. Every time the voices threatened to spill over from her subconscious to her conscious mind, Dee forced herself to focus on Edina and Patsy's adventures in Harvey Nichols. Joanna Lumley was so *thin*, she thought enviously. She smoked – that had to be the secret.

The Christmas special was so rib-crackingly funny that Dee had managed to quell her misery quite successfully when she heard Gary open the front door at half-ten. At the sound of his arrival, she turned off the TV nervously.

Gary didn't shout 'I'm home!' the way he usually did when he was late and wanted to reassure Dee he wasn't a cat burglar. He simply slammed the front door and marched into the sitting-room.

'Hi,' she said anxiously. 'I was worried about you.'

His eyes were slits of disgust as he took in the Absolut Citron bottle on the coffee table.

'Drinking again?' he said harshly.

'Actually, no . . .' began Dee.

'Don't bother with excuses,' he snapped. 'You can do what you like: drink and eat yourself into oblivion for all I care. I'm leaving in the morning.'

He left the room abruptly and marched upstairs.

Dee exhaled slowly. He was going after all. There was nothing she could say to change his mind. She sat and stared at the blank TV screen for a few minutes. It was happening – what she'd dreaded all day. Gary was leaving.

Dee didn't know why, but she didn't break down and cry. Normally she cried at the drop of a hat. But for some reason she was totally calm now that the earthquake she'd feared had actually hit. In the kitchen, she made herself a cup of tea and drank it sitting at the kitchen table while she made a list in a reporter's notebook.

When was he going to London and what were they going to do with the house? Did he want to keep paying the mortgage or should she sell it and split the money?

Protracted banging noises from the spare bedroom told her Gary was sleeping there tonight. Dee felt strangely relieved. She felt too fragile for a night in the same bed, cold shoulders at either edge of the bed, determined not to touch. He hated her, really loathed her.

She had seen it in his eyes when he'd come home, his face a mask of hostility as he stared at her in disgust. Sleeping on the street was preferable to sleeping in the same bed with a man who was repulsed by you.

When Gary arrived downstairs a few minutes later, Dee nervously handed him the list of topics to be discussed.

He looked suspiciously at her tear-free face before he glanced at the notebook.

'I thought we should talk about the practicalities,' she said calmly.

'Er . . . yes,' he stuttered.

'What do you want to do with the house?'

'Sell it,' he said, quickly recovering his composure. 'I'm moving out tomorrow. If you want, you can arrange things with the estate agent and phone me to keep me up to date. The sooner we sell it the better.'

'When are you going to London?' Dee asked, amazed at how cool she was being.

'The end of September.'

'Oh,' she said. Around about the time they were supposed to be going to Amsterdam. Dee thought briefly about wandering around the pretty Dutch capital and visiting Anne Frank's house, somewhere she'd wanted to go since reading the famous diary when she was a teenager. What a terrible life it had been, living in fear all the time, scared that the Nazis would find the family and drag them apart forever. Imagine losing the people you loved most in the world like that.

Losing people you loved . . . Dee felt a lump in her throat and, terrified that she was going to blub after all, dumped her cup in the sink and ran upstairs. She didn't want him to see her crying.

Dee hardly slept that night. She heard Gary go to bed at one, after a couple of hours watching soccer on TV. She heard him brushing his teeth in the bathroom, familiar noises that normally meant he'd soon climb into bed beside her. Tonight, he switched off the landing light and went into the spare room instead.

She lay in the dark, worn out with misery but unable to sleep. Sometimes she cried, hot, hopeless tears that burned her cheeks as they slid down her face. Dawn was creeping into the room when she finally dozed off, her eyes heavy with exhaustion.

At seven in the morning she woke up, feeling instantly awake. Most Mondays she blindly thumped the snooze button and staggered out of bed at half-eight to be in work by ten. Today, she made coffee and toast and brought them back to bed in order to avoid Gary, who worked more traditional office hours. She couldn't face him; couldn't face his fierce, implacable loathing. Not with puffy, red eyes.

She heard him shower at half-seven, have breakfast at ten to eight, and leave the house at five past. When he was gone, she got up, tuned the radio to a loud, energetic rock station and got ready for work. She didn't feel like putting on much make-up. Why bother? Her face was pale and exhausted; her eyes sad and swollen from lack of sleep.

Dee half-heartedly applied eye-shadow and mascara. No make-up could make her look even halfway decent, she decided, gazing at herself sourly. Her dark eyes were dull and lifeless and her usually creamy skin pasty and unhealthy-looking.

She hadn't the energy to iron the grape-coloured silk blouse she'd planned to wear that morning, so she pulled on an old white shirt she hardly wore any more along with the inevitable black palazzo pants. A long-line black velvet waistcoat that covered a multitude of sins pulled the outfit together. It wasn't exactly *Vogue*'s Ten-Most-Enduring-Classics, but it'd do.

Her hair was still damp and frizzy from the shower but it was too much trouble to tame it with anti-frizz stuff. So Dee clasped it back in a scrunchie without bothering to free a couple of strands to hang flatteringly around her face. She'd looked better, she thought as she passed the hall mirror and saw the pale face with the scraped back hair. A lot better.

Maeve danced up to Dee's desk, her face aglow. 'Hello. Isn't it a wonderful morning? And, no,' she said with a broad grin, 'I'm not this happy because gorgeous Karl bonked me senseless all last night. I'm happy because I've found him – *the* one, the man of my dreams! Knock on wood.'

She looked properly at Dee for the first time and her smile faded. 'Dee? Oh my God, what happened? Are you all right?'

Dee managed a wry grin. 'I'm fine. Single, disengaged – or is it un-engaged? – and looking for a new place to live. But otherwise I'm fine.'

'Oh, no.' Maeve put her arms around Dee and hugged her tightly. 'You poor thing. What happened? Or do you not want to talk about it?'

'I don't know if I could talk about it,' Dee explained. 'I don't want to burst into tears in the office *again*. It's becoming a bit of a habit. I'll tell you everything at lunch.'

'OK. Can I get you a cup of coffee or something?' Maeve asked solicitously.

'Yes, that'd be lovely.'

After sitting on her own for a moment while Maeve went to get the coffee, Dee realised that she desperately wanted to tell her friend everything at once. She took her handbag – if she blubbed, at least she'd have her make-up bag handy for repairs – and headed for the kitchen.

Maeve met her halfway with two cups of steaming coffee.

'Have you got your fags?' Dee asked.

Maeve nodded.

'Come into the loos. I'll be able to tell you everything if I can have a smoke.'

The story took three Silk Cuts each. Various women went in and out of the six-cubicle toilet, while Maeve and Dee seamlessly switched to mundane topics of conversation when there was anybody else present. To her amazement Dee still didn't cry, even when she got to the bit about selling the house immediately.

'Jesus, he's a cold bastard,' breathed Maeve.

'I was pretty cold myself,' Dee pointed out.

'That was shock. You cry your eyes out when you see a dead cat on the side of the road. The only reason you didn't go hysterical was because you were in shock. But it'll hit you like a sledgehammer later, I'm warning you.'

'Maybe.' Dee thought about it for a moment. 'I feel sort of frozen, as if none of this is really happening.'

'Like it's a dream sequence? You've been watching too much *Frasier*.'

They both laughed weakly.

'That's pretty true,' Dee said. 'He's a psychiatrist with a disastrous personal life. I'm an agony aunt with a disastrous personal life. Do you think I could sell my story as a sit-com script?'

'I don't see why not.' Maeve glanced at her watch. 'Look at the time! I'd better do some work or I'm history. I'm not like you lucky deputy editor types who can swan in and out when you please,' she said, giving Dee an affectionate hug. 'Please tell me if you feel bad later. I'll get an hour off and we can go to Magee's for a quiet chat, all right? I don't want you suffering in silence, Dee. Promise?'

Dee hadn't another moment to think about Gary until lunchtime. The new editor, Malley McDonnell, spent the morning in Ted Holt's old office – now Eugene Flynn's office – with him, meeting various departmental heads and discussing the changes that were to be made. Apart from the absence of Nigel, Ted and his gossipy secretary, Marion, who had left with her boss, everything was to be the same. *For now*, was the unspoken comment.

'We're bringing in a few new departmental heads,' Eugene explained smoothly when Isabel, Phil Walsh, Maeve, Dee and the other features/women's pages team were getting their pep talk. 'We're appointing two editorial directors – one responsible for the news side of the paper and one for the features/women's/miscellaneous sections.'

Miscellaneous? So that's all they were, Dee thought crossly. She really didn't like Eugene Flynn. He looked like the sort of man who'd pull the legs off a daddy longlegs. And exactly what sort of new managerial system was he creating? *Editorial directors*?

That was a new title. Where did they fit in – directly under the editor and above the different departmental editors? Who knew? The way Flynn was organising the *Sentinel*, there'd soon be ten chiefs to every Indian and nobody would get any work done because there'd be so much executive squabbling about who was in charge of what.

'Jack Carter wanted to be here to tell you how the place was going to be run but he had to go to Belfast on business,' Malley interrupted.

Dee noticed that for some reason Isabel relaxed in her chair at that point. She'd been sitting bolt upright since they'd been in the MD's office, as if she was preparing for a deportment exam and was practising sitting ramrod straight with books balanced on her head.

'Chris Schriber is the editorial director of news, while Tanya Vernon is the editorial director in charge of you lot,' Eugene said. He buzzed his secretary. 'Send Tanya in.'

The door opened. The combined features and women's pages departments looked at their new boss with interest – and amazement.

Tanya Vernon was everything Dee longed to be but wasn't. She was tall, slender, striking-looking, and could have stepped straight off the pages of a high fashion magazine. Her shiny jet black hair was cut into an elegant crop that clung to her perfectly shaped skull and made her Slavic cheekbones stand out. The picture of elegance, she wore a very up-to-date white suit with spike-heeled grey suede shoes, a silver choker, and nothing visible under the buttoned-up jacket. The skirt was short, emphasising the sort of legs that sent grown men into a frenzy. On anyone less striking, the effect would have been that of sex kitten extraordinaire. But Dee sensed that only a very foolish man would ever assume Tanya Vernon was a bimbo.

Her pale grey almond-shaped eyes, dusted with charcoal grey shadow, surveyed the waiting journalists as if she was figuring out who to fire first. Then she smiled, a cool and utterly confident smile.

'I'm Tanya Vernon. And you are?' She held out a hand to Phil, who introduced herself and the rest of the group.

Dee tried to analyse her neutral accent as Tanya politely shook hands with everyone. She couldn't quite place it. Tanya wasn't American but there were traces of the West Coast there – or was it a hint of Australian?

There were no empty seats in the office so the new deputy editor leant against the wall behind Dee and Isabel while Malley and Flynn talked about their plans for the paper.

Dee didn't know if she was being paranoid or not, but she could feel Tanya's hard eyes boring into each of them in turn, sizing them up.

When the meeting was over, she and Isabel were the first to leave.

'I hate someone standing behind me like that,' Dee whispered as they went upstairs to the newsroom. 'I could feel her staring at me all the time.'

'Me too,' whispered Isabel. 'And somehow, I don't think she was very impressed with what she saw. She looks like one very tough lady.'

Dee was amazed. She hadn't thought Isabel would share her opinion. Isabel always seemed so confident and self-assured, not the sort of person to let anyone bother her, even someone as intimidating as Tanya Vernon.

'Have you heard of her before? Has she worked in journalism in this country?' Isabel asked in a normal voice once they reached the newsroom.

'No. And I can't figure out where she's from either,' Dee replied. 'Her accent is weird. In fact, she doesn't have an accent. Maybe she didn't grow up on earth at all,' Dee joked. 'She just dropped down from space one day, shaped like a supermodel.'

Isabel laughed. 'If she's an alien, I hope she's one of the ones who come in peace. I've been having nightmares about vicious new bosses firing half the staff and giving the rest of us coronaries with an increased workload. I'm praying the real thing is nothing like my nightmares.'

By three in the afternoon, Dee had reached the conclusion that Tanya Vernon hadn't been sent down to earth in a spaceship – she'd been sent up in an express elevator straight from hell.

Five minutes after stalking into the newsroom, Tanya had taken over the cubbyhole beside the windows that the photographers used for making phone calls and doing their expenses. 'There's already a photographic office downstairs,' she dismissively told Fred, the head photographer, when he arrived to find her dumping his stuff haphazardly into a document box. 'You don't need this.'

She cancelled lunch for the features and women's departments – 'We're having a meeting in the conference room. Send out for sandwiches.' And she commandeered Jackie as her assistant until her own arrived. 'I only need her for a week,' Tanya coolly told Phil and Isabel. 'You can manage until then.'

Phil's eyes narrowed at this but she said nothing at the time.

'*Her own assistant*, my backside! If she's going to behave like this all the time, I can foresee either a mutiny or mass redundancies,' Phil muttered to Dee when Tanya had gone off in search of a swivel chair that suited her.

'No time for lunch, huh?' Maeve said as she walked by Dee's desk. 'Do you want to go for a drink tonight?

I'm meeting Karl in town at eight but we've got at least an hour to talk.'

'Great,' said Dee weakly. She'd thought of asking if she could stay in Maeve's flat. She wasn't sure if she'd be able to face going home. Gary had said he was moving out today and Dee could imagine how bare the place would look with all his stuff gone.

The more she thought about it, the more depressed she got. The coffee table was his, a reject from his mother's house. So was the Waterford crystal lamp in one corner of the sitting-room.

The curtains had come from one of his elder brothers' houses. When Dee and Gary had bought their house a year ago, they'd been too broke to have curtains made, so Dan had donated brown brocade ones from his old house. Dee had hated them at first but she'd grown so used to them she'd never bothered to replace them.

Without all Gary's stuff, the house would look empty. Without Gary, it would feel empty.

'Dee.' Tanya's crisp, slightly sarcastic voice was impossible to ignore. 'We're having our meeting now. Are you interested?'

She jumped. 'Of course.'

Jackie had bought the sort of sandwiches Dee adored. Soft brown bread filled with chopped egg saturated in mayonnaise, chunks of Cheddar cheese accompanied by generous helpings of coleslaw, and salad sandwiches filled with cherry tomatoes, potato salad and cheese slivers. None of it exactly low-fat thanks to thickly spread full-fat butter and lots of mayonnaise.

It was ages since breakfast so Dee tucked in, heaping her plate with sandwiches. What was the point of dieting when her boyfriend had left her? If food comforted her, she might as well eat.

Tanya barely touched her cheese sandwich. But she drank several cups of black, sugarless coffee as she ran through a list of new ideas.

Dee found it hard to concentrate. As Maeve had said, the shock of Gary's departure had left her numb. Now, a day and a half after he'd announced he was leaving, it was finally hitting her. She stuffed the rest of her last egg sandwich into her mouth.

Tanya was talking to her again. 'If you're quite finished, Dee, perhaps we could continue our meeting?' she said in a chilly voice. 'I just asked you a question.'

Dee felt like a fat child who'd been caught with one pudgy hand in the biscuit tin after eating every single biscuit in it. Her face flamed.

'Tanya, pass the coffee, please,' said Isabel in a voice a few degrees colder than their new boss. 'If we're having lunchtime meetings, let's actually have some lunch.'

With eyes as hard as agates, Tanya shoved the coffee pot down the polished table.

'I'm not a big lunch eater,' she said snidely, gazing at Dee.

'*Chacun à son goût*,' replied Isabel in a flawless French accent.

Tanya stared at her blankly and then two pinpoints of crimson appeared in the otherwise impassive, high-cheekboned face. She hadn't a clue what Isabel had said, Dee realised with delight. She herself had loved French in school and had translated the remark easily.

'Each to his own. *In French*,' said Phil with a smile as she patted Tanya's arm in a glorious gesture of condescension. 'I think I'll have another cup of coffee too. Isabel's right, Tanya. If we're going to work during lunch, we may as well eat.'

Everyone relaxed, the sandwiches were passed around

again and Phil sent one of the office runners out to buy a packet of biscuits. 'Chocolate ones OK?' she inquired genially, as if they were all about to go on a picnic and were keen to discuss the merits of Hob Nobs versus chocolate digestives.

At the top of the table, Tanya glowered.

She soon got her revenge.

'I think we need more lively articles in the paper, ones aimed at younger women,' she said. 'I'd like to run a series on the modern Irish woman, her goals, her heroines – that sort of thing. I want to start with a lifestyle piece on gyms. You know, which are the most popular. Interview women who are committed to keeping healthy, slim, that sort of thing.' Tanya looked directly at Dee. 'That's your assignment for the next couple of days – a two-part feature on the gym industry and young women in particular.'

Dee could feel her insides somersault. Go to gyms and talk to slim, fit women about why they worked out? Her? All eleven stone four pounds of her? Or was it five now? She hadn't had the heart to stand on the scales that morning.

'Bring along a photographer and get some pictures of yourself talking to the subjects,' Tanya added. 'I like that touch in an article – seeing the person who wrote the piece gives it a kind of immediacy and credibility.'

Dee knew exactly what a picture of her beside a couple of Lycra-clad, size eight aerobics addicts would do. It would make her look like a fat, ugly heifer, which was exactly what Tanya intended.

'I'm not sure that's necessary for a feature like this,' Isabel said smoothly. 'This won't be an article about Dee's reaction to the subject, it's about the *women's* reaction to it. I hate the sort of journalism where the

261

journalist is pushed forward more than the interviewee. It's presumptuous. Readers don't want to know about us,' she stressed. 'They want to know about the people we're supposed to be writing about.'

Dee felt a glimmer of hope. Maybe she'd be let off the hook.

But Tanya wasn't having any of it. 'No,' she said decisively. 'I want pictures of the interviewer.'

Dee kept her head down and scribbled endless notes on her A4 pad for the rest of the meeting. Tanya didn't bother addressing any more remarks to her and Dee tried to keep as low a profile as possible. By three everyone was worn out, apart from Tanya who unfurled her long, lithe body, smiled at the pale-faced women around the table, and marched out of the room at her usual fast pace.

'I didn't think you could power-walk in stilettos,' remarked Phil, watching Tanya's slim departing figure. Emily, the features freelance, grinned. 'She probably practises walking all over her staff in them, so marching around on office carpet isn't too difficult.'

They all laughed, but quietly. Nobody wanted Tanya to hear them.

Isabel gently touched Dee's arm as they returned to their desks.

'I hope you didn't think I was interfering earlier, Dee, but I got the impression you weren't all that wild about posing for the gym pictures,' she said quietly.

'You can say that again,' muttered Dee. 'I can't think of anything worse, apart from wearing a sandwich board walking down Grafton Street with Tell Me If You Think I Need To Lose Weight written on it in big letters. What a bitch that woman is. This really isn't my day.'

Isabel looked at her with kind eyes. 'If you want to

talk about it anytime, I'm here. I mean that,' she emphasised, 'I'm not just saying it.'

'Thanks,' Dee said, 'and thanks for sticking up for me at the meeting. I've got the feeling you've made yourself an enemy. Ms Vernon doesn't look like the sort of woman who's used to people disagreeing with her. Or making a fool of her, for that matter.'

They both grinned, remembering Tanya's face when Isabel had embarrassed her by speaking in French.

'Don't worry,' she said, 'I can handle Tanya. She's a bully and you've got to stand up to bullies. She may be in charge but it would be a mistake to say "How high?" when she says "Jump".'

'She could recommend us for the high-jump,' Dee joked.

'*She* might but I'm not so sure about the new editor. Gerry Deegan reckons Malley is a decent, hard-working woman so I can't see her letting Tanya rule with an iron fist in her Gucci glove.'

'I don't share your optimism,' Dee replied gloomily. 'The way my life is turning out, Tanya Vernon is probably already figuring out how soon she can fire me. Or perhaps she's going to humiliate me so much I'll resign first, which will eliminate the need for any severance pay.'

The moment she opened the front door, Dee knew that Gary had moved out. His assorted jackets and raincoats were no longer hanging on the overloaded coat stand. Only Dee's pink velvet floppy hat and her black mac hung there limply.

He'd taken all his stuff from under the stairs apart from a battered sports bag with an empty shower gel container in it. He couldn't even be bothered to put the bag in the bin, Dee realised.

At least he'd left the curtains in the sitting-room. The coffee table was gone along with his CD player, most of the CDs – Dee only owned five of her own – and the video machine.

She sat down heavily on the settee and stared at the mantelpiece. What was missing? Of course, the engraved silver frame with the picture of them at a New Year's Eve party.

Dee had loved that picture: she was at her thinnest in it, dressed in a slinky blue dress with her hair up. It was an incredibly flattering shot, taken at just the right angle so she had cheekbones and no hint of a double chin. Gary, handsome in a dinner jacket, clung to her, laughing at the camera and waving a glass over his head.

His mother had given them the frame as a Christmas present, which was probably why Gary had taken it. It was his, like the silver cutlery which he'd no doubt taken too, and the intaglio Indian blanket chest that had stood underneath the bookshelves.

He'd left the pottery hedgehogs Dee had bought in Kerry and the fat beeswax candles she liked to burn when planning a romantic evening in. There was something else there, she realised. A piece of paper, a note? Dee got up and walked over to the mantelpiece. Lying face down was the New Year's Eve photograph. Stripped from its frame, it lay forlornly on the bare wood.

He hadn't wanted the picture, hadn't wanted a reminder of them at their happiest. Gary had never been the sort of man to carry photos around in his wallet. And if he *had* been, it'd probably be a picture of his soccer team, victorious after winning some match or other.

Dee had two pictures of him in the credit card bit of her purse. They'd have to go, she decided firmly. There was no point being maudlin. Gary was gone, their relationship was over.

She tried to be positive. Think of all the extra wardrobe space. Think of the dieting possibilities – she need never keep fattening foods on the premises ever again. The 'Gary can eat what he likes and I can't deprive him of biscuits, butter and ice cream when I'm shopping' defence was gone. From now on, it was going to be Ryvita by the crate-load, raw carrots in the fridge for those snacking emergencies and plenty of mineral water.

Without him, she'd reinvent herself as a thin, organised, ultra-confident woman. That was it.

CHAPTER THIRTEEN

Isabel stood at the entrance to the Lionceaux restaurant's dining-room and looked around her in amazement. The usually spartan room had been transformed into a winter-cum-autumn scene. Fake snow-covered branches hung over the round tables at one end. Branches covered with russet-toned leaves dangled from the tables at the other. The tablecloths were in the blackberry and damson hues of autumn. Garlands of leaves and berries hung on the walls and a large basket of logs and pine cones stood beside a roaring fire. Even though it was August outside with blue skies, a sweltering sun and a temperature of at least seventy degrees, the interior of the city-centre restaurant resembled a cosy country house in the middle of November.

'Do you like it?' asked Penelope, the PR of the fashion company whose show Isabel had come to see. 'We thought it would be fun to make the autumn/winter show look . . . well . . . autumnal and wintry!'

'It's lovely.' Isabel admired the room. 'So long as I don't have to sit beside the fire, or I'll melt.' Most of the tables were full, apart from one right beside the blazing fire, where Isabel most definitely didn't want to sit.

'That's the only problem,' Penelope admitted, screwing up her pretty face in dismay as she looked around for a spare seat. 'When I planned this in July, the weather was so awful and wet I couldn't imagine its ever being hot again. The poor models are going to roast in their winter coats. And I'm afraid the only table left is the one beside the fire,' she said apologetically. 'But I'll get the waiters to move it away a bit.'

By fanning herself with a menu and drinking iced water, Isabel managed to keep reasonably cool during the show. The models all looked a little flushed during the last minutes of the performance, she noticed.

'This floor-length suede coat with sheepskin lining will see you through the coldest December day,' purred the show's commentator, as a tall blonde girl sashayed across the room, perspiring heavily.

'That coat costs a month's pay,' whispered a scandalised Joe, the photographer who'd accompanied Isabel to the fashion show.

A gaunt and rake-thin fashion journalist at their table shot him a vicious look.

'You're not supposed to comment on the extortionate prices,' Isabel whispered back loudly, and winked at him. 'You're supposed to tell your readers that the coat is beautifully cut; that it's this season's *must-have*. And then you refuse to cough up the full price yourself and demand a huge discount from the designer because you wrote about it in your fashion pages.'

Joe grinned and the frosty-faced journalist sniffed loudly.

Isabel hadn't planned to stay for the lunch but Rhona McNamara, who'd arrived late and watched the show from the door, squeezed into the seat on the other side of Isabel and insisted.

'Otherwise, it'll just be me and those two harpies,' she murmured in Isabel's ear. 'They'll bitch about the entire show, complain about the food, the wine and the temperature of the room, and then smile sweetly at the PR person on their way out of the door in order to get their post-show pressie. Which should be a trowel for applying orange-tinged foundation!' she added wickedly.

Isabel had to smother a giggle. The 'harpies' were two notoriously bad-tempered fashion journalists who ruled the fashion journalism world and carried on like prima donnas. Only slightly older than Isabel, they'd both taken the dual cults of being thin and tanned to the extreme, so their gaunt, brown faces looked far older than they really were. They intimidated young fashion PRs, demanded massive discounts on everything they wrote about and whined for weeks afterwards if they didn't like the gift that fashion companies traditionally gave to fashion writers after shows.

Dressed today in little-girl pastel suits, with Barbara Cartland-style eyelashes over gimlet eyes, far too much blusher, vast paste earrings, solid helmets of big hair and unimpressed expressions on their emaciated faces, Vera and Linda had indeed bitched throughout the entire show.

Vera imperiously ordered one poor model to stop at their table so she could finger the material of the girl's brocade jacket. Her subsequent look of disgust showed she wasn't impressed.

Isabel loathed the pair of them. When they weren't busy snubbing her, they made disparaging remarks about the *Sentinel* and how the contents of the fashion pages had deteriorated since *darling* Antonia had left.

Isabel had groaned inwardly when they'd headed for her table and seated themselves ostentatiously opposite her, which had the effect of making every normal fashion writer avoid that table like the plague. *Why* they sat near her, Isabel couldn't understand – unless they actually enjoyed being bitchy.

'If you hadn't turned up, I wouldn't have stayed,' she told Rhona.

'Quite right,' she muttered out of the side of her mouth. 'The embalming fluid might have leaked across the table and the next time I saw you, you could have turned into a third Bride of Frankenstein.' She smiled sweetly at Vera and Linda and raised her glass in a toast.

While Joe went off to get photos of the models in outfits Isabel had picked earlier, she and Rhona talked – sotto voce, so Vera and Linda couldn't hear.

'How are Naomi and Robin?' Rhona asked, lighting up a menthol cigarette. She was always trying to give up smoking. 'If I didn't smoke, think how much weight I'd put on,' she always said whenever anyone criticised her twenty-a-day habit. A generous size fourteen with a wicked sense of humour and a down-to-earth manner, Rhona was great fun to be around. She'd been the life and soul of the party when the two friends were at college, and she hadn't changed a bit.

'Are they settling into Bray and the new house?' she asked.

'I think so,' Isabel answered. 'Mind you, after saying that, I'll probably go home tonight to find Robin in a right royal mood, giving out because I've dragged her away from her home, her friends, etc, etc, and ruined her life . . .'

'You poor dear.' Rhona patted her arm sympathetically. 'I'm dreading the day my lot turn into teenagers.'

'It's not necessarily anything to do with being a teenager,' Isabel pointed out. 'Naomi's nearly thirteen and she's wonderful. I don't know what I'd do without her, in fact. Mother was on the warpath the other night, something to do with Robin being rude to her. Naomi answered the phone and told her I was in the bath so I couldn't talk. Then she left the phone off the hook for the rest of the evening.'

'Clever girl. Perhaps she'd fancy being my secretary when she's older. I need someone who can lie at a moment's notice. Stressed out or not, you look good.'

Rhona admired Isabel's outfit, an indigo silk ribbed tunic she wore with navy trousers and a filigree silver and onyx necklace. 'And you're still slim! If I wasn't so fond of you, Isabel, I'd have to hate you for being exactly the same shape you were when we were in college. The only part of me that's still as slim is my bank balance.'

Isabel grinned. 'What about the mansion in Wicklow? And the designer wardrobe?'

'What designer wardrobe?' asked Rhona innocently, batting her eyelashes. 'Oh, this,' she exclaimed, looking down at her Lainey Keogh knitted dress. 'Is this designer stuff? Silly me!'

They chatted happily throughout the meal.

'What's this Tanya Vernon like?' asked Rhona.

'Spawn of the devil,' replied Isabel, as she cut into her monkfish. 'She picks on poor Dee O'Reilly dreadfully. I don't know why. She's just got a thing about her. The latest idea is to send Dee on a scuba diving holiday in Donegal.'

'Ouch!' Rhona said. 'Nobody looks good in neoprene and I know that Dee's like myself – on the voluptuous side.'

'Dee even said she'd already tried scuba diving and hated it,' Isabel pointed out, 'and that Emily – one of the feature writers – longs to try. But Madam Vernon has her heart set on sending Dee. The thing is,' she said thoughtfully, 'I'd love to stand up for Dee but I'm not sure she wants me too. She's always a little stand-offish with me, probably because she wanted the women's editor job. But she's so sweet, I'd love to help her.'

'Maybe you should talk to her about it,' suggested Rhona.

'I don't know. I think Dee's just broken up with her boyfriend. Sorry, fiancé. So she might simply be a little sensitive right now. Which is immaterial really, because Tanya Vernon would send even the most confident, happy person in the world insane and screaming for Prozac. She's amazing looking – tall, model-girl body, great cheekbones, the whole nine yards. But she's as hard as nails and she'd walk all over you.'

'Wow! She must be bad. I've never heard you talk so vehemently about anyone.'

Isabel raised her eyebrows. 'You have no idea what she's like. She's frighteningly ambitious – not that I'm saying there's anything wrong with that. It's just that ambition makes her ruthless. And she sucks up to Eugene Flynn like nobody's business. Mind you,' she added reflectively, 'at least when she's in his office, she's not harassing the rest of us!'

'You sure they're not . . . er . . . discussing Ugandan affairs?' Rhona asked, citing the old euphemism for illicit sex.

'I don't know. But she looks like the sort of woman who'd be into S and M and a dominatrix outfit. And as there are no manacles on the walls of Flynn's office, I'd rule sex out.'

'Why is it,' demanded Rhona, 'that so many tough, successful career women feel they have to pick on other women? I mean, we're all thrilled to see a female editor of an Irish national newspaper at last and the McDonnell woman certainly sounds decent.'

'She is,' said Isabel.

'Right, so that's one decent female boss. But her next-in-command *female* member of staff is a fascist cow. We've been complaining about horrible, sexist male bosses for years and yet when some women get a bit of power, they're just as bad as the old-fashioned male bigots.'

'Worse. I can't see too many male bosses sending a female reporter on a job purely to embarrass her about her size,' Isabel pointed out.

Rhona shuddered. 'That's low. I think we'll have to investigate Ms Vernon. You say you've no idea where she came from?'

'None.'

'Sounds suspicious to me. Let me dig a bit. She must have some dark secret somewhere and when you're as much of a bitch as she is, there's bound to be someone ready to spill the beans. Have you met Jack Carter yet?' Rhona inquired, abruptly changing the subject. She drained her glass of wine and looked around for a waiter. 'I've seen him a few times but never met him. He's very attractive, it must be all that power.'

Isabel suddenly became very interested in slicing up a spear of broccoli. 'Er, I met him briefly – very briefly at a party in their house.'

'Temple Isis, isn't it? Is it as grand as it looks in the interiors spreads?' Rhona smiled at the young man who was filling her glass with Burgundy.

'Just as grand,' said Isabel with relief, delighted to be off the awkward subject of Jack Carter. She'd thought about him many times since their first meeting. Far too many times. The man was her boss, married and obviously not interested in her.

'The ballroom is massive, very grand, and the place is awash with oil paintings.'

'Not prints in clipframes, I presume?'

'No. We're talking the real thing. And the floors are all marble. When I think how much the carpets for the girls' rooms cost me, my mind boggles to think of what marble floors cost per square metre,' Isabel added.

'I have heard,' Rhona lowered her voice, 'that Elizabeth Carter is over fond of nose candy.'

'You're the second person to say that to me,' Isabel said in astonishment. 'I wouldn't have noticed it myself, but one of the girls from work said she'd know the signs a mile away. Elizabeth certainly drank a good deal while I was watching her but she didn't come back from the loo with white powder all over her nose. Although she's hardly likely to be that dumb. Where did you hear that, anyway?'

'Jo Denton, my deputy editor, is married to Mark Denton – you know, the publisher? He knows Jack Carter quite well and has been at plenty of charity events with both of them. He told Jo that Mrs Carter is a regular coke head. It's not common knowledge, so don't spread it around,' she warned. 'The circles they move in are full of discreet people. You know, "I won't tell anyone about you if you don't tell anyone about me" sort of thing?'

'Dessert, ladies?' inquired a waiter.

'Oh, yes,' Rhona said enthusiastically.

'We've got Grand Marnier soufflé, strawberries and cream, champagne sorbet, almond tartlets with raspberries and Chocolate Surprise.'

'Chocolate Surprise sounds wonderful. What's in it?' Rhona asked.

'It's a surprise,' the waiter replied firmly.

'I love surprises and I love chocolate. I'll have it.'

'Dessert, Rhona?' asked Vera contemptuously.

Rhona smiled beatifically at her. 'Well, Vera, you know what they say – after a certain age, you've got to choose between your face and your figure. If you choose to keep your face looking good, you have to be prepared for a certain voluptuousness. If you choose your figure,' she gazed pointedly at Vera's skeletal limbs, 'you end up looking like a wrinkled old crone! I'll have cream on that chocolate surprise,' she added to the waiter.

'That's one way to get rid of the harpies,' Rhona said a moment later when Vera and Linda had departed in high dudgeon, clutching Kelly bags – 'Which they've had from the first time Kelly bags were fashionable,' as Rhona sniped.

Isabel was still shaking with mirth. 'That was priceless, Rhona,' she said, wiping her eyes with her napkin.

'I know it was bitchy,' her friend admitted, 'and I know that my wickedness on earth will undoubtedly result in my joining Tanya Vernon's beloved daddy in the bowels of hell when I die. But . . .' she grinned '. . . it was worth it!'

In the taxi back to the office, Isabel thought about Jack Carter. When she'd heard that he'd been called away on business and couldn't visit the *Sentinel* offices the week after the party, she'd been shocked at how let-down she'd felt. She'd *wanted* to see him again, wanted to see if she'd imagined that spark between them.

I do so want to see him again, pleaded one voice in her head. Forget him, said the voice of reason firmly. Back at her desk, she pushed Jack Carter out of her mind and concentrated on the feature she was writing.

'Tanya was looking for you before lunch.' Phil arrived at her desk with a fruit scone and a cup of coffee. 'Apparently, the captions for the bikini spread are all wrong, she needs to see you urgently about a holiday competition for next Saturday's paper, and she's all in a flap because Jack Carter is due in at half-three. That woman never stops – it's perpetual motion. She's been like a cat on a hot tin roof ever since she heard the big boss was coming into the office to meet the staff . . .'

Isabel wasn't listening. *He* was coming into the office in – she glanced at her watch – exactly twenty-five minutes. And she looked like a disaster area! Her face was probably flushed thanks to the glass of Burgundy she'd drunk at the fashion show, *and* she'd eaten that garlic mushroom thing for a starter. She must reek.

'Excuse me, Phil,' she blurted, shoving her chair back. 'I must go to the loo.' She grabbed her handbag and raced off, with Phil staring open-mouthed behind her.

In the loo, Isabel quickly rubbed on some fresh foundation to tone down her red face, sprayed buckets of Ô de Lancôme down her cleavage and did a repair job on her eye make-up. She didn't have a toothbrush with her, so she sucked the elderly Polo mint that had been lurking at the bottom of her handbag for days.

A loo flushed. Isabel hadn't thought there was anyone else in there but her. A cubicle door opened and Tanya emerged, handbag in hand. From the overpowering smell of Chanel No. 5 and her shine-free complexion, Isabel knew that Tanya had been primping in the privacy of the loo.

Phil was right. She *was* in a flap over Jack Carter's arrival. But then, aren't we all? Isabel thought wryly.

'You wanted to see me earlier?' she said.

'I'll talk to you outside,' Tanya said hurriedly.

Isabel shrugged. 'Fine.' She went to the door, glancing back in time to see Tanya extract a small bottle of mouthwash from her Moschino handbag.

Mouthwash? What the hell was she planning to do to Jack Carter? Isabel thought crossly. Snog him? The bitch! Was that how she'd crawled up the promotion ladder so quickly?

Isabel marched back to her desk, stopping off at the kitchen to get a Diet Coke from the drinks machine. She felt very hot for some reason and a cold drink might cool her down. Only the knowledge that her article on childcare was needed for the following morning prompted her to keep working, but her fingers felt clumsy on the keyboard and she kept typing words backwards.

Jack Carter *could* be one of those men who flirted with anything with a pulse and a skirt. Or perhaps he merely liked a bit of mild flirtation with women at parties.

A few teasing words in the garden hardly constituted an invitation to an affair, now did it? There were men who communicated with all women in that way – a bit of flirtatious banter and a smidgen of gallantry.

Anyway, he was married, Isabel reasoned. Her roots needed doing, she was hardly a sex symbol compared to his Cindy Crawford lookalike wife, and what man was going to be turned on by a tired, separated thirty nine year old with two kids? Well, practically forty year old with two kids. Jack didn't even have kids, probably hated them. Why would he be interested in her? Especially if he liked the Tanya Vernons of this world.

The more she thought about it, the harder she banged her keyboard keys. *Stop thinking about Jack Carter!*

'Isabel and Phil!' called Jackie breathlessly. 'Jack Carter has arrived. He's in Eugene Flynn's office and he's due up here in a minute.'

Isabel's glass of Burgundy started doing the tango in her stomach along with the garlic mushrooms. She stared blankly at her computer screen, willing herself to be calm.

She longed to glance in a mirror to see if she looked OK but couldn't, not with the resolutely vanity-free Phil sitting beside her. It was quite possible that Phil didn't look in the mirror before she left home in the morning, as her hair was often standing on end and she never bothered to remove the coating of Red Setter hairs. If she saw Isabel peering into her compact and doing things with lipstick, she'd definitely figure something was up.

'He's here,' said Jackie in a stage whisper.

The staff gathered in the newsroom, talking and joking among themselves. They were nervous at the thought of what the new boss would have to say, but no one would dream of showing it.

'Keep your wig on!' shrieked the news editor from his office.

'Some things never change,' remarked one of the young male reporters, who'd positioned himself near the features department so he could eye up Jackie.

'I hope our new lord and master has something interesting to say,' Maeve murmured as Isabel stood beside her.

'Mmm, yes,' she said absently, and craned her neck to watch Jack Carter enter the room. She needn't have bothered. She could see him perfectly. His big figure dwarfed Eugene Flynn's and he was even taller than Malley, who had to be at least five eleven.

The moment he walked into the newsroom, a hush descended upon the room. He had that effect, Isabel thought, almost proudly.

Dressed in a navy suit, blue shirt with a white collar and red tie, he looked every inch the successful, self-made man – and then some. The tawny hair was greying at the temples, she noticed, and the grey emphasised his tan. But it wasn't his height, the trappings of success or that vulpine tawny hair brushed fiercely back from his strong face that made him stand out. It was something else – something indefinable.

As Jack Carter scrutinised the staff with those piercing eyes slightly narrowed, you could have heard a pin drop. Isabel stared at him, longing for him to notice her. Then Jack's eyes reached hers. Her breathing stopped for the few seconds he stared at her, and then his eyes moved on, without even a hint of recognition.

She barely listened to his speech to the staff. She heard his voice, its low rich timbre filling the room. But if anyone had asked her afterwards to repeat even a word he'd said, she couldn't have.

However, she did see Tanya Vernon talking to him afterwards, standing much too close. And Tanya's suede mini-clad pelvis was thrust blatantly in his direction. Isabel watched icily as the other woman gave a girlish laugh, flicked back a non-existent strand of hair and put a hand on Jack's arm. He grinned down at her. The way he'd grinned at Isabel in the garden.

She turned away, deflated. Tanya's waft of Chanel had obviously had the desired effect.

'I like him,' Maeve said as everyone returned to their desks. 'He's a real no-bull-shit boss. Not like slimy Ted

Holt, who was always looking for someone to rub his greasy fat hands all over.'

'You mean, Ted was a groper?' asked Isabel, shocked out of her misery.

'Groper wasn't the word.' Maeve shuddered. 'He never went for me, mind you. But he loved Dee. He always made a bee-line for her at office parties. Said he "loved a girl with a bit of meat on her".'

'Charming!'

'Poor Dee, she doesn't have the best of luck with men,' Maeve sighed.

'I've been meaning to ask you about that,' Isabel said hesitantly, in a low tone. She wasn't sure if she should say anything to Dee's best friend, but she felt she had to do *something*. Her deputy had been red-eyed and quiet for the past week and Isabel wanted to help.

'Is Dee having some sort of problem at home? I'm only asking because I'm a bit worried about her. The way Tanya is picking on her can't help either.'

'That cow!' spat Maeve. 'If Dee wasn't so down in the dumps, she'd be well able for Bitch Vernon. But Gary, Dee's fiancé, has left her. She's devastated, although she's doing her best not to show it.'

'Poor Dee,' Isabel said with feeling.

'Yeah. She's refusing to face facts right now, living in cloud cuckoo land and hoping that if she doesn't think about it, it'll all go away.'

'I know you're her friend. That's why I asked you,' Isabel said quickly. 'But if there's anything I can do, please ask. I don't want to bulldoze through and tackle Tanya on Dee's behalf, but I'm very unhappy about the way she treats people . . . well, bullies them. I hate that sort of behaviour – it's not management, it's terrorism. I'd stand up for Dee, no problem.'

'Thanks.' Maeve smiled grimly. 'I know you mean it, too. Let's give Ms Vernon a little rope and see if she hangs herself.'

'With someone like Tanya, you could be waiting a long time.' Isabel's phone rang. 'I'll talk to you later,' she told Maeve, before hurrying to her desk. 'Hello, Isabel Farrell speaking.'

'Isabel.'

His voice made the hairs stand up on the back of her neck.

'I wanted to talk to you privately,' Jack Carter continued, 'but there was no chance of that a few minutes ago. What are you doing for lunch on Friday?'

Isabel didn't need to glance at her diary. On Fridays, she did the weekend grocery shopping at lunchtime and bought a sandwich to eat at her desk afterwards.

'I don't think I have any appointments,' she answered cautiously.

'Good. I'll meet you in the restaurant in the Herbert Park Hotel at half-twelve. I'm looking forward to it,' Jack added.

'Marvellous,' Isabel said. ''Bye.'

She put down the receiver and stared at the phone. Half an hour ago he'd practically ignored her at the meeting, plunging her to the depths of misery. And now he'd asked her out to lunch.

I wanted to talk to you privately . . . I'm looking forward to it.

Her heart soared. He wanted to meet her for lunch, was dying to take her to lunch. And it couldn't be about business, because whatever he'd wanted to say, he couldn't have said it to her earlier because they weren't alone! Isabel knew she was behaving like an infatuated schoolgirl but she didn't care. After all she'd been through, this was a wonderfully liberating sensation.

She tapped merrily at her computer as if she was playing the piano.

Phil glanced at her inquiringly. 'You all right?' she asked.

Isabel looked at her colleague with dancing eyes. 'I'm marvellous,' she said. 'Bloody marvellous!'

CHAPTER FOURTEEN

Dee stared at the picture in the paper, unable to take her eyes off it even though it was the most horrible picture of herself she'd ever seen. She stood, smiling cheerily in bright sunlight, on a tiny stone quay wearing a navy and red wetsuit as she held her diving flippers aloft. Damp hair streamed down over her shoulders, her make-up-less face looked scrubbed and clean, and every inch of her body was cruelly outlined by the clinging rubber wetsuit. It was like the 'before' picture in a slimming magazine – only there were no gorgeous 'after' shots of her in a size eight dress, grinning as she held up the wetsuit and saying she could now fit into it *twice*, she was so thin.

There were other pictures of Dee's diving weekend in the wilds of Donegal – underwater shots of astonishing, rainbow-coloured fish swimming through her gloved fingers, and pictures of the picturesque hamlet where she and thirty-nine diving enthusiasts had stayed when they weren't flinging themselves into the freezing Atlantic. There was even quite a nice picture of Dee and one of the diving instructors – the hunky one who looked as if he should have been a model – sharing a plate of cod and chips in the pub. She was wearing her black velvet T-shirt and with her hair fluffed out around her face, and low pub lighting, she'd looked almost decent.

But the picture that stood out was the one where she looked like a beached whale on the quay. It was so truly horrible that Dee couldn't keep her eyes off it. And, naturally, it was by far the biggest on the layout.

The freelance photographer, a keen diver and underwater photography expert, had promised Dee he'd send the photos straight to her so she could censor any awful ones before she sent them, and the article, to the sub-editors. But Tanya Vernon had rung the photographer, had somehow made him send the pictures to *her* first, and had picked a selection of the most horrific for Saturday's paper.

'What's wrong?' demanded Mick, the sub-editor, when Dee had cried out in shock as she saw which pictures he was using. 'They're top shots. The underwater ones are amazing, the colour is great.'

'That's not what I meant,' wailed Dee, horrified. She'd known the tight rubber diving outfit didn't suit her but, as the purpose-built diving hostel didn't have any full-length mirrors, she'd had no way of seeing how deeply unflattering it was. Until five days later in the *Sentinel* offices when she noticed Mick at work on her feature.

'Can't you use other ones?' begged Dee. 'There *must* be other ones. He took loads of pictures . . .'

Mick looked mulish. 'These are all I got,' he said, gesturing to the six photos on the desk in front of him. 'Tanya particularly wants to use these ones.'

'But I don't want you to,' Dee said tremulously. 'He promised he'd send them to me first . . .'

'Sorry, Dee. These are all I've got and Tanya wants them in the paper. She's not here so I can't ask her about them. You look great,' he added in a soothing voice.

'I'm so glad you think so,' she said tremulously before rushing from the newsroom.

Dee wasn't working on Saturday but she got up early and went straight to the newsagent's to get the paper, even before she'd had her first cup of coffee. She had to see how awful she looked. The pictures drew her like a magnet.

Once she'd bought the paper, she hurried outside the shop and riffled through the pages until she came to the diving article. It was worse even than she'd imagined. There she was in all her enormous glory – huge, lumpy and bulging out of her wetsuit. It might have been better, Dee thought miserably, if she'd looked even slightly gloomy or aware of her own bulk. But no, she was smiling as if she'd just been given the Hope diamond by a besotted boyfriend, blissfully unaware that she looked like the back end of a bus.

Maeve phoned while she was on her third bowl of Special K.

'Hiya, Dee,' she said with more-pronounced-than-usual cheeriness. 'What are you up to?'

'So you've seen the diving pictures?'

'Yeah,' Maeve admitted. 'Are you OK?'

'Delirious. I'm going on a diet tomorrow. I need to starve myself totally. Nothing but grapefruit, water and five-mile hikes. After six months of that, I might look halfway decent.'

'Oh, Dee, you look fine. You're so hyper-critical of yourself. Nobody but you would look twice at that picture.'

Dee shuddered. 'They wouldn't want to. I look enormous. No wonder Gary left me.'

'He left you because he's a spoilt brat who deserves to be colonically irrigated every morning with a kilo of Vindaloo powder,' Maeve told her vehemently. 'And I wish I could be the one to do it. Pig! Have you heard anything from him?'

'No. It's nearly two weeks since he left and he hasn't even rung me about selling the house. I don't know where I'm supposed to get the time to organise it,' Dee said. 'I haven't a moment to phone estate agents and all that.'

She didn't add that she'd been putting off phoning an estate agent, still hoping against hope that Gary would arrive on the doorstep with a bag of dirty laundry in one hand, a bunch of roses in the other and an apologetic expression on his face.

She'd pictured the scene endlessly, especially when she was lying in the big double bed at night, arms wrapped around herself so as to pretend she was being cuddled.

'Dee, are you still there?' asked Maeve. 'I was asking if you want to go out tonight with myself and the girls? We're going to get a pizza and go clubbing. Please say you'll come?'

She hesitated. She wasn't sure if she was up to a night out with the girls; a night where her newly single status would be highlighted every time the DJ played a love song and she had either to head for the loo or the bar in case she looked desperate for a dance with some neanderthal.

'I don't know,' she said slowly.

'O'Reilly, you're coming if I have to drag you out myself,' Maeve said firmly. 'You can stay with me tonight if you don't mind sleeping on the horrible sofa bed. The only problem is that Nancy and Ronnie refuse to sleep anywhere else, so don't get a fright in the middle of the night if you wake up with two heavy lumps taking all the space.'

Ronnie and Nancy were Maeve's beloved cats, one mink-coloured and one tabby.

'They don't have to sleep somewhere else,' Dee protested. Two warm, soft bodies curled up against hers would be a thoroughly enjoyable experience after a fortnight of singledom. Unfortunately for her, Smudge was one of those cats who hated sleeping with her owner. She preferred to snooze downstairs, no matter how often Dee tried to coax her into the lonely double bed. 'They can sleep on top of me, if they'd like. I'd love them to.'

'Brilliant. Will you come to my place then, say at about half-seven?' Maeve asked. 'And wear something devastating.'

'How about a wetsuit?' asked Dee wryly.

'Forget about that. Chalk it up to one of life's rich experiences, courtesy of Bitch Vernon. I swear that woman is just asking for trouble. Anyway, I've got plans for her.'

'You mean, you're making a wax doll to stick pins in?' inquired Dee.

Maeve sniggered. 'The thought *had* crossed my mind, I can tell you. Gathering bits of her hair for a doll wouldn't be hard, she spends so much time in the loo brushing it. You'd think she was auditioning for a hair commercial. She loves herself, doesn't she? Well, somebody has to. See you later or I'll come and get you,' she commanded.

Dee hadn't yet managed to summon up the energy to scan her wardrobe for something devastating when the phone rang again. It was Millie, her one-time future sister-in-law.

'Dee, I'm so sorry about you and Gary.' Millie's voice was full of warmth and sympathy. 'I just heard. How are you coping?'

Until that moment, Dee hadn't been doing too badly. That picture of herself in a disgusting diving suit had taken her mind off her other problems. But Millie's kind, familiar tones made her tearful.

'Fine,' she muttered, groping around in her pocket for a tissue.

'You don't sound fine. I'm coming over to see you.'

'No,' shrieked Dee, briefly shocked out of her misery. The house was like a pit. Smudge's fur was everywhere, the kitchen looked like the scene of a particularly wild heavy metal party, with dishes, glasses and cups every-where, and she hadn't bothered cleaning the bathroom in ages because she was out of every cleaning fluid known to woman. 'Can we have a coffee somewhere instead?'

Millie was the picture of blooming pregnancy when she arrived at the Yacht. Her pale, freckled face glowed, her eyes sparkled and she looked very jaunty in a pair of pregnancy denim dungarees worn with a blue floral T-shirt.

'I know, it's a bit hippy-ish and the entire outfit is screaming "I'm pregnant",' she said, giving Dee a big hug, 'but the subtle, gathered-under-the-boobs mater-nity dresses make me look like I'm on my way to some very posh garden party. I hate all those interesting details on the collar meant to take your eye away from the bump. I mean, where else are you going to look?'

She pushed back a bit of strawberry blonde hair that had escaped from its casual ponytail. 'What'll you have? Tea, coffee? I know it's too early for lunch but I'm having a toasted cheese sandwich. I've got such a craving for cheese all the time. I ate an entire packet of mature Cheddar for my lunch yesterday, followed by two bags of shrimp cocktail crisps and some kiwi yoghurt.'

Ensconced on a curving bench seat at one of the picture windows with tea and coffee in front of them, Millie gave Dee's hand a quick squeeze.

'I didn't know you'd broken up with Gary until last night,' she began. 'Dan's been away on a course and his mother is barely talking to me because I didn't tell her about the baby immediately,' her hand slipped unconsciously to her belly, 'so she hasn't rung me. It was sheer fluke that Adrian rang us from London looking for some phone number or we'd never have found out.'

'Adrian knew?' asked Dee. He was the Redmond brother who came between Dan and Gary, a high-flying stockbroker who lived in Muswell Hill with his equally high-flying wife, Natasha, another stockbroker.

Dee had only met them a couple of times and had felt immediately intimidated by Adrian's glamorous half-Indian wife, who was petite, exquisitely beautiful and supposedly an amazing cook to boot.

'Gary's moving in with them next week when he starts work,' Millie continued. 'He was going to stay in a hotel when he moved to London but Margaret *had* to stick her big nose in, and begged Adrian to put him up for a month or so. I can't see Natasha being too impressed,' she added. 'Gary and a clutter-free minimalist apartment don't sound like ideal partners to me.'

Dee stirred her coffee silently and thought about how things had changed. Two weeks ago, she was getting married to Gary Redmond. Now, his sister-in-law was telling her what he'd been up to, filling Dee in on his life, his plans, where he was living and when he was going to start his new job. It was like some particularly nasty dream and she longed to wake up from it.

'Sorry, that was tactless.' Millie looked up from her tea to see Dee's frozen face. 'I thought you knew where he was. I thought you'd have spoken to Gary . . .'

'He hasn't rung me,' Dee said simply. 'Since he walked out of our front door, I've heard absolutely nothing. Zilch.'

'Oh, Dee, I'm sorry. I just can't believe you've split up, everything seemed to be going so well. What happened? No,' Millie said quickly, 'don't tell me. I'm not here on a fact-finding mission. I just want to help.'

'It's OK, I don't mind telling you,' she said.

But even as she said it, she realised that she *did* mind telling Millie. The things Gary had said to her still filled Dee with a secret, burning shame. She was fat, ugly, hopeless and an embarrassment to him. How could she tell that to a woman whose husband – Gary's brother, at that – worshipped her? Millie wouldn't be able to understand it. Dee certainly didn't. Telling her everything would be too humiliating for words.

For a brief second she almost hated Millie, which was unbelievable because nobody could hate her. It was just that she had everything Dee had once had. Well, to be honest, Millie had more. She had an adoring Redmond man for her husband, a man who wouldn't let his old biddy of a mother be nasty to her; she was pregnant with a much longed for baby; and she was loved. Loved, appreciated, treasured and adored.

Dee wondered if she'd ever understood how important those words were until now, when they didn't mean anything to her. Correction: when they didn't mean anything to the man in her life, the man who was supposed to make her feel loved, treasured, appreciated and adored.

'It's hard to talk about it all,' she admitted shakily. 'But Gary left me, not the other way around.' She blotted her eyes with a crumpled bit of loo roll. 'I'd still have him back, you know, but I haven't heard anything from him. I rang his mobile phone last week but he has it switched to the answering machine, so I left a message and asked him to phone me.' She hadn't even told Maeve that. 'He didn't return my call.'

Millie didn't say anything.

'So what does Dan think about all this?' Dee asked, anxious to change the subject. Telling Millie what she'd done made her feel even more hopeless and needy than ever.

Only the worst kind of losers rang their ex-boyfriends, begged for a phone call and then stared at the phone longingly for hours, willing it to ring.

Only complete failures would break their new diets by eating an entire tub of strawberry shortcake ice cream afterwards in anguish.

'Dan is shocked,' Millie said. 'He tried to talk to Gary about it on the phone but he wasn't too forthcoming. He's been staying with Margaret before he goes to London,' she added.

'I bet *she's* thrilled,' Dee said bitterly. 'She always hated me. I wasn't good enough for her precious son. Now he agrees with her. If she wasn't a tee-totaller, I'm sure she'd be breaking out the champagne.'

'Don't let Margaret come between you,' Millie said earnestly. 'You two were made for each other, you know it. You've got to get back together.'

'Millie, you don't understand,' Dee said fiercely. 'We didn't have some trite argument about who did the hoovering. Gary decided he was sick of me, he told me I was a fat bitch and he was ashamed of me.'

She heard Millie's sharp intake of breath but ignored it.

'He was offered the job in London and decided to take it. The engagement's now off and he wants me to sell the house. That's it, that's what happened. If you think we're likely to get back together despite all of this, then you're the only one who does!' Dee's voice broke and she sank her head into her hands.

'You poor thing.' Millie pushed her untouched sandwich aside and put an arm around her. 'I had no idea. I'll kill him. Dan will kill him.'

'I don't want people to know what happened,' sobbed Dee.

'It's OK, nobody else has to know, but I've got to tell Dan. He loves you and if anyone can give Gary a good kick in the behind, it's Dan. We won't sit by and let Gary ruin both your lives.'

Dee raised her head to look at Millie. 'Promise me you won't tell Dan? Promise me?' she begged. 'And I don't want *her* to know what happened, his mother. I couldn't bear it. She'd love to know exactly how I got my comeuppance, please don't tell her.'

'As if I would,' said Millie. 'I wouldn't tell that bloody woman what time of day it was if she asked. It's all her fault that Gary is as spoilt as he is. She ruined that boy. If he hadn't been Mumsy's little pet for so long, you wouldn't be having so much trouble with him. Now listen, Gary loves you, Dee, even if he's managed to forget it. He'll come back, I'm sure of it.'

'I'm not.' Dee had stopped crying. She'd been doing so much sobbing that her internal reservoir could only manage short bursts of tears, which was just as well or she'd have had permanently red-rimmed eyes. 'It's over, Millie. I know that for a fact. I simply don't know what to do about it or with myself. I'm lost.'

'Of course you're not lost,' she said briskly. 'You're not the sort of woman who's lost without a man.'

'I'm not?' Dee asked with a catch in her voice.

'You're not. You're going to dust yourself off, get out there and enjoy life. And when Mumsy's boy comes running home with his tail between his legs, you'll be the one calling the shots.'

It was a satisfying thought and one which Dee had regularly. Unfortunately, just as regularly, she had visions of herself as a greying, unwanted hulk that no man would ever look at again.

'I can't see it happening, Millie,' she sighed. 'I might have had some chance of getting back with Gary if he'd gone to stay with you and Dan when he left me. But Lord knows what Margaret has been filling his head with while he was staying with her. She's always thought I was a jumped up, lower-class scrubber who wasn't fit to clean her floors, never mind marry her son,' she said venomously. 'She's got the perfect chance to tell him that over and over again now. Did I tell you about the first Christmas I was going out with Gary and she gave me a pack of sports socks as a present? My poor mother saved up and gave Gary a beautiful designer tie.'

The memory still had the power to enrage her. That Christmas morning was engraved on her soul: the formal present-giving ceremony in the Redmond's equally formal house where even the Christmas tree didn't dare to shed its needles.

She'd carefully wrapped up Margaret's gift in gold wrapping paper. Typically, Gary had left it up to her to buy his mother's present.

After several months with him, Dee had finally got the measure of his mother and would have *liked* to have bought the old cow a book on manners, underlining any apposite sections on how to behave civilly towards your son's girlfriend. Instead, she kept her feelings in check and bought a big bottle of Joy, Margaret's favourite perfume.

Dee loved giving presents and had been happy to see how thrilled Margaret was to get the perfume, even if she did ostentatiously kiss Gary and tell him he was a wonderful son. He adored his striped polo shirt and had left the room to try it on while Dee ripped open her parcel and found two pairs of pink and white aerobics socks.

'I wouldn't have minded so much, but I think she'd figured out by then I wasn't an aerobics sort of girl.'

'My first Christmas present was a poinsettia, which promptly died,' Millie said. 'So the following year she bought me a book on how to care for houseplants!'

'Miaow!' laughed Dee.

'I knew I'd cheer you up. Tell me, what are you doing tonight? Please come round to have dinner with us? Although I should warn you that Dan is cooking Mexican food, so be ready for red hot chilli alert. Bring Smudge and stay the night with us.'

'Actually, I can't come tonight,' Dee said.

'You're not sitting at home on your own, I won't let you.'

'No, I'm not,' she protested. 'I'm going out with some girls from work. With Maeve actually. We're going clubbing.'

'Come and have dinner with us tomorrow night, then.'

'Can't. I'm going to my parents' house.'

'Have you told them?' Millie asked.

'Yeah. They were great. I thought they'd start giving out stink about Gary and tell me I was better off without him, but they didn't.' Dee grimaced. 'I think my mother doesn't want to say anything bad about him in case we get back together.'

'You will, I know you will,' Millie said enthusiastically.

Dee drank her coffee. She wouldn't put a bet on it.

'It's perfect for you.' Maeve tugged up the zip of her red Lycra top and looked at Dee, who was trying to figure out whether she should let the long, silky leopardskin cardigan hang open or close it with the tie belt.

'I've never seen you wear anything leopardskin before, it really suits you.'

'I went a bit mad in town,' she said, still fiddling with the cardigan's tie belt. 'It looked great in the shop but I'm not sure now . . . I look like an old, fat Spice Girl.'

'You look great.'

Dee examined herself critically in Maeve's bedroom mirror.

Worn over a clinging black knitted dress, the cardigan was very over the top and made her look like a voluptuous blues singer who was just about to burst into 'Cry Me A River' in a dark, smoke-filled jazz club. The sales assistant in Big Babes had been the sort of person who didn't believe bigger women should hide under vertically striped marquees.

She'd been very persuasive and insisted Dee swop the baggy shirt she'd been going to buy for the slinky knitted dress and cardigan. But what looked nice in a carefully lit shop with an admiring, size twenty sales assistant egging her on, wouldn't necessarily measure up in the cold light of a nightclub populated by *Elle*-slim girls.

'You're wearing it, you look great,' repeated Maeve, who could tell exactly what was going through her friend's mind. 'You don't look fat, I promise you. You look like a sex bomb and you'll need man repellent to keep the blokes away from you tonight.'

Dee grinned. She knew there was no chickening out. Maeve would insist she wore her new outfit. It was either that or the grey sweat suit she'd brought along for the next day.

'Tina Turner?' asked Maeve, poised by the CD player.

'Yeah. Play "Better Be Good To Me".' Dee loved that song. 'A special request for horrible bastard Gary Redmond!'

'You got it, girl!'

The music blasted into the room and Dee had to stop herself from moving to the beat as she applied a last coat of mascara. With plenty of sooty eye make-up for the heavy-lidded look, and a tiger's eye pendant just dipping into her cleavage, she was dressed to kill. Or would be by the time she'd consumed Maeve's Dutch courage concoction – a lethal mix of peach schnapps, vodka and orange juice.

'Is this a real cocktail or just the dregs of your drinks cabinet?' Dee took another sip and screwed up her face.

'It's a Vestal Virgin. Actually, I'm not totally sure if I've made it correctly – I've lost the cocktail booklet. But one of those will loosen you up a bit.'

'Loosen will be the word,' Dee pointed out. 'Maybe I'll give booze a miss till we order some wine in the restaurant. I don't want to drown my sorrows any more, Maeve. I've been doing that too much these days.'

'Don't let Gary dictate to you now that he's gone.'

Maeve stopped applying lip gloss to impart her warning. 'He's a bully and he's history,' she said crossly. 'So there's no need to pay any attention to all the rubbish he was always moaning about. You like the odd drink, so what?'

Dee decided that lip gloss was a good idea and swiped the tube off Maeve.

'He *was* right about that,' she said earnestly. 'I always got drunk at parties . . .'

'Because you felt self-conscious and unsure of yourself,' interrupted Maeve. 'Gary never even *knew* why you drank too much. The man had the sensitivity of a rhino.'

'Well, he sort of knew. He knew I was self-conscious. But that wasn't a proper excuse. Because I had one problem, I could have ended up giving myself a worse one, which would have been awful.'

Dee had been thinking about this for ages. She'd remembered all the times she'd had too many drinks to cover up her enormous insecurity complex. Pouring vodka into herself hadn't helped, and it certainly hadn't made her thinner. If anything, it had made her more depressed than ever when she woke up and remembered the daft, flirty things she'd said to people she hardly knew when buoyed up with five or six screwdrivers.

'I'm not drinking so much any more and I've got to do something about my weight,' she said decisively. 'There's no point hiding. I've got to *do* something. I'm joining a gym – I've got an introductory session next week. I'm going to do a step aerobics class.'

Maeve stared at her. 'Are you serious?'

'Deadly.'

'I'm thrilled, Dee. I'd love you to get some exercise

but you should do it because you want to be healthy not because you want to lose weight, in the hope,' Maeve hesitated, 'that Gary will come back to you. I'm sorry.' She sat on the bed and looked at Dee earnestly. 'I want to be a proper friend, so I don't want to see you throwing all your energy and dreams into this plan only for it to fail miserably.' Maeve reached for a Silk Cut. 'I want you to do this for yourself, not for some man who doesn't deserve it. Have I said too much?'

She looked up anxiously.

'No. You *are* a good friend, but I do know what I'm doing, Maeve. Honestly.' Dee sat down on the bed beside her. 'I think I need to change my life. And I do want Gary back. I know you think I shouldn't, not after everything . . .'

'Hey, it's your life and your decision,' Maeve interrupted, 'not mine. You love him and you want him back. I don't want to see you getting hurt again, that's all.'

Dee shrugged. 'I'm hurting now. I feel only half-alive, I can't work properly and I want to sit in the corner and cry every five minutes. What could be worse than that?'

Maeve took a deep drag of her cigarette and reached for the ashtray to stub it out. 'At least now, you're *hoping* Gary will come back. What happens if he makes it clear that no matter what you do, he won't?'

For a moment neither of them said anything.

'Let's talk about something else,' Dee said finally.

Romance was in the air, Dee realised mournfully as she peered over the top of her menu at the diners in Luciano's Pizzeria. The place was jammed with loving couples sharing twelve-inch pepperonis and bottles of Chianti. They all seemed to be gazing lovingly at each other over the garlic bread. She could imagine the conversations: 'I'll only have garlic bread if you have it, too.' 'OK, let's share . . .' 'Oh, you're *so* romantic!'

She sighed. Sitting in a restaurant on a Saturday night with a group of women was like shrieking out loud that she was manless. She might as well rent a small plane to fly over the city with an advertising flyer streaming behind it: 'Dee O'Reilly Is Single, Desperate And Gagging For A Man'.

It didn't matter that Chloë, Geraldine and Evie were single too. *They* didn't mind. They were in their late-twenties and genuinely preferred hanging around with their girlfriends. They didn't seem to feel the shame of being manless.

But then, Dee reflected, they didn't know the bliss of renting a video, ordering Chicken Tikka for two and sitting in front of the telly with their man, sharing connubial bliss and pitying all the people who didn't have what they had.

Dee used to pity Maeve and the girls, for God's sake! How often had she watched her friend tart herself up in the loos after work, for a fruitless night out on the pull?

Perfumed, painted and dressed up to within an inch of her life in the tightest of trousers and T-shirts you could buy in Morgan, Maeve would head off into the night and encounter nothing but the sort of pre-historic men who thought two whirls around the dance floor and a couple of Bacardis meant they owned shares in your Wonderbra. It was hell out there and Dee simply wasn't up to it.

Now Maeve had a boyfriend – one who didn't throw a wobbly when she went on her wild girls' nights out – and Dee was the manless one. Destined for endless parties where the main objective was quietly to size up every man in the room as potential boyfriend material.

What a nightmare. How could Gary do this to her? She desperately wanted to go home, back to the familiar four walls where she felt insulated from the horrible, dog-eat-dog world. But at home she missed Gary even more. She missed his soccer stuff dumped all over the bedroom floor, his voice in the morning telling her to get out of bed, and she missed his arms around her. She missed that most of all, his presence.

Dear Annie,

Last month, I thought I had everything. A great job, a great boyfriend, everything really . . . My boyfriend suddenly dumped me and it's as if my whole life has disintegrated. I've never had much self-confidence but I haven't a shred now. He gave me lots of reasons for leaving but what it all boils down to is he thinks I'm fat and he's ashamed of me. I always thought I was fat too, but he told me I was being silly and that he loved me as I was. Finding out that he didn't really love me for what I was has been like a huge slap in the face. It's as if everything we did together for four years was a lie, as if he was kidding me all the time.

I feel so let down, so hurt. I can't tell people how I really feel. I'm supposed to help others solve their problems and I can't solve my own. I feel such a failure, a fraud. And I'm lonely. My boyfriend and I were together for a long time and I'm scared stiff at the thought of being on my own again. I've tried talking to him but he won't even return my calls. What should I do? I've thought of simply turning up on his doorstep – even though he's moved abroad – but I'm not sure what he'd do. Should I risk it?

Lonesome

'That's a big pepper grinder,' remarked Maeve, as the waiter proffered a black pepper grinder that was at least two feet long.

The girls exploded with mirth. The handsome waiter, who was used to this reaction, gave her a saucy smile.

'Pepper?' he asked.

Maeve nodded and he ground some out on to her seafood pasta.

'Would you like some?' he asked Dee, giving her an appreciative look.

'Yes, thanks.' What was his game? she wondered. Was it the 'chat up the spinsters of this parish' night? Did the waiters get paid more if they flirted with the single girls, like the male dancing partners laid on for lonely older women on cruises? Well, she wasn't in the mood to be patronised. She sat stonily while he sprinkled far too much pepper on to her food.

'I don't think ground pepper was the only thing he was offering you, Dee.' Chloë nudged her in the arm when the waiter had left.

Cue another explosion of giggles.

'I told you that outfit would work,' Maeve said, raising her glass in Dee's direction.

'God, I wish I had boobs like yours, Dee,' groaned Geri enviously, adjusting her pink ruffle shirt over her non-existent bosom. 'Men love boobs.'

'Correction,' Mara said. 'Men love enormous boobs on stick-thin girls, which, as we all know, doesn't happen in nature. Except in California.'

'True,' agreed Geraldine. 'Nature gives us skinny top halves with flat chests and balances it with hips so enormous you need a "wide vehicle" sign on your bum.'

'You could always get a boob job,' Maeve suggested. 'What do you think, Dee?'

Dee, who hadn't been paying attention, blinked. 'Sorry, I was miles away.'

'Boob jobs. Are you in favour or not?'

Dee relaxed and grinned. 'I've never had to think about a boob job,' she joked. 'But I've thought about liposuction more than once.' She twirled some pesto sauce and mushrooms on to her fork. 'Perhaps the only surgery I need is having my jaw wired so I can't pig out on gorgeous Italian food.'

Chloë's eyes lit up at the mention of the word liposuction. 'Would you have it? I've often thought about it for my thighs.'

Maeve shuddered and reached for the bottle of red wine. 'I can't even bear to think about that.'

'That's because you don't need it,' Chloe pointed out. 'You're naturally thin.'

'You're thin too!' Maeve retorted.

'I've fat thighs,' Chloë said. 'You can't tell with bootleg trousers.'

'I'm not against surgery,' Maeve explained. 'I just don't like pain, blood or needles.'

'I could put up with a bit of pain to have all my fat bits vacuumed away,' Chloë replied.

'Liposuction does sound magical, so far as results are concerned,' Dee said. 'Imagine – one minute you're fat, the next you're a waif. Still, I always feel that if I'm ever going to be thin, I've got to suffer to do it. You know, spend hours on jogging machines.'

Geraldine ate the last morsel of her pizza and licked her fingers. 'Delicious! I must admit, I like fast results. I prefer the idea of exercise routines that promise you'll look five years younger after five hours of doing their exercises. Not that I've ever got round to actually *doing* any of those exercise plans. But when I need to, I'll go for the five-hour one rather than the lifetime-of-pain variety.'

'Call me a cynic,' Mara said, 'but so far as I'm concerned, the only five-hour process that'll make you look five years younger is one that involves a scalpel, a talented plastic surgeon and ten grand in cash.'

'Talking of fat, who wants dessert?' asked Maeve as she pushed her plate away and lit up. 'They do the most amazing cake with marscapone cheese here.'

'Grab the waiter and get the dessert menu,' Geraldine said.

Their waiter rushed by, again wielding the enormous pepper mill.

'What is it with the enormous pepper mill?' Chloë demanded. 'Is it a status symbol? Do Italian waiters fight over who's got the longest one?'

'It's a mating ritual,' Maeve insisted. 'See how he waved it at Dee. If that's not a strong come on signal, I don't know what is.'

'I don't think we should let her come out with us any more,' Mara said with a wicked grin. 'She's too sexy. There'll be no men left for the rest of us!'

Dee got an attack of the giggles. 'You're quite safe, you know. Maeve sprayed me with man-repellent earlier.'

'Brilliant!' whooped Chloë. 'That'll come in handy later when we decide which of the lads we fancy and which ones we want to get rid of. OK, who's for more wine?'

CHAPTER FIFTEEN

Isabel burrowed her head into the pillow to block out the sound of next door's dog barking manically. She was so tired, it was only around six in the morning and she really wanted to get another three-quarters of an hour of sleep. Especially as she'd spent hours staring at the luminous green numbers on her clock radio the night before, watching half-one crawl sluggishly towards two before she was able even to doze.

It was her nerves. Nerves at the thought of going out to lunch with the chairman of Roark International, the big boss; nerves because she felt like a star-struck teenager just *thinking* about him; and nerves because he was *married*, after all.

Stop thinking and go back to sleep, Isabel told herself. At your age, you need all the beauty sleep you can get.

Rudy yapped on. A sweet black mongrel who danced around her feet when he was out on the street, he had the most irritating bark imaginable when Isabel was at home or trying to sleep.

'Please stop, Rudy,' she moaned. She wished she could summon up the energy to drag her other pillow across the bed and cover her ears with it. But she was too tired to do anything.

What the hell was he barking at, anyway? It was too

late for burglars and too early for visitors. Rudy usually only got into his barking stride when the postman arrived at around eight-fifteen.

A dart of shock penetrated Isabel's brain. The postman . . . Eight-fifteen . . . Just then, she heard the familiar twang of the brass letter box banging shut. She sat bolt upright in the bed, stared at the clock and witnessed the little green number on the end change from five to six. Not eight-fifteen, eight-sixteen.

'Oh, no! I can't believe I've overslept, today of all days! What's wrong with you, you bloody clock radio?'

Isabel leapt out of bed and ran downstairs in her enormous marl grey T-shirt, flicked on the kettle, grabbed a yoghurt from the fridge and ate it on her way to get the post. More bills. And a flyer for an ironing and house cleaning service. Some hope of that, she thought wryly, wishing she could ignore the dust on the hall table.

She didn't have time to do any serious housework during the week and certainly didn't have the cash to get someone else to do it. Just as well neither she nor the girls was asthmatic. There was dust on the dust and the kitchen floor was screaming out for a good scrub. Isabel loathed dust and dirt. As she hurried upstairs, she promised herself she'd do a mammoth spring clean the next day.

Fifteen minutes later, Isabel was showered, her hair was half-dry and beginning to curl around her face, and she was panicking.

The fitted white cotton waistcoat she'd decided to wear wasn't in her chest of drawers. She'd been sure she'd washed and ironed it. She'd seen it only the day before. Cursing, she dragged out all the other white things and dumped them on the bed, anxiously sorting through them. This was ridiculous! It was bad enough that the house was over-run with dust mites, now they had clothes-eating gremlins as well. Isabel stood up straight. She didn't have gremlins after all. She had a fifteen-year-old daughter who loved her mother's clothes.

'Robin, have you seen my white waistcoat, the fitted one?' Isabel pushed open Robin's bedroom door and looked around at the clothes strewn everywhere.

'Whaa?' moaned her daughter, moving like a caterpillar in her duvet chrysalis.

'My white cotton waistcoat, the one with the eyelet embroidery.' It was a beautiful waistcoat, one she'd bought in a tiny boutique in Portugal. Almost prim in its pristine whiteness. Yet the eyelet embroidery could be ever-so-slightly revealing – and very sexy – if you didn't wear a slip underneath. Worn with her business-like fitted navy linen suit, Isabel thought the waistcoat would look wonderful. A perfect fusion of career woman and real woman.

Then she noticed it, screwed up into a bundle at the foot of Robin's bed, half wrapped in a pair of inside-out jeans. It must have looked great worn with them, she thought furiously.

'Robin, next time you want to borrow something of mine, could you please ask?'

'You weren't here,' Robin mumbled from the depths of her bed. 'I wanted to wear something nice yesterday, we went to Dalkey.'

'I wanted to look nice today,' Isabel said tiredly, 'and I'd decided to wear the waistcoat. Now I've nothing ironed and I'm late.'

The lump in the bed made no response. Isabel massaged the bridge of her nose and hoped the rest of the day wasn't going to be like this. She pulled a pale pink sleeveless cotton blouse out of her wardrobe. Verging on the frumpy and nowhere near as sexy as her beloved waistcoat, it'd have to do. Her multi-stranded necklace of seed pearls would finish the outfit and, Isabel thought as inspiration struck, rich red lipstick would add some glamour. With her usual pale pink, she'd look too boring for words.

She stuck her head in Robin's bedroom again before she left for work.

'Will you dust the house today? Just do the downstairs and run the hoover over. Get Naomi to wash up your breakfast things and water the plants. Mrs McCarthy is coming at ten to take Naomi and Julie to day camp and I expect you to be here when she gets back at five, OK?'

Isabel hated getting the girls to do housework in their summer holiday, but she needed a hand around the house. And at least if Robin was tidying, she couldn't spend too much time hanging around Bray with unsuitable girlfriends. Isabel was convinced she'd smelt smoke on her elder daughter's clothes the previous week. But she hadn't wanted to start an argument while Robin was so deeply uncommunicative.

If Isabel said one word about the link between cancer and smoking, Robin would almost certainly buy two hundred untipped coffin nails and smoke them until her lungs were frazzled. So Isabel was biding her time.

The newsroom was abuzz when she arrived at work, much later than usual. Tanya Vernon lounged on her swivel chair like an *Elle*-dressed piranha, phone jammed against one ear as she watched Isabel's progress across the office. If anyone else had arrived half an hour late,

Tanya would have berated them loudly. But she always trod carefully with the self-assured and poised women's editor.

'Did you bring the evening paper with you?' joked Phil, who had no such scruples.

'No, they were all sold out,' replied Isabel easily.

She switched on her computer, opened her briefcase and flicked open her Rolodex.

Jackie arrived with a sheaf of messages.

'I love your outfit, Isabel,' she said enthusiastically. 'That lipstick's very glam. I've never seen you wear red before. Are you going anywhere nice for lunch?'

Isabel coloured. 'Not really,' she replied, as off-handedly as she could manage. 'I'm meeting an old friend for a sandwich.'

The morning flew by. Isabel's phone never stopped ringing and she barely had a chance to drink the cup of coffee Phil brought her for elevenses. She'd only left herself twenty-five minutes to get to the hotel by the time she finally left her desk, and hadn't even had a chance to freshen up.

'I want to talk to you,' said Tanya as Isabel raced past her, handbag flying.

'I'll be back later,' she said, ignoring Tanya's snort of disapproval.

The traffic was brutal, the day was a scorcher and the fan in Isabel's car could only manage 'hot' or 'hotter'. She unwound the window the whole way down and hoped she wouldn't sweat on to her cotton top.

She nearly missed the turn into the Herbert Park Hotel car park and then almost bumped into a Mercedes coupé which was reversing out of a parking spot as she sped in.

Get a grip, Isabel, she told herself firmly. You're like a

lovesick teenager. She brushed her hair vigorously, glad that she'd recently had it cut and highlighted so that the tell-tale mousy roots were gone. It fell in silky blonde waves to her shoulders. She ran some blusher over her high cheekbones and slicked more lipstick on her full lips. Her naturally dark eyelashes framed her big blue eyes and meant she didn't need much mascara, so she simply brushed a subtle beige over her eyelids. Finished, she examined the results in the car mirror. She looked good. Or was the ruby red lip colour overdoing it?

In the lift up from the car park, she looked at herself nervously. The lip colour was too trollopy, she was sure of it. Certainly too much for a business meeting.

But then again, what sort of meeting were they having? Business or pleasure? Jack Carter hadn't said and she hadn't asked. She'd better not assume too much.

The lift opened and Isabel had taken one step towards the ladies' when she was confronted by the man himself. He stood like a prop forward blocking her way. He was immaculately dressed in a pristine white shirt and smart tie beneath a dark navy suit. Tall, handsome and very male. Isabel felt her pulse speeding like a racehorse.

'I decided to meet you here,' said Jack, holding out one large hand, 'as I guessed you'd be coming up from the car park.'

'Hello,' Isabel said tremulously. She shook his hand and drew hers away again quickly. Had she held on too long?

'I thought you'd like this place,' he added as they walked towards the restaurant. 'The food is good and it's never as crowded as some of the city-centre restaurants.'

The maître d' smiled, murmured 'Mr Carter, Madame' and led them to a quiet table for two.

Isabel sat down, fiddling with the collar of her blouse before making eye contact with Jack for the second time since they'd met.

His eyes looked different. They weren't the gun-metal grey she'd remembered from the meeting in the *Sentinel* office. Instead, they were a clear pewter colour, alight with interest and warmth. He was more attractive than she'd remembered too, the strong-boned face more relaxed and a smile playing around the corners of his mouth. He seemed a little nervous, almost edgy, Isabel thought. She was probably imagining it. Why would the head of a multinational corporation be scared of her?

'Does this meet with your approval?' he asked anxiously, eyes briefly sweeping over her. 'I wanted to find somewhere that wasn't too crowded or hot.'

He'd remembered *exactly* what she'd said that night in his garden, Isabel realised with a start. Then she noticed the glint in his eyes, an amused glint that told her he was teasing.

'This is perfect, although I quite like picnics,' she answered softly. 'Talking and eating outside can be so relaxing, and you could have brought the dogs.'

'Sir, a message came for you. It's urgent.' A waiter handed Jack an envelope.

He ripped it open and his face clouded.

'Sorry, Isabel. I didn't want to be disturbed but something always comes up. I just have to make one quick phone call, a *very quick* phone call,' he added. 'Do you mind?'

'Not at all,' she said, waving one hand. 'Would you prefer to be alone?' She pushed back her chair, ready to leave the table.

'No, please stay. I'll only be a moment.'

He fished a mobile phone from his jacket pocket and punched in numbers.

After a few minutes, it became apparent that when Jack Carter did something, he gave it his complete concentration. It was as if she wasn't there, as if he was sitting in his high-rise office at his desk having an important conversation, instead of a restaurant with a woman he barely knew sitting opposite.

Isabel studied him surreptitiously as he spoke on the phone. He ran one strong hand through his hair, raking the tawny strands back from his forehead impatiently, streaks of silver appearing under the rich brown.

His eyebrows were drawn down heavily over his eyes and Isabel noticed a faint, silvery scar running from his left eyebrow to his left temple. It hadn't tanned as well as the rest of his face.

She idly wondered where he'd got his tan. Lying beside a bronzed and oiled Elizabeth in the South of France? Or splayed out on a millionaire's yacht, with a gang of other wealthy pals, all sipping elaborate cocktails, Greek islands in the background?

'Sorry about that,' Jack apologised as he switched off his mobile phone. 'Have you decided what to order?'

The faint rapport they'd had when talking about picnics had evaporated. It was like talking to a stranger again.

They both studied the menu.

'Would you like wine?' he asked.

Isabel thought about it. If this was a business lunch, maybe she should stick to mineral water. But would he be offended if she said no to wine?

'A glass of red, perhaps?' she said.

'Are you racing back to work?' He stared at her intently as if the waiter wasn't standing beside them.

Isabel was sure she wasn't imagining it. His look said, 'Don't rush back to work.'

'No.' She smiled. 'I'm not.'

'A bottle of number thirty-five,' he said to the waiter. 'I'm not rushing either and we may as well have a bottle while we're at it. Doesn't Malley let you have long enough lunch breaks?'

'I don't have time for long lunch breaks,' Isabel said. 'I'm too busy.' She stopped, aware that she sounded like a sycophantic employee looking for praise. 'That sounded wrong,' she said. 'It's just that since I've taken over the women's editorship, I haven't had time for long, leisurely lunches.'

'I understand.'

They talked about the perfect length for lunch and ate their bread – well, Jack ate his and Isabel nibbled a corner of tomato and fennel bread. She'd felt ravenous earlier, now she wasn't a bit hungry. She felt confused, nervous and excited, all at the same time. No matter what banal thing she said – to her shame, she'd actually blurted: 'Maybe we should have a cookery section every week and tell people how to make delicious bread like this' – Jack listened to her intently, concentrating on her every word as if she'd just revealed some fascinating piece of insider information.

His eyes never left her face, he looked fascinated by her, enthralled. But all he wanted to talk about was business.

By the time their starters arrived, she'd come to the unwelcome conclusion that Jack Carter had invited her to lunch purely to discuss the *Sentinel*.

It was work all the way. For the first half an hour, they discussed women's magazines in Ireland and the changing face of the newspaper industry. Jack was very interested in what she had to say, particularly in relation to her experience in magazines in the UK.

By the time she'd consumed her Caesar salad and given him a description of the reader profile of the magazine she'd worked on in Oxford, Isabel had got her appetite back, even though the feeling of excitement inside her had dimmed from supernova brightness to forty-watt-bulb level.

'Where do you see the women's pages going?' asked Jack, his voice serious.

Isabel took a sip of wine. She enjoyed talking about her job but not when she'd been hoping to spend lunch gazing into the eyes of such an attractive man. Over her chicken and his Dover sole, they moved on to politics, which Isabel hated talking about. Jack wanted more political content in the paper. Not wanting to point out that political articles had absolutely zilch to do with her, Isabel nodded sagely and wondered why her romantic antennae had been so off target.

Not that she'd been exactly looking for dates recently. After splitting up with David, the last thing she'd wanted was another man. But she'd been so incredibly attracted to Jack and so sure that he'd felt the same way. And now they were talking about politicians and by-elections like a couple of world-weary political hacks in Buswell's hotel. Boy, had she got it wrong.

'Is your chicken nice?' asked Jack, suddenly.

Isabel looked at him in surprise. He sounded anxious again, as if he was genuinely worried whether she was enjoying herself.

Sitting in the garden with his beloved dogs at his feet, he'd been supremely relaxed, the master of the situation. Now, he was anything but.

'It's lovely,' she said, smiling at him. He smiled back.

He really was so attractive, she thought ruefully. She stared down at the table, eyes alighting on Jack's hands. She loved his strong wrists and the way the little hairs curled around them, dark beside the silver of his watch. You could tell a lot by a man's hands. His were workmen's, strong and capable. Not manicured and buffed to a high sheen. That wasn't Jack Carter's style at all. She dragged her eyes away.

'So, who do you think should tackle the increased political coverage in the paper?' she asked, determined to be businesslike.

'Er . . .' Jack appeared nonplussed momentarily. 'I'm not sure. Who do you think?'

Isabel racked her brains frantically. It was like being interviewed for her job all over again. She lurched into a conversation about different styles of political reporting, in the hope that Jack wouldn't think she was only interested in her section of the paper. As they finished the wine, Isabel realised that she'd better get back to the office soon.

She didn't want the boss to think she took incredibly long lunches given the slightest opportunity to do so.

'That was lovely,' she said briskly, putting her napkin on the table. 'But I really must be getting back to work.'

'You sure you don't want dessert?' Jack asked, his voice sounding panicky. 'They do a very nice mousse thing here . . .'

Isabel had been about to pick up her handbag from the floor. She stopped.

Jack leant forward across the table and put one large hand on her small one. 'Please don't go so soon.'

'Oh, OK.' She sat back in her chair while he called the waiter over.

'We'll have dessert now,' he said.

'Of course, sir.'

She wasn't in the least bit hungry any more, but Isabel ordered tropical fruit salad and Jack plumped for apple crumble. She couldn't see any mousse on the menu.

'I've been thinking,' he said, after taking his first bite of crumble.

Isabel's heart stopped for a second. What was he going to say now?

'I've been thinking of increasing the size of your department,' he said finally.

She couldn't keep the surprise out of her voice.

'That's wonderful, thank you, Jack. Is that what you invited me here to say?'

He dug his spoon into the crumble but didn't eat any. Raising his eyes to hers, he gave her a long, soul-searching stare. Then he pushed his bowl away, leant both elbows on the table and steepled his hands together thoughtfully.

'Actually, I didn't have any plans to give you more staff until a few seconds ago,' he admitted, taking a deep breath before continuing. 'I didn't know what else to say to you. I wanted to keep us talking, so that you'd stay here with me, but you're making me tongue tied, Isabel, and I don't know what to do. Can you believe it?'

He gave a low, ironic laugh and sat back in his chair, waiting for her to say something. Isabel gazed back at him, excitement flooding into her heart. *He liked her. She made him tongue tied!* She knew she hadn't imagined that spark of attraction after all. She hadn't been dreaming, she hadn't been wrong.

Her cheeks felt flushed and warm. 'I thought you asked me out to lunch to talk about business,' she said slowly.

Jack didn't hesitate. His eyes bored into hers. 'I asked you out to lunch because I haven't been able to stop thinking about you since that night in the rose garden.'

He gave her a long, scorching glance. 'I wanted to phone you first thing on Monday morning after the party, but urgent business took me abroad. Today was the first chance I've had to see you alone again. And as soon as I did . . .' He looked faintly sheepish. 'I didn't know what to say. You were so calm and composed sitting there, I couldn't think of how to say what I felt. Until just now, when I thought you were leaving and I knew that if I didn't come clean, I'd spend more sleepless nights thinking about you.'

Isabel felt the hairs on the back of her neck stand up and the butterflies in her stomach swooped, landing with a resounding thud, like a team of gymnasts who'd just performed the most difficult movement perfectly and were confident of full marks from the adjudicators.

'Did you really think this was meant to be a business lunch?' he asked.

She played for time and took a sip of luke-warm coffee before answering. She thought of lying, but changed her mind. Why hide the truth?

'Well, I had hoped it would be more than just business,' she answered simply.

They both laughed, the tension evaporating.

'What a captain of industry,' Jack mocked himself. 'None of the people I do business with would believe it if they saw me right now. I've got a reputation for being as tough as old boots.'

'So I've heard. But I'm going to hold you to that promise about extra staff,' said Isabel, smiling.

'You can have anything you want,' Jack said fervently.

'Anything? OK, I want a chauffeur-driven limo, a

CATHY KELLY

corner office and . . . only kidding.' Isabel speared a bit
of papaya. 'Somehow I feel as if I've been too honest
about my feelings, but you look like the sort of man
who respects honesty.'

'I do, but it doesn't always pay off. I had to be honest
with you, though, Isabel. You know about me, you know
I'm married. You know I shouldn't be here. But,' he
looked at her helplessly, 'I couldn't stop myself.'

That was exactly the way she felt too. Drawn to him,
knowing she shouldn't be, but unable to stop herself. 'I
shouldn't be here, either.' Isabel abandoned her fruit
salad. 'My husband was unfaithful and that hurt me. His
affairs would have hurt me a lot more if I'd really cared,
of course,' she added wryly, 'although I didn't know I
didn't care until earlier this year. Our marriage broke
down a long time ago but I couldn't accept it. But I
know enough about how it feels to be betrayed to hate
the idea of doing that to anyone else . . .'

Somehow, her openness felt right to her. It was as if
she'd known Jack all her life.

'I know what that feels like too,' he said quietly. 'My
wife had an affair once. It was a long time ago. It was so
long ago but I still remember how much it hurt, even if
she can't.'

Isabel said nothing. She was a little shocked by how
bitter he sounded. Why wouldn't his wife remember?

The waiter arrived, looking utterly distraught. 'Was it
not satisfactory?' he asked at the sight of their two
practically untouched desserts.

'It was excellent,' Jack said smoothly.

'Lovely,' added Isabel, feeling guilty for leaving so
much of such a delicious fruit salad. 'I think our eyes
were bigger than our stomachs.'

The waiter whisked the plates away.

'I don't normally get into conversations like this,' Jack said suddenly. He leant back in his chair, and gently rubbed his fingers across his chin. 'I'm known for keeping my innermost thoughts to myself.'

Isabel smiled. 'That's pretty much what they all think of me in the *Sentinel*. No one really knows me.'

Having changed the subject, she thought it might be wiser to stay away from talking about partners and ex-partners. Especially when she felt she already knew too much about Elizabeth Carter. She wished Phil had never mentioned the rumours that Jack's wife was a habitual drug user. It was information she'd prefer not to have known.

'I want to know everything about you,' Jack said, leaning across the table and taking her hand in his. His skin was warm, his fingers gentle as they stroked her hand, exploring the soft skin, reaching up to encircle her slender wrist. 'I want to know about your life, your daughters, what you like, what you hate, what makes you happy, what makes you sad. Everything.'

'How do you know about my daughters?' she asked, suspiciously.

He looked guilty. 'I asked about you. But I did it subtly . . .'

'What do you mean, you asked?' she demanded, withdrawing her hand. 'It must have been a dead giveaway.'

'It wasn't, I promise you,' he protested softly. 'I talked to the editor about *all* the senior staff. I wanted to know more about you but I knew that would have been too obvious.'

Isabel relaxed. 'Sorry. I'm just so scared of causing a scandal in the office. Of course I'll tell you about the girls.'

319

She talked about sweet, kind Naomi, who longed to be a journalist like her mother, and about pretty, highly strung Robin who was going through a rebellious stage. 'You know teenage girls,' Isabel said wryly.

'I don't know any teenage girls,' Jack remarked. 'Elizabeth and I don't have children,' he added quietly.

Isabel waited, silently.

'We planned to have children, naturally. Who doesn't?' Jack sighed. 'But it never happened. It changed things between us. It wasn't the only thing that changed either,' he added enigmatically. 'That's the way it's been for around ten years now. Live and let live.'

'Is that why you're here now?' she asked gently.

'I'm here because of you, because you're unlike any other woman I've ever met.'

She gave him a questioning look. Was that a throwaway line, the pitch of an experienced Lothario who had so many notches on his bedpost that it resembled a Hindu carving?

'I've met plenty of women who wanted to become involved with me . . .' Jack said, fiddling with the stem of his wineglass.

'And did you succumb?' Isabel asked cynically. She didn't want to hear about other women. But there *must* have been others. Jack could have had his pick of scores of women and not just because he was a powerful man. He was attractive, charismatic. The sort of man who drew women like a magnet.

But while Isabel preferred to know the truth, it still cut her to the bone to think about the other women.

'No. Except once.' His gaze never wavered as he looked at her. 'I had an affair seven years ago, the first time I ever did. I was always faithful, anachronistic though that may seem these days,' he said.

'This woman was very special, she'd been my friend for many years and we ended up sleeping together one night . . .' he hesitated, searching for the right word '. . . because we were lonely, I suppose. That's the only way I can describe it. We were together for about six months.'

'Did you love her?' Isabel asked in a low voice.

'Yes, as a friend and a lover. She lived abroad and I could have moved and lived with her but I didn't.'

'Why?'

Jack shrugged. 'I don't know. I asked myself that question every day for a year when we broke up, every day when I felt sad and alone. But the moment was gone and there was no going back. She's married now herself,' he added. 'She's very happy, has twins. Little terrors, she says.'

Isabel fiddled with her napkins.

'I'm not telling you this because I still love her,' Jack said urgently. 'That's all in the past. I'm telling you because I don't want you to think that I have played around with scores of women. I haven't. What I feel about you is special; something I've never felt before. That's what I'm trying to say in my clumsy way.' The pewter eyes were earnest now, the proud face open and vulnerable.

'Isabel, look at me.' His voice was gentle and demanding at the same time. 'You're beautiful, fascinating, sophisticated, clever and more than a little reserved. But I feel as if I can see past all that, past it to the passionate woman inside. I want to know that woman.' His hand grabbed hers.

'I want to know you too, Jack. But this is madness, you know it is.' Isabel spoke quietly. 'I can't deny what I feel about you but I still can't believe we're here, why we're even thinking of doing this. Are we mad?'

'Probably.'

They drank more coffee and as they continued to talk, time flew.

When Isabel finally looked at her watch, she was horrified to discover that it was a quarter to four.

'Oh, God, I've got to get back to work!' she exclaimed.

'I wish you didn't have to,' Jack said earnestly. 'When can I see you again?'

Isabel felt flustered. She couldn't see him over the weekend. How could she hide this from the girls? It would be impossible. They were supposed to go to visit Rhona on Saturday and to her mother's on Sunday.

'The earliest I could see you is Monday,' she said, apologetically. 'I'm sorry . . .'

He held her hand across the table. 'It's OK. Let's not rush things. We could have a pub lunch on Monday, take a couple of hours to talk?'

'That would be lovely.'

He kissed her gently on the cheek in the lift down to the car park. When he touched her, Isabel had to quell the desire to put her arms around him and kiss him properly.

'I'll phone you on Monday,' he said tenderly, looking down at her, his face just inches away from hers. He walked her to her car and stood there, smiling until she started the engine. When she drove up the car park ramp, Isabel could feel his eyes on her still.

On Monday, Isabel felt ecstatic, joyous almost. She'd spent the weekend thinking about nothing but Jack, replaying their conversation over and over again in her head. She'd thought today would never come so she could see him again.

But now they sat side by side on a wooden bench in the Queen's in Dalkey, drank soup, ate toasted cheese sandwiches and went through several glasses of white wine.

Yes, she knew she was crazy to see him again, but she couldn't help it.

She felt utterly relaxed with him, chatting easily about her weekend, telling him about the funny things Naomi had done. He loved hearing her talk, even her story about the search for the perfect hamsters.

'Naomi wanted two females but it's impossible to figure out which sex they are and we went to three pet shops before we were guaranteed we were getting two girls,' Isabel explained. 'Even now, I'm not convinced. Cindy and Barbie will probably turn out to be Sid and Ben.'

'Or Sid and Barbie,' grinned Jack, 'which will mean a bigger cage.'

'There is no such thing as a bigger cage than the one we got,' she pointed out. 'We bought the penthouse-with-a-river-view of hamster enclosures. It's got about four different rooms, tunnels, a hamster gym and a big plastic ball for exercise outside.'

'A plastic ball?' he asked, confused.

'You put the hamster in the ball, close it – it has air holes – and she can run around on the carpet safely without escaping into the settee and living there forever.'

He laughed. 'You learn something new every day.'

Isabel swirled her wine thoughtfully. Jack's thigh lay beside hers on the bench. When he moved – or laughed – he touched her, his leg close to hers. She was intensely aware of it. Calm down, Isabel, she told herself. He thinks you're cool and collected.

By the time the waitress proffered dessert, they'd finished their wine and were too sated to think of eating anything else.

'Just coffee,' Isabel said. She glanced at her watch. It was half-two, time she was on her way back to the office. Time for the real world.

Jack leaned closer. 'What have you got to do this afternoon?' he asked softly.

Isabel sighed. 'Lots of little bits and pieces. Tidying up really.'

'Call the office and tell them you won't be back,' he said suddenly. 'For once in our lives, let's play truant. It's a beautiful day, we could go for a drive.'

Isabel gazed at him. His face was animated, eager. He looked like a kid dying for a long-promised trip to Disneyworld.

What the heck? Faced with an afternoon spent arguing with Tanya Vernon over some trivial matter in the meeting the other woman had demanded, or else spending it with Jack Carter, Isabel knew what she wanted to do. There really was no contest.

She was sick and tired of being the responsible one, of always doing the right thing and never letting her heart rule her head.

'I'd love to,' Isabel said.

They walked under the dark tunnel and down the sloping lane to Killiney beach, as gulls and guillemots wheeled above their heads. A couple of people walked their dogs along the sand; a small group of women and children sat on a bright red blanket, having a picnic in the August sun.

The tang of the sea hung in the air, reminding Isabel of summer days in childhood spent on the beach, running into the water and searching for shells among the pebbles.

Her shoes weren't built for walking here, so she took them off and walked in her bare feet.

'Give them to me.' Jack took her shoes in one hand and reached for her hand with the other. He stroked her palm gently with his fingers.

Isabel felt warm and content inside. It felt utterly natural to be walking along the beach with Jack, holding hands and letting the gentle sea breeze sweep over them.

She *should* have been in the office, and in fact couldn't believe that she'd taken an unannounced afternoon off. She, Isabel Farrell, the most conscientious person she knew, bunking off. But she was having such a glorious time with such a wonderful man, that she didn't care.

It might do Tanya Vernon good to be stood up. It might also do her good to see Isabel walk along a beach with Jack Carter, she thought with an evil little grin. Serve the other woman right for being such a vicious cow.

Isabel looked up at Jack and smiled, wanting him to know how much she was enjoying herself.

He grinned back and tightened his grip on her hand. He'd left his suit jacket in the car and had rolled up his shirt sleeves to feel the sun on his arms.

'I haven't been here for years,' he said. 'It's funny how you can live on an island and never go near a beach until you go abroad.'

'My parents sometimes brought us here when we were small, myself and my brother,' Isabel said. She kicked the sand with her feet, loving the sensation of it between her toes. 'Luke – he's a surgeon in LA – loved the sea and was always bringing boats down here to see if they'd float. I used to collect shells. Everywhere I went, I collected shells or pebbles. It sounds silly, doesn't it? I was always ruining the pockets of my clothes dragging pretty pebbles and rocks home in them. It drove my poor mother insane.'

Isabel couldn't resist looking down at the sand, keeping an eye out, just in case.

'There's a lovely one!' she exclaimed and stooped, still holding Jack's hand, to pick up a fragment of opalescent pink shell. 'Isn't that beautiful?' she said, showing it to him. 'I'd love to be able to paint my bedroom that colour – a pearlised pinky-purple. I've never seen anything like that in the paint catalogues.'

Jack let go of her hand, slid one strong arm around her waist and gave her an affectionate squeeze. 'You see, Isabel, this is what I like about you. If you were one of the women I normally meet, you wouldn't be happy wandering along the beach, picking up shells.' He kissed the top of her head. 'You'd be demanding to know when I was going to fly you to Paris in the company jet.'

'You mean, Paris in the company jet was the other option?' she joked.

'It's always an option,' Jack said. 'You simply aren't the sort of woman who'd want to do it.'

'Does that mean I'm a pushover?' she asked. Tanya would have been packing for Paris before Jack had managed to finish saying, 'Do you want to come to lunch . . .'

'No,' he said. 'It means you're one of the few unspoiled and truly genuine women I've ever met.'

Isabel shrugged off the compliment, faintly embarrassed.

'I don't know how I'd fit in a flight to Paris and still be home in time to cook dinner for my daughters tonight,' she said. 'Not to mention cooking up something for the two new members of the family, Cindy and Barbie.'

'Here's another shell for your collection,' said Jack.

Grateful for the change of subject, Isabel examined the shell, a perfect white scallop.

They walked and talked for half an hour, stopping occasionally to pick up interesting pebbles and shells. Then, tired thanks to a combination of lunch, wine and walking in the afternoon heat, they sat down on the high wall at the bottom of the cliff.

Isabel placed her shells on the bit of wall between them. They both bent at the same time to pick one up and banged their heads together.

'Ouch!' Isabel groaned.

'Sorry. Your poor head.' Jack put a hand on the back of her neck and kissed her forehead where he'd bumped into her.

Isabel caught her breath. His face was inches away from hers, she could smell his aftershave and feel the heat of his breath. He moved downwards. His lips touched hers, gently at first, then passionate and fierce.

Jack's arms slid around her and he held her tightly, pulling her closer, Isabel couldn't resist, she didn't want to. She clung to him, kissing him just as fiercely, just as passionately.

It was like being consumed by someone, feeling his mouth bruising hers. He moved away from her mouth, kissed her cheekbones, her eyelids, her jaw, her neck, like someone who'd been denied human contact for years. She leant into him, loving the sensation of his mouth on her skin. Her fingers splayed across his neck and shoulders, touching and caressing. And still they kissed, deeply, passionately, hungrily.

'Isabel.' He said her name raggedly as he pulled away abruptly. 'I'm sorry, have I rushed you?'

She cradled his face in her hands, amazed and yet not

amazed at what she felt for him. 'Don't be sorry. I've been thinking about this all weekend.'

'Me too.'

They fell on each other's mouths again, hungry for each other. When they stopped kissing, Isabel's mouth felt bruised. She was sure she'd have beard rash later from his five o'clock shadow.

Jack held her hands in his.

'I have to see you again,' he said, his gaze direct. 'Soon, not in three or four days' time.'

'It's difficult . . . with Robin and Naomi. Who do I tell them you are?'

'I don't know. I'm sorry, this isn't fair. I just want to see you again.' His fingers caressed her hands, gently stroking the delicate veins that showed through the skin. 'Can I phone you tomorrow?'

'Yes. I'm not working, though. I've got a day off in lieu of the Saturdays I've worked. We'd better go,' Isabel said. 'It's late.'

'Let me drive you home,' he said. 'You're over the limit and I don't want you to lose your licence.'

'Yes, please,' she said. More time to spend with Jack before he drifted back into his world and she sank back into hers.

Naturally, it was the one evening when Robin *wasn't* in her bedroom listening to her stereo. When her mother arrived home, she was at the front door saying a protracted goodbye to her friend Susie. As Jack's silver Jaguar pulled up outside number 12, the two girls stared at it intently. Isabel could see her daughter's eyes widen as she recognised who was sitting in the passenger seat.

'Robin?' Jack asked, looking at the tall, slim girl in faded jeans and Isabel's indigo silk cardigan.

'Yes. I can't imagine what she's going to make of this,' Isabel groaned.

'I'll resist the temptation to kiss you then,' he said. Instead, he slid one hand across to squeeze her thigh.

'I'll phone you tomorrow.' He stared straight ahead to all intents and purposes admiring the terraced houses on Isabel's street. 'Thank you for the most incredible afternoon.'

''Bye.' She got out of the car. 'Thanks a million for the lift. I hope I didn't put you too much out of your way,' she said loudly to Jack before she slammed the door as casually as she could.

Then, she arranged her face into what she hoped was a normal smile for the benefit of her daughter and walked nonchalantly to the door. It was hard looking normal after the sheer excitement of the day. She wanted to dance with delight, to yell from the rooftops that she'd fallen madly, desperately in love. But she couldn't.

'Hi, Mrs Farrell,' said Susie, a blonde vision in PVC jeans and a tiny black T-shirt. 'I'd better go, Rob. 'Bye, see ya tomorrow.'

'See ya,' Robin said. 'Where's the car, Mum?' she demanded, turning back to her mother. 'I wanted you to drive me to Cheryl's house this evening. She lives in Monkstown.'

Isabel thought of her car, sitting forlornly in the Queen's car park.

'I ended up having a couple of drinks with the gang from work,' she improvised. 'So I left the car there. I didn't want to drink and drive. One of the guys offered to drive me home, to save me the taxi fare.'

'But you promised to take me shopping tomorrow,' her daughter started indignantly. 'You know I need new stuff for autumn. Who was that, anyway?'

'Someone from work. We'll get the train to Dalkey in the morning, get the car and then drive into town,' Isabel said.

'I thought you said you went for a drink after work?' Robin said suspiciously. 'What's the car doing in Dalkey?'

Isabel gave up. 'It just *is*, Robin, all right? Now I've got a headache. Can you make something for yourself and Naomi for dinner?'

'I'm not surprised you've got a headache. It's very early in the evening to be plastered,' Robin sniffed disapprovingly.

'I'm *not* plastered,' said Isabel. 'I had a few glasses of wine at lunchtime. And, Robin, if one of us is destined to turn into my mother, it's supposed to be *me*, not you.'

'It's your life.' Robin stalked off into the kitchen.

That's supposed to be my line too, Isabel thought as she went tiredly upstairs.

'Hiya, Mum.' Naomi was at her bedroom door, clad in her school sports outfit and almost bouncing with excitement. 'I won my tennis match this afternoon! I'm through to the semi-finals.'

'Well done, darling. I'm thrilled.' Isabel gave her a huge hug. 'I've got an awful headache and I'm going to lie down. Come into my room and talk to me.'

She lay on the bed, propped up with pillows, and listened to Naomi recounting every shot.

'The summer camp coach thinks I should have private lessons at school this year. Could we afford them, Mum? I know it'll be expensive,' Naomi said earnestly.

Isabel felt her heart melt. Poor little Naomi. She was so scared they hadn't enough money, she was afraid to ask for tennis lessons.

Damn David! Isabel had worked long and hard to make a good home for the girls and thanks to his business disasters Naomi felt she couldn't have the sort of things all the other girls she knew had. Well, she'd have tennis lessons for the rest of her life, if Isabel had to slave for the money.

'Of course you can have tennis lessons, Naomi,' she said now. 'We're not broke at all any more. We've got plenty of money,' she lied. 'I want you to have the best of everything. And if you happen to turn into Martina Hingis, then so much the better!'

'Naomi!' yelled Robin from downstairs. 'Dinner. Now.'

'I asked Robin to make you something for dinner,' Isabel said. 'I'm sorry, I know I should be cooking . . .'

'Mum, you make dinner every night,' protested Naomi. 'You can't do it all the time. Will I bring you up some toast and tea?'

'No, Naomi. I'm not hungry. I'll just lie here and rest for half an hour.'

When Naomi raced downstairs, Isabel thought about Jack. How could they have a proper, normal relationship under such circumstances?

Do I want a love that's measured out in lunchtimes? she wondered. Do I want to be the other woman, always on the end of the phone but never fully with the one I love? And didn't know the answer to her own question.

331

CHAPTER SIXTEEN

'She put on nearly five kilos, can you believe that? If I ever got that fat, I'd kill myself.' Two lean, Lycra-clad women strolled into the gym changing room and dumped their towels and mineral water bottles on the wooden bench in the centre. The red-haired one slumped down on the bench, leaning back on the bare boards and stretching languorously.

'But that's what you get when you don't work out,' she added.

'I'm just amazed. I thought she was so into her body that she'd never let herself go like that.' The dark-haired girl slid her white leotard over shoulders damp with sweat and dragged it down her perfectly toned torso. Underneath, she wore a sports bra and grey cycling shorts that were moulded to slim thighs. The white G-string leotard bisected her behind into two flawless, taut globes.

Dee tried her hardest not to look and failed. She pretended to tie her laces but couldn't resist peering up at the other woman's body in amazement. It was like watching a ballet dancer rip off her tutu to reveal a physique crafted by years of sweat and effort. The red-haired girl executed an effortless sit-up and off the bench.

'I put on four pounds once when I missed training for a month,' she said, reaching round for her water bottle. She glanced briefly at Dee, who was stuck in the corner, trying to hide her bulk behind several open locker doors.

Dee looked down at her trainers hurriedly. God, they'd think she fancied them if she stared any more. But she couldn't help herself. Both women were amazing looking, toned and beautiful. What she wouldn't give to look like they did! The little mermaid had given up her voice for legs – Dee felt as if she'd give ten years of her life for a body like theirs.

'Are you going out tonight?' asked the red-head, ripping off the rest of her workout clothes.

Dee gazed at her and considered crying. So that perfect body wasn't all thanks to the great god of Lycra. The red-head girl had *thighs* that were slim and a flat stomach, not just vacuum-packed cycling shorts making it look as if she did.

'Yes,' replied the other woman, 'one of the girls from work is getting married and we're going clubbing.'

Not content with looking perfect, they had boundless energy too, Dee realised mournfully. She'd only driven here from work and changed into her new sports clothes and already she felt exhausted. She couldn't imagine how shattered she'd feel *after* an aerobics class.

Shuffling down the corridor in her stiff new trainers, Dee began to get a sense of what the word 'humiliation' really meant. There may have been other overweight, unfit people wandering around the ultra-modern Fitness Studio, but she couldn't see them. Everyone appeared to be slim and glowing with health, instead of at least three stone overweight and glowing with embarrassment.

Eyes down, she negotiated the coffee bar and made it to the gym where her Fit For Life consultation was to take place. Fit For Nothing more like, Dee thought to herself.

The gym was packed. Dozens of shiny-faced, lean people jogged, cycled, stepped and rowed to a pulsing beat. Televisions suspended high up on one wall showed everything from *Emmerdale* to MTV and as she looked nervously around, Dee heartily wished she was at home watching her own television. Maybe she could just cut out the mini Mars Bars and she'd lose weight. She'd start walking, stop eating chocolate digestives, she didn't need a gym . . .

'Dee O'Reilly?' asked a kind voice.

Dee turned to see a tall, very muscular young man in an acid yellow polo shirt and shorts standing behind her. Twenty-something, around six four and incredibly attractive in a Scandinavian rock star way, he was the sort of man to make your knees go weak. As Dee's knees were already weak with nerves, she simply stared at him blankly.

'I'm James,' he said. 'I'll be doing your Fit For Life consultation because Danielle's out sick.' He took her hand in a firm, one-hundred-and-fifty-five-kilos-on-the-bench-press grip. Dee smiled weakly.

It wasn't enough that she was going to be officially shamed into finding out how unfit and slobby she was – she was going to be shamed by a very good-looking man into the bargain. What a perfect evening this was turning out to be. Why didn't she simply strip down to her bra and knickers in front of the entire gym and humiliate herself completely?

'How did you know it was me?' she asked, seconds before her brain realised this was a very dumb question indeed. How the *hell* did she think he knew? Because she was the only person on the premises who looked like an opera singer as opposed to a fit, gym-going person.

'I didn't recognise you and I know everyone else in the gym tonight,' James said cheerily. 'C'mon, let's get started. This takes about half an hour.'

'Fine,' said Dee. 'So I'll be too late to make the step aerobics class,' she added hopefully. With any luck, she'd leave after the consultation without going anywhere near the aerobics department, could grab a video en route home and collapse in front of the box with some chocolate. And never go near the Fitness Studio ever again.

'No, you'll be in time,' James reassured her.

'Oh, goody.'

After five minutes' hard pedalling on the bike in the consultation room, Dee felt she'd had enough exercise for one night.

'Now that you've warmed up a little, I'll increase the resistance and you've got to keep pedalling at the same speed,' James explained, checking that the wrist bands reading her pulse were working properly before he fiddled around with the bike's control panel.

Warmed up? thought Dee. She already felt heated up to about gas mark five. How much hotter did she have to get?

James sat down at the computer again and watched Dee's pulse rate on the screen.

'How much longer do I have to keep going?' she panted. Her thighs were burning with the effort of moving the pedals and she didn't think she could keep it up much longer.

'Only ten minutes,' he said breezily.

Another ten minutes! Dee's energy flagged suddenly. The last time she'd done anything this energetic, she'd been hoovering the stairs when Smudge had moulted fur everywhere and dinner party guests were due any second.

'You're going below the speed limit,' James warned. 'Get those legs moving! You can do it!'

Dee really didn't think she could.

'I haven't done any exercise for a long time,' she wheezed, her thighs in agony.

'How long?' inquired her torturer.

'Never, really,' she said, biting the bullet in the hope that he'd stop the test on medical grounds. A totally unfit person could pass out with the strain of fifteen minutes on a bike.

'You're doing very well, Dee, in that case,' he said encouragingly. 'Most people who've never exercised before can barely cycle. You've done . . .' he glanced at his stopwatch, '. . . nearly nine minutes. Only six to go!'

When the time came for her to sit on the ground for the flexibility tests, she sank on to the carpet gratefully and wondered if it would be bad form to curl up on it and beg for a rest. She was sweating madly, the stray bits of hair around her face were plastered damply to it, and she felt weak from the unaccustomed effort of cycling.

'Put your feet together and stretch out as far as you can,' ordered James.

Stretching she could do, no problem. The only difficulty was that she might pass out on the floor when she was supposed to be reaching her feet. Next, James measured her inner arms and thighs with little callipers that pinched painfully. Then he tested her lung capacity.

Dee had just about stopped panting and had thought the test was practically over when the worst bit came.

'Hop on the scales, Dee,' said James, not even looking up from the computer screen where he was typing in her details.

She reeled in shock. 'The scales?'

'Yeah, and then we're finished. You're just in time for the aerobics class. It's a beginners' one, you'll be well able for it. You did very well on the exercise bike.'

'I don't want to be weighed,' Dee said suddenly.

His expression was sympathetic. 'I understand. Lots of people don't want to be weighed, but we have to do it. That's how we assess your physical fitness and we can't let you join the club properly until we do that.'

Dee said nothing. She felt like crying. It was bad enough weighing herself in the privacy of her own bathroom, away from prying eyes. But to be weighed publicly, in front of such a gorgeous man . . . He'd think she was a total pig when he realised how much she actually weighed. Then he'd put her weight into the computer and it would be official – Dee O'Reilly: Tank Girl.

Maybe other people in the gym would be able to look her up on the computer and see how fat she was. It was too awful for words. She shouldn't have come here.

'You don't have to look,' James offered. 'I'll just weigh you quickly and I won't tell you. C'mon, it'll all be over in a minute and you can get to that aerobics class.'

His voice was wheedling. He patted her shoulder.

'I'm not letting you out the door until we finish this, and I'm a strong bloke,' he joked.

Dee dithered for an instant. He was so nice, so friendly.

'OK.'

'Great.'

He kept his hand over the panel that showed her weight. Dee stared at the wall, not wanting to look in his direction. But he didn't gasp in shock or curl his lip in disgust.

'Off you go,' he said cheerily after a couple of seconds. He pushed a button and removed his hand from the now-blank panel. 'See, I told you I wouldn't let you see.'

Relieved, she got off the scales.

'I'll have your assessment in two days,' James said. 'If you want to come in then, I'll make out a programme for you – you know, gym work, what machines you should use and what areas you need to work on.'

'Everywhere,' Dee remarked wryly.

'It always seems so daunting at first, but it's not,' he said encouragingly. 'In six weeks, if you come regularly, you won't know yourself. You can achieve amazing results in that time. And, let me tell you,' he grinned at her, 'there isn't a woman in this gym who likes being weighed, so you'll fit right in.'

'Thanks for the encouragement.' Dee smiled. 'You've been really kind. I was dreading this. Now, which way do I go for aerobics?'

Dee's entire body was weak with exhaustion as she unlocked the front door and nudged it open with her hip. She dropped her gym bag on to the hall floor, followed by her handbag and coat.

All she wanted was an enormous plate of sausages and chips, something to give her back even a fraction of the energy she'd had earlier in the day. Step aerobics had been hell. How did women do it week in, week out, for years? She was shattered after a beginners' class and couldn't imagine what the advanced 'power workout' must be like. From the moment the throbbing beat had boomed out of the aerobics studio speakers, it had been torture. The luminous pink Lycra-clad demon at the top of the class had leapt around like someone on a particularly bad acid trip, merrily shouting commands to the assembled beginners.

At least they'd all been pretty dreadful too. There'd been several overweight women in the class, bundled into long, baggy T-shirts with long, baggy sweat pants designed to hide everything. Just like Dee.

Thankfully she wasn't the only person who didn't know what a 'jumping jack' was either. What felt like twenty million jumping jacks and a few billion grapevine steps later, she wished she still didn't know.

Dee bent, painfully, to pick up the letters on the mat inside the front door. Junk mail about discount oil refills didn't interest her, nor did a flyer for a crêche. Then she found a letter that shocked her out of her exhaustion.

She'd have known Gary's writing anywhere. That familiar sloping script that had decorated birthday and Valentine cards for four years.

To my darling Dee, love you forever, always, with all my heart, Gary . . .

Could he have had a change of heart? she wondered, staring at the envelope. Did he still love her desperately, want to come home and make everything the way it had been before?

For a moment, Dee held the precious letter close to her chest, longing for the words to be the ones she hoped to read. That *had* to be it. Why else would Gary write to her?

She ripped open the envelope, tearing through the London postmark. Inside was one thin sheet, only half-covered with Gary's almost illegible scrawl.

Dee,

I'm writing to find out why you haven't put the house up for sale yet? My mother says there's no estate agent's sign up. I want to sell it and unless you plan to buy my half, then see an estate agent.

If you won't, I will. I don't want my money tied up in a property I'm not living in. Sort it out.

Gary

She scrunched up the letter in one trembling hand. Why would he write to her, indeed? Because he was too much of a coward to phone her and demand to know why she hadn't put the house on the market. The bastard!

After four years together, he didn't even have the decency to phone her. All she got was a short, sharp letter that contained not one shred of kindness. After all they'd been through together . . . One lousy phone call, that was all she'd wanted.

It wasn't as if she'd bawl her eyes out on the phone or scream at him if he rang. No way. She simply wanted the chance to talk to him, person to person. What did Gary take her for? Some demented bunny-boiler who'd lost her mind because her man had dumped her and would screech down the phone, begging him to come back? Hardly. She was a successful career woman, the deputy women's editor of a leading newspaper, no less. Not a fool. Not the sort of woman to disintegrate in front of him. She wouldn't mind so much if he'd even made an effort to be polite on paper, but he hadn't. The letter was blunt verging on rude. Never mind verging, Dee thought angrily, it *was* bloody rude.

She stomped into the kitchen, opened the pedal bin and dumped the letter in it. Bastard! What she'd like to do to Gary-bloody-Redmond if she ever got her hands on him again! As for his bitch of a mother . . . Sneaking round looking for estate agent's signs, indeed. She'd bet a tenner the old cow had stuck her ugly head up to the front window to see if the house had gone to rack and ruin since her beloved Gary had left, to check if his investment had deteriorated.

In fact, it was much more likely to have deteriorated while he was living there, Dee thought venomously, since he was a lazy, useless sod who'd never cleaned up in his life.

She wrenched open the fridge, seeking solace. The large slab of Edam cheese, iceberg lettuce and family pack of diet yoghurts didn't fit the bill. Neither did the neatly stacked Lean Cuisines in the freezer. The small boxes of microwavable chips were another matter. So much for the diet to end all diets, Dee muttered to herself as she stuck one box of chips in the microwave and poked around in the cupboards for the ketchup.

After demolishing three boxes of chips, four chocolate digestives and a can of Diet Coke, Dee fished Gary's letter out of the bin and smoothed it out carefully. She re-read it several times, to make sure she hadn't imagined its nasty tone. She hadn't. *Sort it out.* Gary had managed to stop himself from adding *or else* but it was clear that was the message. Dee wondered what the 'or else' would be?

Would he send his mother round armed with a baseball bat, or would he simply get his lawyer to write a stinker of a letter threatening the courts if she didn't sell up sharpish?

Their lawyer, actually. Although he was Gary's friend, so it was obvious which of them he'd choose to represent in a battle. She'd better organise her own legal adviser in case things got nasty. Dee sighed. Perhaps she and Gary should have drawn up some sort of pre-engagement contract to sort out the fine details in the event of a break-up.

But when you were madly in love, you didn't think about breaking up. You thought about picnics on the beach, sharing romantic dinners and spending the rest of your life with the man you adored. Sometimes you day-dreamed about having his babies. You certainly didn't anticipate the day when he'd hot-foot it to London, order you to sell the joint home immediately and then send his mother round on a reconnaissance mission to see if you'd started flogging the house yet.

Smudge's elegant marmalade-coloured face appeared at the kitchen window. She miaowed plaintively and Dee let her in.

'Where have you been, Smudgy?' she demanded, picking up the cat and trying to hug her.

Smudge was not the sort of cat who took kindly to hugs. She wriggled out of Dee's arms and landed daintily on the worktop beside the white ceramic dish with her name painted on it in black.

'You only come home for dinner,' Dee grumbled, opening a tin of cat food. 'Why can't you be more like Ronnie and Nancy? They love cuddles and they adore Maeve. Hell, they like *me* more than you do.'

Smudge looked the other way in disdain, arching her graceful neck to signify that she was bored with conversation and was waiting for her dinner. After breaking up the chunks of cat food to the consistency that Smudge required, Dee placed the dish in front of her.

The cat glanced at it briefly with amber eyes then shot off the worktop into the sitting-room. Dee sighed. Even Smudge hated her.

Making a cup of tea, she took another couple of chocolate digestives and followed the cat into the sitting-room. She flung herself tiredly on to the big armchair and thought of all the things she'd say to Gary next time she saw him. And it wouldn't be anything nice.

Dressed to kill and looking devastatingly slim, she'd throw a drink in his face before marching off with her new boyfriend, some six-foot hunk of pure muscle who worshipped her. A six-foot hunk who'd then spend the evening wrapped around her so tightly they practically qualified for Siamese twin status.

Dee smiled grimly to herself. A new boyfriend . . . that'd show Gary. She knew just how to make sure he found out about Mr Wonderful too. Millie was holding a dinner party in a couple of weeks' time and had begged Dee to go. Dee would – but not alone.

Dee could hear them shouting long before she reached the conference room. Tanya Vernon's voice carried the entire length of the corridor, its previously accentless quality coloured by rage.

'You piece of shit!' she screamed in a strong Midlands accent. 'Don't you ever dare to countermand an order I've given!'

'You have no authority over my staff,' yelled back Chris Schriber, editorial director for news. 'How dare you tell that kid that your assignment took precedence over mine?'

Dee belted past the conference room and into the safety of the newsroom where the early-morning staff were clustered near the door, necks craned, listening avidly to the row.

'I'm glad *somebody's* standing up to that bitch,' said

Noel, one of the young news reporters, fervently. 'She's a thundering cow.'

'What happened?' asked Dee, wriggling past the fascinated throng.

'She made the fatal error of bullying the new free-lance into doing an assignment for the features department when Chris had given him an urgent news story. Big mistake,' said Noel joyfully. 'Because Chris looks so easy going and laid-back, she thought she could walk all over him. She'll learn.'

Tanya's voice went up an octave.

'You fucker!' she screeched.

'Have you noticed her accent?' Belinda, the gossip columnist, was rubbing her hands together with glee. 'It didn't take long for the posh Dublin 4 sounds to disappear. I wonder how long she spent trying to lose her real accent?'

'I wonder why she bothered?' said Dee. 'She should be proud of where she comes from instead of trying to cover it up. Silly cow reminds me of my ex's mother, always trying to pretend to be something she's not.'

She walked past the empty desks to her own. Isabel was the only other person not listening to the Vernon/Schriber match. She sat at her desk, concentrating fiercely on her computer screen.

'Morning, Isabel,' Dee said.

The other woman looked up, her expression tense.

'Oh, Dee, hello. I didn't hear you come in. I'm supposed to have this damn' article finished and I just couldn't write for toffee yesterday.'

'I know what that's like,' Dee replied with feeling, dumping her bulging briefcase on her desk. She'd found it impossible to write even the simplest article recently. Staring at the blank computer screen was the perfect opportunity to dwell on all the misery in her life. 'You must have great powers of concentration, though, Isabel,' she added, 'as you're the only person on the premises not glued to the bout of the century.'

Isabel raised her eyes heavenwards. 'If I listened, I'd be tempted to rush in there and join in,' she said. 'That woman would try the patience of a saint.'

Dee was amazed. 'But you never seem the slightest bit upset by her. You're always so calm and cool.'

Grinning, Isabel swivelled the chair away from her computer and stretched her arms above her head to loosen the tension in her shoulders. 'I count to a hundred backwards, that does the trick. But one day . . .'

'One day you'll finish her with a sawn-off shotgun?' suggested Dee, laughing.

Isabel pretended to consider this. 'It's an interesting thought but I couldn't face the time in jail. You get life for premeditated murder. No, one day I'll give Ms Vernon a taste of her own medicine. And when I'm finished with her, she'll be sorry.'

'Can I watch?' Dee begged. 'I'll hold your coat. I hate her guts.'

'So you should,' Isabel said. 'Tanya's utterly vile to you, although I don't know why.' She left her chair to sit on the edge of Dee's desk. 'You let her bully you too much, you know. You've got to stand up to her. I'll back you up any time you want to do it, but you have to make the first move.'

Disconcerted by the suddenly serious tone of the conversation, Dee said nothing.

'Er . . . thanks,' she stuttered after a moment.

'I mean it,' Isabel emphasised. 'I hate seeing her pick on you but I haven't really discussed it with you before because . . .' She hesitated and looked around the office.

There was still nobody down their end of the newsroom, everyone was hanging around the door, glued to the ongoing row '. . . because I knew you resented my getting the women's editor job, and I didn't think you'd appreciate any interference from me. But we get on now, we work well together and I feel we should sort things out. That includes Tanya. What do you think?'

The concern on Isabel's face was so genuine that Dee knew she was serious. She wasn't surprised by Isabel's kindness, not really. Deep down, she'd always known that Isabel was a decent woman. She just hadn't wanted to face up to it. It was easier to hate her for taking Dee's job than to think about what sort of person she really was.

Dee stretched out a hand and patted Isabel on the arm. 'Thank you,' she said. 'I know you mean it.' In an instant, her eyes flooded. She could cope with rows and horrible letters from Gary. It was compassion and sympathy she couldn't take.

'Sorry,' she sniffled, looking blindly around her desk for a spare tissue. 'I've just been having a bit of an awful time recently and I feel all messed up. Your being nice to me sets me off.'

'You poor thing,' Isabel said fiercely. 'I know just what that's like.' She put her arms around Dee and hugged her, the way she hugged Robin and Naomi. 'I was just the same when my husband and I split up. All I did was cry.'

'You know about me and Gary?' Dee asked in surprise.

'Maeve told me. I asked her,' Isabel added hurriedly. 'She wasn't breaking a confidence, I'd just figured out that something awful had happened to you and I wondered if I could help.'

'It's OK, I don't mind you knowing. It's just . . .' Dee started to sob '. . . everything's so messed up. He hasn't contacted me since he left, then last night I got a letter from him wanting to know why I hadn't started selling the house,' she wailed.

'That's appalling,' Isabel said with feeling.

'I know.' Dee sobbed even harder.

The newsroom door slammed loudly and people started moving back to their desks.

'Come into my little cubicle,' Isabel urged, taking one look at Dee's blotchy face. 'I'll keep everyone out while you stop crying. Otherwise they'll all want to know what's wrong.'

She made strong, sugary tea while Dee sat facing the window and tried to repair her face with a fresh dollop of Number 7.

'Tanya's on the warpath,' Isabel announced, putting a mug in front of Dee. 'She's in Malley's office now and as soon as she gets out of there, she'll be down here like a shot, looking for fresh meat. Pretend you're on my phone and sit looking out of the window until you feel better. I'll get rid of her if she storms down here.'

But Tanya never came back into the newsroom. After fifteen high-decibel minutes in the editor's office, she marched out of the building to whoops of delight from the newsroom.

'Way to go, Chris, my man!' yelled Noel when Chris Schriber left Malley McDonnell's office a moment later.

'You socked it to that cow!' yelled another news reporter.

'Seems we're not alone in loathing Ms Vernon,' Isabel remarked drily to Dee.

'There are probably more people in the *Sentinel*'s We

348

Hate Tanya Club than there are in this branch of the NUJ,' Dee said, with only a trace of a snuffle.

She drank her tea gratefully and waited for her face to return to its normal colour.

'Thanks, Isabel,' she said warmly as she finally left the safety of the women's editor's cubicle to return to her own desk.

'What are you up to tonight?' Isabel inquired on the spur of the moment.

'Oh, I dunno. The men in my life are fighting about who gets to whisk me off to Guilbaud's for a slap-up four-course meal,' Dee quipped with a touch of her old sparkle.

'If you're not doing anything, I'd love you to come out to my house for dinner,' Isabel offered. 'It'd just be simple food in the kitchen, nothing fancy, I'm afraid. You could meet my daughters.'

Dee was touched. 'That would be wonderful,' she said. 'I'd love to.'

'It's a deal then. You can come out with me after work, if you want, then you can have a couple of glasses of wine and get a taxi home.'

Dee groaned. 'That sounds fabulous. Food, wine *and* company.'

Dee pottered around Isabel's kitchen, admiring all the little homely touches. She picked up the smallest of the family of crimson and gilt dolls that sat on the window next to a pretty variegated ivy.

'I love these little things,' she said. 'They're so cute. Are they Russian?'

'Yes.' Isabel turned round from the sink where she was washing mushrooms. 'David, my husband, brought them back from Moscow.'

For a brief moment, Isabel wasn't in the kitchen in Eagle Terrace. She was hundreds of miles away in her cosy kitchen in Oxford, with its familiar distressed wooden cupboards and the warm terracotta tiles on the floor. She was looking beyond David to the Russian dolls, concentrating on them instead of on the husband she was about to leave.

It all seemed like years ago; years since she'd seen his face. Now the face she dreamed of in the middle of the night was Jack's. *His* arms enfolded her in her dreams, *he* kissed her languorously and drove her insane with passion. Not David.

'The painted plates are lovely too,' Dee added. 'They suit the room perfectly. Where did you get them?'

Isabel dragged herself back to reality. 'They're Portugese. We went on holiday there a lot.'

'Oh, God, I'd love to be on a beach in Portugal now,' Dee said dreamily. She sat on one of the stools at the breakfast bar. 'Can you imagine it – the sun on your skin, sand between your toes, and no work?'

Isabel thought of the last time she'd felt sand between her toes, that magical afternoon she and Jack had spent a mere three days ago on Killiney beach. Merely thinking about it sent shivers of excitement through her body. He'd phoned her twice since then but they hadn't managed to meet up because Naomi had developed a sore throat and Isabel skipped lunch every day so she could rush home early to look after her.

Isabel couldn't wait to see Jack again, to feel him hold her tight and kiss her passionately. What would it be like to make love to him, to be made love to by him . . .

'Are you *sure* you don't want me to help you with dinner?' asked Dee, seeing the way Isabel kept stopping washing the mushrooms to stare into space.

'No.' She flushed. 'I didn't invite you out here to make you cook your own dinner. You need a little pampering. It's only a simple pasta dish, anyway, so it's not exactly difficult to make. The girls will lay the table when they come home from the video shop. I want you to sit there and relax. Have another glass of wine.'

The front door banged shut. 'Sorry it took so long,' sang Naomi from the hall. She stuck her head round the kitchen door. 'Robin spent *ages* talking to the guy in the shop.'

'I did not!' she protested hotly, following her sister into the kitchen.

'You did. He's gorgeous,' Naomi sighed.

'Oh, no,' joked Dee. 'A battle between sisters for love of the hunky video shop guy! That was the one advantage of having a brother. No competition.' Robin and Naomi laughed. 'Not that the bloke in my video shop looked twice at me!' Dee complained.

'I'm sure he did,' Isabel said firmly. 'You just wouldn't have noticed. Girls, will you lay the table?'

It was lovely eating as part of a group again, Dee realised as she tucked into the delicious meal Isabel had whisked up. The three Farrells joked and talked easily. Even Robin, whom Isabel had warned was going through rather a spiky stage, was relaxed and chatty.

After dinner, the girls sat on the old squashy settee and watched their video, while Isabel and Dee sat at the breakfast bar and finished the bottle of rosé Dee had brought.

'That was delicious, Isabel,' she said. 'You are a marvellous cook. I couldn't conjure up anything like that in half an hour.'

'I love cooking. Well, most of the time,' Isabel amended. 'Sometimes it can be a bit of a drag, cooking every evening. I long to have toast and marmalade because I'm exhausted, but I've got to make something nutritious and interesting for the girls.' She lowered her voice. 'I'm so paranoid about Robin developing an eating disorder that I insist we eat together every evening. She doesn't show any sign of it so far but she's so aware of her body and very fashion conscious. You can't be too careful with girls of her age, I've read some awful health reports about bulimia and anorexia. The stress of the break-up could easily push her into it.'

'She ate everything and she didn't race off to the bathroom afterwards, either,' whispered Dee, who was familiar with the signs of eating disorders.

'I know, I just can't help worrying.'

'Listen,' said Dee, 'I do nothing but worry. If I didn't have something to worry about, I'd get worried!'

She got up to go to the bathroom and Isabel sat and finished her wine. She really was enjoying Dee's company. She'd forgotten how lovely it was to have a female friend over for the evening.

Since moving home to Ireland, she'd desperately missed all her close women friends in the UK and had more or less blocked everyone else out. It had been an instinct for self-protection, she imagined. She'd shut herself off from people to give herself time to heal from the pain of her marital breakdown. Now it was time to let people back in.

When Naomi went to bed and Robin retreated to her bedroom to listen to CDs, Isabel and Dee moved on to the settee. Isabel opened another bottle of wine and produced some bowls of cheesy popcorn.

'I love this stuff,' she admitted, kicking off her shoes and curling her feet up under her on the settee.

'So do I,' said Dee. 'The only difference is that you

can eat it and stay skinny, while I can't. But,' she added positively, 'all that's going to change now that I'm joining a gym.'

She kept Isabel in stitches telling her about the beginners' step aerobics class.

'I thought I was going to pass out with exhaustion. The instructor was like Barbie's taller, slimmer, better-looking younger sister while most of the class were the same shape as your little Russian dolls, all wearing far too many clothes. From what I saw yesterday, the slimmer you are, the tinier your sports clothes become. So if you've a size eight figure, you wear precisely four inches of leopardskin Lycra. I think I'd better purchase four metres of the stuff!'

Somehow she didn't mind discussing her size with Isabel. 'Which is weird,' Dee said out loud, utterly relaxed thanks to the second bottle of wine they were sharing, 'because I hated you at first for being so slim and sexy.'

'Me, sexy!' gasped Isabel. 'Nobody has ever called me sexy before. *You're* the sexy one, Dee. Haven't you noticed the way every man in the office watches you when you sashay across the newsroom? Poor Tony Winston's going to have a heart attack some day watching you, especially when you wear that little black velvet mini. His eyes are out on stalks looking at you.'

Dee giggled. 'He looks like a rabbit with myxomatosis every time *any* woman walks past. He's a walking hormone, that man. But you *are* sexy, Isabel. You're classy and elegant. You could have any man you wanted.'

Isabel thought of Jack. She wanted only him.

'I'm falling in love with a married man,' she said dreamily and sipped her wine, her eyes dark, briefly wondering why she was telling Dee all this. To hell with it, she needed to tell *someone* and it was very easy to confide in Dee. 'I suppose, when you're wearing your agony aunt hat, you'd advise me against it?'

Dee gave an ironic little laugh. 'Being an agony aunt, and having the right answers to questions about life, the universe and everything, are two vastly different things,' she said. 'I spend hours telling other people what to do in succinct, pithy answers that make it sound as if I'm some sort of bloody oracle, while my own life is a complete mess.'

'Your answers are always excellent, you give great advice,' Isabel interrupted. 'Everybody thinks so. You'd have made a great psychologist, Dee.'

'Yeah, but I'm a disaster when it comes to my own problems. "Physician, heal thyself." So I'd be the last person to tell you what to do, Isabel. How serious is it?'

The other woman shrugged. 'Well, we haven't done anything yet, if you know what I mean. We've only just met, to be honest. But I'm crazy about him, I can't help it. After breaking up with David, I can honestly say I didn't think I'd give a hoot for any man ever again.'

Dee nodded in understanding.

'But this is different,' Isabel added. 'He's special.'

'Be careful you don't get hurt,' warned Dee. 'It's easy to rush into things and forget about the future.'

'I think about the future all the time,' Isabel said softly.

CHAPTER SEVENTEEN

Isabel sat in the lobby of Moran's Red Cow hotel and tried not to stare too fixedly at the car park visible through the wall-to-wall glass front. Jack had said he'd be there by nine-fifty a.m. He was always on time, and it was now a minute past ten. Where was he?

She couldn't concentrate on either her cooling cup of coffee or the magazine in front of her, and felt as if she had 'secret assignation' written in giant letters all over her forehead.

The man opposite, who was pretending to leaf through the *Star*, was certainly eyeing her up speculatively. Maybe he'd been able to see through her disguise and knew that she wasn't a businesswoman meeting a contact for an important commercial discussion, but was instead a nervous thirty-nine-year-old separated mother-of-two about to meet a married man so they could escape for a mid-week break.

It was too difficult to get away for the weekend, as Robin, not to mention her mother, would be bound to ask lots of questions.

Isabel could imagine it: 'A newspaper conference in a country hotel *at the weekend*? Sounds ridiculous to me,' all said in Pamela's ringing, imperious tones. A Tuesday-till-Thursday conference on the future of the *Sentinel* sounded much better, although it had been difficult packing her suitcase the night before for a supposed three-day business convention with Naomi and Robin marching in and out of the room at inappropriate moments.

'What do you want this for, Mum?' asked Naomi innocently, extracting a cinnamon-coloured push-up bikini from the case, moments after Isabel had hurriedly jammed it into one of the side pockets.

'Did I put that in there? I must be totally losing my marbles,' Isabel said, grabbing it. 'Naomi, could you get me my . . . er . . . tweezers, please, and the big nail file? They're both in the bathroom.'

The second Naomi swung out of the door, Isabel folded the bikini, wrapped it up in the middle of a T-shirt and shoved it back into the case.

Robin sauntered in, eating a very messy peach and wearing the silky kimono dressing gown Isabel had carefully washed, ironed and stored in the airing cupboard, especially for the trip.

Determined not to lose her temper, she said mildly: 'Robin, I'm actually taking that dressing gown with me.'

'Whatever for? Who's going to see you?' she said truculently.

Isabel counted to ten. 'Nobody, but I'll need a dressing gown and that's the lightest one I've got so it'll take up less room in the case.'

Robin shrugged it off, stomped into her own room and returned, wearing her own pink towelling dressing gown, to supervise the packing with an eagle eye.

'Do you want your tampons, Mum?' asked Naomi helpfully, dropping the tweezers and the nail file on the bed.

Hopefully, no, prayed Isabel. Although it would be

just her luck that she'd get the curse on this, her first night away with Jack. Bad luck or God seeking retribution for the crime of going away with another woman's husband. No, there was being prepared and there was asking for trouble and bringing tampons would be like asking for trouble.

She folded up a voluminous cotton nightie she had no intention of wearing with Jack around. Pink-striped and with a colourful teddy on the front, it had been a long ago Mother's Day present and would kill any lustful longings stone dead. Mindful of her audience, she ostentatiously placed it on top of the pile of packed clothes.

Now, from her vantage point in the hotel, Isabel scanned the car park anxiously and again thought of all the items she'd *planned* to bring with her – a suitcase full of frou-frou bits of lingerie, lacy push-up bras to emphasise what cleavage she had, sexy little wisps of knickers and even a long-forgotten suspender belt, if only she could remember to buy stockings to go with it.

Naturally, in the last-minute panic involved in taking three days off work and organising everything so that the girls went to stay with their grandparents complete with a wardrobe-full of clean, ironed clothes, and plenty of frozen meals so nobody could complain about eating food they didn't like, there hadn't been time for shopping for stockings.

Which was just as well, she thought ironically, as with two sharp pairs of eyes watching her every move, there was no way she'd have been able to pack anything in the sexy underwear department.

In the end, she'd given up and packed a suitcase of her usual elegant work clothes, with one evening outfit:

'Just in case the editor decides to finish off the conference with a posh dinner,' she'd lied to the girls. Which was why she had a *second* bag – this one an enormous Marks and Spencer's plastic carrier – sitting in her car beside the suitcase, stuffed with bras, knickers and the silvery spaghetti-strap evening dress she only wore on very special occasions. Lord knew how squashed it would be by the time they reached Ashford Castle.

She hated lying to Robin and Naomi. Guilt pierced her intestines and caught them in an iron grip every time she thought about it. What sort of mother did that make her? A lying, horrible one who was joyously excited at the prospect of practically three whole days with Jack. *Three whole days* . . .

Isabel poured herself some more coffee, sat back in the armchair and sipped it, staring out into the car park for his car.

He'd never been late before. He was always early, in fact. *She* was the one who'd been late last week when she'd got stuck in traffic behind a broken down bus on her way to Cooke's for lunch. Jack had been white-faced when she got there, twenty minutes late.

'Thank God,' he'd said fervently, catching her hand in a vice-like grip. 'You're so utterly reliable, I was sure you'd had an accident when you didn't turn up on time.'

He hadn't let go of her hand for ten minutes, crushing it tightly in his until the colour came back into his face.

That was it, Isabel thought in horror now. He'd had an accident.

Visions of car wrecks flickered on and off in her head. Jack sitting in a pool of blood in his crumpled up car, desperately hurt and terrified, with no way to contact her . . .

'Phone call for Isabel Farrell at reception,' announced a cheerful voice over the hotel tannoy.

Isabel practically ran to the reception desk, grabbed the courtesy phone and gasped into it: 'Yes?'

'Isabel. I'm sorry I'm late . . .'

'But you're OK, aren't you? Has something happened . . . you haven't had an accident?' she said, the words coming out garbled.

'I'm fine, darling. I'm so sorry you were worried,' Jack said apologetically. 'I was on a long-distance conference call and couldn't get away. Listen . . .' A voice interrupted him, a female voice saying the conference call to Australia was set up. How could Jack manage to take several international conference calls when he was supposed to be miles away from his office, driving her into the depths of County Mayo to stay in a glorious thirteenth-century castle set amid acres of woodland and the calm shoreline of Lough Corrib?

He was going to cancel, Isabel realised. The wonderful trip she'd longed for wasn't going to happen. Her heart sank down to her cream and navy leather sling backs. Misery washed over her as she wondered why she'd let herself become so utterly involved with a married man when it would inevitably mean trouble.

'Isabel,' he was back on the line. 'Sorry about that. This is one of those days. I'm very sorry but I'm going to be delayed here for at least another hour.'

She knew what was coming next. *Can't go, we'll do it again soon, I promise.*

'So I had a brainwave,' he was saying. 'Let's go down by helicopter. We can fly directly to Ashford Castle and arrange to have a hire car waiting for us if we want to drive around. The only thing is, you'll have to drive to the airport to meet me, is that OK?'

'Fantastic!' said Isabel, her eyes dancing. 'That's wonderful. I thought you were going to say you couldn't go at all?'

'I haven't thought of anything else for the past week,' said Jack, in a low, husky voice that made Isabel feel as if she was dive-bombing naked into a huge feather bed.

'Me neither,' she answered, aware that the hotel receptionist was staring at her curiously.

Isabel drove too fast along the M-50, hurtling towards the airport as if afraid the helicopter would leave without her. It was ridiculous to feel this girlishly excited about the trip; ridiculous how often she'd played the whole scene over and over in her head, imagining what a wonderful time they'd have. It had been Jack's idea. They'd planned it after their fifth lunch, this one a picnic in the Dublin mountains for which they'd both taken the afternoon off work.

After consuming an horrendous quantity of pâté, crackers, French bread and Cheddar, watched by around a hundred interested ants, they'd hoisted themselves up on a huge rock halfway along the pony track and gazed out at the city spread below them. It had felt like the most natural thing in the world to be sitting there together, Jack's sweater-clad arm around her shoulders, her hand resting on his thigh.

Something flashed in front of Isabel, a dart of grey plumage with a hint of the darkest pink.

'That was a bullfinch, I'm sure of it!' she cried, twisting her body round to see if she could see the rare bird. She'd leant on Jack, both hands on him as she peered over his shoulder at the trees behind the rock.

'I don't know how much longer I'm going to be able

to take this birdwatching,' he said in a strangely high voice.

Isabel stared at his watering eyes then glanced down. In her attempts to track the progress of the bird, she'd leant on Jack so that one hand was on his upper thigh, the other jammed into his groin, flattening him in what had to be a particularly painful place.

'Sorry!' she yelped, moving her hands.

'That's better. I don't mind being this close to you,' he said in a low voice, 'but I sort of hoped it would be in a more comfortable setting than this.'

Isabel could feel a brick red colour flood rapidly up her chest to cover her face. She knew exactly how it looked – ugly and hot, as if she'd been hanging over the cooker for half an hour making hollandaise sauce.

'I've put my size ten feet in it again,' he said immediately. 'I'm so sorry, Isabel. Making jokes when you're nervous is one thing, but that was unforgivable.'

Isabel said nothing, praying her colour would tone down. She never flushed like this normally, except when she was very hot. But Jack had such an extraordinary effect on her.

'Sorry,' he repeated tensely. 'I'm pushing you too fast – I didn't mean to. I don't know what to do or what to say, I'm so useless at this.' He raked back his hair again, eyebrows pulled into a dark line.

'No, you didn't do anything wrong.' Isabel was amazed at how firm she sounded. She could feel her skin cool down and was immediately calmer and in control. 'Honestly.' She squeezed his arm affectionately. 'I don't usually go puce all the time either, but when I'm with you, nothing is normal.' She laughed.

'Is that good or bad?' he asked, his face lighting up.

'Good. Very good,' she replied.

Jack shifted into a better position on the granite rock so that he was almost facing Isabel, eyes boring into hers. He'd taken both of her slender hands in his larger ones, caressing them almost unconsciously. 'Tell me, how do I make things not normal? How do I make you feel, Isabel? I want to know.'

She studied him closely. 'I thought I'd never want another man,' she said, speaking softly as if they were sitting somewhere with people close enough to hear, instead of on a deserted hillside surrounded by birds, trees and without another human being in sight. 'After David, I though there'd never be another man in my life. I know that sounds drastic,' she admitted, 'but it made sense to me. Our marriage was unravelling for years though I tried to ignore it. I loved David and hated him at the same time. Do you know what I mean?'

Jack nodded and she felt his fingers increase their pressure on her hands; strong fingers kneading the soft fleshy part at the base of her thumbs. They got so sore and tired from constant typing and he seemed to know that, without her even telling him. Isabel closed her eyes briefly, loving the sensation of the massage, luxuriating in how it relieved the ache in her hands.

'Go on,' he urged her.

'I remember commissioning an article once about marriages that were too bad for you to stay in them and not bad enough for you to leave. At the time, I thought that's what my marriage was.'

Isabel allowed her gaze to move, focussing idly on the hillside behind him. It was rampant with gorse, the spiny branches clustered with a profusion of acid yellow flowers, but she didn't see any of it. She was seeing herself a year ago, lonelier within her marriage than she'd ever been out of it but afraid to take that first giant step.

'When I left, I was so tied up with worrying about the practical side of things at first, the girls and money, that I didn't really think about what I'd done,' she continued. 'I'd left my husband.'

'I'm so very glad you did,' Jack said suddenly. 'Or I'd never have met you. And I can't imagine anything worse than not having met you.'

'It wouldn't have done you much good to have met me in the beginning,' she said wryly. 'I was a mess. When I eventually realised what I'd done, I went to pieces.'

'And nobody ever knew because you kept all the pain and fear locked inside,' he said softly. 'Everyone thinks you're the epitome of calm, the sort of woman who can handle anything, but that's merely the façade you show the world. What's inside is very vulnerable.'

He knew her so well, Isabel thought, not really surprised. Everyone *did* think she was firm, unshakable, dependable. When on the inside she felt like she was on an emotional rollercoaster half the time. Jack knew this when so few other people in her life did. David, her mother, her father, even Robin, all thought Isabel could cope with the sinking of the *Titanic* without ever losing her quiet confidence.

'And then I met you,' she continued, 'and you turned my carefully ordered world upside down. I couldn't stop thinking about you. I still can't,' she admitted quietly.

Jack took her face in his hands and looked at her lovingly. He traced the curve of her cheekbone, and touched the full rosebud mouth.

Isabel stared back, deep into his eyes. He put his arms around her and they clung together tightly.

'I didn't mean to be crass earlier,' he murmured, his face buried in her soft, blonde hair.

'You weren't,' she said. 'Not at all.'

Jack moved so that his face was right beside hers, so close she could feel his breath against her skin. His eyes sought hers, warm dark eyes looking for the answer to a question he wasn't going to ask outright. Isabel reached up and rested one palm against his cheek, feeling the warmth of his skin, tracing the strong-planed face with gentle fingers.

She loved Jack's face.

'Despite the fact that I blushed like a schoolgirl earlier, I *am* ready, you know,' she said carefully. 'If you want me . . .'

'Want you?' he said fervently. 'You have no idea how much I want you, Isabel. But I want it to be right – the right time. I don't want to rush you. I feel that I keep saying the wrong thing, I'm so eager to say the *right* one . . .'

Isabel moistened lips dry with nerves. Jack was looking at her with a passionate yet anxious expression. She smiled, letting him see the warmth in her eyes. Then he kissed her and she felt herself melt. It was a strong, urgent kiss, their mouths eager. Isabel closed her eyes and gave herself up to the sensations coursing through her. She felt his body hard and tense against hers, the taut wall of his stomach muscles.

'I want you too, Jack,' she whispered into his ear.

'Will you come away with me for a few days?' he asked, his voice low and throaty. 'Next week. I want to take you somewhere beautiful. We could go to Ashford Castle, do you know it?'

Of course she knew it. One of Europe's most exclusive five-star hotels, a castle that probably had four-poster beds, vaulted rooms hung with medieval tapestries and roaring great fires to lounge in front of, wrapped in fluffy white bathrobes, until it was time to make love . . .

'Will you?' he asked again, anxiously this time, as if he'd taken her silence for hesitation. It was funny to hear him sound unsure, this man used to ordering other people around for a living.

For reply, Isabel wound her fingers round his neck and kissed him open-mouthed, letting her tongue gently explore his mouth. Jack groaned and kissed her in return, arms circling her to hold her in a crushing embrace.

'I'd love to,' said Isabel finally, when she'd caught her breath after the ferocity of their embrace.

Now she threw the toll-bridge money into the machine's gaping mouth and put her foot to the floor when the green light appeared on the traffic lights. Jack probably wouldn't even have left his city-centre office yet, but she wanted to be at the airport before him. She turned the car radio up loud and sang tunelessly along to the Bee Gees, doing her best falsetto as she shrieked out the words to 'Tragedy'.

She opened her window to enjoy the August sunshine and the wind blew her hair back in a rippling blonde mane. A van driven by a long-haired youth overtook her and the driver beeped his horn loudly as he whizzed past, an admiring grin on his face. Isabel smiled back delightedly, for once not caring that she'd been eyed up by a kid young enough to be her son. It was a glorious day and she felt just thrilled with life in general. If a twenty-year-old kid liked the look of her with her hair rippling free and wearing a very grown-up cream double-breasted trouser suit, then Jack had to love it!

He was waiting for her beside the helipad, face creased up into a smile as she hurried to meet him.

Isabel wondered if he'd shake hands with her, anxious to maintain the pretence that this was a business meeting and they were flying to Mayo on Roark International business, especially in front of a row of helicopter company employees who probably knew his itinerary better than she did.

Instead, he grabbed her suitcase and set it down on the ground before sweeping her into a hug that crushed the breath from her body.

'Wow!' she gasped.

'Wow is right,' Jack said. 'You look wonderful.' He stood back to admire her, taking in the colour in the high cheekbones and the sparkle in her huge blue eyes. Isabel was glad she'd worn her elegant Mondi trouser suit and the multi-stranded pearl necklace that emphasised her slender neck.

She just wished she had a fortune to spend on clothes to make herself beautiful for Jack, and didn't have to rely on a wardrobe of things that were either several years old or second-hand designer stuff she'd cleverly altered and updated to make them look new.

'You look pretty good yourself,' she replied.

Jack's mouth curved into an even broader smile. 'Nobody's ever told me that *I* look good.'

She patted his pinstriped arm consolingly. 'Poor Jack. Well, you *do*.'

He did. With his wolf's hair brushed sleekly back from his forehead, the tanned face relaxed and the narrow, pewter eyes warm and tender, he looked nothing like the corporate giant who ran his company with an iron hand. Apart from the well-cut grey suit that sat beautifully on his big frame.

When they climbed into the helicopter, Isabel squeezed his arm excitedly. 'I've never been in one of these before,' she said. 'This is an adventure.'

Jack put his big hand over her slender one. 'The first of many, I hope.'

As the helicopter dipped down on the approach to Ashford Castle, Isabel leant forward eagerly in her seat to get a first glimpse of the legendary hotel.

The trip had been so quick she still hadn't tired of staring out through the giant glass bubble at the lush greenness below. Miles of sun-drenched Irish country-side had sped by underneath the helicopter's rotors; winding country roads snaking through patchwork fields, swelling into villages, towns and sprawling cities. She'd adored the trip and Jack had seemed happy to share her enthusiasm, pointing out landmarks and admiring pretty farmyards.

'I could get used to this,' said Isabel when they'd soared above a snaking queue of cars backed up in the heat.

'So could I,' he answered, with feeling.

'That's Cong,' Jack said as they passed the tiny village that nestled on the outskirts of the castle's demesne.

'They filmed *The Quiet Man* here. You know, the John Wayne, Maureen O'Hara movie?'

'I love that film,' said Isabel. 'My grandmother adored John Wayne and I remember seeing it with her one Christmas on TV . . .'

Then Ashford Castle filled the horizon, cutting Isabel off in mid-flow. It wasn't listed as one of the most notable hotels in numerous travel guides for nothing. The castle rose majestically from the distance, a sprawl-ing, craggy edifice, battlements thrusting into the sky as they had done for the past three hundred years.

Lough Corrib glittered in the midday sun. The stately oaks, beech trees and undulating private golf course splayed out in front of them, creating the perfect setting for the castle. If it hadn't been for the scattering of luxury cars parked in the castle forecourt, and the sound of the helicopter humming in their ears, they could have been stepping back in time by at least a hundred years.

Nothing much had changed since then, Isabel was sure, looking at the weathered grey stone of the castle and the elegant, neatly clipped shrubberies surrounding it.

The helicopter hovered over the moat and the pilot brought it down expertly on the helipad, blades whirring slowly as the giant bird settled on to the ground.

'Welcome to Ashford Castle,' murmured Jack.

It was like stepping back into another era, Isabel thought as she admired the exquisitely panelled entrance hall with its rich old furnishings, suits of armour and gigantic oil paintings.

Everything seemed bathed in a warm, golden light, as if candles still burned in the wall sconces. Even reception was nothing like your average hotel's, being a low desk without a 'Have a Nice Day' sign in sight.

Every inch of the hotel screamed taste, opulence and olde worlde charm. Isabel was enchanted simply walking around.

Their suite was furnished with lovingly polished antiques, an enormous carved bed and a giant brocade-covered couch so comfortable you could curl up and sleep on it. The stone-edged arched windows looked out past the ornamental gardens on to the lake at the back, where a small boat sat among the reeds, slowly making its way over the gleaming, smooth surface.

Isabel sank on to the couch, closed her eyes and leant back.

'I love this place,' she said, breathing in the scent of the flowers on the table. 'I feel like a Victorian lady who's arrived by chaise from the station and is about to command her maid to unpack her tea gowns.'

'If you were a Victorian lady,' said Jack, 'my valet would be doing the same for me, *in a separate room.* So I'm thrilled you're not Victorian. Tea, however, is a great idea. I'm starving. Come on, Milady.' He hauled her to her feet.

They sat on a vintage leather couch in a richly decorated ante-room off the very grand dining room, ate the most delicious chicken and salad sandwiches and drank fragrant coffee. Isabel hadn't realised she was so hungry until she'd taken the first bite. When they'd devoured one platter of sandwiches, they had to order more.

They talked eagerly and smiled at one another as they ate, laughing at each other's jokes and trying to figure out where their fellow diners came from. The three elegantly dressed women at the next table were tanned, well-heeled, determinedly ash blonde and could have come anywhere from Arizona to Australia, but they spoke so quietly it was impossible to tell.

The large group of men in bold checked trousers at the far end of the room had to be golfers.

'American,' guessed Jack, hearing a Boston Brahmin accent and discussions about the golf course in Augusta.

Next they did the quick version of the crossword in the paper, amazed to finish it in seven minutes.

'I've never done the cryptic one,' Jack said, sitting back on the couch once they'd figured out that blue dye had to be 'anil' because nothing else would fit.

'Me neither. Although Phil in the office does it in about fifteen minutes every morning when she's eating her breakfast.'

'Clever woman,' he remarked. 'Isn't she the one with loads of children and horses?'

'You left out loads of dogs and a rabbit,' Isabel pointed out. 'Phil is the ultimate earth mother. She adores minding small creatures. I always feel as if I could talk to her about anything and she'd look after me.'

'Is she good at her job?' Jack asked in a matter-of-fact tone.

Isabel took a sharp intake of breath. She didn't want to discuss her friends and colleagues with Jack. This had to be out-of-bounds. It would be wrong to talk about the people she worked with. Not because she'd colour his view of the ones she loved, but because she'd undoubtedly change his impression of the ones she didn't like. Tanya, for example.

'Yes, Phil is wonderful at her job,' she replied quickly. 'Let's go for a walk,' she added, finishing her last sandwich. 'I feel so full of energy and this place is so beautiful, it would be a pity to waste a lovely day.'

Back in their suite, Isabel grabbed some clothes and, in a moment of shyness, retreated to the bathroom to change. What are you like, you fool? she asked her reflection in the mirror. Some laid-back woman away with her lover you are! You can't even take off your clothes in the same room as him – how are you going to cope when it's time to go to bed? Because there's only one bed in this room, no matter how inviting the couch looks. What's he going to think of you now, running away like a scared kid to change clothes?

She splashed water on her flushed face, took a deep breath and pushed open the bathroom door.

'Isabel, look.' Jack was standing beside the window in the sitting-room, stripped to the waist. He wore only a pair of jeans, his bare tanned back tapering down from strong shoulders to lean haunches. Isabel stared at the strong muscled back and the rich dark hairs growing coarsely from his arms.

'Swans.'

She stood beside him, only mildly diverted by the sight of two snow white birds skimming across the water. She could smell the lemony scent of his bare skin beside hers. She'd known him for a month now, yet this was the closest they'd ever been. More than anything else, she wanted to touch him, to feel that warm skin next to hers, nipple to nipple in the big, old bed, with no mobile phones, conference calls or the day-to-day traumas of life to interrupt them. Just clean, fresh-smelling sheets wrapped around them and nothing between them.

'I can't wait to walk around the grounds,' Jack said eagerly. 'There's bound to be loads of wildlife out there.' He pulled on a grey sweatshirt. 'Ready?'

They walked companionably past the turrets that guarded the moat and down the rolling drive, keeping an eye out for wild creatures all the time. But apart from a surfeit of birds and a bedraggled sheepdog making his muddy way across a marshy bit of bog behind the hotel, they didn't see anything.

'Not even a rabbit,' Jack said in disappointment, putting an arm around Isabel as they trudged back up the drive.

'It's this new perfume,' she said, wiping her hot brow. 'Eau de Sweat. Animals run a mile when they smell it.'

'It's lovely.' He buried his nose in her neck, sniffing like a bunged-up person inhaling Friars Balsam. 'Lovely.

But I can't smell it properly outside. We need some shelter.'

Laughing, she let him drag her into one of the turrets, up the stone stairs and on to the top of the small battlement.

'I thought you needed shelter?' she laughed.

Eyes glittering, he pulled her close and kissed her long and hard. Isabel pressed herself against him, not caring that any member of staff could look out and wonder at the people who'd flown down in such style and were now embracing on top of the turret. It was bliss; sheer, unadulterated bliss. She could feel Jack hard against her, feel how turned on he was. Her insides turned to mush the way they always did when he held her closely.

'Let's go back,' he murmured. 'I want to lay you down on that glorious bed and make the most wonderful, exciting love to you.'

Isabel could feel her stomach fluttering with nerves as they walked back to their suite. This was it. The moment he saw her saggy thirty-nine-year-old body. The moment when only the second man in eighteen years saw it. And it wasn't even dark, so she couldn't hide her stretch marks or the cellulite that dimpled her bum by making him turn the lights off.

'I've got to go to the loo,' she said suddenly and bolted for the bathroom. Inside, she sat on the edge of the bath and took a deep breath. God, she was nervous. It was ridiculous, she knew.

After all, she was crazy about him, desperately in love with him. She wanted to be there, he'd hardly twisted her arm to make her come along. But she felt so insecure, so unsure of her own attractiveness. Even though Jack knew she was much softer emotionally than she let people realise, he still thought she was poised, calm and confident. How could he know that she'd lost all of those things and that she was surviving on just a wing and a prayer?

'Isabel, are you all right?' he asked from outside the door, his voice anxious. For a moment, she thought of all the things she *could* say – it had all been a terrible mistake, she felt too guilty about Elizabeth. But she didn't want to say any of them.

She was crazy about him. Had lain in her lonely bed at night, imagining what it would be like to have Jack beside her, his arms around her. Since she'd met him, she hadn't been able to keep him out of her head or her heart, Elizabeth or no Elizabeth. She couldn't just back out now because of an attack of nerves.

Isabel opened the door. 'Sorry. I just felt . . .'

'It's all right,' he supplied gently. 'It's scary, isn't it?'

She nodded.

'Come here,' he said tenderly, enveloping her in his arms. 'I *do* want to make love to you, desperately, if I'm honest. I want to make love to you and make everything right in your life . . . But only if that's what you want too, my love?'

Isabel half-laughed, half-gulped at his words.

'You're beautiful, gorgeous and I adore you,' he said softly, stroking her hair. 'I wouldn't want to be here with anyone else but you.'

Isabel hugged him then and as they began to kiss, all her worries about cellulite and how long it had been since she'd made love vanished. They stood like that for a few moments, enjoying the closeness and the warmth of their embrace.

'I think you need a few distractions to help you relax,' announced Jack as he pulled away reluctantly. 'Let's explore this place.'

They spent the afternoon wandering around the castle, admiring mementoes of the heads of state and long-dead European royalty who'd visited in style at the turn of the century. With the help of a guide book, they tried to figure out which bits were genuine thirteenth-century and which bits had been restored a hundred years ago.

At seven, they went to dinner in the Connaught Room restaurant. Isabel wore her silvery spaghetti-strapped dress with her hair piled on top of her head so that her elegant neck and shoulders were bare.

'You look beautiful,' Jack said slowly when she emerged from the bathroom in her finery.

After a wonderful dinner, they walked slowly around the gardens, breathing in the scent of the woods and enjoying the night air.

And when Jack carefully shut the door to their suite, Isabel was more than ready. They stood wordlessly at the end of the bed, her arms encircling his neck, his hands clasped around the base of her spine. Jack bent his head and their lips touched, slowly, like two people unsure of each other.

As their kiss deepened, their bodies responded with passion and the uncertainty melted away. Isabel felt herself bend towards Jack, her body arched sensuously into his. His strong hands caressed the small of her back through the silky dress.

'Oh, Isabel,' he murmured hoarsely. 'I've waited so long for this, it's like I've waited all my life.'

'I know,' she replied simply. 'I feel exactly the same.'

And she did. Safe in the circle of his arms, with his lips nuzzling her, she was content. Perfectly and utterly content.

She let her fingers stroke his neck lovingly, one hand

massaging the muscles of his shoulders. She loved the feel of his body close to hers. Used to being the tallest woman in any room, Isabel loved feeling so petite beside Jack. He towered over her, could clasp both her hands in one of his. He made her feel what no other man had ever made her feel: dainty and adored. It was a new and wonderful sensation.

Jack feathered kisses over her face before softly tapering down towards her neck. Tenderly, he left a trail of kisses along her collar bones, his lips hot against her skin, burning her with restrained passion.

Finally, Isabel moved so she could loosen his tie and open his shirt to rain her own tiny kisses on his neck and throat. But still he held back. It was as if he didn't want to let himself go fully, Isabel thought. As if he thought he'd scare her away.

Didn't he realise that nothing could scare her away? Not now. Slowly, and with great deliberation, she unbuttoned his shirt.

She quickly undid his gold knot cufflinks and he helped her slide the shirt over his shoulders. Then, she wrapped her arms around him, and pressed her body against his, loving the feel of his skin against her bare shoulders.

'Isabel, Isabel,' he moaned, 'you're incredible, so sensual. I'm afraid to . . .'

'Don't be,' she replied, breath warm against his satiny skin. 'I won't run away, Jack, my darling. Make love to me.'

He gently unzipped the long, silvery dress. Isabel stepped out of it, no longer nervous at the thought of Jack seeing her in her white silk panties and nothing else.

When they clung to each other, bare skin to bare skin,

she knew she'd finally come home. Jack's lovemaking erased all thoughts of everything but the moment itself. She loved him back with just as much passion and vigour until finally they slept in each other's arms.

It was a magical couple of days. When they weren't making love, they walked miles around the estate, visited the tiny, picturesque town of Cong or simply sat and talked. They talked about their childhoods, their families, and all the funny things two people in love want to hear about each other. Like favourite colours, favourite foods, first record, first kiss, first love. Jack delighted in painting Isabel's toenails, while she giggled at his attempts and made him smudge the pearly pink.

She spent an hour massaging his shoulders, kneading away the knots under his shoulder blades while he groaned appreciatively under her expert touch. Then he insisted on returning the favour, leaving Isabel limp after his hands had worked their gentle magic on her.

'Have you ever thought of taking it up professionally?' she murmured, face down on the bed, too exhausted even to move.

'Only if you're my sole client,' said Jack, starting on her feet.

On their last morning, they had breakfast in bed and, propped up against the pillows as they finished their coffee, Jack finally talked to Isabel about his wife and her drug addiction.

'I didn't even know Elizabeth was taking drugs for a long time,' he said sadly. 'That sounds stupid, I know, but I just didn't realise. Her sister was the one who mentioned it to me. She phoned me one day and said that Elizabeth was in hospital because she'd crashed the car. Then she said it was a miracle nobody else was hurt because Elizabeth had been so stoned, she could have killed someone. I was shocked.'

Isabel squeezed his bare arm. He still looked a little shocked, even at the memory.

'I had no idea, can you believe that? She'd been using drugs for at least two years and I had no idea.'

'When did the accident happen?' Isabel asked quietly.

'Eleven years ago. We'd been married for four years at the time. She gave up then, got one hell of a fright. She was brilliant about giving up. Elizabeth is very strong-willed when she wants to be,' he explained.

'But about seven years ago she started again and she hasn't stopped since. She's quite careful now, doesn't do it every night. But I can read the signs these days. The way her eyes glitter. The way she tries not to look at me in case I notice.'

'Why don't you send her for treatment?' asked Isabel.

Jack raised one eyebrow. 'She's been to half the treatment centres in the US and UK, and simply books herself out when the going gets tough. You can't make someone give up drugs if they don't want to.'

'What about the money – surely you can stop her having the money to pay for the drugs?'

'Elizabeth has her own money, her father was wealthy. I can't control her allowance.'

They sat quietly for a moment, both lost in thought about a woman with the funds to feed her drug habit and not the slightest inclination to give it up. Isabel knew it was very difficult for Jack to talk about his wife's problem. It was a measure of his feelings for her that he could open up about the subject at all.

'Do you know how she started or why?' Isabel asked.

'It was not being able to have children. I'm not guessing here, I know it for a fact. She told me one night

– screamed it at me,' Jack said wearily. 'Like it was my fault. In the beginning, we kept trying for a baby and nothing happened. I thought of having tests done when nearly two years had gone by and Elizabeth wasn't getting pregnant, but she wouldn't hear of it. All her side have large families and she was convinced it was just a matter of time. She said she was only thirty-two, it was early days. Finally, she gave up and we had the tests.'

He sighed. 'I'd almost hoped it was my fault because no matter how difficult it would have been for me to think I was to blame, I knew it was going to be worse if it was her fault. She was so *convinced* she was well able to conceive. She adores kids.'

'What happened?'

'The doctors discovered she has an abnormally shaped uterus, which meant it would be very difficult for her to carry a child to full term. And she has blocked fallopian tubes, which was why she'd never conceived in the first place. "A freak" was what she called herself when she found out. "I'm just a freak of nature, Jack." ' He massaged his temples tiredly. 'She said it over and over again.'

Isabel was shocked. 'How awful for her. She must have been devastated.' She remembered how the loss of her beloved baby had nearly destroyed her, and she'd already had two precious children. How much more unbearable would it be to be told you'd *never* have any children at all?

'She was more than devastated,' he recalled. 'She was destroyed mentally. For about a month after we found out, she went on a complete bender. She was never sober. And then, she seemed to get over it. Of course,' Jack reached over to the tray and poured them both more coffee, 'I now know that she *didn't* get better. She just switched from booze to drugs.'

'It must have been very difficult for both of you,' Isabel said gently.

'It was. But it doesn't matter so much any more, not since we've drifted so far apart. You grow harder when you live with an addict. Eventually you care less and less until there's no love left at all. I love her in my own way,' he admitted. 'We've been together a long time. But it's hard to love a drug addict, Isabel. They take all you can give, twist it and throw it right back in your face. You get tired of it eventually.'

She moved the tray and the coffee so she wouldn't upset them, and hugged him tightly. She didn't want to ask any more questions because it was obviously so painful for Jack, but as she held him in her arms, she felt a tremor of fear about what the future might hold.

Dee threw the property supplement down on the kitchen table in disgust. There was nothing there she'd like to buy – or could afford to, for that matter. House prices had gone berserk. Wearily, she got up from the table and boiled the kettle. Unfortunately, she wasn't making another coffee so she could lounge around reading the papers. She was boiling more water to clean the woodwork in the sitting-room. She'd scrubbed every part of the kitchen until her fingers were raw and resembled prawns a few hours out of the freezer. Now, after an enjoyable ten minutes' rest, she had to tackle the sitting-room and hall. What a way to spend a Friday morning off!

But there was no way she could let an estate agent put one Gucci-tasselled loafer past the front door unless she did a spot of spring cleaning first. And as Gary would undoubtedly send more notes threatening Mafia-style retribution if she didn't get the house on the market very soon, she had to get down to some serious house scrubbing.

If temper made a person clean and polish faster, Dee would have been finished much sooner because vitriolic thoughts of Gary filled her head to the exclusion of all else.

Bloody, bloody Gary! she raged, rubbing away at a bit of candle grease on the skirting board in the sitting-room. It was blue candle grease at that. Only stupid Gary would buy bright blue candles when the room was painted in warm amber colours, the settee was brown and the carpet beige. The moron never could co-ordinate anything. He only managed to wear the correct ties with each shirt because he bought every-thing matched up at Next, although he would have died before admitting it. Dee would have loved to have told everyone this. Not to mention all his other little peca-dilloes.

For a few happy moments, she envisioned a vengeful ex-files newspaper, one written by disgruntled, dumped partners where they got to spill the beans on the dumper.

'My boyfriend never put the loo seat down, picked at his toenails every evening in front of the news, and the only culture he ever consumed came from yoghurt.'

'Really? *Mine* worshipped the ground his mother walked on, believed that the sheets only needed to be changed when there was a full moon, and thought that the clitoris was one of a group of islands under French colonial rule in the eighteen hundreds.'

Dee grinned to herself and carried on scrubbing. By twelve, her leggings and T-shirt were grubby, she was hot, exhausted and hungry, and wanted to take the rest of the day off. At least she didn't have to be in until after lunch. She took a deep draught of Diet Coke and decided she'd have a long bath and a toasted cheese sandwich before ambling into the office. She was taking things out of the fridge when the phone rang loudly.

'Dee.' Jackie sounded flustered on the phone, as she always did when Tanya Vernon was prowling round the office like a leopard looking for a baby antelope that had strayed from the herd. 'Tanya's having an editorial meeting at half-twelve and she wants you there.'

'Half-twelve!' squawked Dee, thinking of her greasy hair, empty stomach and the pile of unironed clothes on the bed. 'Why didn't you phone me earlier?'

'Sorry,' Jackie said apologetically. 'It's just that Tanya only called it now. Sorry.'

'It's not your fault,' sighed Dee, sorry for snapping. 'Tell Isabel I'm on my way in but that I may be ten minutes late, OK?'

There was no point in telling Tanya she might be late – the other woman would be at the door with a stopwatch and a smirk on her face that said, 'You're fired.'

What a manipulative cow she was, Dee thought as she ripped off her clothes and clambered into the shower. There had been no mention of an editorial meeting the previous evening; everyone had been too busy concentrating on getting stuff ready for the extended Saturday edition of the paper. Tanya just liked throwing her weight around by calling an extra meeting, hoping to upset Dee – because she knew Dee had the morning off and wouldn't be in till half-two – and Isabel – because she had taken a few days' holiday and might possibly be in late. With Isabel absent, Tanya could really boss everyone around. But Isabel was sitting serenely at her desk when Dee rushed into the news-room at twelve-thirty-five, damp ringlets flying.

'I thought Jackie said you weren't due in until after lunch?' said Isabel, smiling when she spotted her deputy.

'I'm not supposed to be,' snarled Dee, 'but the Bitch From Hell called a half-twelve editorial meeting and got Jackie to ring up and summon me to it.'

Isabel's mouth formed a perfect oval. She winced. 'Oh. You're not going to believe this, Dee, but Tanya's cancelled the meeting. She and Eugene Flynn have gone out to lunch instead.'

'The cow!' shrieked Dee at the top of her voice. 'I've just raced in here at ninety miles an hour and she's *cancelled the meeting*? I'll kill her!'

'Join the queue,' said Phil Walsh, arriving at her desk carrying a pile of stationery with a cup of tea balanced dangerously on top. 'Apparently, Chris Schriber is out for her blood and rumour has it she's only gone out to lunch with Slasher Flynn to try and charm him into taking her side if there's a war between the two departments.'

'Really?' Both Isabel and Dee were fascinated.

'Go away for three days and you miss everything,' Isabel remarked.

'Tell you what,' said Emily, the pretty freelance who now worked almost exclusively for Isabel and Dee in the women's section, 'now that we've been reprieved, why don't we all go out to Magee's for a spot of early lunch and you can fill us in on the gossip, Phil?'

'Brilliant idea,' she said. 'I didn't feel like drinking that tea anyway.'

Dee was the last into the pub as she'd taken a call on

her mobile phone and had stood outside to finish it. She hated walking into pubs and restaurants talking on her mobile, it always felt so stupid and pretentious. Narrowing her eyes to get used to the dark atmosphere of Magee's, she stuck her phone into her handbag and walked straight into a tall man who'd just got up from a bar stool.

'Sorry,' she muttered, jerking backwards.

'My fault, Dee,' said a familiar voice. She peered up, eyes still not accustomed to the light in the pub. Whoever he was, he was at least six foot tall and he knew her.

'It's Kevin Mills, the photographer,' he said sardonically, black eyes crinkling up with amusement. 'I know we haven't worked together for a few months, but I didn't think you'd forget me that easily.'

'Sorry, Kevin, I couldn't see you in this light. Hi,' she said, conscious that her hair was flapping wetly around her face like rats' tails. She hadn't seen him since they'd joined forces on the story about Chazz, the singer who'd trashed his hotel room in the Conrad.

Kevin was dressed in his customary casual clothes: a tan suede shirt, jeans and Timberlands. He'd had his dark hair cut very short so it clung to his perfectly shaped skull. It suited him, highlighting the gypsyish good looks and broad shoulders that got worked out by constantly dragging an enormous camera bag around with him.

'Haven't seen you for ages,' he said, his shrewd photographer's eyes travelling slowly over her face and body.

Dee silently cursed Tanya Vernon again. If that horrible woman hadn't dragged her out of the house at top speed, she might have ironed something nice to wear instead of being caught in a crumpled indigo silk wrap shirt and a matching skirt she only wore when she was desperate.

'I'm working in the women's section now,' she explained. 'I've been promoted.'

'To deputy women's editor,' he said. 'I know. Congratulations.'

Dee couldn't believe it. How did he know she'd been promoted? Paparazzi photographers rarely got too involved with what went on in individual newspapers. They worked for themselves and preferred to keep to themselves, so the hirings and firings in the *Sentinel* wouldn't be of much interest to him, she'd assumed.

'Now that you're in management, I guess we won't be doing any more jobs together,' he said with a hint of regret.

'No,' said Dee. He had a lovely voice, pitched real low and sort of growly. She wondered who he was seeing these days? Probably some catwalk cutie.

Photographers often ended up dating models, and with a photographer as ruggedly handsome as Kevin, the models would be queuing up to date him, instead of the other way round.

He turned to go then looked back at Dee abruptly. 'We never had that drink,' he said. 'Remember, the day we did the story on Chazz?'

Dee remembered all right. She'd been flattered when Kevin had asked her if she wanted to join him for a drink in the Conrad bar. She'd nearly gone with him but hadn't, stopping herself because she was cross with Gary and didn't want to put herself in temptation's way by spending time with a man who looked like Kevin Mills.

They'd never have that drink now, not unless they

ended up on a story together, which seemed unlikely.

'Give me a ring sometime when you're free and we'll get together,' Kevin said.

Dee blinked at him. *He* was asking her out for a drink?

'Yeah, I'd love that,' she said, brown eyes as wide as saucers.

He gave her a heart-stopping grin. 'See ya round, kid.' And he was gone.

Maeve was loading up her tray with lasagne, chips and a pint glass of milk.

'I saw you talking to the delectable Kevin Mills,' she said, taking her change from the barman.

'You're not going to believe this, but he asked me out for a drink!'

'Why wouldn't I believe it?' demanded her friend. 'The way you go on sometimes, O'Reilly, you'd swear you were the Hunchback of Notre Dame's uglier sister. You look great, you silly eejit! You're the only one who can't see it. Well,' Maeve said darkly, 'you and that prat of an ex-fiancé of yours. I wish Kevin Mills would ask *me* out for a drink.'

'He didn't mean it *that* way,' Dee protested. 'It's just that we were supposed to go for one before and we didn't.'

'God, give me strength,' muttered Maeve. 'Get yourself some lunch and we'll talk about this later. I swear you need therapy, Dee. If only we could remove some of Tanya's excess superiority cells and inject them into your head, then maybe you'd both be normal. She wouldn't be so big-headed and you might start appreciating yourself.'

'I do, it's just that . . .'

'Just nothing!' interrupted Maeve. 'You're always running yourself down, Dee, and it's not good for you. If

385

you keep saying all sorts of negative things about yourself, other people will eventually believe them, even though they're not true. Lecture over. So when are you going out with Kev?'

Dee chewed her full bottom lip. 'He said to give him a ring sometime.'

Maeve raised her eyes to heaven. 'If Kevin Mills asked me out for a drink, I'd demand to know when, where, and watch him write it down in his diary. Run after him this second and pin him down.'

'Have you got your lasso handy?' asked Dee, with a smirk.

Maeve stuck out her tongue at her.

'You're an awful nag, Maeve, do you know that?' she said good-humouredly, nicking a couple of chips from her friend's plate. 'If you weren't my best friend, I think I'd have to kill you.'

'You couldn't,' Maeve replied. 'I'm too valuable to society. Who else would lay out Carol-Anne's dreadful articles in the paper or zip you into your man-pulling black corset if it wasn't me, huh?'

'Point taken.' Dee stole some more chips. 'I'm just going to get a sandwich. Don't start gossiping without me.'

Over soup, sandwiches and lasagne, Isabel, Dee, Phil, Maeve, Emily and Jackie chatted, bitched and gossiped to their heart's content, concentrating on Tanya Vernon whom they all loathed.

Everyone had something to say, apart from Isabel who sat quietly listening, barely touching her bread roll or her mushroom soup.

Dee couldn't help staring at her. Isabel's face simply glowed with some inner joy and the corners of her rosebud mouth were permanently upturned, as if she was remembering a glorious private joke.

Dee wondered if Isabel's few days off had included time spent with the mysterious married lover. It must have, she decided, watching the way Isabel's eyes misted over dreamily during even the juiciest bits of the conversation. She really was miles away.

'Apparently, Tanya has gone so completely over the departmental budget with her spending on freelances and photographers, she's going to have to eat into the news freelance budget, which is why Chris Schriber is going mad,' Phil explained, spreading mustard liberally on her ham sandwich.

'Before Tanya left, I saw her in the loo plastering on the Estée Lauder and that horrible Moschino perfume she wears,' Emily revealed. 'She brushed her teeth *and* flossed. I can imagine what she's planning and it's not lunch.'

Maeve's eyes narrowed. She loathed Tanya. 'Obviously planning to seduce Slasher in the hope he'll give her more cash to spend,' she pronounced.

'I don't know though.' Emily's cat-like eyes glowed wickedly. 'If you saw the way she canoodles with our glorious leader, Jack Carter, I'd put money on it that she hopes *he'll* turn into her sugar daddy.'

If she hadn't been reaching over for the milk, Dee wouldn't have noticed Isabel stiffen imperceptibly and blanch at the mention of Jack Carter.

So *that* was it, Dee thought, shocked, surreptitiously studying Isabel's white, stunned face. Her married man had to be Jack Carter. But he couldn't be, could he? They'd only just met and Jack was the boss, after all, *the* big boss.

Dee went through the whole thing in her head but still came up with the same answer. Isabel had looked as

if somebody close to her had died when Emily mentioned Jack and Tanya in the same breath. What else in
the conversation could have produced such an extreme
response? Hardly Tanya being over budget.

Dee pretended to eat her lunch but kept an eye on
Isabel. The other woman's hand shook ever so slightly as
she raised her soup spoon to her mouth. The colour had
drained away from her face and the rosy glow had gone.
She *had* to be having an affair with Carter, why else
would she react so violently to the conversation?

Poor thing, Dee mused. Jack Carter probably eats
decent, hard-working women like Isabel for breakfast.

Emily was getting into her stride now. 'You should
have seen the way Tanya was all over him last month
when he came to give us the speech,' she continued,
revelling in the story. 'She was practically sitting on his
lap afterwards, according to my spies. There's a big
company hooley next week in the K Club where
they're all going to be patting themselves on the back
over the smooth takeover and the rise in circulation. I
bet you a tenner Tanya gets to first base with Big Jack
that night.'

'Who do we know who's going to the K Club?'
demanded Maeve, eyes alight with glee. 'We need a
source to tell us exactly what happens. That's one story
I really want the inside track on. Do you think we could
get pictures?'

'We want the negatives,' joked Phil. 'You could barter
a great job for yourself with the opposition if you
brought them a scoop like that. The rival chairman –
married chairman, I should point out – canoodling with
a jumped up, beautiful though tarty member of staff at
a corporate do, while his lady wife does her bit for
charity . . . The *Globe* would love that story.'

Isabel was so pale she was almost white now, the veins on her neck a milky blue. Dee felt a surge of protectiveness towards her. She couldn't begin to imagine what it must be like to hear this sort of thing about a man you were secretly involved with. It must be hell.

Dee moved to let the waiter refill her coffee cup. Whatever Isabel saw in Jack Carter, it had to be serious because she wasn't the sort of woman to jump headlong into a relationship with a married man.

Isabel had to be crazy about him. She'd said so the night she'd had Dee over for dinner. She'd fallen hook, line and sinker, she'd said. Which wasn't that surprising, Dee thought, because Jack Carter was very attractive, charismatic, and had an aura of quiet strength that would make any woman fall for him. Dee could understand how Isabel felt, all right.

But she was pretty sure that Isabel hadn't bargained on hearing her married lover discussed cold-bloodedly at the office as if he was some cheating rock star with the morals of an alley cat. Nor had she thought about the implications of having an affair with a man who ran a newspaper. It was a cut-throat business. Rival papers would indeed kill for a story like that – a thought which obviously hadn't even occurred to Isabel.

If Dee had been having an affair with Jack Carter, she'd have been scared to look crossways at him in public in case some rival snapper was there with his long lens, snapping a magical Kodak moment of infidelity for the next day's front page.

She only hoped Isabel and Jack were being cautious when it came to dates and weren't forgetting that high-profile, wealthy business magnates like Carter made great story material.

'I'd love to see the sort of dress Tanya will wear to

that party,' Emily was saying. 'Liz Hurley's ultra-revealing Versaces will look like a couple of demure sacks beside it, I shouldn't wonder.'

Everyone laughed.

Dee glanced at Isabel's taut expression and knew she had to say something to get the conversation on to safer ground before Isabel's increasingly shocked demeanour made it obvious to everyone what was wrong.

'Get real, girls,' she said briskly. 'Jack Carter isn't the slightest bit interested in Tanya. He's got taste, for God's sake. She's just a complete slapper who'd sleep with her grandad and his German Shepherd if she thought it would get her somewhere. Put her in the same room as any powerful man and she'll be oozing compliments all over him like cheap musk oil.'

'That's true,' muttered Maeve.

'If Tanya was all over Jack Carter like a cheap suit at any gathering, I'm sure it was only because he was too decent to push her away,' added Dee.

'I can't imagine where she thinks she's going to get by going out to lunch with Slasher all dolled up,' Phil said. 'I think the only thing that turns him on is filthy lucre.'

'Funnily enough, that's the only thing that turns Tanya on too,' Dee couldn't resist saying.

But Emily was not to be deflected from Jack Carter. She must fancy him, Dee thought briefly.

'I hear Elizabeth Carter has a serious drug problem,' she said.

Phil glanced at Isabel.

'Mrs Carter doesn't have a drug problem,' Maeve quipped. 'She can afford it.'

'This might not be the wisest subject to talk about in the pub across the road from the *Sentinel*,' Phil reminded them in a low voice as the guffaws died down.

Gossiping in Magee's was a dicey business as you never knew which member of staff was sitting unnoticed behind a banquette, ears wiggling like Bugs Bunny's for any stray comments that could have nuclear repercussions if repeated in the wrong company.

'It's OK, I looked around when we came in, there's nobody within earshot,' said Jackie eagerly.

'I've heard she takes cocaine by the bucketload,' Emily whispered. 'They say the cops caught her once but Carter had it sorted out so she was never even charged with possession.'

'Why doesn't he book her into detox?' demanded Maeve. 'It's not as if they haven't got the cash.'

'Maybe he prefers her stoned out of her mind,' said Emily with a shrug. 'Then he can have it off with the Tanya Vernons of the world.'

Isabel's hand jerked and she spilled coffee all over the table. Everyone shoved back their chairs so they wouldn't get dripped on.

'I've got to get back to work,' announced Dee, standing up. 'You have too, haven't you, Isabel?' she asked blandly.

'Yes.' Unable to look at anyone, she got unsteadily to her feet and banged into the table clumsily. They all stared at her. Isabel Farrell was the least clumsy person they knew. She usually glided through the newsroom as elegantly as if she moved on rails.

'Isabel, are you getting one of your migraines?' asked Dee loudly. 'You shouldn't have come in if you thought you were getting one. Maybe you should go home to bed.'

Isabel glanced up, looking horrified as she realised what Dee was doing. She squeezed Isabel's hand silently.

'You poor thing. You should take the rest of the day off if you're getting a migraine,' said Phil in a concerned voice. 'I was wondering why you were so quiet during lunch. You've been doing too much. You should have taken a longer break. Three days off isn't enough.'

'I'm fine, really. Just a bit headachey,' lied Isabel, recovering her composure somewhat. 'I'll take the long route back to the office, it might clear my head.'

She walked off with Dee close behind her. As soon as they were a few feet away from the girls, she turned, her face a mass of questions.

'How did you know?'

Dee put a finger over her mouth.

'Not in here,' she murmured. 'The place is probably bugged.'

Outside, Isabel leant against the pub wall tiredly.

'I had to say something to put them off the scent,' Dee said quietly. 'Emily would be on to you like a shot otherwise. Not that she'd rush off and tell people, because Emily adores you for all the work you've given her and how nice you've been to her. But the more people know, the more chance your secret has of getting out. And believe me, Isabel, this would be the office gossip of the century.'

'How did *you* know?' asked Isabel, ashen-faced.

'I saw your face when Emily started talking about Jack and Tanya and I thought of what you told me that night at your house. I reckoned either you'd suddenly remembered you'd left the gas on at home this morning, or you were upset by what she'd said. I didn't need to be Einstein to figure out why. Actually,' Dee said, 'I *still* don't know for definite. You're having an affair with Jack Carter, aren't you? Or am I totally off beam?'

'I am.' Isabel sighed. 'I'm not very good at this,' she

said weakly. 'I'm too transparent.'

'Not a good poker player,' agreed Dee. 'But you'd better learn how to be from now on. People are always going to be talking about Jack Carter and if you look as if you're going to faint every time it happens, someone will cop on. I'm not going to tell anyone, you know that,' she added reassuringly. 'But you've got to be careful.'

Isabel still looked drained. Dee took her by the arm. 'We should walk back to the office. Do you want a bar of chocolate? It always helps me when I've had a shock.'

Isabel shuddered. 'No, I couldn't eat a thing.'

Dee grimaced. 'That's the difference between you and me,' she said. 'When I'm upset, I head straight for the fridge or the sweet shop, one or the other. You can't eat. That,' she patted Isabel's arm kindly, 'is why you're reed thin and I'm on the cardboard diet.'

'The cardboard diet?' asked Isabel, fascinated in spite of the knot in her stomach.

'Yeah. Cardboard. Whenever you feel hungry late at night, you get a bowl of whatever fibre-rich breakfast cereal reminds you most of cardboard and you eat a huge bowl of it, soaked in hot water. It's horrible but filling.'

Isabel burst out laughing.

'You're a tonic, Dee,' she said. 'And a real friend. Thanks.'

'It was nothing. You'd do the same for me,' she said firmly. 'If you want to talk about it at any time, you know where I am. But please be careful.'

They reached the *Sentinel*.

Tanya's silver Mazda was back, Dee noticed with a shiver. Obviously the planned long, liquid lunch with Slasher Flynn had backfired and become a short, sharp meeting and now she'd be like a bear with a sore head for the rest of the afternoon.

As they climbed the stairs to the newsroom, Dee considered saying something to Isabel about not being up to Ms Vernon's customary tantrums that afternoon. But Isabel was back in her dreamworld, going into the ladies' loo with her mind a million miles away.

Dee engaged in a little daydreaming herself. Kevin Mills had asked her out for a drink. That was the second time. What did he mean by it? Did he mean it in a friendly, platonic way? Did he know that she and Gary had split up?

Or, she thought morosely, there could be a third reason. Kevin himself might be planning a career away from the front line of paparazzidom and he might think that the recently promoted Dee was in a position to give him other work, like fashion shoots or cushy portraits. She sighed. Perhaps that was it. He wanted to bend Dee's ear about his plans and thought that a couple of Jack Daniel's and Cokes would have her eating out of his hand.

It didn't take long for Tanya to appear, breathing fire and brimstone. Dee had only just arrived back at her desk when she heard Tanya's steel-tipped stilettos tapping out an angry beat as she marched down to the features end of the newsroom.

'I want to talk to you,' Tanya snapped.

The unnerving thing about Tanya, Dee thought, looking up at the editorial director apprehensively, was that she was breathtakingly beautiful even when she was mad. But because she was such a fiercely confrontational person, you stopped noticing her beauty within two minutes of meeting her.

Today, the hard little face was even more spiteful

than usual. Tanya's almond-shaped eyes glittered with temper but didn't detract from the symmetry of the perfectly shaped glossy pink mouth and Slavic cheekbones set off by a flawless complexion.

She stood beside Dee – Tanya never sat when she could tower over someone and intimidate them with her height – and started an angry tirade.

'I want to know why you've been hiring freelances for jobs you could perfectly well do yourself?' she snapped. 'It's sheer laziness. We're way over budget and we've got to cut back. I don't want to see any more expenditure on unnecessary items. That article on the TV soap star from *Coronation Street*, for example. You could have done that yourself instead of getting Emily to write it.'

'I couldn't,' Dee defended herself nervously. 'Isabel was away, I was busy with the fashion pages *and* the interview piece. There was no way I could fit another interview in. The actress was only in Ireland for one day. It was take it or leave it.'

'You should have left it then,' said Tanya. 'I'm trying to run these departments efficiently and cost-effectively and you're ruining my good work. I want you to consult me in future before you hire anyone to do any job.'

Dee goggled at her. If that was the case, she'd be in and out to see Tanya every five minutes because the women's department was incredibly understaffed. She and Isabel relied totally on a panel of freelance journalists, which meant they hired people on the spur of the moment every single day.

Dee was about to point this out but Tanya had swooped on to another subject, like a hawk spotting a well-fed rabbit. 'And as for spending money on that beauty salon spy thing, that's a waste of time!' she snorted derisively.

'Now that the government has tightened up regulations surrounding hygiene in beauty salons, I thought it would be a good idea to see if the salons are actually putting the new rules into practice,' explained Dee, eyes darting towards the newsroom door to see if Isabel was on her way back from the loo. Tanya would certainly shut up when she appeared. Isabel, where are you? she prayed.

'Oh, please,' Tanya drawled snidely. 'I suppose you only came up with that idea so you could get free treatments yourself?'

Dee was stunned. 'Of course not,' she said, horrified. 'I wouldn't dream of it!'

'Gimme a break,' Tanya snarled. 'You think you've got it all sorted out, don't you, Dee? You don't want to do any work. You simply want to sit on your big fat backside and get the freelances to do what you should be doing, while you swan off and get your blackheads squeezed. You think you've walked into a cushy number with this job, don't you?' She jabbed one manicured finger in the direction of Dee's chest.

Unable to speak, she sat there bewildered. She couldn't believe all the appalling things the other woman was saying to her. She felt as if she'd been suddenly transported back eighteen years to Saint Veronica's Secondary School, with a gang of kids cruelly taunting her about her weight. Dee had always frozen up then too, unable to speak from shock and misery.

'All you lot who've been here for years think the *Sentinel* is a cushy number, a retirement home for crap journos who couldn't get a job anywhere else. But it's not.' Tanya leant forward until her face was inches away from Dee's, so that she could smell the sickly acidic smell of her breath. 'People like me are going to drag this paper kicking and screaming into the future, with a circulation you wouldn't even dream of. And you and your lazy ways aren't going to stop me.'

'I don't want to,' mouthed Dee ineffectually.

'You better not!'

With that, Tanya straightened up and marched off in the direction of the editor's office. Feeling like she'd just gone ten rounds with Lennox Lewis, Dee sat in her chair, utterly dazed.

Why does she hate me so much? she asked herself tearfully. What have I done to make her so vile, malicious and horrible to me? Dee couldn't come up with a reasonable answer. There was no point in remembering Maeve's opinion that Tanya hated everyone and picked on people because she was a bully and could get away with it. That didn't make Dee feel any better.

Because Tanya didn't pick on Maeve, she picked on Dee. And on Jackie, when Isabel and Phil weren't around. She picked on the people who wouldn't answer back, and she got away with it. Now she'd done it again. And Dee had sat there, like a mute and let Tanya slander her senseless. Dee had said nothing. Not one word.

Hot tears of humiliation burned beneath her eyelids. Once again she'd been used and abused, and she'd let the bully do it. Practically given her permission for it. Coward, coward, coward!

Isabel hurried into the office, looking a little more relaxed than she had ten minutes earlier. Dee longed to tell her everything, all the appalling things Tanya had said, about how she was sitting there on her 'fat behind' and how lazy she was.

But she couldn't. Tanya had always been snide and attacked Dee by subtle means up to now. This full-frontal assault was something new. Isabel would be utterly shocked to learn that Dee had taken all those remarks without answering back.

Isabel was brave, she had self-confidence and self-respect. Dee didn't want to be diminished in her eyes by revealing just how lacking in those qualities she was.

'Tanya was here, giving out yards about us hiring freelances,' she said in a small voice. 'She says we should be doing the work ourselves.'

'Nonsense,' Isabel said briskly. 'We're so understaffed that we wouldn't have a paper at all if it wasn't for the freelance contributors. That woman is a menace. She wants us to suffer when she blithely spends the budget elsewhere. Where is she?' Isabel looked around inquiringly.

'She went into Malley's office,' Dee said.

'Right.' Isabel marched off to do battle.

Dee watched her silently.

Five minutes later, Isabel was back, her mission successful. 'Tanya is all talk,' she sighed. 'She caves in like a shot if you push her. Don't let her bully you about her problems, Dee,' she advised. 'If she hadn't overspent, she wouldn't be hassling us now.'

'You're right,' Dee said in a quiet voice. She sat at her desk and tried to write, but she kept typing dyslexically, all the words coming out backwards because her concentration was shot and her hands were shaking. She worked quietly all afternoon, not wanting to leave the safety of her desk in case she bumped into Tanya again. But eventually she had to go to the bathroom.

There was no sign of Tanya as Dee walked past the conference room where the other woman routinely held court when she wasn't at her desk in the newsroom. In the ladies', Dee put on some lipstick to bring back some colour into her face. She was nearly out of her favourite colour, a rich coffee shade. She'd go shopping later. Buying cosmetics always cheered her up. Some of that new waterproof mascara would be nice too, and maybe bubble bath. Passion fruit aromatherapy stuff. Feeling somewhat happier, Dee went back to the newsroom and nearly collided with Tanya, who was coming out of the editor's office.

When Tanya walked by, she smirked knowingly at Dee, a smirk that said, 'You didn't tell anyone that I called you a fat, lazy lump, did you?'

Dee felt sick to the pit of her stomach. She'd failed again. Somehow she'd let Tanya get the upper hand and unless she did something about it, Tanya would ruthlessly exploit that power for all it was worth. What was the point of vowing she'd never let someone like Gary walk all over her again when she let someone do it every day in the office?

Why didn't Tanya pick on Maeve? Dee knew the answer. It was because her friend wouldn't take it. One moment of speaking to Maeve like that and Tanya Vernon would be flat out on her Prada-clad back with Maeve's fist imprinted in her face. Well, she'd get a verbal lashing anyway.

Tanya respected people like Isabel, Phil and Maeve. She didn't respect Dee one little bit. Why would she, Dee thought bitterly, when Dee wouldn't even stand up for herself? You're a spineless coward, O'Reilly, she told herself.

Isabel barely noticed how quiet her deputy was all afternoon. Her mind was full of Jack Carter, the discussions about him and Tanya, and the fact that Dee had so easily cottoned on to the identity of Isabel's married man.

She didn't know whether to be relieved or not about the latter. She knew that Dee wouldn't tell a soul but the whole incident had given her a scare, let her see what she was really taking on.

Everyone had spoken so coldly about Jack, as if he was bound to be having flings with every woman who threw herself at him. Isabel didn't know what to think. Did they all know something she didn't? And how could she ask without attracting raised eyebrows and knowing stares?

Isabel looked out of the window blankly. She was stunned to find that she still felt unsure about Jack. The wonderful warm feeling in her belly after their glorious holiday in Mayo had disappeared totally, to be replaced by the gnawing emptiness to which she was used. The emptiness of being with a man who was as faithful as a cat in a tuna fish factory.

CHAPTER EIGHTEEN

Robin looked at her watch ostentatiously and sighed, the sort of sigh a mother was supposed to hear from about twenty feet away.

Isabel, sitting a mere foot away with a much-needed cup of tea in front of her, ignored it. Her feet ached from traipsing around Dublin's city centre looking for new clothes for Robin and she wasn't about to be blackmailed into getting up from the coffee shop seat a mere five minutes after she'd sat down.

With another great sigh, Robin shoved her half-empty glass of Coke away from her. Isabel went on sipping her tea, while Naomi delicately bit into her cream bun. Isabel hadn't bought her half the clothes she'd got for her demanding elder daughter, but Naomi still sat there happily, nose buried in a teen magazine. *She* hadn't moaned and complained for the entire day, sulking when she couldn't find the exact type of black PVC schoolbag she wanted. It was Naomi's turn next, Isabel decided firmly. The next hour would be dedicated to buying clothes for *her*. Isabel wasn't going to make a distinction between her two daughters.

'Susie will be waiting for me outside Oasis!' said Robin in exasperation after another minute's silence.

Isabel gave her a grim stare. 'She won't be. It's at least another ten minutes until we have to leave. I'm not budging until then. Thanks to you, we've spent my Friday off walking miles looking for exactly the right clothes that won't disgrace you before your pals. Now I'm going to enjoy this chance to sit down.'

'I can meet her on my own,' Robin said crossly. 'It's only a bit up the street from here. I'm hardly likely to get mugged between the Jervis Centre and Oasis . . .'

'You won't,' Isabel interrupted. 'I want to meet Susie to find out who's picking you up from the disco tonight – her mother or me,' she added, enunciating each word crisply and dangerously.

'Suit yourself.' Robin, recognising that tone of voice, turned her attention to the numerous carrier bags strewn on the floor around their table. Her face lit up as she examined the two tiny strappy tops and the fake leather jacket she'd bought in Miss Selfridge's, courtesy of a generous gift cheque from her father.

Isabel would murder David when she saw him. It was a ridiculous sum of money to send to a teenager, especially when he'd insisted Robin spend it on 'fun stuff' for herself, instead of boring old school clothes being the implied message.

Isabel had just bankrupted herself buying boring old school clothes for both girls as the autumn term started in ten days.

Not that something so mundane would ever occur to David. Oh, no. He probably thought school uniforms came free instead of being so ridiculously expensive you'd assume John Galliano had designed them. Isabel simmered as she thought of all the things she had to say to him. The only good point was that she wouldn't have to wait very long as he was arriving in Dublin first thing the following morning, to spend the weekend with Robin and Naomi.

Apart from its providing her with the opportunity to tell him some home truths, Isabel dreaded it. The few times David had visited the girls previously, he'd only been able to stay in Dublin overnight, which meant he'd spent a day with them and she hadn't set eyes on him. On this occasion, he wasn't flying back until Monday evening, so he'd be dropping in and out of the house all weekend, picking up the girls and dropping them off whenever it suited him. He'd even had the temerity to ask could he stay in Eagle Terrace, which Isabel had flatly refused. Her mother had raged at the idea when Isabel had inadvertently told her.

'That wastrel deserves to be shot, and now he wants to stay with you?' Pamela had shrieked down the phone. 'The nerve of the man! The sooner you get divorced from him the better.'

Isabel couldn't agree more. Unfortunately, whenever she thought about divorce these days, she thought about Jack Carter and how desperately she longed for him to get divorced from Elizabeth. She thought of nothing else. They'd never even discussed it, of course. How could they? Jack was crazy about her, she was sure of it, but he'd never mentioned the word 'love'. And Isabel loved him. Madly and desperately. But all she could do was wait.

'Mum, it's nearly time!' said Robin impatiently. Isabel finished her tea. In this mood, Robin would drive both her and Naomi insane.

Susie stood outside Oasis, hopping from one foot to the next and shivering like a whippet in a skimpy T-shirt that wasn't suitable for a chilly late-August day. She had goosebumps on her arms and had her enormous fake suede handbag clasped to her chest as if it was a hot water bottle. Isabel idly wondered when her daughter and her friends would realise it was more sensible to arrange to meet *inside* a shop than outside it.

'Hiya, Susie!' cried Robin, magically transformed from sulky teenager to smiling, merry one. She pushed her dark blonde hair back off her face as she delved into the carrier bags to show off her bounty.

'Fake leather!' squealed Susie in delight, the cold forgotten. 'Rob, you babe!'

They giggled in unison as Robin ripped the tags off the jacket and put it on to be admired.

'Susie, what's the story about the disco tonight?' asked Isabel, who didn't want to stand outside all day.

'My mom can't pick us up, she's got a dinner party. She says she knows it's her turn but she's sorry,' Susie said, without taking her head out of Robin's Miss Selfridge bag.

Great, thought Isabel glumly. Another person with a social life. That means Dogsbody Farrell will have to stay awake till half-one in the morning to ferry home four hot, sweaty, excited teenagers even though it isn't her turn for the disco car pool. Marvellous.

'Well, I'll see you all at half-one outside the gate,' she said firmly. 'Don't be late.'

'We won't. Thanks, Mum,' said Robin, eyes shining as if she hadn't just spent the past two hours in a vicious sulk.

'And lend Susie your new jacket, she's freezing. Come on, Naomi,' Isabel said, putting on a bright, forced smile for her younger daughter. 'What are we going to buy *you*?'

As she drove home two hours later, shattered and broke, Isabel thought about Friday nights in the lives of women in love with married men. Tonight, Jack was at one of his wife's charity fundraisers, the sort of party where the only people who didn't arrive in limos were the waiters, and where only the finest wines, champagnes and hors d'oeuvres were served.

She, on the other hand, would be sitting at home in leggings and a sweatshirt as she flicked through the channels and contemplated doing the ironing. Thanks to Susie's mom and her dinner party, Isabel couldn't have a couple of G & Ts and go to bed early either. She'd have loved to be going to a dinner party, to get dressed up and talk to new people instead of watching TV on her own. But going anywhere without Jack would be horrible – so horrible that it was easier to stay at home and think about him instead of go out and look sadly at the other happy couples who could afford to be seen together.

This affair thing wasn't all it was cracked up to be. If she wasn't so in love with Jack Carter, there was no way she'd have been able for it.

At home, she rustled up a speedy dinner of stuffed chicken breasts for herself and Naomi and wondered what people had done before Marks and Spencer made ready-cooked meals.

'This is lovely, Mum,' Naomi said, eating twice as fast as she normally did. 'Can I go out to the park? We're playing rounders tonight.'

'Sure. But be in by half-seven,' Isabel said, kissing her on the cheek. 'The evenings are getting darker and colder.'

With Naomi gone, the house seemed very empty. Isabel washed the dishes and wondered if Jack would phone her. He'd said he would. Then again, with a glamorous party to go to, he might forget.

He *could* have phoned while she was shopping, although Isabel had told him she'd be gone most of the day.

What if the only chance he'd had to phone had been while she was out? She imagined the phone ringing plaintively in the empty house, while she, who longed for it to ring now, had been stuck in rush-hour traffic day-dreaming about Jack.

Depressed, Isabel decided the only solution was to clean the place. She'd been letting the housework slide and with David destined to drop in and out all week-end, she didn't want him to think they were living in squalor. Not that it mattered to him, she thought testily.

So far, he hadn't contributed one penny to the girls' upkeep and she hadn't heard a word about The Gables or whether he'd managed to sell it or not. She could have had a red bulb outside the door for all he seemed to care.

Forget David, she told herself sternly. You're on your own now. Being broke is just part of separated mother-dom.

Just then, a picture of Elizabeth Carter slipped into her mind. Elizabeth in a seductive red dress that had probably cost more than Isabel's salary, pre-tax. How could she compete with that? Jack wouldn't ring. Why would he?

Isabel fought the impulse to run upstairs and take one of her anti-depressants. She'd managed to cut down the number she used by over half and planned to stop taking them altogether within the next couple of months. Falling in love with Jack had given her the boost she needed to give them up. And falling in love with Jack sometimes made her need them more than ever . . .

Isabel took a deep breath and started on the kitchen, methodically cleaning the worktops, hob and sink. Then she washed the kitchen window until it sparkled and mopped the floor. The back garden was still a disaster zone but the pretty china pots of pink and white geraniums she had arranged on the windowsill meant your eye was distracted from the weeds. Or so she hoped.

It would be just like David to peer outside and make some fatuous remark about getting a man in to do the back garden, when she didn't have the spare cash to do any such thing.

When the kitchen gleamed, she attacked the hall and stairs. Would she hear the phone over the roar of the vacuum cleaner? she wondered anxiously.

An hour and a half later, the small house shone and Isabel was dog tired. There was nothing like house-work to take your mind off emotional problems, she thought with satisfaction. Five minutes of encounter-ing balls of dust under the furniture and in the corners soon had you cleaning manically – along with idly wondering how much those overhaul cleaning firms charged for a day-long, reclaim-your-home-from-the-dust session.

Glancing at her watch, Isabel saw it was nearly time for the start of a new TV mini-series set in the forties. She loved programmes set in the past and felt like getting immersed in somebody's fictional life. It might make her forget her own.

Upstairs, she washed the dust from her face and carefully reapplied her moisturiser. You're getting old, Isabel, she told her reflection. You'll be forty next month. Forty!

She gazed at her face morosely, not seeing the fine

bone structure that gave her an elegant, classical air. She didn't notice the clear, ocean blue eyes but saw only the fine lines around them and the dark shadows that only a vat of Touche Éclat would camouflage.

When the phone rang, she thought it might be Robin, ringing to say they were all going to a different disco and could Isabel pick them up there? It wasn't. It was Jack.

'Hello, Isabel.'

Her heart leapt at the sound of his voice.

'Jack.' She said his name with pleasure. 'I hoped you'd ring.'

'I phoned several times but nobody answered. I had to talk to you.'

'I was hoovering,' she explained. 'I thought I'd be able to hear the phone but obviously . . .'

'I miss you,' he said, voice low and deep. 'I wanted to talk to you so badly all day. I knew you were out this afternoon but I kept phoning, hoping you'd be back early.'

'Darling.' Isabel sat on her bed and smiled. 'I spent the whole day thinking about you, too.'

'I wish I could see you tomorrow.'

'But you've got to go to the K Club,' she said miserably. The executive conference in the plush Kildare hotel, where Emily, Phil and Maeve had joked that Tanya Vernon would put the moves on Jack.

What was it Emily had said?

I bet you a tenner that Tanya gets to first base with Big Jack that night.

She didn't believe it but the little bud of jealousy had already sprouted in Isabel's heart, sending spiteful shoots into her subconscious. Tanya and Jack, it said. Jack and Tanya . . .

'I'm leaving very early in the morning but I'll be back on Sunday by lunch,' he said. 'Could I see you then?'

Isabel wanted to curse. 'I'm having lunch with my mother,' she wailed. 'She invited me because the girls will be with David. What about later?'

He groaned. 'I've got to fly to London at half-three.'

Neither of them said anything for a moment. Adultery was worse than co-ordinating Middle Eastern peace talks, Isabel thought bitterly. When one side could manage a date, the other one couldn't. Perhaps he didn't really want to see her. Perhaps it was more convenient this way.

'I'm back in the office on Monday,' she said, her voice cooler. 'You can phone me there.'

'You mean, I can't phone you at home?' he asked, suddenly anxious.

'It's difficult,' she said slowly. Two could play at that game. 'Robin is so very curious and if she answers the phone, she's going to wonder who the hell this strange man is who's suddenly phoning her mother up.'

'Isabel, my darling.' Jack's voice was like a caress, touching her over the phone line. 'I want to see you so badly, you must believe that, but this weekend is impossible what with the conference. I'd come over early tomorrow but I'm flying down with Malley McDonnell, Eugene Flynn and Tanya Vernon.'

Isabel took a sharp intake of breath, sick with envy.

'Can I see you on Tuesday?' he was saying.

'I don't know. I might be busy. You know, parties to go to, conferences to attend,' she said off-handedly to hide her hurt. He was flying down with Tanya! How could he? Had the girls in the office been right?

'Don't be like that, Isabel,' he pleaded. 'I know this is difficult for you. Christ, it's impossible for me . . .'

She could imagine him running a hand through his hair impatiently and for a brief second she weakened. Poor, darling Jack. She loved running her fingers through his hair.

Then she imagined Tanya Vernon sitting limpet-like beside him in the helicopter, where Isabel had sat on their trip to Ashford Castle.

She envisaged Tanya's hot little hand snaking along Jack's thigh at dinner; her giving him a half-lidded, tempting look from those cold, calculating eyes. A come-and-get-me look. Men were all the same. They never could resist temptation. David had never even tried to.

Thinking of him, her heart hardened. He had made a fool of her for years; it wasn't going to happen again.

'Phone me at work, Jack,' she said in the brusque tone she used with Robin when she was playing up. 'And remember to enjoy yourself, won't you? I'm sure you'll find Tanya great company.'

She hung up and immediately regretted sounding so bitter, so much like a spoilt child.

Damn! But she couldn't help it. She felt so jealous, so scared and hurt. Had Jack any idea what it was like to sit at home and long to be with him with all her heart? Did he know how it felt to think of a man morning, noon and night, and know that he was with someone else? No, was the answer. And he never would.

The phone rang again, shrill and insistent. Isabel stared at it but refused to pick up the receiver. Inside, she wanted to. Desperately. She wanted to hear Jack's voice telling her he was crazy about her and that he understood how difficult it was for her.

The phone stopped ringing. A minute later, it started again, the shrill sound drilling into her skull. Isabel wanted to lie down on the bed and sob her eyes out.

'Mum, I'm back. Sorry I'm late. I was batting.' Naomi was home.

'Hi love, I'll be down in a minute,' Isabel called downstairs. 'I'm just answering the phone.'

She picked it up hesitantly.

'Isabel, what's wrong?' Jack asked. 'You're not worried about Tanya, are you? That's ridiculous.'

'Why is it ridiculous?' she asked hotly. 'It's common knowledge that Tanya Vernon is madly keen to get you into bed . . .'

'Common knowledge?' yelled Jack in astonishment. 'It's the first I've heard of it, Isabel. Tanya's an ambitious junior executive I've barely spoken to before this and I'm only giving her a lift in the helicopter because I want to talk to Eugene Flynn who said he was driving her down to the conference.'

'Oh.' Isabel felt incredibly foolish.

'And if Ms Vernon fancies the idea of sleeping her way to the top, then she's in the wrong company. Eugene Flynn has no interest in women unless they have a bank balance bigger than his, and I'm not interested in hustlers like her. Why would I want to look twice at Tanya when I've got you, Isabel? Don't you understand that? Don't you trust me?'

'Yes,' she said slowly, feeling awful. She'd let her own insecurities mess things up dreadfully.

'Shit!' Jack cursed. 'I wish I could see you tomorrow, Isabel. I hate leaving you like this. I know it's impossible for you. But I want you to understand that I've always been totally truthful with you, about how I feel for you and . . .' He hesitated briefly.

'We can't talk about this over the phone. I must see you, soon.'

There was no mistaking the urgency in his voice or the emotion.

Isabel felt very emotional herself. She hadn't meant to say she didn't trust him. It was just so difficult. Where did she stand? Why had she fallen for him so hard when there didn't appear to be any future for them?

'If you don't want me to phone you at home over the weekend, Isabel, please phone me on my mobile?' he begged.

She grinned for the first time. 'You *can* phone me at home,' she relented. 'I was just being stupid, saying you couldn't.'

His voice relaxed too, changing from slightly strained into the rich, warm tone she loved.

'I'll get you back for that, you brat,' he warned. 'Which is the worst place for tickles – your sixth rib or your feet?'

'You tickle my feet and you're dead!' she joked back. 'Jack, I'd better go. Naomi has just come in and she'll be upstairs in a moment. I'm sorry about earlier . . .'

He cut her off. 'Don't say sorry, Isabel. You've absolutely nothing to be sorry for. I know it's horrible seeing me waltz off to this party without you. I'd hate it if it were me waiting at home, thinking about you with lots of strange men ogling you. So I can understand perfectly. But you've no reason to be jealous, honestly.'

'I'm glad, really glad. I'll talk to you tomorrow, then. 'Bye, Jack.'

'Goodbye, my darling.'

Isabel stared at the phone for a long time before she left the bedroom. She'd nearly done it when she'd said goodbye. Nearly said, 'I love you.' She did love him but she couldn't say it, not when he'd never said it, not when it would have meant so much to her if he had.

If he didn't love her, where was their relationship going? She laughed mirthlessly. Even if he *did* love her, where was their relationship going?

Further along the road of a double life that would include long illicit lunches and stolen nights in five-star hotels?

All she wanted were cosy evenings in, waking up in the same bed in the morning, eating breakfast in companionable silence, sharing their lives, normal lives.

But he belonged to another woman and after the things she'd been through, Isabel knew how much it hurt when the man you loved strayed . . . Or did she really mean that any more? She realised with a jolt that she'd stopped thinking of Elizabeth in quite the same charitable way. Elizabeth was like a spoilt child, a creature who lived entirely for pleasure and put more money up her nose than would feed a small African village for a month. Isabel wasn't sorry for her. In a way, she despised her for wasting her life. And she hated Elizabeth for being married to Jack.

Isabel loved him, adored him: it was every woman for herself.

'Did you have a nice time, Naomi?' she asked, taking a few deep breaths to calm herself as she went downstairs.

After a sleepless night where she wondered over and over again if Jack loved her or not, Isabel finally drifted off to sleep as dawn was creeping in at the bedroom window. She awoke to the sound of Robin's yells.

'Dad's here! He's here!'

Isabel groaned and massaged her head, feeling a headache of Krakatoan proportions rumbling at the base of her skull.

'Let him in and make him a cup of tea,' she croaked, peering round her bedroom door. 'I'll be down in a few minutes.'

She stumbled into the bathroom. A hollow-eyed face stared back at her from the mirror over the sink. This hadn't been part of her plan.

She'd intended to be at the door to greet David, beautifully dressed, perfumed and carefully made up, with her handbag and car keys in her hand so he'd realise she was on her way out and that he wasn't being invited into 12 Eagle Terrace.

Her night of anxiety over Jack had completely screwed up that plan. Now she looked like she'd been in bed with the 'flu for a month and it was going to take more than ten minutes to salvage her sleep-ravaged face. Which would give David plenty of time to snoop around downstairs, letting his overexcited daughters entertain him while he idly riffled through electricity bills, her briefcase and anything else personal he could lay his hands on. Blast!

'Naomi, take your dad into the sitting-room,' Isabel yelled with a flash of inspiration. She'd barely finished decorating it and there was nothing even vaguely private there apart from swatches of curtain fabric.

'He says he's fine here, Mum,' replied Naomi.

Double blast!

Isabel jammed her shower cap on – she couldn't meet David for the first time in months with her hair plastered to her head – and had the quickest shower of her life. Ten minutes later, she went downstairs as calmly as she could, dressed in a cream trouser suit David had never seen before. She'd quickly applied all her war paint and a generous spray of Ô de Lancôme. She didn't care that it looked odd to be so formally dressed at half-nine on a Saturday morning. She wanted to look businesslike so that David didn't even attempt to mess her around. For, as she admitted to herself with that final shaky breath before she pushed open the kitchen door, she *was* nervous. Seeing your husband for the first time after such an acrimonious split wasn't going to be easy.

'David, hello,' she said to the back of his head.

He turned from looking out of the kitchen window and smiled broadly at her. Naomi and Robin flanked him, Robin clinging to his arm while Naomi made coffee.

Isabel had forgotten how tall and lean he was, how graceful he looked in casual clothes like the pale chinos and rich green polo shirt he was wearing now. The light coming in at the window burnished his dark hair to a rich shade of chestnut.

His hair was shorter and his face thinner but otherwise he was still the same old David: totally relaxed despite the tension of the whole situation. Isabel had often felt that he'd have made a master criminal. Now she was sure of it. His face was as untroubled as if he'd been away for a few days on business and had just returned home to an ecstatic welcome. He didn't look like a man who was seeing his estranged wife for the first time in her new home, a home where he wasn't particularly welcome.

'You look wonderful, Izzy,' he said warmly.

Isabel steeled herself to remain self-possessed. She threw him a calm, poised look and ignored the comment.

'What are your plans for today?' she asked.

David ruffled Robin's hair playfully, not noticing that she'd braided it into intricate little rows and that ruffling messed it up.

'Dad!' She ducked and immediately started smoothing it with her hands.

'Sorry, Robin,' he said contritely. 'For that, you get to pick what we do today. What do you say – bowling and burgers?'

She shot him a scathing look and Isabel smothered an impulse to laugh. It was about time that David discovered that his precious little kitten had grown into a teenage lioness during the summer holidays, a lioness always ready to unsheath her claws.

The Robin who'd have been happy to spend Saturday bowling and eating burgers was nothing but a memory. The new Robin wanted to be taken shopping or into elegant restaurants for her lunch so she could pose up a storm.

'I'd love to go bowling, Dad,' said Naomi eagerly.

Ever the peacemaker, Isabel thought fondly.

'For God's sake, bowling is for kids,' snapped Robin.

'Come on.' David put an arm around both of them and drew them together. 'I don't want my two beautiful girls fighting.'

Robin was mildly pacified at being described as beautiful.

'We can go bowling if you like, Naomi,' she conceded, 'if we can go to the Clarence for lunch. U2 own it and all the movie stars stay there. A girl from school went there for dinner and said she saw Leonardo DiCaprio in the bar. Please, Dad?'

'Of course, Robin. Anywhere you want.'

'Well, that's settled,' Isabel said briskly. She glanced at her watch and started picking up her briefcase and papers. 'I've got to head into the office for a meeting and then I've a lunch to go to. What time will you bring the girls back this evening?' she asked David.

'I don't know . . . nine, ten?'

'Be more specific,' she said, trying to keep the hostility out of her voice but failing.

'Are you going out tonight?' he inquired silkily.

'That's none of your business,' she snapped. 'I expect the girls back by eight.'

''Bye, Mum.' Naomi came over for a hug but Robin walked out with a blithe, 'See ya.'

David waited until the girls had left the kitchen before he spoke. 'I'd hoped we could have a drink sometime this weekend, Izzy. We've got things to talk about.' He looked at her with big, hangdog eyes.

Isabel would have loved to have told him to take a running jump, that she had no plans to talk to a man who hadn't even mentioned maintenance for his daughters. But she couldn't do that. He was the girls' father and he was right – for once. They *did* have things to discuss.

'Tomorrow evening when you bring the girls back. We can go out for an hour,' she said firmly. By Sunday night, she might be able to cope with him on a one-to-one basis.

'Great. I'll look forward to it,' David said breezily. He walked past and kissed her on the cheek before she'd had time to step back. Furious with herself for not seeing it coming, Isabel wiped her cheek angrily as he sauntered out of the room, calling to the girls. The front door slammed and she was alone, wondering whether she was far too overdressed to do her supermarket shopping.

The leg of lamb was, naturally, perfectly cooked. Pamela Mulhearn was an excellent cook. Floury potatoes, minted peas, broccoli spears and carrots just the right side of *al dente* all tasted beautiful and were a testimony to Isabel's mother's habit of getting up before eight on Sunday mornings to put lunch on before she went to Mass.

'I don't hold with staying in bed late at the weekend,' she always said.

But Isabel simply wasn't hungry. Not wanting to hurt her mother's feelings, she pushed everything round her plate and tried to hide the uneaten lamb under a couple of bits of potato. She'd had another miserable night thinking about Jack and couldn't face food.

Breakfast had been a cup of coffee and half a slice of brown toast on her own because David had picked the girls up at eight to take them to Wexford for the day.

Isabel felt weary and lonely without them. A proper Sunday lunch was her idea of hell at that moment.

'More peas, Isabel?'

'No, thanks, Mother,' she said, hoping her mother wouldn't notice her largely uneaten meal. But for once, Pamela didn't seem interested in making her daughter eat up every morsel of food. She was animatedly talking about her new project, a charity clothes shop nearby where she'd started working.

'They simply don't know how to run that place. As I said to your father, they've organised it all wrong. There's no proper book keeping system, they never know how much stock they have in at any time and they don't even have an iron in the back to run over items that come in crumpled!'

'I didn't know you knew much about stock control and book keeping, Mother?' Isabel said with interest.

'I did some book keeping in the doctor's office where I worked before I married your father,' Pamela answered. 'And you only have to watch one of those real-life television shows about shops and businesses to see that stock control is vitally important. I don't know how that shop keeps going.'

Seeing that her mother wasn't interested in her lamb consumption, Isabel gave up pretending to eat and sat back holding her glass of white wine.

'Who's running the shop?' she asked.

'Mrs Jewison used to run it and she was very good apparently but she broke her hip so Mrs Flaherty took over. And, believe me, that woman shouldn't be in charge of a supermarket trolley.'

Pamela's face was animated and happy, eyes glittering behind her bi-focals as she explained her plans to turn the tiny one-time dry cleaner's into the most successful charity shop on the east coast. Her enthusiasm was infectious. The normally gloomy Sunday lunchtime atmosphere was replaced by something approaching gaiety.

Isabel's father wasn't chewing his lamb with a wary expression on his face in case he made the wrong sort of noise and had Pamela demanding to know what was wrong with her cooking. She was transformed, Isabel thought with amazement.

There were no disparaging remarks about the stringiness of the meat or the deterioration of the butcher's shop now that 'nice Mr Hill has gone and left it to that untalented, gormless son of his.'

Pamela ate heartily and even drank some of the white wine Isabel had brought, though she rarely drank anything other than sherry.

'I think we need to be more choosy about the clothes we accept,' she was saying. 'Otherwise shoppers with money will give us a wide berth because they'll think we stock nothing but junk. And we'll get better quality clothes if we get a better quality of customer. The richer ones will give their old clothes to us, so we'll get all the good labels.'

'You're really enjoying it,' Isabel said encouragingly, pleased to see the positive change in Pamela. 'You should have done something like this years ago.'

Her mother looked slightly shamefaced. 'I know. I regret not getting more involved. People were always asking me to help with the Vincent De Paul and the local charities. But I wanted a proper job, do you understand?'

Isabel shook her head. 'Not really.'

Pamela sighed. 'I was proud, you see. I always thought I was so clever and that a job where they'd take *anybody*, like in a charity, would be beneath me. That I was better than that. So I wouldn't help out. After all those years, I now find it's fun and I'm good at it. And,' she smiled ruefully, 'that charities need clever people just as much as proper businesses do.'

For the first time in years, Isabel leant over and gave her mother a spontaneous hug. Her mother wasn't a huggy person, she wasn't keen on affectionate kisses and tactile people. Even now, she held on to Isabel woodenly, not quite sure what to do with her arms. But it was still a hug.

'Well done, Mother,' Isabel said warmly. 'I'm so proud of you. If anyone can make that charity shop work, you will. I know it.'

Pamela beamed, the smile lighting up her normally stern face. She patted her perfectly coiffed frosted curls. 'I hope so. Now why didn't you eat your lunch?'

The day passed with painful slowness. Isabel felt lost without Naomi and Robin. She tried to occupy herself by sorting out the garden but it was such a hopeless task, and pulling up weeds simply gave her more time to think about Jack and their relationship. A relationship that was going nowhere fast.

As she stuck her trowel into the hard, compacted soil, determined to uproot a particularly resilient dandelion, Isabel kept seeing Elizabeth Carter's face smirking at her. Elizabeth . . . rich, privileged, idle – well, not that idle, Isabel conceded. She did a lot of charity work. Although she couldn't somehow see Elizabeth standing in a small charity shop sorting through second-hand clothes with Pamela telling her what to do in the background.

Elizabeth's sort of charity involved big parties, designer dresses, people telling her she was 'Wonderful, darling!' and the odd line of coke in the bathroom afterwards. And Jack by her side, handsome in his dinner jacket, eyes crinkling up when somebody made a joke.

Isabel stabbed the trowel into the heart of the dandelion. Bloody weeds!

David arrived back with the girls at half-eight. Isabel forced herself to say nothing about their being home an hour later than he'd promised. Instead, she calmly got her jacket, told Robin there was a pizza in the freezer if she or Naomi was hungry, and told David he could follow her in his car to the Harbour Bar. That way he could drive back to his hotel afterwards without going back to Eagle Terrace.

In the Harbour Bar, Isabel found them a seat in a corner and let David go off to buy her a white wine spritzer.

The pub was bustling, jammed with locals who'd been going there for years, and with tourists who liked the cosy atmosphere of a genuine Irish bar. A pretty girl with lustrous black hair and a pair of trousers practically sprayed on to curvy hips eyed David as he stood at the bar ordering the drinks. Isabel watched her watching him and knew that David, even though his back was turned to the girl, was aware he was being watched. He'd always had a sixth sense for things like that.

The girl nudged her female companion, whispered something and they laughed – high girlish laughs. David turned his head a fraction so that he could see where the laughter was coming from. The girl smiled shyly at him and he smiled back.

Isabel looked away, not wanting to be caught watching. God, it was like a French farce. She was watching her husband flirting with another woman on an occasion when he'd brought her out for a drink to try and reconcile their differences. Because she was sure that's what it was all about. David thought he could wangle his way back into her life, even if on a part-time basis.

Why else had he pumped Naomi for information about Isabel's social life the last time he'd visited, and why else had he been so very pleased to find out that 'Mummy doesn't go out much' as Naomi had innocently put it?

He placed the drinks on the table and took a deep draught of his Guinness.

'I needed that,' he said, wiping his mouth with his hand. 'It's been a hectic weekend.'

'What did you want to talk about?' Isabel said abruptly.

'Us, the girls, the house.'

'There is no "us", David. You know that. As for the girls, I'd like to know when you're going to start paying maintenance for them? It's been over six months and you haven't paid a penny. I'd also like to know what the position is with The Gables? Do we still own it, and, if so, when are you selling it? I need the money.'

He reacted to her bluntness in his usual way. 'Hold on, Izzy. You're always in such a rush. Let's not talk about selling The Gables yet . . .'

'Why not?' she said.

'Listen, Izzy.' He put down his glass and moved closer to her so that his knees were almost touching hers under the small table. 'The new agency is doing well. Freddie reckons we'll be in the black in a few months and then we'll be in the money. I'm still holding out for that villa in Portugal. You know, the one we talked about? Down the coast from Lisbon so we're near the city but still in the countryside . . .'

'David, you still don't get it, do you?' Isabel asked in exasperation. 'This isn't about a second home in Portugal or about how well your ad agency is doing. Frankly, I don't give a damn about that so long as you agree to pay maintenance for your daughters.

'This is about *us*. You want us to be a couple again and it just isn't going to happen. Understand?'

She'd raised her voice as she was speaking and the couple sitting at the next table glanced in their direction curiously. Isabel flushed; she hated being watched.

'You're certainly not beating around the bush,' David said flatly.

'No. There's no point.'

'Listen . . .' He tried to take her hand in his but Isabel pulled it back rapidly. She knew his tricks.

'Isabel,' he said, his voice wheedling.

She knew he was serious when he started calling her 'Isabel'.

'Listen to me,' he repeated, without any attempt to touch her. 'Don't cut me off, please. I've been thinking about you so often recently, wishing I could turn back the clock. We had some great times, didn't we? Remember this time last year, when we all went to Scotland for a week?'

Isabel remembered the utter peace of the cottage they'd taken for five days, and the glorious two days they'd spent in Edinburgh. They'd been – on the outside, at least – like any other family, two parents and two daughters. Not one struggling parent with one sweet daughter and one difficult one.

David reached for her hand and this time Isabel didn't jerk it away.

For a fleeting moment, she thought how nice it was to sit in a pub with a man and not have to worry about who saw them. David didn't have to rush home to his wife; *she* was his wife. Then she remembered what it had been like being his wife. The arguments over bills; the crazy, money-making schemes; his ability to shut out reality and live in fantasy land; her inability to live like that.

And she thought of Jack, darling Jack whom she loved so much. It was time she told him, she decided. The next time she saw him, she'd do it. He could make his decision then about their future, but at least she'd have been honest with him. And if he couldn't cope with hearing that she loved him, that was his problem. Isabel would walk away, agonising though it would be, knowing she'd done the right thing.

'We've been through so much together,' David was saying softly. 'I can't believe you can simply throw all that away, Isabel. Can you?'

His eyes were beseeching, almost irresistible in his boyish face.

Isabel gazed at him, wondering how she could have

even momentarily listened to a word of his nonsense, and resisted. 'I'm not throwing it all away, David, it's already gone. We're separated and I want to get divorced.'

This time he snatched his hand away. 'You can't be serious?' he said shortly.

'I'm perfectly serious. I'd like us to be grown-up about this, for our sakes and for the girls'. They don't need their parents at each other's throats.'

David sat and scowled into his pint.

'We should try and sort out issues like visiting rights before we see our solicitors. It'll make things easier,' Isabel said, matter-of-factly. 'They could visit you for half term, it's a long weekend in October. Or,' she paused, hating the very idea, 'if that doesn't work out, perhaps you'd like to see them for Christmas. I *do* have them all the time, I suppose. Although I'd miss them so much . . .'

'I don't think Christmas would work out,' he said quickly. 'I've . . . er . . . already fixed something up.'

Isabel lost her temper again.

'I can't believe you came here, begging me to come back to you, when you've already made arrangements for Christmas,' she said angrily. 'How did you plan to tell me? Were you going to announce it after we'd got back together? "Sorry, Izzy. Sorry, Robin. Sorry, Naomi – I'll be away for Christmas. Your presents are under the . . . oops! Forgot to buy presents. Still, there's always next year." '

'Don't be so vicious, Isabel,' spat David. 'It doesn't suit you. The Christmas trip is business, and it'll probably be as boring as hell. How else are we supposed to build our client list if we don't keep them happy and give them what other agencies give them? That's what the Jamaican trip is all about. I don't know why you've never understood that. Why you've never been able to support me when it comes to business trips.'

'You're right, David,' she said coolly. 'I never could support you. Not when I knew that the trips were eating up the company's profits – profits our family could have benefited from if they weren't being frittered away on expense account lunches for clients who grow obese on five-star cuisine.'

'You're so short-sighted, Isabel,' he said scathingly. 'You don't understand at all.'

'On the contrary,' she replied, pushing her unfinished drink away from her, 'I'm being far-sighted. Our marriage is over, David. If we can't have a civilised discussion after fifteen minutes in each other's company, it's hardly likely we'll manage a few more years of blissful togetherness, is it? Now, let's talk about The Gables. I want to sell up.'

On Monday morning, Jack was on the phone at half-nine. Isabel had only just arrived in the office and Jackie stood beside her waving a sheaf of phone messages.

'I've missed you so much,' he said.

'Really?' Isabel said in a bright tone, conscious that Jackie stood about six inches away, writing another message on her notepad.

'Morning,' muttered Phil, dumping her briefcase on to her desk beside Isabel's. 'Malley wants us in an editorial meeting in five minutes, I met her on the way in.'

Isabel nodded. 'I'm afraid I can't really talk right now, er . . . Susan,' she said into the receiver.

'*Susan?*' laughed Jack. 'Couldn't you have pretended I was a man, at least? Juan, Philippe, Dirk . . . something

426

masculine, something to make them all wonder who your exotic lover is?'

Isabel bit her lip to stop herself giggling. 'That would be inappropriate under the circumstances, *Susan*, but if you want, I'll take out an advert in the paper – we get a staff discount – and mention your name over and over again!'

'Great idea,' Jack said suddenly. 'That's exactly what we should do. I'm sick of this clandestine assignation stuff. Anyway, as you obviously can't talk right now, I'll ring you at home tonight. 'Bye, darling. Have a good day.'

Isabel was still too stunned by thinking about the implications of what he'd said to pay very much attention at the editorial meeting.

The rest of the day turned out to be so hectic that she had no time to sit quietly and wonder what Jack had really meant earlier. It was only as she drove home to Bray that evening, exhausted after a ten-hour day where *everything* had gone wrong, that she went over the conversation in her head again.

I'm sick of this clandestine assignation stuff.

So was she. But what had he meant by that? Was he going to leave Elizabeth? Or was he merely being flip, fed up with the bizarrely one-sided conversations they were forced to have when other people were present?

At home, Robin had defrosted and started re-heating a home-made aubergine lasagne, while Naomi had laid the breakfast bar for dinner. Wonderful smells emanated from the oven and Isabel, who hadn't had time for anything more than a yoghurt for lunch, realised she was hungry.

'Sit down and I'll make you tea,' offered Robin solicitously.

Isabel suspected that her elder daughter's weekend with her father had not been a huge success. But she knew better than to probe her about this. When Robin felt like talking, she would.

After dinner, she disappeared up to her room and Naomi and Isabel watched TV. When the phone rang, Isabel was too tired to move from the chair and let Naomi run into the hall to answer it.

'It's for you, Mum,' she said a moment later.

Isabel sank on to the bottom step and picked up the phone.

'You sound tired,' Jack said. 'Bad day?'

'Exhausting. Well, it wasn't just today,' she admitted. 'It was the whole weekend. It was such a strain. David and I went out for a drink,' she said tiredly, pulling the pins out of her chignon. She ran her fingers through her hair to settle it.

'You did?' Jack asked tautly.

'Yes. He said he wanted to talk about the girls but he got on to some long-winded story about the business and a villa in Portugal he wants to buy for us.'

'A villa in Portugal?' Jack's voice was raised now. 'I hope he was joking? I thought he was bankrupt?'

'Not according to him,' Isabel remarked. 'I don't understand it. But talking about a villa in Portugal when he doesn't have a bean is pure David.' She raised her eyes to heaven. 'He's talked about buying a place there for years. He loves it and we went there for holidays a lot. The idea was pie in the sky, naturally. He always spent every penny so there was never enough even for necessities, never mind second homes.'

'What do you think about all this – the villa?' Isabel recognised more than a hint of jealousy in his voice and she smiled to herself.

'I'm not sure,' she said playfully. 'I've always fancied the idea of a holiday home somewhere hot, somewhere you could wear nothing but a bikini all day long. And I love Portugal.'

'Oh, I see.' Jack sounded crestfallen.

'David can buy all the villas in Portugal he wants,' she said, relenting, 'I won't be visiting him there. He was looking for a reconciliation, actually. That's why he asked me out. But I told him I wanted a divorce.'

'Thank God,' said Jack with relief. 'For a moment, I thought you were trying to tell me you were going back to him?'

'I know, I'm sorry. I thought you knew there was no chance of that, Jack?'

'I do,' he muttered. 'But . . . hell, I don't know, Isabel. I suddenly felt so terrified that's what you were saying: that you'd had enough of me, enough of the secrecy and lies.'

'Don't be silly,' she said softly. 'I wouldn't look at another man, don't you understand that?'

'I know, thank you.

'I'll tell you what,' she said, wanting to cheer him up, 'let's go out tomorrow night, to dinner? We can go somewhere discreet . . .'

'Mum, aren't you off the phone yet?' shouted Robin, thundering down the stairs. 'I want to ring Susie.'

Isabel sat bolt upright on the bottom step. 'Er . . . just a minute, Robin, I'm talking to Phil. I've got to go,' she said apologetically to Jack. 'I'll see you in work tomorrow. We can talk about it then. 'Bye,' she added in a falsely bright tone.

There was no point in continuing the conversation with Robin hanging on her every word, but as Isabel hung up, she felt utterly miserable. She hated all the subterfuge, hated lying to Robin and pretending to be talking to someone else on the phone. Why couldn't she and Jack have a normal, out in the open relationship like other people? Was that too much to ask?

CHAPTER NINETEEN

'You'll enjoy yourself, you know you will.' Maeve reached around the back of her computer and switched it off. 'Fiona would love you to come and you know she always gives amazing parties. What were you planning to do tonight?'

'Go to the gym,' said Dee, leaning against her friend's desk. 'I've got to go to three aerobics classes a week and I missed Wednesday's.'

'There's no point in being incredibly fit and thin and living till you're a hundred if you have such a boring life you never go outside the front door,' Maeve pointed out.

'After one week of aerobics, I'm hardly incredibly fit and thin,' Dee answered. 'But I've lost five pounds.' She ran a hand over her hips, wondering if she looked noticeably slimmer or if she was the only person who was aware of the difference.

'You look great,' Maeve said encouragingly. 'A veritable man trap. Which is all the more reason to come out tonight and flirt with all the hunky single men at Fiona's birthday party.'

They left the office and walked out to the car park together, Dee weighed down by the armloads of papers, supplements and freelance articles she planned to read as she had the weekend off.

'Is Karl going?' she asked. 'I don't want to play gooseberry.'

She didn't say that she couldn't face an evening as the only single girl at a party chock-a-block with besotted couples, all talking softly to each other and sharing couplesy jokes and Eskimo kisses. She couldn't bear an evening like that.

Maeve unlocked the door of the classic Triumph Herald that cost her a fortune in garage bills. 'He's going to be late because he's working until half-nine tonight, so I need moral support. Please come with me?' she pleaded. 'It'll be fun. You know what'll happen if you don't, Dee. You'll come back from the gym and be bored rigid sitting in front of the box all night.'

That was true, Dee realised. A low-cal fish meal with a green salad, two glasses of Californian Grenache and, as a special Friday night treat, a ninety-five-per-cent-less-fat chocolate mousse awaited her, along with the TV guide and a mediocre detective film she wouldn't have dreamed of watching if Gary had been around. Another thrilling Friday evening in the life of Dee O'Reilly, glamorous journalist incarnate. If she really felt healthy, she might slop on a bit of that sauna face mask, pluck her eyebrows and paint her toenails. Whoopee!

'I'll go,' she said suddenly. 'Will we drive or get a taxi?'

Dee noticed him long before he saw her. She and Maeve had just arrived at the party and Dee had followed her friend down the stone steps into the vast kitchen when she spotted him. Dressed in head-to-toe faded denim, he lounged against a giant fridge, eating ice cream and looking at the only two other people in the room, who were kissing each other with the passion of teenagers on a first date.

He was blond, with a boyish, finely sculpted face, sea blue eyes and a full-lipped mouth more suited to a girl than a twenty-something man. But his athletic, lean-hipped figure looked anything but feminine. Maybe it was the after-effects of the bottle of Frascati she and Maeve had shared when they'd met up at Maeve's house earlier. Or maybe it was because she'd lost five pounds and felt pretty fabulous in her black silk skirt and dainty, caramel-coloured crochet cardigan, but Dee felt like behaving recklessly.

And as she watched the young man's laughing mouth curve around the ice cream, for a moment Dee wished she were that chocolate-covered ice lolly.

'Dee, Maeve! You made it at last!' shrieked their hostess, appearing from the door into the garden with bits of twig in her hair and a handsome black guy in tow.

He was at least a foot taller than Fiona who, dressed in black leather jeans and a spray-on purple rubber T-shirt, with auburn hair extensions rippling down her back, looked more like an MTV heavy metal show presenter than a thirty-year-old advertising agency executive.

'Hi, Fiona. Sorry we're so late. We got held up. But we brought booze. And . . .' Maeve held up a parcel wrapped in flowery paper, tied with a big pink bow '. . . your birthday pressie!'

'You darlings!' Fiona squealed with delight. 'Thank you. I hope it's sexy undies! Everyone else has given me crystal fruit bowls and house stuff, or perfume I don't like. Now, I must introduce you to Fabio. He's the best birthday present a girl could have. For once, my hopeless brother got me something I really needed – a man!'

She dragged him out from behind her and wrapped both arms around his jeans-clad waist happily.

'Fabio, meet Dee and Maeve. Maeve and I were at college together, Dee works with Maeve and they shouldn't be allowed out together!' she trilled, obviously tipsy.

'Hi.' Fabio grinned. 'Pleased to meet you,' he said in a soft accent.

'You're American?' said Dee in surprise. She'd assumed that with a name like Fabio, he had to be Italian.

'My mom loved Italy,' he explained patiently as he picked bits of twig out of Fiona's bird's nest hair. Dee wondered what they'd been doing in the back garden.

'My dad was overseas when I was born, so she got to name me before he got home. Otherwise, I'd be Luther.'

'I much prefer Fabio,' growled Fiona, sliding one hand into his jeans pocket. 'My brother Conor's back from South America,' she explained to the girls. 'He was on a college expedition in Ecuador, Chile . . . well, *everywhere*. He arrived home yesterday with four of the guys from the expedition, including Fabio. Joey's upstairs trying to sleep in my room because he's jet-lagged, and keeps screaming at us to turn off the music. I think Che is in the conservatory rolling joints as big as carrots. And Daryl . . .' She peered over Dee's head towards the fridge where Mr Ice Cream was licking his fingers lasciviously. 'Daryl is eating us out of house and home. I keep trying to get him to go upstairs and join the party, but he says he likes hanging out in the kitchen. I think he's shy.'

'Where's Daryl from?' asked Dee, trying to sound as

nonchalant as possible as she eyed up the handsome, golden-haired guy.

'Texas,' Fabio said. 'We called him Cowboy on the trip.'

Perfect name, Dee thought, taking another quick peek in Daryl's direction. All he needed was the Stetson – he had everything else, from the big buckle on his leather belt down to the dusty brown cowboy boots.

'Fiona, I think I'll put this in the fridge,' Maeve said, holding up a bottle of white wine.

Fiona wasn't listening. She was staring raptly at Fabio. 'And what was *your* nickname?' she purred.

'Come on, Dee,' urged Maeve. 'You've got the beer.'

She pushed Dee in the direction of Daryl, who had finished his ice cream and had his head in the fridge trawling for more food.

'He's a bit of all right, isn't he?' Maeve whispered in Dee's ear as they admired Daryl's muscular figure.

'You can say that again,' she murmured, unable to take her eyes off him. She loved the way his narrow hips gave way to broad, strong shoulders, the way the denim shirt stretched over his muscles.

'He's gorgeous.'

'Go for it, then,' Maeve hissed. 'There's only one way to get over a man, and that's to get another one, pronto. A quick fling with Daryl is just what you need, my girl.'

'Don't be daft, he wouldn't look at me . . .' began Dee.

Suddenly, Maeve pushed the bottle of wine into her arms and rushed off. 'Must go to the loo,' she said quickly before disappearing upstairs.

Dee stared blankly at Daryl's rear end for a moment until he extricated himself – and a large tub of potato salad – from the fridge.

'Well, hell-o,' he said in a soft, Southern drawl as he straightened up, turned round and looked at Dee appreciatively. 'What would your name be, honey?'

Dee went weak inside. The way he said *honey* sounded like he'd just suggested they strip off and do something wild and sexy on the floor. Something that was illegal in the Bible Belt. Something that involved strawberries, ice cubes . . .

'My name's Dee,' she gulped, unable to think of anything else to say.

He held out both golden-skinned hands towards her. 'I'm Daryl.'

Was he looking for a hug? Dee thought, bewildered.

'Let me take some of those cans and put them in the refrigerator,' he said instead.

'Of course.' Flustered, she looked down and realised she was still holding Maeve's six-packs and a bottle of wine.

When the beer was safely stowed, Daryl cracked open a bottle of Budweiser and offered it to Dee. 'Thanks,' she said, even though she rarely drank beer.

He opened a second one, took the potato salad and a fork and sat down at the table.

'You want some?' He gestured with his fork.

Dee shook her head.

'Why don't ya'll sit down and keep me company while I eat?' he said. 'I don't know anyone at this party, and I feel kinda lonely.'

Dee dropped on to the chair beside him, making the kissing couple look up briefly from their session. Upstairs the party was obviously in full swing. She could just hear Hot Chocolate's 'You Sexy Thing' being played. It was probably being belted out at full blast but the old stone walls of Fiona's Georgian cottage meant you were insulated from upstairs noise when you sat in the basement kitchen.

Maeve and all her college buddies were upstairs, chattering, drinking and dancing, while she was downstairs with a complete stranger and a couple of youngsters who were obviously stoned out of their minds and in danger of getting lip lock. Was she mad? Dee decided that she must be.

She sipped her beer and watched Daryl. He was all sun-toned colours – the blunt-cut hair that fell over one eye, the hairs gleaming on his slim, finely muscled arms, and the skin visible through the open-necked denim shirt. Like a honey-skinned child who'd played outdoors in the sweltering Pan Handle sun from birth, and probably thought sun cream was for sissies.

Daryl plunged a forkful of potato salad into his mouth, displaying ultra-white teeth and a pink tongue. Dee had never seen anyone eat the way he did. He didn't just eat – he devoured the food, making the entire procedure look like the most sensuous experience she'd ever witnessed.

God, he was sexy! An utterly laid-back, effortlessly gorgeous cowboy, who could – and probably did – have anything he wanted in life. She was very attracted to him. It was intense, exciting and utterly mad. It felt strange to be openly flirting with a man. She still felt so *attached*. At the back of her mind, she half-expected Gary to appear from upstairs, take one look at Daryl, and drag Dee out of the party, lecturing her all the way home on the dangers of talking to strange men.

Dee, really! How many times have I told you? You're too friendly for your own good. You're as undiscriminating as a Labrador puppy. Who knows what that man must have thought? He could have believed you were chatting him up, do you realise that? I can't leave you alone for a second . . .

Daryl regarded her from sleepy blue eyes.

'You don't talk much, Dee, do ya? I like that in a woman, I gotta admit.'

She quivered inside.

'Sure you don't want some food?' He proffered the fork in her direction, a soft pulp of salad glistening on it.

Dee, who was on the sort of murderous diet which meant she could only eat Lean Cuisines, low-fat cheese, rice cakes and fruit, drooled. And not only for what was at the end of Daryl's fork.

She leant over towards him, opened her mouth slowly and ate the potato salad. Her eyes never left his.

'My kind of girl, all right,' said Daryl, letting his face slide into a big, sunny grin.

Dee gave him her hottest come-hither look and was gratified to see it was having the desired effect. He held out another forkful of food and she ate it, even more slowly this time.

Then she panicked. What the hell was she doing? She was supposed to be moping at home, thinking about her ex-fiancé and sobbing whenever she heard a sad song on the radio. Which was what she'd done for the past two and a half weeks. Instead, she was flirting with a stranger at a party, licking his fork like she was auditioning for a part in a Thai sex show.

And he could be doing this for fun, teasing the big fat girl and making her think he fancied her until – *kapow!* he left with some willowy eight-stone goddess who'd been in the bathroom for most of the party putting on more eyeliner.

Daryl grinned at her and winked.

'I love your outfit, honey. It sorta moulds you. Whaddya call that stuff?'

438

Dee beamed back at him. 'Crochet.'

Oh, what the hell? She could sit here all evening, nervous as a turkey at Christmas, wondering if he *really* fancied her or if he was only *pretending* to fancy her for some nefarious reason – and totally miss out on having any fun.

All she ever did was over-analyse things and where did it get her? Nowhere. So stop analysing. Maybe this sex-on-legs cowboy actually fancied the knickers off her and she'd waste her opportunity wondering why.

After all, they could be keen on bigger women in Texas. And Gary wasn't here. He was in London, probably propped up on a barstool in Wardour Street, ogling girls and telling everyone that leaving Ireland was the best thing that had ever happened to him.

'So . . . what do you do, Daryl?' Dee asked brightly.

'Ah'm studying South American Culture in college in New Mexico,' he said, taking a slug of beer. He wiped a trace off his mouth with the back of his hand and Dee gazed, transfixed. He might as well have said he was studying cows on Pluto.

'What about you?' he asked.

'I'm a journalist.'

He looked interested. 'That's cool. Whaddya write about?'

'I work in the women's section of a daily newspaper, so I write about everything and anything. I do features, health reports, interviews . . .'

'Bet you're real good at it,' Daryl said, giving her his lazy smile once more. 'Bet you're real good at everything.'

There was no mistaking what he meant, 'specially as he'd taken one of Dee's hands in his and was paddling the inside of her palm with calloused fingers.

'Did you get those in South America? she asked nervously, staring at his work-roughened hands. 'Tell me about it?'

Daryl needed another beer for the story. While he opened the fridge, Dee fretted. She should have asked him about his college degree but was too uptight to ask him anything about South American culture. She didn't know the first thing about South America and didn't want to appear stupid. Then again, he hadn't asked her anything particularly rocket-scientist-clever about her job.

Daryl lounged back into his chair, one denim-clad knee nudging Dee's thirty-denier-covered one companionably.

'A college professor I know in San Antonio was working with this film maker and they wanted to make a film on religious ceremonies in South America. It was all low-budget stuff so they needed volunteers. Hell, it was the chance of a lifetime, so I signed up,' he said in his drawling voice. 'It wasn't a paid vacation or anything like that, but it was pretty exciting all the same.'

An influx of partygoers arrived in the kitchen, noisily demanding booze and crisps.

'Fiona said she had Hula Hoops stashed away somewhere,' said one girl, pulling open cupboards frantically. 'I'm ravenous.'

'Daryl, you eaten everything on the premises yet, huh?' said a voice and Dee looked up to see a cigarette-slim dark-eyed man sink into the chair beside Daryl.

'Dee, honey, meet Che, one of our expedition leaders, a man who knows South America like the back of his hand. Che, meet Dee.'

He stretched across the table, took Dee's hand and kissed it, Spanish-style.

'Pleezed to meet you, *cara*,' he said, flashing black eyes giving Dee the once-over.

She glowed with delight. 'Lovely to meet you, Che.'

She was enjoying this evening. It sure made a change from the ones she'd spent with Gary's cronies where the only terms of endearment used were when someone – usually Dee – was required to hit the shops for more beer and Pringles.

'You got the munchies, Che?'

'Yeah. Real bad.'

Daryl handed him the potato salad container and the fork. He took Dee's hand in his and stood up.

'Whaddya say we have a dance, Dee? I was tired earlier but I'm gettin' my energy back now. I musta been hungry.'

Thanks to her newfound enthusiasm for exercise, Dee was able to run up the stairs with Daryl without disgracing herself by panting *too* heavily at the top.

Upstairs, it was noisy, crowded, and the air was scented with the dual party smells of booze and smoke. People sat on the stairs or on the floor, chattering loudly and drinking out of bottles, mugs and the odd glass. Dee peered into the gloom of the sitting-room looking for Maeve but couldn't see her friend anywhere.

'Come on.' Daryl pulled her into a large room which had been turned into a make-shift disco, complete with flashing lights near the sound system and a big mirrored ball on the ceiling. Nina Simone was on the CD player; fragrant non-cigarette smoke filled the air and couples mooched slowly around the centre of the room, locked together as they danced to the slow, melancholy music.

Dee was determined not to notice that most of the dancers, Daryl included, were about eight years younger than she was. It was Fiona's party after all, and if she, just two years younger than Dee, liked having twenty-something-style parties, complete with dope heads and snogging couples now that she was in her third decade, then Dee wasn't going to get upset about it. What was that saying? You're as old as the man you feel.

Daryl was around twenty-four so Dee would have to be twenty-four for the night too. She wasn't going to tell him she was thirty-two and had just become disengaged.

'I love this kinda music,' he said, sliding his arms around Dee and gently pulling her close to him. He wasn't as tall as Gary. In fact, he was the perfect height for Dee. Even wearing high heels, her head was on a level with his biceps, so she snuggled close to his chest while he buried his head in her hair and inhaled deeply.

'You sure smell nice. You feel pretty nice, too,' he drawled.

Dee forgot about feeling fat and frumpy. She forgot about Gary and how she still sobbed every time she thought about how cruelly he'd destroyed her self-confidence and their relationship. She forgot everything except the sensation of being held tightly in a man's arms. A man who clearly fancied her rotten. After nearly three male-free weeks, it was a wonderful feeling. Daryl's shirt felt soft against her cheek and she closed her eyes contentedly as she leant closer to him. He smelled of apple shampoo, fresh male sweat and some sort of cologne she didn't recognise.

They swayed gently together, not really dancing, just trundling around slowly to the music. Daryl's arms held her close, one hand under her crochet cardigan, stroking the small of her back through her silky camisole. Nina Simone gave way to Billie Holliday huskily asking where her lover boy was.

Dee grinned silently. An hour ago, she'd have wanted to cry into her Budweiser on hearing that song. Now, locked in an embrace with a handsome, albeit young, Texan demigod, she didn't give a damn about her ex-lover boy. She merely hoped he fell off his London barstool and sprained something.

'Dee!' hissed a familiar voice.

She opened her eyes to see Maeve, circling the dance floor slowly with Karl, giving her an energetic thumbs up sign.

'Way to go, babe,' she mouthed encouragingly.

Dee grinned back, feeling like a teenager at her first dance. Karl swivelled his head round and winked bawdily.

After an hour of dancing, drinking copious beers and holding CD covers up to the light to see what track to play next, Dee was feeling very tipsy and needed to sit down. Daryl agreed.

He looked down at her with sleepy, blue eyes.

'Shall we sit this one out?'

The couple on the bench in the crowded conservatory hooched up so Dee and Daryl could squeeze into the last space available. 'Squeeze' being the operative word. Their thighs were jammed together like cellophaned packets of chicken breasts in the supermarket and neither of them could move their arms.

'Hold on,' Daryl said. He wriggled around, grabbed Dee by the waist and lifted her effortlessly off the seat before plonking her on his lap. She was stunned. He'd actually lifted her up and hadn't given himself a hernia!

And he wasn't gasping as though he'd been flattened by a steam roller, the way Gary always had when space had been tight and she'd ended up sitting on his lap.

'I'm not squashing you, am I?' she asked anxiously,

convinced that once Daryl knew how heavy she really was, he'd go off her like a shot. She vainly tried to lever herself off him so he wouldn't feel her full weight. 'We can always go back to the kitchen. There's sure to be loads of room there.' She got one foot on to the floor and with a hand on the back of the bench, could just about hoist herself off Daryl . . .

'Relax, honey. This is perfect. Cosy, dontcha think?'

He swept her arm from the bench and held her body so her entire weight was on him and her feet could no longer reach the floor. He settled her on to his lap and enveloped her in strong arms.

When his lips closed on hers, Dee thought her heart would explode, it was beating so fast. Surely he could hear it, beating furiously because she was so hopelessly excited?

But Daryl didn't appear to have heard any such thing. Instead, he kissed her leisurely, the pool-drain lips melting against hers as though they'd been made for each other. Dee kissed him hungrily in return, letting her tongue play with his while his mouth devoured her the way he'd devoured his ice cream earlier. His lips scorched hers, burning every place they touched.

He tasted slightly salty with a hint of peppermint mingled with beer. Dee tried to remember if she'd brushed her teeth before going to the party, but soon gave up all rational thought as Daryl kept kissing her, his mouth insistent.

One hand cradled her head, pulling her closer to him, while the other explored the contours of her breasts through her cardigan. She couldn't feel the callouses on his hands, just the touch of his fingers brushing her bare skin.

'I love your body,' he murmured huskily, moving

away from her mouth for a brief moment.

Dee felt her loins melt with a mixture of lust and gratitude as his hand made it inside her cardigan, navigated the cream camisole and burrowed inside her underwired bra. His fingers tweaked a nipple gently, making it rise like a pressure-cooker trivet on 'cooked'. He liked her, fancied her and hadn't passed out at the weight of her on his lap. What a guy!

She kissed him even more passionately and let her own hand sneak furtively inside his shirt to caress his smooth, tanned chest. His skin was warm and satiny. In the dim recesses of her brain, Dee was aware of being glad that it was almost dark in the conservatory and that most of the other couples in the candle-lit greenery were doing exactly what they were doing, apart from the ones concentrating on smoking joints.

But, amazingly, she wasn't too worried about being spotted snogging a strange man at a party. It felt good. Damn' good. Maeve was right: she deserved some fun.

Daryl was languorously licking her earlobe. He sucked it, sending rockets of excitement cruising through Dee's body straight to her groin. Little explosions went off inside her with every caress.

'Oh, Dee,' he murmured. The hand that wasn't stroking her gently was moulding her closer to him. Daryl moved his mouth from her ear to her neck and slowly along her throat, trailing hot, passionate kisses as he went.

She couldn't take it any more. She wanted him so badly, she thought she'd spontaneously combust. He was just as excited as she was, that was obvious.

But not like this, Dee thought suddenly. Not at a party with loads of other people. She couldn't believe she was doing this at all, groping a strange guy thanks to a few compliments and several beers, even if he was the most gorgeous one she'd seen in years and even though she was feeling pretty abandoned right now.

No, she couldn't see herself having a one-night stand with Daryl in someone else's bedroom on top of all the coats while the party raged on around them.

If they didn't stop, that was exactly what was going to happen. Not that the other partygoers would mind as nobody was paying them the slightest bit of attention.

Gently disentangling Daryl from her, Dee sat up straight on his lap, raked her hair out of her eyes and gasped for breath.

'Wow! That was something else,' she breathed.

'Yeah, you can say that again.' Daryl regarded her hazily through pupils black with desire.

'I just don't know . . .' She paused, at a loss to know how to say this. After all, *she'd* been wriggling around on his lap like a sex-starved trollop simply gagging for some lurve action. Daryl would hardly be too impressed when she said she wanted to call a halt to the proceedings even though they were both saturated with lust.

'I . . . I . . . just don't know if I want us to have a quick bonk here,' she stammered, face pink from a mixture of desire and embarrassment. 'I'm not used to that sort of thing. I know it's old-fashioned but I've been involved . . . sorry, I *was* involved with someone for a long time and I'd feel a little uncomfortable just . . . you know.'

'I know.' Daryl ruffled her hair affectionately. 'You're one hell of a sexy lady, Dee, d'ya know that? I thought we were both a gonner there, I thought I'd have to drag you into the flower garden and rip this knitted thing off.' He fingered her cardigan.

Dee's breath quickened at the thought.

'But, hey,' he continued, 'we can arrange a date so we get to know each other a bit better. I'd like that.'

'You would?' she asked, utterly astonished. 'You mean that?'

'Sure. I've only been here two days. You can show me around Dublin. Whaddya doin' tomorrow night?'

'It's like being a teenager again!' Dee told Maeve delightedly. 'Actually, I never did anything like that when I *was* a teenager, because I was fat, self-conscious and . . . yeuch, I don't even want to *talk* about then. But tonight, it was like being a teenager for the *first time*!'

She pirouetted around Maeve's tiny sitting-room gaily, hugging herself with delight. 'So *that's* what it felt like to be groped at a dance by someone you'd never met before?' she crowed. 'When I was in college, the girls used to talk about it and I'd pretend to know what they were talking about, but I hadn't a clue, really. I used to nod and look like I'd done it too. I even invented a guy who snogged me senseless at one party after I did my Leaving Cert exams. But,' she looked up at Maeve, her face momentarily sad, 'it never actually happened to me.'

'Well, it has now, you floozie,' said Maeve, giving her a poke in the ribs. 'I thought we were going to have to have him surgically removed from your body like the face-hugger in *Alien*. He was glued to you.'

'Oh, yes,' murmured Dee, remembering. 'Daryl can be glued to me any time. He has the most amazing body. He's all muscle, as hard as nails . . .'

'Hard?' asked Maeve. 'I should hope so, Ms O'Reilly, after all you were doing to him. If he *wasn't* hard after an hour of you sitting on his lap doing the Dance Of The Seven Veils And One Cardigan, I'd be worried.'

Dee grinned. 'I don't mean *that*,' she said. 'I didn't want to feel him up too much on our first date. I'll wait for the second.' Her eyes sparkled with glee. 'He's taking me to the movies tomorrow night and then we're going for a meal!'

'If you manage to get a seat in the back row in the cinema, you'd better book a take away for dinner,' advised Maeve, 'because if tonight's performance was anything to go by, the pair of you'll never make it to the restaurant. It'll be home. Wham, bam, thank you, mam. And, "Have you got anything to eat, honey? I'm ravenous." ' She mimicked Daryl's Texan drawl.

'I don't know if I could bring another man home to bed yet, not in mine and Gary's,' Dee said, sounding uncertain.

'Damn Gary. He swanned off and left you,' said Maeve belligerently. 'You could have it off with an entire army band in that bed and it's none of his bloody business. You should have brought Daryl home with you tonight and had mad, passionate sex in the bedroom, in the hall, in the front garden and on the kitchen table. That would have exorcised bloody Gary's po-faced ghost.'

'If I'd had any more to drink at Fiona's party, Daryl and I would've certainly ended up on the kitchen table,' joked Dee, 'but I'm glad we didn't. He's so lovely,' she added with a dreamy look in her eyes. 'I'd love to go out with him.'

'Don't book the church just yet,' warned Maeve. 'He may be one of those men who peak at two dates, you know. And don't forget, he's only here on his holidays. He might have a girl in every port and a few at home in Texas for spares.'

'I'm perfectly aware of all that and I don't care,' Dee

said happily. 'He's absolutely stunning and he wants me.' She had a flash of wicked inspiration. 'Do you think I should bring him to one of the pubs Gary's mates go to?'

Maeve cackled with delight. 'Brilliant idea! Please do. Can I come along and watch? I'd love it. Wear something utterly sexy and spend the evening wrapped around delectable Daryl, sticking your tongue in his ear. I bet you a tenner Gary will hear all about it before you've slammed the door on the taxi outside the pub.

'I've just had a better idea,' Dee breathed. 'Millie's dinner party . . . I'll bring him to that.'

CHAPTER TWENTY

Dee threw the tenth outfit on to the bed and despaired of ever finding anything utterly sexy for her date with Daryl. Everything looked horrible, especially the black jeans she'd bought at horrendous expense that morning. She abandoned the search for the perfect, irresistible outfit and looked in the mirror for what felt like the ninetieth time. The pale coral lace teddy – another credit card splurge earlier – was surely one of the most flattering pieces of underwear she'd ever worn. It'd need to be, she mused, it had certainly cost enough. Delicately laced under-wired cups were finished off with satin ribbon fashioned into tiny rosebuds, while the control panel that held in her tummy was covered in the same rose-patterned lace. Seriously high-cut legs completed the sexy but classy effect.

Even Dee, who'd been known to cry at the sight of herself in bra and knickers, was impressed. She hoped Daryl would be too. And for once, she'd managed to apply the fake tan evenly so that she wasn't mottled white in places and the colour of an elderly Jaffa orange in others.

Maeve had phoned that morning, strongly recommending a post-horrible-fiancé bonk.

'It'll do you good. There's nothing to beat the love of

a good, hunky Brad Pitt lookalike to make you feel better about life in general,' she urged. 'And stop panicking about AIDS. You've got your Dutch cap, you've got condoms. Just don't let him try anything with handcuffs.'

Dee had laughed uproariously but hadn't mentioned her fuck-me undies or her ruinously expensive new jeans. She still hadn't quite decided if she was up to having sex with another man after so many years with Gary. She wanted to make that decision herself, at the last minute.

The jarring ring of the doorbell interrupted her mental debate.

'Yes?' She peered out of the front bedroom window.

'Taxi, love,' roared up a middle-aged taxi driver. 'You going out in that?' he added with a salacious wink.

Dee wrenched her dressing gown off the bed and wrapped it around herself.

'You're early,' she yelled down at him, and glanced at her watch. 'Fifteen minutes early.'

'There's a concert on in the Point tonight, love,' the taxi driver retorted. 'I've got a booking for that and you won't get a taxi for love nor money then. So it's now or never.'

'All right. Give me five minutes,' Dee grumbled. She slammed the window shut and stared at the mess on the bed in horror. What the hell would she wear? Damn, damn, damn! It'd have to be the jeans. She'd already found everything to go with that outfit and if she decided on anything else, who knew how long it would take her rummaging around in drawers for the perfect tights to go with that perfect skirt or whatever?

Cursing, she dragged on the jeans, a slinky white low-cut T-shirt and her black leather jacket. She found her mercilessly high ankle boots – the only ones that looked good with jeans because they gave her some much-needed extra height – and pulled them on. Pausing only to fluff up her hair and give herself another squirt of Obsession, she ran down the stairs and was in the taxi a mere six minutes after it had arrived.

The taxi driver, a grizzled man who wore a tweed cap pulled disreputably down over one eye, grinned at her. 'I preferred the first outfit, love.'

Dee sniffed and looked out of the window. That was all she needed – a lecherous driver chatting nineteen to the dozen for the entire journey. But he didn't attempt any more conversation and drove at breakneck speed into the city centre, getting her to the Savoy cinema twenty-five minutes before she was due to meet Daryl. She couldn't hang around O'Connell Street that long, Dee realised. She'd be arrested for loitering with intent.

So she bought an evening paper, went into Madigan's and ordered a mug of coffee, resolutely ignoring the lure of the cheese and onion crisps that everyone else in the pub seemed to be eating. When she arrived at the Savoy again, Daryl was waiting for her, wearing his jeans, a white cotton T-shirt and a huge fisherman's sweater that looked like it had been knitted from Shredded Wheat. His blond, freshly washed hair flopped engagingly over his eyes and he kept having to flick it back with one hand.

'Hi, Dee.' He enveloped her in a huge bear hug, the sweater arms swamping both of them. He must have borrowed it. 'How're ya doing?'

'Fine.' She beamed up at him. 'Looking forward to this.'

'Me too.'

Arm in arm, they walked into the cinema, bought

their tickets, a vat of buttered popcorn and sat in the darkness waiting for the movie to start. Dee barely concentrated on the film, she was so conscious of Daryl sitting beside her in one of the cinema's few double seats.

She tried to sit as thinly as possible, holding her stomach in and keeping her crossed leg lifted off the one underneath, so it wouldn't look as if she had fat thighs.

Daryl didn't appear to notice all this effort on his behalf. At first, he merely held her hand, but when the scary bits started and Dee involuntarily shrank into the seat, he put one arm around her shoulders and held her close. She cuddled up to him and, even if she was going to have a crick in her neck from sitting at a slightly awkward angle, she wouldn't have moved for anything. Eventually, she abandoned her thin-thigh exercise and let her stomach flop out naturally. It *was* dark after all. He wouldn't be able to tell anyway.

Afterwards, Daryl was all praise for the director, a horror flick *wunderkind* he loved.

'Nobody does violence the way he does, he's so cool,' he enthused, as they strolled down O'Connell Street for Temple Bar.

Dee nodded, determined not to let on that she couldn't stand horror movies. She hadn't really cared what they'd gone to see. If he wanted to see a scarefest where everyone and their granny ended up as dog meat, then she wasn't going to argue. This was a *date*. You had to suffer for love, she thought happily.

Why else had she spent hours watching Gary's team play football on freezing Saturdays or endured hour after hour of European football when she really wanted to watch the romantic comedy on the other channel?

Temple Bar, Dublin's trendy Left Bank, was buzzing by the time they got there, Daryl's long left arm draped around Dee's shoulder, her arm around his waist.

Music poured from the open doors of the bars and pubs, and revellers spilled out on to the pavements, drinking their pints and eyeing up the talent that walked by. As on so many Saturday nights, the cobbled streets were jammed with half-plastered hen and stag parties from other countries, all giggling as they lurched from atmospheric pub to pub, intent on drinking too much Irish booze, grabbing a quick bite, and finally clubbing until the wee small hours.

As a result, the myriad restaurants that lined the streets were all full and by the time Dee and Daryl had made their way from the Elephant And Castle down as far as Bad Bob's via Fat Freddy's, Dee was beginning to wonder if she should have booked somewhere.

If all else failed, she decided, they'd squash their way into the madly popular Oliver St John Gogarty and order Guinness and lots of crisps to keep them going until the stag parties staggered off to Club M to dance the night away and the restaurant tables freed up.

'What about this place?' asked Daryl, spying a small Italian place down a laneway.

The tiny Italian restaurant had one empty table left and Dee sank into her seat gratefully. Her feet were killing her in the stiletto boots, she was ravenous, and the scent of garlic bread drifting out from the kitchen was doing unmentionable things to her taste buds.

They shared a basket of bread, drank a carafe of house wine and both had the special: clam linguine, which came with ciabatta and roasted peppers into the bargain.

Looking at his clean, faded denims, the cotton T-shirt

CATHY KELLY

that had obviously been washed to within an inch of its
life, and his plain old Timex with the worn leather strap,
Dee reckoned that Daryl didn't have much money. She
didn't want to embarrass him by ordering anything
expensive.

He was determined to pay for the meal.

'You got the movie and the popcorn, dinner is my
treat,' he'd insisted earlier.

She loved watching him eat and he certainly loved
Italian food, twirling the coiled strands of pasta like an
expert.

'Back home, my momma and grandmomma are into
local American food so we don't go in for much foreign
cooking. My brothers and I love this sort of food,' he
said, forking pasta into his mouth with gusto.

'How many brothers do you have?' she asked. 'And
what do they do? I don't know anything about you, do
you realise that?' By the second hour of their second
date, Dee had known everything imaginable about Gary,
from the size of his family to how good he was at soccer
and the highest break he'd ever had playing snooker.

Daryl was different. He wasn't a talker, had no real
interest in telling her about his life. And she wasn't sure
he was that curious about hers. To someone as incorri-
gibly inquisitive as Dee, that was strange indeed.

In fact, the more they sat there, drinking their spicy
red wine and mopping up the tasty pasta sauce with the
extra bread, the more Dee realised that she and Daryl
had practically nothing in common. She was a reporter,
permanently on the lookout for a fresh piece of gossip
and eager to know everything about the handsome guy
sitting across the table from her. He was happy to spend
the entire evening with her without once asking her a
personal question. She was a worker bee, constantly

thinking about the next thing she should be doing and worrying if she wasn't achieving it. He'd drifted his way through college, had finally gone back to finish his degree at the age of twenty-five – he was, she was amazed to discover, twenty-seven – and wanted to travel the world for the rest of his life.

The South American trip was his third adventure. Before that, he'd spent six months in Alaska on an environmental protest – 'It sure was cold and there wasn't much to do where we were staying' – and several months in a commune in Mexico. His next trip was a year-long one to Nepal.

Dee felt her life story was horrendously boring by comparison.

'Going to work directly after college and staying in the same job for six years sounds like vegetating when I look at what you've done,' she said ruefully. 'I never wanted to leave Ireland. For good, I mean. I love travel and I'd love to be able to go all over the world but I don't know if I have the guts to do what you do, to work anywhere. I sound like a coward.'

'Hey, different strokes for different folks,' Daryl remarked, pushing his empty plate away from him. 'My two older brothers are married with kids, one in Austin, one in San Francisco. There's nothing wrong with it, I just don't want that sort of life.

'But,' he leant forward and wiped a smudge of sauce from her mouth, 'don't run yourself down for what you do. You've got a great job, a home, a life. Who knows? I may end up with nothing more than a worn-out back pack and some tropical disease that's eatin' me up from the inside out when you're a happily married woman with kids.'

Dee smiled wryly, thinking of how she'd screwed up

her most recent chance of being married with 2.5 kids. Spending four years with her had sent her last boyfriend hotfooting it to London. Perhaps she should hire herself out as some sort of incentive scheme for reluctant emigrants: Date Dee And Get The Courage To Leave Home And See The World.

'Fiona was tellin' me about this guy you were going to marry?' Daryl said.

Dee stared at him in surprise. She couldn't believe he'd asked Fiona about her, that didn't sound his style. No, Fiona must have brought it up when she heard he was going out on a date with Dee. She wasn't sure she wanted him to know about Gary. It was all too recent, too painful.

'You mentioned it last night,' he added, 'about how you'd been with this guy for years, so I wanted to know about him. He sounds like a complete asshole, that's for sure.'

Dee grinned. 'You said it.'

'Thing is,' Daryl looked faintly uncomfortable for the first time all evening, 'I don't wanna be moving in on you if you're still cut up about this guy. I don't wanna be an asshole too. You might need some time without another guy in there.'

Dee was incredibly touched. This handsome Texan drifter she fancied like mad, and with whom she'd practically had sex the previous night in someone else's conservatory, was behaving like the perfect gentleman.

He might only be in the country for a few weeks, but he didn't want to rush in, break her heart and then dump her. Her boyfriend of four years hadn't been that considerate.

'You're the least asshole-like guy I've met for a very long time,' she said softly.

Their eyes met over the flickering red candle that had melted halfway down during the meal. Dee knew how it felt. She'd been wondering what to do all evening and now sweet, thoughtful Daryl had shown her the way.

'If you like, we could skip coffee here and have it in my place?'

His eyes lit up wickedly and the handsome, golden face creased into one huge grin.

'I'd sure like that.'

By the time they got to Dee's house, she felt the taxi driver should have been paying *them* for the in-cab entertainment they'd provided on the trip home. Daryl had taken up where they'd left off the previous night, kissing Dee passionately as soon as they got into the taxi. When he'd slid his hand up inside her T-shirt, she could see the taxi driver's eyes drinking in the scene from his rear-view mirror.

'Nice place,' Daryl said, taking his mouth from hers briefly while she unlocked the front door and let them in. Then he was kissing her again, tongue probing hers, hands pushing off her leather jacket.

They practically fell on to the stairs, limbs everywhere as they grabbed at each other. By the third step, his Shredded Wheat jumper was off and Dee's T-shirt was around her armpits as Daryl kissed her body from her belly button up.

Halfway up the stairs, he unzipped her boots and wriggled her out of the skin-tight jeans.

He was so enthusiastic and so passionate that she didn't stop to worry about the red marks on her skin from wearing tight jeans. She was concentrating on pulling his T-shirt over his lean, muscled torso. Sitting up straight to pull it over his head, Dee had a chance to admire the flat, six-pack stomach tanned the colour of peanut butter, before he was pressed against her again, hungrily kissing her. His mouth was wide and desperate, his tongue thrusting against hers frantically.

The wool of the stair carpet was wiry and harsh against Dee's back. She moved uncomfortably, trying to settle herself into a decent position but it was impossible. With Daryl lying on top of her, she was being squashed into the stairs. It was a nice way to be squashed, but it was still uncomfortable.

'Let's go to bed,' she murmured into his ear.

Without saying a word, Daryl helped her up and followed her up the remaining stairs and into the bedroom, holding her hand tightly with one hand. The other was travelling over her coral-lace-covered bum.

Dee grimaced as she saw the bed covered in all her earlier discarded outfits – skirts, trousers and skimpy tops flung around haphazardly. She hadn't had time to put it all away. The place looked like a tornado had passed over.

But Daryl didn't appear to notice. He was engrossed in nuzzling her neck and sliding the straps of the teddy over her shoulders. Dee picked up a bundle of clothes, dropped them messily on the bedroom chair and turned back to him.

'Where were we?' he growled, pulling her to him and sliding the teddy down with one hand.

'You're beautiful,' he said, gazing at her full breasts, uncovered for the first time. He sat on the bed, pulled Dee towards him so that she was standing between his knees and buried his face between her breasts.

As he kissed, licked and sucked, Dee wrapped her hands around his head and let the desire flow through her. She felt wanton and earthy, a sexual and desirable woman.

Daryl touched her greedily, anxiously, as if she was a fantasy woman who was going to disappear if he didn't make love to her as if his life depended on it. Dee felt wanted and beautiful: an aphrodisiac cocktail that no amount of oysters, strawberries or champagne could equal.

Lovemaking with Daryl was a revelation. She was used to Gary's tried and tested methods which consisted of passionate snogging for five minutes followed by a further ten of foreplay and then another ten of energetic sex. A swift and exciting session, like a quarter of an opera, starting with slow song and moving up to a triumphant finale.

But if Gary's technique was one brisk, expertly executed movement where the conductor had one eye on the clock to avoid paying overtime, Daryl's was the entire opera with an award-winning symphony orchestra playing their hearts out as they recorded an album with Pavarotti.

He started gently, and after two hours reached a bed-shaking crescendo. By the time he finally slid inside her, Dee was damp inside and out, had already enjoyed two shattering orgasms and couldn't wait to feel him plunge into her quivering body. Moving in and out of her with long, precise strokes, Daryl waited until she'd come an unbelievable third time before he let himself go, his lean body shuddering with pleasure as he came.

'You're beautiful, Dee, so sexy,' he groaned, sinking on to the pillow beside her. 'That was somethin' else.'

'You're telling me,' she purred. Her body felt exquisitely tired, muscles warm and relaxed. She nuzzled into his shoulder, loving the feeling of his long arm draped comfortably over her waist.

She closed her eyes happily and waited for the

inevitable snores. Gary always fell asleep immediately after sex. It was better than Mogadon, he joked. But Daryl didn't drift off, leaving Dee on her own on one side of the bed as he settled on to the other with his back towards her. Instead, he moved until his mouth was beside hers and he could kiss her softly. His lips brushed her mouth, then her forehead and eyelids. His hands stroked her hot, damp skin tenderly. Cuddled up beside him like two spoons in a drawer, Dee was utterly content.

Sated and exhausted, they fell asleep a little after one a.m., limbs wrapped around each other, totally comfortable in the other's presence.

Dee awoke at three, hot, sweaty and thirsty. Moving in the bed to untangle herself from the mess of sheets and duvet, she woke Daryl up.

'Where are you goin', honey?' he murmured, stretching for her as she climbed out of bed.

'To get some orange juice, I'm so thirsty. Do you want some?'

'Yeah. Don't be long now.'

He welcomed her back to bed with the ardour of a round-the-world yachtsman who hadn't seen a woman for a year.

Dee found that half a litre of orange juice and a passionate lovemaking session put the kibosh on a burgeoning hangover far better than a pint of water and two paracetamol before going to bed ever had. And waking up with a warm, aroused body beside hers was infinitely more fun than being woken up by the blistering ring of the alarm clock.

Millie and Dan lived in a large semi in Malahide in the sort of housing estate that was perfect for kids. A large green dominated the centre of the estate, complete with adventure playground. As Dee and Daryl drove slowly into The Maples the following Saturday, gangs of kids playing football on the road stepped back to let their car pass. It was nearly eight on a balmy August evening and there was at least another hour of decent light left. The game restarted once they'd driven by, loud yells and squeals puncturing the calm.

Dee remembered watching the kids on her street playing five-a-side when she was young. She'd never joined in. Instead, she'd hung out of her bedroom window, stared at all the skinny kids racing up and down after the ball and wished she could play sports. Her brother Shane had been admitted to the football-on-the street club when he was old enough. He was always getting into trouble with their mother for using clean jumpers for goalposts and getting tar on them when the road surface melted in the sun. The only stains Dee ever got on her jumpers were from ice cream.

'Dan's a good cook, right?' Daryl asked when they stopped outside a neat, well-maintained house with a gleaming brass number 20 on the door. 'I'm starvin'.'

Dee laughed. 'You're always starving, Daryl. I don't know where you put it.'

He gave her a lopsided grin. 'My momma says she thinks I have a tapeworm inside me, that's the only reason I can eat so much!'

'Gross!' shrieked Dee as she pushed open the small white gate. 'I won't be able to eat a thing thinking about that.'

'Great.' He pinched her bum. 'We can go home then.'

'No, we can't.' She wheeled round and slapped his wrist.

Dan had obviously been busy in the garden, Dee realised guiltily as she and Daryl walked up the path past a tiny, beautifully manicured lawn and weedless flowerbeds. Dee's own garden was looking more like a butterfly sanctuary than ever. Not that it had been any better when Gary still lived with her.

Why was it that Millie had got one of the keen on gardening, keen on tidying-up and utterly responsible Redmond brothers, while she had ended up with the housework/gardening-phobic one?

Millie met them at the front door, her round face wreathed in a welcoming smile. 'Dee! I'm so pleased you could make it,' she said, giving Dee a sideways hug so as to avoid squashing her bump. At six months pregnant, Millie was the shape of a round-the-world balloon and nearly as big, as she joked herself. Tonight, she was dressed in a black silky cardigan that was stretched across her stomach revealing a pale blue T-shirt dress underneath. She'd put on loads of weight and looked as if she was ready to pop at any moment. Her strawberry blonde hair shimmered lustrously, her skin glowed and her freckles were more pronounced than usual thanks to hours spent in the back garden soaking up the summer heat.

Dee pulled Daryl into the Laura Ashley-papered hall. 'This is Daryl,' she said, a shade nervously.

'Hello, Daryl, welcome,' said Millie, and gave him a friendly peck on the cheek. 'I hope you like lamb *tagine*? Dan has been cooking for hours and he'll have a fit if you don't all love Moroccan food.'

'I love Moroccan food,' Daryl assured her.

Millie pushed open the dining-room door and led them in. Two other couples were seated around the glass-topped wrought-iron table. Dee's heart sank when she realised she didn't recognise anyone. She said a little prayer that nobody tactlessly asked how she'd met their hosts.

'Did you tell Dan I was bringing someone?' she asked Millie out of the corner of her mouth.

'Yes,' Millie whispered back. 'I think he got a bit of a shock.'

'Not half so much of a shock as I got when his beloved brother dumped me,' muttered Dee, rattled by the idea of introducing her new lover to her ex-fiancé's elder brother. This entire evening was a big mistake. Why had she ever thought she could pull it off? Dan would probably try to strangle Daryl between the lamb *tagine* and the Sambucca.

'Relax,' Millie said. 'You're entitled to bring anyone you want, Dee. Gary left you and that's what I told Dan. He's fine, don't worry.'

Dee felt so apprehensive she was almost nauseous but it was a bit late to back out at this point, so she said nothing. The last time she'd been in this house, Gary had been with her and they'd been celebrating Millie's birthday. It was only a few months ago but it felt like years. The memory was crystal clear. Gary had got plastered on illegal poteen from Millie's Donegal home-town and they'd ended up staying the night in the spare room on an ancient double bed that squeaked every time you moved an inch.

The next day, Dee, Dan and Millie had had a whale of a time teasing Gary about how much he'd drunk, asking him if he wanted a 'hair of the dog that bit him' hangover remedy purely for the fun of watching him turn forty shades of green at the very thought of touching alcohol . . .

Millie guided Dee to a seat beside the head of the

table and Daryl, ignoring the dinner-party etiquette which would have placed him opposite, sank into the seat beside her.

'You okay, honey?' he asked, knowing how uptight she was.

'Fine.' She gave his arm a grateful squeeze.

Millie made the introductions, instructed Daryl to pour the wine and made for the kitchen, from where the most amazing scents were drifting, along with the odd curse and the sound of saucepans clashing. Whatever Dan was cooking, it required lots of attention and he remained in the kitchen for ages.

After two gulped back glasses of red wine and the arrival of the last guests, Dee had almost forgotten how nervous she'd been about turning up on Millie and Dan's doorstep with a new boyfriend in tow.

Chrissie and Pat, newly married and unable to keep their eyes off each other, worked in the bank alongside Millie and kept finishing each other's sentences as they told how Chrissie could barely make toast and Pat had to do all the cooking.

'She's ruined one kettle already,' he said fondly, gazing across the table at his new wife with adoring eyes.

'Clever move,' remarked Jane, an attractive blonde woman who owned a dressmaking business. 'I wish I'd done that when we moved in together.' She shot Clive, a partner in Dan's firm, a meaningful look. 'Clive thinks housework is one of the great feminine mysteries, like waxing your legs and dyeing your eyelashes.'

Dee giggled into her wineglass. 'I used to go out with someone just like that. Thanks to an adoring mother, he thought housework was beneath him,' she said, before she realised where she was and who she was talking about.

At that instant, Dan appeared at the dining-room door, wearing an apron, a rather silly chef's hat and a frazzled expression.

'Hi, all,' he said. 'Sorry I haven't been talking to you but something went a bit wrong in the kitchen and I've been trying to sort it out. A man's work is never done.'

Dee blanched and hoped to hell he hadn't heard what she'd just said. But Dan wasn't looking at her. His eyes were on Daryl who was lounging back in his wrought-iron chair, heavy glass goblet in one hand and a proprietorial arm around Dee's shoulders.

Dan's eyes narrowed. In another sloppy jumper – this time, an enormous moss green one – black jeans faded to a shade of grey and with several thin leather bracelets wound around one wrist, Daryl looked like a street musician, a million miles away from Gary, the king of Next chic.

'Hello, Dan, lovely to see you,' said Dee gamely. 'This is Daryl.'

Dan said nothing for a moment.

Millie, watching everything over her glass of mineral water, prodded her husband with one finger.

'Hi, Dee. Hi, Daryl,' he said evenly, and loped around the table to give Dee a rather strained hug. For a dreadful moment, she thought he was going to say something about being sorry she and Gary had split up. But he didn't. He straightened up and held out a hand to Daryl.

Dee could see that Dan's mouth was set in a tight line. Not unlike his mother's, she thought absently. Gary had looked like that sometimes, generally when he was doing something he resented. The two men shook hands. Dan then sat down at the head of the table and poured himself a glass of wine.

'Cheers,' said Chrissie, who was sitting on his right.

'Cheers.' Everyone raised their glasses and the uncomfortable moment passed.

'What are you cooking?' Jane asked. 'And whatever it is, could you take Clive into the kitchen and show him how to make it?'

'He should show *you*,' snapped back Clive.

Dee winced and wondered if she and Gary had often brought their quarrels out with them, carrying the private war into other people's homes.

Probably.

The dinner party was anything but plain sailing. Clive and Jane bickered throughout the meal, and even though everyone else appeared to be used to their constant sniping, it unnerved Dee who felt more wound up than a clockwork toy.

It had been a mistake bringing Daryl here, she decided anxiously. It didn't matter that Gary had dumped her – Dan was still his brother and, as such, was watching Dee and Daryl with the disapproving countenance of the head nun at the second years' first mixed disco.

But eventually, lubricated with plenty of red wine, he loosened up and began to play the part of the genial host. He was helped along by Millie, the peacemaker, who kept refilling his glass with wine. The first course – lots of unusual dips with crudités, pitta bread and tortilla chips – was wonderful and spicy enough so that everyone but Millie and Dee, who was driving, drank far too much.

The lamb *tagine* melted in Dee's mouth, in much the same way as Daryl's right hand melted on to her flesh as it made its way under her mini skirt and headed north to the tender skin revealed by her stockings. It was a bit over the top to wear a charcoal suede mini skirt and sheer black hold-ups to an ordinary dinner party, but she hadn't been able to stop herself. Daryl made her feel so sexy that she loved dressing up for him and seductive lingerie drove him wild.

From the moment he had discovered what she was wearing under the suede mini, he'd been unable to keep his hands to himself. His fingers were like a mole on a timer, burrowing under her skirt every ten minutes.

When he was doing it, he didn't look at her, merely forked up his succulent lamb and appeared to listen intently to what was being said. Dee didn't know how she stopped herself from gasping while Dan recounted some long-winded story about a motorbike he'd once owned, because Daryl's long fingers were wickedly twanging the elastic on her knickers. He never stopped, she thought a little wearily. He had sex on the brain.

'Gosh!' she said, bright-eyed with interest as she pushed Daryl's hand away. He pushed right back. Dee could feel herself going pink in the face. She had to stop this. It was like sitting beside a horny octopus and the other guests were bound to notice soon. Hanky-panky in the bedroom was one thing, but Daryl didn't seem to realise that there was a time for everything. And this wasn't it.

She slid her fingers down to his knee and caught it in a vice-like grip, hoping he was ticklish. She squeezed expertly, fingers tightening on the sensitive hollows. He jumped, hit the table with both knees and all the glasses and the wine bottles vibrated noisily from the impact.

'Are you all right, Daryl?' inquired Millie.

'He's fine,' smiled Dee, thumping him hard on the back. 'A bit went down the wrong way, didn't it, darling?'

She gave him another thump for good measure.

'Sure.' He grinned back at her.

By dessert, Dan was nicely drunk and Daryl had wisely given up groping Dee's thighs in favour of running his fingers up and down the arm closest to him, occasionally sneaking in a quick stroke of her boob.

More relaxed because she figured Dan was too merry to care what Daryl got up to, Dee stopped minding and sat with one hand resting on his thigh.

When he and Jane weren't bitching at each other, Clive was a wonderful raconteur and had them all in stitches with a selection of stories and jokes. Dan's eyes were glazed by the time he served dessert, a summer pudding that was laced with *crème de cassis* and was truly lethal. Dee took one look at her heaped plate, covered with an over-generous dollop of cream, and vowed to eat nothing but grapefruit the next day.

'This is beautiful, Dan,' said Pat, licking his spoon appreciatively. 'I wish I could cook like this.'

'Darling, you can,' cooed Chrissie across the table.

Jane caught Dee's gaze and raised disbelieving eyes to heaven.

When they all retired to the sitting-room to drink coffee and liqueurs, Dee decided that she and Daryl would make their excuses after ten minutes.

'Fine by me, honey,' he whispered. 'I just wanna get you home and take a good look at those stockings.'

'Shush!' hissed Dee, conscious that Dan was right beside them, unsteadily placing bottles of Bailey's and Drambuie on the coffee table.

'D'ya want some help?' asked Daryl.

Dan gave him a hard look. 'I think you've got your hands full already,' he slurred.

Dee felt her heart skip a beat. Oh, no, there wasn't

going to be an argument, was there? She hated arguments. They shouldn't have come. It was a bad idea.

Spending time with Millie and Dan was one thing when she and Gary had been dating, but spending time with them now was a recipe for disaster. She and Millie had things in common and genuinely liked each other. But Dan, while he liked Dee, loved his brother and would probably never be able to look at her without thinking 'if only'.

'Dan,' interrupted Millie judiciously, 'boil the kettle, love. We need another cafetière of coffee. There are eight of us, you know.'

Dan left and Millie sank on to the settee beside Daryl and Dee. 'Poor dear, he's not taking it too well,' she said, watching her husband's lanky form shuffle into the kitchen.

'Dee didn't leave Gary, he left her,' pointed out Daryl helpfully.

'I know, but don't say that to Dan,' warned Millie. 'He'll go ballistic. He's very easy going normally but he's lost his sense of humour over this. He was convinced you two were meant for each other,' she added to Dee.

She sighed wearily. 'We'd better go,' she said. 'I don't want a fight and I reckon that's the way things are heading.'

'Don't go yet,' begged Millie, pale blue eyes filling up. 'I wanted us to have a lovely evening together. I don't want to lose touch with you simply because you're not going out with Gary any more . . .'

Dee put her arms around her. 'We won't,' she said, more hopefully than she felt, and handed Daryl the car keys. 'Do you want to go out and wait in the car while I say goodbye to Dan?'

'Sure.' He kissed Millie, said his goodbyes and left.

Dee made her way reluctantly to the kitchen. She didn't know what to say to Dan and wasn't in the mood for a drunken lecture on how she and Gary should get back together. Hell will freeze over first, she thought.

But Dan seemed to have got over his fit of pique. He was staring drunkenly out of the kitchen window into the moonlit garden, ignoring the steaming kettle beside him.

Dee cleared her throat. 'We're going, Dan,' she said awkwardly.

'Dee,' he muttered and flung his arms around her.

She felt a lump in her throat. Damn it, she didn't want to cry. Why was she even thinking about crying?

'I love you, you know,' he mumbled into her shoulder. 'You're like the little sister I never had.'

That did it. Dee felt a fat tear roll down her face.

'I love you too, Dan,' she said brokenly. 'Gotta go.' She tore herself away from him and marched into the hall, wiping away tears savagely.

''Bye, Millie. I'll phone you,' she called into the sitting-room before she banged the front door behind her.

'Why do they all behave as if *I'm* the one who broke up the bloody relationship?' she raged to Daryl as she climbed angrily into the car. 'Gary's the one they should be giving the guilt trip to, not me.'

'Hey, they're never gonna change the way they think,' he said pragmatically. 'You should keep out of their way. It's over and that's it.'

'You're right.' She crunched the car into first gear. 'I've had it up to my tonsils with the Redmonds.'

Morning was streaming in through a gap in the curtains when the phone rang beside her head. Dee opened one eye groggily, reached for her bedside table and dragged the receiver from the phone.

'Hello,' she croaked, barely able to talk from exhaustion. She and Daryl had made love for hours when they'd returned home. It had been at least two in the morning before Dee had turned out the light.

'Dee.' His voice made her sit bolt upright in the bed.

'Gary!' What was he phoning her for at . . . she glanced at the clock radio . . . ten-thirty on a Sunday morning? The answer was blindingly obvious – Dan had rung to tell him all about the previous night's dinner party, and, no doubt, the handsome young American who'd been all over Dee like a rash.

'I rang you in the office but they said you weren't in. I hope I didn't interrupt anything?' Gary said in a bitingly sarcastic voice, obviously having no clue as to what he *was* interrupting. 'You're not hungover *again*, are you?'

'I took today off,' she said.

Suddenly, Dee shot up in the bed again as she felt Daryl's hot, naked body stretch up from the bottom of the bed to press seductively against hers. His long arms reached up to caress her breasts, while his tongue jammed itself into her belly button, flickering kisses against the tender skin.

'Aaah!' she gasped in pleasure as his head went lower.

'Dee, what's going on?' Gary demanded.

She stifled a giggle. Maeve would adore this scenario – one man making love to her while her ex threw a tantrum over the phone, demanding to know what was going on. Gary would never in a million years think she was in bed with Daryl: it simply wasn't the sort of thing Dee did. Well, the *old* Dee wouldn't have. The new Dee was relishing the experience.

Daryl's tousled blond head appeared beside her and he kissed her deeply before turning his attention to her breasts. He attacked one nipple voraciously, sucking it into a little hard peak.

Dee moaned again and started stroking the back of his neck with one hand. The other hand, the one holding the phone, slipped down absently on to the pillow.

'Dee!' Gary sounded utterly outraged now, his voice was at that, 'What have you boil washed my football jersey for, you stupid cow!' tone. It was all she could do not to burst out laughing and tell him exactly what she *was* doing. How hilariously ironic.

A week ago she'd have been on the edge of her seat with nerves if Gary had rung, desperate for him to say he was coming back and that he still loved her. But four dates with a charming, polite, admiring and devastatingly sexy man had given her a whole new perspective on things. Gary had dumped her unceremoniously and now Daryl, lovely, sexy Daryl who was stroking her intimately with his clever, probing fingers, had given her back her confidence and made her feel like a desirable woman again, instead of a lump of lard who wore too much eye-shadow.

Tough bananas, Gary, she thought triumphantly. Yes, I *am* in our bed with another man and it's wonderful.

She sat up, kissed the top of Daryl's head gently before motioning him to be quiet and jammed the phone to her ear again.

'What do you want, Gary?' she asked, thrilled to have the upper hand for once.

'I want to know what's going on?' he demanded.

Dee's eyebrows lifted in amusement. 'What do you mean, "you want to know what's going on?" ' she said.

'I'm in bed, right? I was out late last night and now I'm tired. I've got the day off so I can spend all day in bed if I want to.'

Daryl's mouth turned up at the corners at this and he went back to kissing her nipple. Dee just stopped herself from moaning with pleasure.

'Anyway,' she continued, 'it's none of your business what I'm doing.'

'Who were you out with?' Gary asked.

Dee grinned to herself. He was playing games. He knew perfectly well. 'A guy.'

'A guy! What guy?' Gary demanded.

Daryl's white teeth gently nibbled her nipple, making her squirm excitedly. God, but he was good at that.

'You don't know him. He's American, a friend of Fiona's brother.'

'*American!*' Gary's voice was at screeching point now.

'Texan, actually,' Dee said. She was enjoying this.

'From Austin,' supplied Daryl loudly.

Dee sniggered.

'He's there now, isn't he?' Gary's voice was a howl of outrage. 'He's in bed with you, in *our* bed. I don't believe it. How could you?'

Dee lost her temper. 'What the hell do you mean, how could I?' she raged. 'You complete bastard! You left me nearly a month ago and I haven't heard from you since, apart from a bitchy note telling me to sell the house. You have no rights over me any more. We've split up.'

'Well, *I* haven't been out screwing around,' howled Gary angrily.

'And I haven't been screwing around either,' yelled Dee into the receiver. She felt Daryl place a calming hand on her shoulder and he kissed her softly on the cheek.

'Don't let him get to you, honey,' he whispered into her ear.

She nodded and took a deep breath. Why was she wasting her time even having this conversation with Gary? He had no right to ask her what she was doing now or who she was seeing. How dare he?

'I'm only screwing one person,' she announced calmly. 'We're sleeping late because we're exhausted. We were at it like rabbits all night. Satisfied, Gary?'

She listened to his outraged splutter for a couple of seconds.

'Anyway, I don't know why you're pretending you don't know about Daryl,' she emphasised his name, 'because I'm pretty sure Dan was on the phone to you at first light, filling you in on all the details of his dinner party.

'I just wish you'd tell your family that *you* left *me*, not the other way round, so they'd stop feeling responsible for getting us back together,' she hissed. 'It's about time I told Dan and Millie what a complete shit you've been. Maybe then they'd get the message.'

She slammed down the phone.

'Well done.' Daryl grinned at her. 'You told him.'

Dee grinned back, feeling like a naughty schoolgirl who'd just been caught round the back of the bike shed with a strange boy. She'd told Gary about Daryl and now he was insane with jealousy and rage. Ha bloody ha! Wait till she told Maeve.

Millie levered herself on to the armchair in Dee's sitting-room carefully and Dee put a cup of tea and a plate of biscuits on the small table beside the chair. Smudge appeared from nowhere and sniffed Millie's ankles with interest.

'Gary isn't impressed,' she said, trying to settle herself comfortably. 'He rang Dan almost immediately this morning, demanding to know everything about this Daryl you were seeing.'

Dee giggled into her coffee mug.

'Dan told him he'd only met Daryl for the first time last night,' Millie added, 'and said it was Gary's own fault if you were going out with some American. He left you after all.'

Dee blinked with surprise. Dan taking Gary to task for dumping her? She'd love to have heard that.

'When you went last night, I gave out stink to Dan and told him he had no right to give you or Daryl such a hard time,' Millie admitted. 'It really wasn't right. So, what happened with Gary?' she asked eagerly.

'It was priceless, Millie,' Dee smiled at the memory. 'He was outraged. I still can't believe I told him Daryl was there in bed with me!'

'That gave Dan a bit of a shock, too, I can tell you,' Millie said. 'He's furious with Gary for breaking up with you but was still hoping you two would get back together and this rather knocked him sideways.'

Dee shrugged. 'I understand, but I can't stop living and wait for Gary to get his act together and decide he really loves me after all. I need a life and I needed Daryl.'

'I agree completely,' Millie pointed out. 'He really is sex on legs. Hearing about him was just what your spoiled ex-fiancé needed. Realising he's got a serious rival might make Gary see sense.'

'I don't know if I want him to see sense,' Dee said blankly. 'I'm having fun, finally. It wasn't fun when Gary left, I can tell you. But Daryl is good for me. I'm not so sure Gary ever was.'

Millie sighed. 'I know what you're saying,' she admitted. 'It's just that Dan would love to see you two back together, it's his little dream.'

Dee didn't look at her for a few moments. She was thinking what a naive man Dan Redmond was.

'I don't know if I want Gary back. You know what he said to me.'

'You told me some of it,' Millie said, 'about your weight . . .'

'That wasn't the half of it,' Dee exclaimed. 'He said I hid behind a ton of make-up and that my clothes were loud, vulgar and not the sort of thing a deputy editor wore. I don't know if he really meant it or not but it was incredibly hurtful. And not very good for the old self-confidence.'

'He's a bastard, isn't he?' Millie said with a sigh. 'I mean, how could he say those things?'

'You tell me. Anyway,' Dee sat back in her chair, 'tell Dan that his precious brother really messed up this time.'

'I will.' Millie sat back with her mug in her hand and stared at Dee. 'I blame their mother, you know. She really got her claws into Gary when their father died. At least the others had some sort of normal home life, but he was Margaret's little pet. She spoiled him rotten.'

'She's welcome to him now,' Dee said flatly. 'More tea?'

When Millie left, Dee pottered around the house, tidying up and thinking about the past few days. When Gary had first left, his comments about her being a fat, ugly, over-made-up slob had cut her to the bone and made her think that everyone else would judge her in the same way. Now Dee was beginning to think that

Gary's viciousness showed just that – that *he* was vicious, not that she was guilty of all the things he'd accused her of.

She really was better off without him.

CHAPTER TWENTY-ONE

Isabel gazed blankly at the carpet. She couldn't concentrate on what the speaker was saying. The subject was Women In The Media and, as she was the next person on the podium to deliver an address to the several hundred delegates in the Burlington Hotel conference room, she *should* have been paying attention to everything the female TV producer was talking about.

Instead, she was thinking about that morning's trio of financial disasters. The bank manager had rung about her overdraft, which was now turning into an Atlantic Ocean-sized trough.

'Mrs Farrell, you should come into the bank so we can discuss things,' he'd said gravely. 'There are a few options I can recommend but we've got to sit down and talk about it.'

Isabel quailed at the thought of discussing her overdraft, particularly as it was December, Christmas was just around the corner, and Robin had put in an order for a computer.

Even worse, the gas boiler had just broken down and would cost hundreds to replace. Hundreds Isabel didn't have and which the bank clearly wouldn't be keen to lend her.

They'd woken up that morning to a freezing house

and no hot water. When Isabel went to investigate the only thing the boiler produced was a worrying belch.

To add insult to injury, she'd brought Naomi on a routine trip to the dentist before lunch to be told that train-track braces were definitely on the cards. Naomi had groaned at the thought of getting braces, particularly as she'd thought she'd managed to escape them while most of her class at school boasted metal mouths. Isabel had groaned even louder at the thought of the bill.

You were always so ready to criticise David's mishandling of finances but you've made just as big a mess of them yourself, she thought morosely as she gave up all pretence of listening to the speaker.

At least she hadn't wasted oodles of cash on any mad get-rich-quick schemes, but buying a Ralph Lauren blazer with matching chinos the previous Saturday – albeit at a designer second-hand shop – wasn't the wisest financial decision she'd ever made, either. The outfit was very classy and would have cost four times the amount Isabel had paid for it if it had been new. But given the crimson colour of her bank balance, it was an impulse buy she now regretted.

And all subconsciously to compete with Jack's wife, a woman who wouldn't put on a nightie unless it had Janet Reger written on it. Elizabeth Carter's make-up bag was probably Prada and Isabel was sure *she* didn't stock up on moisturiser while she was doing the weekly shop in the supermarket, throwing Oil of Ulay into the trolley along with the loo roll and a raft of yoghurts.

Isabel wished she didn't feel the constant need to compete with Elizabeth. It was so ridiculous, childish and unlike her. But she couldn't help herself. Simply hearing that Elizabeth had attended some glamorous party clad in head-to-toe designer clothes was enough to send Isabel into a fit of insecurity where she tore through her wardrobe, looking for something, *anything*, expensive and beautiful to wear the next time she saw Jack.

Not that he ever really talked about his wife, apart from saying whether she was in the country, out of the country, or busy organising some charity event or other. He certainly never discussed what she'd been wearing or how much she spent when she went on her regular shopping trips to Harrods and Harvey Nichols. In fact, his voice was always neutral while speaking of her, as if she was some distant relative whose movements were of little interest to him.

Isabel, however, found that she couldn't avoid hearing or reading about her lover's wife – and about her social butterfly existence and wardrobe to rival Nicole Kidman's.

Never a huge fan of the gossip columns, she was now drawn helplessly to them every day. Elizabeth's name constantly leapt out of the pages of newspapers and glossy magazines.

'Elegant as always in Gucci jersey and Manolo Blahniks to die for, Elizabeth Carter attended the opening of . . .'

'While most racegoers froze in their flimsy dresses and got heels stuck in the muddied grass of the owners' enclosure, Mrs Carter was both warm and effortlessly stylish in a cashmere Jasper Conran coat worn with a rakish Phillip Treacy hat . . .'

The articles were always accompanied by pictures of the fabulously dressed Elizabeth, looking as if a team of stylists had just spent a month working on her. She was so glamorous she made Isabel feel dowdy and dull.

Isabel, who'd never hated anyone in her entire life, found that she almost hated Elizabeth. If she was honest with herself, it wasn't because Elizabeth could afford to spend thousands of pounds on one outfit, while Isabel was worried sick about spending a fraction of that on a second-hand jacket. It was more than that.

Elizabeth had the things Isabel didn't – *she'd* never needed to start over again with no money because she'd had a feckless husband who'd ruined them. She'd been born with a silver spoon in her mouth and a private allowance which meant she had never needed to hold down a job. And she had a wonderful husband whom she didn't appear to appreciate.

That was it in a nutshell: Isabel hated Elizabeth for having Jack and not even appreciating him. Then again, Isabel admitted to herself, she only knew one side of the story. Perhaps Elizabeth adored Jack and was devastated when they'd drifted apart. And now she, Isabel, had practically taken him away from Elizabeth. So she didn't have everything, after all. She didn't have children, either. The poor woman had been denied that. Isabel couldn't imagine life without Robin and Naomi.

The familiar guilt crept into her head and she thought of how horrific it would be if Elizabeth found out about her husband's infidelity. Despite her otherwise charmed life, Elizabeth had had her share of sorrow.

To discover her husband was seeing someone else, was serious about someone else, could destroy a woman as emotionally fragile as her . . .

The sound of applause startled Isabel back to reality and she jerked her head around to the podium where the TV producer was wrapping up her speech with a few comments about how women had to do everything *twice* as well as men to advance their careers.

Isabel closed her eyes, took a few deep breaths and reminded herself never to agree to speak at one of these conferences ever again. She'd said yes on impulse and had been regretting it ever since.

Tanya Vernon had also been asked but had refused. 'Presumably,' Phil Walsh had remarked caustically, because there'd be nobody there she could sleep with to further her meteoric career.'

There was always the TV producer, Isabel thought wryly, as the very masculine-looking woman left the podium, stage lights glinting off glossy black hair that was barely an inch long.

Isabel rose, smiled a professional smile at the delegates and began her speech. As she stared at the interested faces below her, all women who'd battled their way up the career ladder in a male-dominated world, she felt a surge of pride at having won the women's editor's job in the *Sentinel*. She loved her job, loved the work and even the pressure that came with it. Her speech wasn't going to be one of those doom and gloom ones about how hard it was to be a working woman.

Twenty minutes later, after a standing ovation for Isabel's positive woman power speech, there was a break before dinner and the evening session. Now that she'd done her bit, Isabel had absolutely no intention of hanging around any longer. But before she'd managed to sidle out of the door, she was button-holed by one of the organisers, Alva.

'Isabel, you must have a glass of wine,' she announced. Alva was a formidable grey-haired woman dressed in a grey suit. 'I want to introduce you to some of our other panellists.'

Saying no to her was impossible, so Isabel graciously

allowed herself to be propelled towards a group of women in the centre of the room.

She sipped a glass of mineral water and chatted amiably, wondering how soon she could leave without being rude. The discussion wasn't anything to do with women in the media. Everyone was eagerly talking about a hatchet job of a biography that had been written about one newspaper proprietor and was about to be serialised in another paper.

'You can't get your hands on a copy for love nor money,' Alva said. 'There are no review copies available and the author has wisely left the country.'

'I'm sure I could get a copy if I wanted to,' remarked one woman coolly.

Isabel recognised Sophie Walker, a statuesque redhead who wrote a scurrilous diary page for one of the women's magazines. In her early-thirties, she would have been quite attractive had it not been for an over-large, upturned nose and the slightly surly expression on her heavily foundationed face. She was dressed entirely in pale blue, from her knitted jacket and long skirt right down to her glass bead necklace. Isabel suspected that a colour consultant had once told Sophie that pale blue was her 'best' colour. They'd been wrong. Only doe-eyed supermodels could get away with iridescent blue eyeshadow dusted over their eyelids.

'From what I hear from my contacts, the book blows the lid on everything from the way he runs that paper like his own private army, to stories about his many female friends,' Sophie said with heavy emphasis on the word 'friends'. 'They say he makes a big deal about the lack of morality in modern Irish society – and then made one of his girlfriends leave the country in case his wife found out they were having an affair. Are you planning to write anything about the book?' Sophie said, turning sharp eyes on Isabel. 'It'd be just up the *Sentinel*'s street,' she added snidely.

Isabel felt a prickle of unease. There was something about the way Sophie had made that comment, which made Isabel think it wasn't just a throwaway remark from one journalist to another. Definitely not.

She shrugged. 'I don't know,' she said airily. 'That sort of article would hardly be my type of thing.'

'Really?' Sophie's face was disbelieving. 'I thought executive flings in rival papers would be grist to any tabloid's mill? Everybody loves a good gossip and stories about married newspaper bosses having it off with other women will have the whole country spellbound over its Cornflakes.'

Isabel's prickle of unease turned into full-blown, stomach-clenching fear. She was sure the other woman was talking about more than just one newspaper boss. What exactly had she heard about Sophie Walker? That she was a tough cookie with a nose like a bloodhound for gossip. And that an officeful of lawyers went through her articles with a fine toothcomb to make sure she didn't libel anyone – and that she could print as scandalous a story as was legally possible. The words *Sophie Walker* and *dangerous* ran through her head in a jarring refrain.

Unless Isabel was very much mistaken, Sophie knew something about her and Jack. After all, they'd been seeing each other for over four months and it was entirely possible that somebody had noticed something. Did Sophie know the truth or was she only guessing? Isabel dreaded to think of the consequences if she knew the truth.

'We all love reading about affairs, don't we, girls?'

CATHY KELLY

Sophie trilled in an insincere tone.

Feeling rattled, Isabel rapidly ran through her options. She could laugh it off and hope to put Sophie off the scent. Or she could dump her glass and run, letting the gossip columnist think what she wanted to.

Isabel knew which option she'd prefer but she stayed where she was and planted a big fake smile on her face.

Dee had once told her she was utterly transparent. Now Isabel needed an Academy Award-winning performance.

'I'm not sure readers are that interested in affairs these days,' she said in a bored tone. 'It's so sordid, so low-rent. Being fascinated by other people's sex lives always strikes me as rather pitiable. I thought this country had advanced too much in the past few years to be interested in who's doing what to whom.

'Anyway,' she added, staring Sophie Walker down, 'the people who write about that sort of stuff nearly always get it wrong. You have to be so careful of getting your facts right, don't you? Or you and your paper get taken to the cleaner's. The most recent libel case won record damages, so it's not worth publishing if you're going to be damned all the way to the bank.'

'Don't talk to me about libel suits,' groaned a magazine editor. 'They're the bane of my life.'

'Really?' said Isabel interested. She swapped her mineral water for a glass of white wine and watched Sophie out of the corner of her eye. Her ploy appeared to have worked. The other woman looked a little taken aback at the direction the conversation had taken. That cocky look was gone.

She began to tell a bitchy story about an acquaintance's married boyfriend. Isabel pretended to be interested in a long-winded tale of a legal battle. But if anybody had noticed the way she was clutching her glass, they'd have seen that her knuckles were white.

After twenty of the longest minutes of her life, Isabel figured she could leave without giving Sophie Walker pause for thought.

'It was lovely to meet you,' she said, shaking Sophie's hand warmly. 'I'm sure I'll see you again.'

Outside, Isabel breathed in the cool December air and felt her stomach heave. She wanted to retch from fear and anxiety. Every instinct told her that Sophie Walker knew what was going on between her and Jack.

What should she do? Pray that she'd put the gossip columnist off the scent with her blasé act – or she hoped it had been blasé, anyway. Tell Jack? Or say nothing and wait for the inevitable piece in Sophie's column? She could see it now: *Which newspaper magnate has been getting overly involved in his paper, taking one of the tabloid's attractive female management team out to lunch to discuss ways to increase circulation over the Puligny Montrachet and lobster?*

Jack answered his phone on the third ring. Nobody knew the private line number but her and only he ever answered it.

'Oh, Jack, you won't believe what happened,' Isabel gasped into her mobile phone.

'What, darling?' he asked anxiously. 'What's wrong? Have you had an accident? Are the girls all right?'

Relief at hearing his voice made her suddenly emotional. Afraid she would cry, Isabel took a few deep breaths and tried to compose herself before continuing.

'No, I'm fine, and the girls are too. It's nothing like that. I was at the Women In The Media conference and I met this woman, Sophie Walker, a gossip columnist with one of the magazines . . . I think it's *Hype* . . .

Anyway . . .' Isabel took another deep breath . . . 'I think she knows about us. In fact, I'm *sure* she does.'

She shuddered at the thought.

'Isabel, don't panic, please.' Jack's voice was calm. 'What makes you think this woman knows anything?'

Isabel told him the whole story.

'I've heard of Sophie Walker before,' Jack said grimly. 'She's written some pretty nasty things about friends of mine, although she was rapped over the knuckles last year when she made a not-so-veiled reference to a relationship between a trainer and one of his grooms. The magazine was stung for a couple of hundred grand, so she's got to be careful what she writes now. And you handled the situation perfectly,' he said encouragingly.

'I don't know,' fretted Isabel. 'She was so cocky, so sure of herself. What if she writes something?'

'She won't. She was simply prodding you for information. She didn't get any so she's not going to print anything.'

'Are you sure?' asked Isabel. 'I'm so afraid . . .'

'Don't be,' Jack said firmly. 'It'll be OK, I promise. Forget about Sophie Walker. What time can you meet me tomorrow?'

Isabel dried up the last plate and put the stack in the cupboard. She balled up the tea towel and stuck it in the washing machine then surveyed the kitchen. Everything was sparkling, ready for Jack's visit. Eagle Terrace wasn't a palace by any means, certainly not up to Temple Isis standards. But she was proud of it. She'd worked hard to make the small terraced house into a home and reckoned she'd done it more successfully than Elizabeth Carter had with her icy, antique-filled mausoleum.

Stop that, she told herself. She hated being so jealous, so competitive. But she couldn't help it. At the back of her mind there was always the thought that Elizabeth had to have something she didn't . . . Stop it, stop it, stop it! she raged.

Determined to keep her mind off Elizabeth, Isabel rearranged the settings on the breakfast bar for the fourth time. Jack always brought champagne when he came for lunch, so she had bought two pretty champagne flutes to drink it out of. She kept them right at the back of the saucepan cupboard so Robin or Naomi wouldn't find them.

Isabel wasn't sure if she could cope with questions about mysterious champagne glasses when they never had any. It was bad enough coming up with excuses for taking so many calls at night on her mobile phone. Robin was openly curious but apart from giving Isabel knowing looks when the phone rang, she'd said nothing, partly because she was receiving more than a few phone calls from a deep-voiced youth herself.

The doorbell rang and Isabel felt her heart race. He was here. Jack stood at the door, handsome in a grey open-necked shirt worn with a charcoal suit, pewter eyes glinting excitedly. His arms were full of flowers, a huge bouquet of the Stargazer lilies Isabel loved, and stuck awkwardly under his arm was a bottle of champagne.

'Hello, darling, I think I'm going to drop this,' he said. She ushered him in, took the champagne and the flowers and put both on the hall table. Jack grabbed her and threw his arms around her, hugging her to him fiercely as he kissed her.

'I missed you,' he murmured, as his lips sought hers.

'I missed you too, Jack,' she replied before they lost

themselves in an urgent kiss.

Isabel felt a surge of desire as she clung to him, arms entwined. No matter how often they saw each other, and they met up at least every second day, she still felt that rush of passion whenever he held her.

Jack left her mouth and buried his face in her neck, resting his head on her shoulder briefly. She stroked his hair, loving the way the tension seemed to leave his body when he was in her arms.

'You feel wonderful.' He held her at arm's length. 'And you look beautiful, as always. Is this new?' he asked, fingering her red crêpe blouse.

'Yes,' Isabel answered. Well, it was new to *her*. Not telling him about her second-hand clothes foraging was her only vanity.

'You have such beautiful taste, my darling,' he said. 'Mine isn't anywhere near as good, but I bought you a present. It's in the car.'

He went out and returned with a carrier bag and a large white box, carefully tied up with a white ribbon. 'I hope you like it,' he said, handing her the box.

Isabel delightedly opened it, unwrapped several layers of tissue paper and gasped.

There lay the most exquisitely finished ivory silk dress she'd ever seen. She held it up carefully, revealing a beautiful long bias-cut dress that rippled as she examined it. Two delicate straps held it up, crossing over in the most intricate back detail. With her practised eye, Isabel didn't need to look at the label to see that it was a Ben De Lisi, an original from one of her favourite designers.

She'd featured it in her fashion column a fortnight previously, an amusing piece about what a committed shopaholic could buy if money was no object. Jack must have read the article. She felt a lump rise in her throat. Nobody had ever given her such a thoughtful present before.

'It's beautiful,' she said. 'I love it. Thank you, Jack.'

He kissed her forehead tenderly. 'I thought you could wear it in Paris. If you'll agree to come with me, that is?'

'Paris?' she asked, in amazement.

'I thought we could go next month, three days on our own with no interruptions,' he said eagerly. 'As a belated birthday celebration for your fortieth.'

'But we went to Belfast for my birthday,' Isabel pointed out, remembering their three-day September break in the Culloden, the only hotel she'd ever visited where the grown-ups got a rubber duck in the bathroom.

'That doesn't count because we didn't have to fly anywhere,' Jack argued happily. 'And Paris in the springtime sounds so romantic. Please say you'll come?' he begged.

Isabel pretended to look confused. 'January isn't springtime, is it?' she asked. 'Maybe we should wait . . .' She beamed at him. 'I'm only teasing, darling. I'd love to go with you.' Paris in January. It sounded wonderful.

After a lunch of omelettes, crusty bread and champagne, they went upstairs to Isabel's bedroom and made slow, languorous love.

They then curled up together under the duvet and talked, perfectly content in each other's arms.

Isabel kept a wary eye on her alarm clock, nevertheless. The girls got out of school at four, went to her mother's for an hour, and were usually home by half-five. But every time she and Jack had spent the afternoon in her home, Isabel had been nervous that they'd arrive home early for some reason and every noise in the street made her jump. Which was why she leapt frantically out of bed when the doorbell rang at half-three.

'Oh, no,' she shrieked. 'Who could that be?'

'It's not the girls, they've got keys,' Jack reminded her.

'You're right,' she gasped in relief.

'It's probably somebody selling something, Isabel. Don't answer it, they'll go away.'

'You're right.'

But the bell rang again, this time a longer ring. Isabel peered out of the window, trying to see who was below but she was at the wrong angle.

The bell rang a third time.

'Damn!' She pulled on her dressing gown. 'I'd better go down.'

She opened the front door, prepared to give out stink to whatever salesman had rung three times. But the words died in her mouth when she saw who stood on the step.

'Isabel,' said a very smart, forty-something blonde woman in an expensive-looking beige wool coat with a matching hat jammed on her dead straight bobbed hair. It was Robin's best friend, Susie's mother. 'I knew you were here when I saw your car. Are you sick or something?' she asked, staring at Isabel's hastily tied dressing gown.

She felt herself flush. 'No, Amanda,' she lied. 'I . . . er . . . took a couple of hours off to . . . do some housework. The place gets so messy. I was having a bath afterwards,' she said nervously, hoping she didn't look like she'd just got out of bed after a glorious afternoon in bed, glowing from Jack's lovemaking.

This was all she needed. Amanda was anything but stupid and if she figured out exactly what Isabel was doing at home at half-three on a Thursday afternoon,

she was bound to let it slip to Susie, who'd tell
Robin . . .

'I thought you were hoovering or something and
didn't hear the bell,' Amanda said.

'Come in,' Isabel said hurriedly. She was about to lead
the way into the kitchen but remembered that the
debris of a romantic lunch for two was still there, so
pushed open the sitting-room door instead. Unfortunately, it was directly under her bedroom. The floorboards upstairs creaked suspiciously.

Amanda looked up in alarm. 'What was that?'

Isabel blinked. 'A mixture of ancient floorboards and
next-door's cat,' she announced. 'Tiddles sneaks in
through the kitchen window and goes up to lie on the
beds.'

'How awful!'

'What did you want, Amanda?' Isabel asked as
politely as she could. 'It's just that the bath will get
cold.'

'Oh, I just wanted to check if you could pick up the
girls tomorrow night for me? We're going out to dinner
and I hate asking but . . .'

Isabel gritted her teeth. Amanda was always 'just
asking'. But this wasn't the time to refuse.

'No problem,' she said cheerfully.

'Great.' Amanda went into the hall. 'I do love what
you've done with this place,' she added, looking around.
'It's so elegant. My best friend lives five doors down and
her place is nowhere near as nice as this.'

'Really?' said Isabel faintly.

It was getting even worse, Amanda had a friend who
lived down the road – a friend who probably noticed a
strange Jaguar parked outside Isabel's house at least
once a week.

The upstairs floorboards creaked again.

'Bloody Tiddles,' said Isabel, wrenching open the front door. 'Don't worry about tomorrow night, Amanda,' she said brightly. 'I'll pick up the girls. Must fly, I hate cold baths. 'Byee.'

'Tiddles?' said a highly amused voice from the upstairs landing.

'Tiddles will be shot for making so much noise,' said Isabel, climbing the stairs wearily. 'You were like a roomful of cats, not just one.'

'I wanted to know who it was.'

'The mother of Robin's best friend,' she answered, 'who is, no doubt, already planning to ask my daughter what outsized breed of cat our neighbour has, the one that sleeps on the bed and weighs ten times as much as any normal cat?'

'She won't,' Jack said consolingly.

'You don't know Amanda,' brooded Isabel. 'And I don't really know the neighbours here. For all we know, there could be ten rival reporters living across the road, waiting for the day they catch a glimpse of us starkers in front of my window so they can have an interesting front-page splash.'

Jack cuddled her. 'Don't fret, Isabel,' he said softly.

Isabel felt a sense of foreboding from the moment she walked into the Clarence, clutching her coat closely around herself to ward off the freezing cold. A monument to modern design and elegance, the Clarence was all Art Deco, polished wooden floors and minimalist furniture. It was also, she knew, very fashionable and almost always busy.

Not really the ideal spot for a quiet lunch with your married lover, she thought, pushing open the door into the Tea Room restaurant and relinquishing her coat to a waiter.

Having their romantic lunch at home so rudely interrupted the day before had given her the jitters. She'd spent the evening half-expecting Amanda to phone up and say, 'Bath? Pah! You weren't having a bath, were you? My friend saw a man leave your house at half-four . . .'

'This way.' The waiter led her past the other diners to a table where Jack was waiting.

'Isabel,' he said with a smile, rising as she arrived.

'Jack,' she said warmly.

Seeing him relaxed her. What had she been worrying about? Plenty of people met for lunch every day. That didn't mean they were having affairs, did it? So what if the neighbours and nosy Amanda suspected that Isabel was involved with someone who arrived at the oddest hours? It was her business.

She slid gracefully into her seat – and gasped.

Sitting a few tables away, clad in her trademark blue, was Sophie Walker, the columnist who'd been making innuendoes at the Women In The Media conference earlier that week. She wasn't looking at Isabel or Jack but, from the position of her table, she wouldn't be able to miss them. Isabel felt her legs grow weak and sank back in her chair.

'You won't believe who's sitting about fifteen feet away,' she said from between clenched teeth.

'Who?'

'Sophie Walker.'

'You're not serious?' Jack asked.

'I really wish I wasn't,' Isabel said, attempting to keep a fixed smile on her face as she took the menu from the waiter. 'If she sees us – and there's no way she *can't*

497

when she turns away from the man she's with – she'll definitely write about it.'

'Let's look like we're having a business lunch,' Jack suggested.

'Right.' Isabel dragged her chair as far away from his as she could. Then she pulled some papers from her handbag and laid them ostentatiously on the table between them.

'We can pretend we're talking business if she comes over,' she said anxiously, knowing in her heart of hearts that a few papers between the wineglasses wouldn't fool someone like Ms Walker for a nanosecond.

Lunch was hell. Isabel hardly noticed the delicious food, she was so busy concentrating on looking business-like and smiling brightly at Jack in what she hoped was an unlover-like way.

By the time Sophie and her party left, she hadn't looked in their direction once and Isabel crossed her fingers that the other woman simply hadn't noticed them.

'Maybe she didn't see us,' she whispered to Jack hopefully.

But as Sophie pushed in her chair, she turned in Isabel's direction and gave her a little wave, a malicious smile on her normally surly face.

Isabel felt her stomach sink but waved back, her own smile frozen in place.

'I should have known,' she said bleakly. 'We're finished, Jack. That woman will have it on the six o'clock news.'

He walked her back to the car park, doing his best to comfort her. For some reason, he didn't appear to be too put out by the gossip columnist's appearance. He seemed calm and quite relaxed.

'We haven't been that lucky lately,' he said wryly, putting a strong arm around Isabel as they stood beside her car in the high-rise car park.

'No,' she said shakily.

He kissed her on the lips. 'Don't worry, Isabel, it'll be fine,' he promised. 'You'll see.'

She didn't see how it could be, but she said nothing. On the drive back to the office, she thought of their planned trip to Paris. If news of their affair was made public – as now seemed inevitable – she could forget that.

'Mum, can I borrow your crystal drop earrings for the disco?' Robin didn't bother to come downstairs, she simply leant over the banisters and yelled loud enough for Isabel to hear her in the kitchen.

'Sure,' Isabel replied wearily. She didn't give a damn. Robin could borrow her entire wardrobe for all she cared. She sat miserably in the armchair in the kitchen, staring blankly at the TV but not seeing anything. Naomi was upstairs with her friend, Emer, who was staying over for the weekend.

Robin was tarting herself up for the disco. She'd spent an hour in the bathroom and the overpowering scent of bubble bath, deodorant and Isabel's Ô de Lancôme wafted through the house.

Amanda was picking Robin up in half an hour to drive her and Susie to the disco. Isabel couldn't face her and had asked Robin to get the door when Susie arrived.

'I've got a headache. Susie's mother is sure to want to come in and chat and I'm not feeling well enough,' she'd told her daughter.

It was hard to imagine that just a day before she'd

been so frantic at the thought of Robin's meeting Amanda and discussing the exploits of the non-existent Tiddles, Isabel thought glumly. It didn't matter now, not in the slightest. Jack would soon be out of her life, she wouldn't have to cover up any more.

She wiped away the tear that slid down her cheek. It was as if Amanda's interruption had signalled the destruction of everything precious in her life. It had all seemed perfect until Amanda had turned up, and until lunch earlier today. Since then, Isabel's affair had turned from the most wonderful thing in her life to something doomed.

She felt so desperate, so utterly miserable. Seeing Sophie Walker had brought everything to a head. Sophie would spill the beans, Isabel knew it. The *Sentinel* women's editor having an affair with the paper's proprietor was too juicy a story to sit on. It would be plastered all over Sophie's magazine within days, and then all over Dublin.

Isabel couldn't bear to think what would happen when Elizabeth found out about it. She'd give Jack an ultimatum and Isabel was so very scared that he'd choose his wife. Well, of course he would. Which would leave her picking up the pieces of her life. Again.

When Robin left, Isabel heard Naomi and Emer belt into her bedroom, giggling madly. Naomi had suddenly become very interested in clothes and took every opportunity to try on her elder sister's things. Only when Robin was out, naturally, as she wasn't so keen on having her things borrowed as she was of borrowing Isabel's.

'What's yours is mine and what's mine's my own,' Isabel teased her occasionally.

She almost didn't get up when she heard the phone

ring loudly in the hall. It couldn't be for her, she thought morosely, before remembering that it *could* be because her mobile phone's battery needed recharging.

It was Jack.

'Hi,' she said in a monotone, and sank on to the bottom stair. 'How are you?'

'Great, but you certainly don't sound too good,' Jack replied, his voice concerned.

'I'm not,' Isabel said, and suddenly fat tears started to pour down her face. It was as if a dam had broken and all the misery, loneliness and worry came flooding out. 'I'm sorry,' she snuffled, 'so sorry.'

'What's wrong, Isabel?' he asked in desperation.

'Everything,' she sobbed. 'Everything. That woman seeing us today . . . it means it's all over, you know that. She'll write about us and then you'll leave me.' She hated sounding so clinging, so desperate, but she couldn't stop herself. 'I can't bear to think of not being with you, Jack,' she said. 'I love you, don't you understand that? I love you.'

There, she'd said it. It was out in the open. She loved him. There was silence at the other end of the line. Oh, God, what had she done? She'd scared him away. Isabel wiped her face roughly with her sleeve, waiting.

'Isabel,' he said abruptly. 'I need to see you. I don't want to say this over the phone, I want to see you.'

Suddenly, she felt scared. What was he going to say? What could be so portentous that he needed to be with her while he said it? That he'd decided to end their affair – especially as she'd declared her love for him and put him under pressure? She could imagine it: *It was just fun, Isabel, I thought you knew that? I thought you felt the same? I never meant you to fall in love with me . . .* Her heart fluttered painfully in her chest and she felt a fresh flood of tears rise inside her. Please, no . . .

'I love you, Isabel. I'm crazy about you too. And I don't want to spend any longer living this half-life with you. I want to be with you all the time. I want to live with you, if you'll have me?'

'Have you?' she whispered. 'I'd love to be with you, it's what I've dreamed of. I always hoped, I just could never be sure . . .'

'You can be sure now,' Jack said fervently. 'Being with you has made me see what a sham my marriage is. I can't stay with Elizabeth, I don't love her the way I love you. We've just stayed together because it was easier, simpler, to do that than to part. But I can't do it any more.'

Isabel listened joyously. Every word he said was music to her ears.

'I know that we haven't even known each other that long, but it feels like a lifetime,' he said.

'I know,' she replied. 'I can't imagine my life without you. I thought that's what you were going to say just then. I thought I'd scared you off by telling you I love you.'

He laughed, a deep throaty sound. 'I've wanted to say that for so long, but I was afraid of rushing you. I think I've loved you from the moment I saw you, even if that does sound as corny as hell.'

'I don't care,' she said happily. 'You can be as corny as you like when you say wonderful things to me. I feel just as corny – I love you so much.' Isabel searched her pockets for a tissue.

'I don't want us to have to hide how we feel any more. Lunch today made me realise that. I hated you pushing your chair away from me. I hated the fact I couldn't touch you or kiss you in case that woman saw us. So I want all that subterfuge to end.'

Isabel glowed with happiness.

'I need to do one more thing before I leave Elizabeth,' Jack was saying. 'I want to get her into a rehab programme so that she's off drugs. I owe her that much, Isabel. It'll take a little while, but you do understand, don't you?'

'Of course,' she said automatically. Anything was OK so long as she had Jack.

'Oh, Isabel, I love you, I love you, I love you. I'll never get tired of saying it,' he murmured.

'Don't stop then,' she replied.

'I've got to go, I'm afraid,' he added regretfully. 'I'm still in the office and I've got to meet one of the directors from the UK company for dinner.'

'You're still at work?' Isabel asked, shocked. 'It's half-eight, Jack! You'll kill yourself.'

'No, I won't,' he laughed, 'but it's lovely to have you worrying about me, although there's no need to.'

'Of course there's a need to when you work such ridiculous hours,' she fretted.

'I'm crazy about you, Isabel, do you know that?' he asked warmly.

'Yes,' she replied ecstatically.

When they'd hung up, Isabel sat on the step, hugged her knees to her chest and looked around the small hall with pure delight. Everything looked wonderful, even the dusty hall table with its bowl of wilting roses and the collection of trainers, umbrellas and tennis balls under it. Life was wonderful. Jack was wonderful. And he loved her, adored her, wanted to be with her.

He'd finally said it: he loved her. And not just that. He was going to leave Elizabeth. They had a future together, a glorious future. If only Jack could help Elizabeth to get over her drug addiction. He'd do anything to get her off drugs. Isabel felt a quiver of unease. What if he couldn't? What if Elizabeth got worse? Would he leave her then?

CHAPTER TWENTY-TWO

Dee signed the document with a flourish and handed back her solicitor's pen. She'd done it! The house finally belonged to her. Of course, she'd be utterly broke for Christmas, not to mention most of the following year, and had already warned her family and friends not to expect anything but the tiniest presents. But it was worth it.

Ever since Gary had left, he'd been harping on about selling the house they owned jointly so they could split the profits.

Dee had soon realised that she didn't want to leave the pretty little townhouse. She liked living there, she liked the area, she liked her neighbours and she liked being so near to the office. So she'd decided to buy Gary out.

'Signed, sealed and delivered,' she said happily to her solicitor.

'The building society has to amend the documents to show just your name, which may take a couple of weeks, but otherwise, yes, it's signed and sealed,' he answered.

Dee left his office on a high, the sort of high that would normally send her straight to Grafton Street on a shopping binge. Not for the moment, she told herself firmly. Shopping, even her favourite January sales blitz, would have to wait until she'd cleared all the stamp duty and solicitor's bills. Women of property had to be careful with their cash.

She hurried along Baggot Street in her short fake fur coat, a spring in her step. The sight of a pretty girl in glossy black fur, shapely legs emphasised by sheer tights and spindly suede court shoes, a swathe of chestnut curls swinging along behind her head, elicited a whistle from a passing motorbike courier.

Dee winked joyfully at him and then ducked into Searson's pub when she thought he was stopping the motorbike to talk to her. She had to stop being so bouncy and friendly with strangers. It was always getting her into trouble.

Peering around the pub door a minute later, she saw that the courier hadn't stopped after all and resumed her journey, resolving to keep her eyes firmly on the ground.

The house was hers. Yahoo! She need never worry about Gary Redmond again.

A silver Porsche growled to a stop beside her and the driver honked his horn loudly, giving her a shock. What had she done now? Dee wondered in astonishment. Was she giving out invisible Come-and-get-it-big-boy signals or something? It must be the coat. Fun fur seemed to attract all sorts of unwarranted attention. Men thought that 'fun fur' equalled 'fun girl'. It'd have to go.

She flicked back her hair, stuck her nose in the air and hurried on.

'Dee,' roared a low, husky voice she recognised. She stopped and stared at the Porsche's driver. It was Kevin Mills.

'Do you want a lift?' he asked, leaning over towards the passenger window.

Dee hurried towards him. 'No,' she said regretfully. 'I've got my car. It's parked around the corner.'

Trust her to have her car with her on the one occasion when the utterly gorgeous photographer offered her a lift. And he *was* looking gorgeous today. His short dark hair was sleeked back from his forehead, he had a few days' stubble on his square jaw and wore a black polo-neck jumper that made him look like the hero in some hip French movie.

'Where's your car?' Kevin asked.

'Parked beside the canal.'

'Hop in. I'll drive you round,' he said, black eyes glittering.

Suppressing a beatific smile, Dee opened the passenger door. She hadn't realised the seats were so low and practically fell on to the cream leather, ending up with her flirty little chiffon skirt halfway up her thighs, exposing a lot of leg.

Kevin's eyes flickered over her before he turned his attention to the wing mirror and nosed his car back into the traffic.

Dee sat back in her seat gleefully and tried to arrange herself elegantly, pulling down her skirt and adjusting her coat so he'd realise *it* was bulky and not her. Kevin was really going out of his way to drive her back to her car, she thought with pleasure as he pushed through the heavy traffic. It would take at least ten minutes to reach it this way. On foot, the journey would have taken her five.

She flashed him a radiant smile. 'You're very good for doing this,' she said, watching his handsome profile.

Kevin's mouth curved up at the corners.

'No problem. I haven't seen you for ages anyway. You can tell me what you're up to.'

Dee couldn't wait to. 'I've bought my ex-fiancé's half

of the house, so it's totally mine now. I've literally just signed the papers in my solicitor's.'

'Congratulations,' Kevin said. 'He didn't deserve you.'

Dee's smile widened. 'When he left, I realised I liked living there on my own. He wanted me to sell up so we could split the money. He's in London and wants to buy somewhere there, I suppose,' she said. 'This way, I never have to see him again.'

'You've no regrets, then?' Kevin asked, eyes on the road.

Dee briefly wondered why he was asking her that question. 'None at all,' she answered firmly. 'What have you been doing anyway? Any good assignments?'

'Mostly news and celebrity-hunting. I've been offered a skiing junket to Kitzbuhl next month and I'm still trying to work out whether I should take it or not.'

'Skiing,' said Dee dreamily. 'I've always wanted to go skiing. I have this little fantasy that skiing holidays are all adorable log cabins, with roaring fires, soft rugs and big glasses of *gluhwein* when you come in after a hard day on the slopes.'

Kevin stopped the car and ran his eyes over her again. 'That's a very nice fantasy,' he said softly, his voice like hot, dark honey. 'I can picture it right now. Is it a fantasy for one or for two?'

Dee flushed rosily. 'Two,' she muttered, suddenly not knowing where to look. The way Kevin was staring at her, his black eyes drinking her in, was too much.

'I'd better go,' he said ruefully, glancing at the diver's watch on his wrist. 'I'm late for a job.'

'Of course,' Dee said in confusion, and grabbed the door handle.

'Congratulations again, on sorting out your house,' he said. 'I'm happy for you.'

He bent over towards her. Dee expected him to peck her on the cheek but instead he kissed her deliberately on the mouth. Stunned at the feeling of his lips against hers, she did nothing for a moment. Just closed her eyes and breathed him in. He smelled and tasted wonderful, his mouth so warm, so soft.

Kevin moved away slowly, his face only a fraction away from hers.

'I've been inviting you for a drink for months now, do you think you might be free soon?' he asked, eyebrows raised quizzically.

'Yes! Tonight in fact.' Dee could have kicked herself as soon as she'd said it. *Tonight!* He'd think she was desperate. Why hadn't she ever been able to play it cool? But Kevin was nodding. He leant back in his seat and stretched out one long thigh easing the bunched-up muscles with his left hand. Dee tried not to stare.

'Tonight would be wonderful. Will I pick you up?'

'No,' said Dee abruptly, thinking of the mountain of dishes in the sink she'd have to do before inviting anyone in.

'I'll meet you somewhere then. How about eight in Magee's?'

'Perfect,' she breathed.

'I'm looking forward to it,' he said.

She climbed out of the car and waved as he roared off down the road. Wow!

Dee wasn't sure how she drove back to the office without crashing the car, she was on such a high. She had a date with Kevin Mills that evening. Wait till she told Maeve and Isabel.

It was odd that Kevin had never asked about Daryl, even though Dee was sure he knew about her Texan boyfriend. Well, ex-boyfriend. Daryl had gone home over a month ago and while Dee missed his exuberant lovemaking, 'specially when she was alone in her big double bed with nothing but the cuddly seal he'd bought her for company, she was quite content without him.

Daryl had been a lovely, deeply sensual interlude, like the sexy bit in a novel – thoroughly enjoyable for a while but not the sort of thing you wanted all the time. He'd been sweet, charming and lots of fun. But the only thing they'd had in common was sex and after two months of putting up with Daryl's non-stop sexual appetite, Dee was exhausted and, she had to admit, bored.

He was the genuine Martini man, she'd explained to Maeve one day: 'Anytime, anyplace, anywhere.' When Maeve had stopped giggling long enough to inquire what was wrong with that, Dee had pointed out that constant sex was like constant chocolate – eventually, you'd had enough.

'He never stops, Maeve,' Dee explained. 'He wants to make love at least three times a day, and if we go out anywhere, his hands are everywhere.'

'I've noticed,' Maeve said. She'd seen Daryl in action and knew that he liked to keep his hands busy, normally burrowing under Dee's clothes with scant disregard for who was watching or where they were.

'We never talk, all we do is go to bed, and there are times when I'd like to have a pizza in front of the telly and a conversation instead of a sexual marathon,' Dee complained.

Thankfully, there hadn't been any scenes or uncomfortable moments when the inevitable split had come. One day, Daryl had simply said he was going back to the States. After a night of tender lovemaking when they talked about how they'd enjoyed spending time with each other, Dee drove him to the airport and waved him goodbye.

She'd cried, naturally, as he ambled off past the security gates, rucksack in hand, and had spent that evening sniffing miserably and wondering if she'd been wrong to let him go, if she shouldn't have made him stay. Then her natural resilience came into play and she settled down to do the chores she'd ignored while he had been there.

Sorting through the laundry basket and realising that she hadn't worn a single piece of underwear for eight weeks that hadn't been either a G-string, all lace or designed for immediate removal, Dee grinned to herself. Daryl *had* been wonderful but a relationship based totally on sex couldn't work in the long term.

He'd done wonders for her self-confidence though. Thanks to him, Dee's long-absent belief in herself had reappeared. When he was around, she'd felt gorgeous, sexy and desirable. She was thrilled to discover that those feelings didn't vanish when he did.

Now she was going out with Kevin Mills. Tonight. Whatever would she wear?

'A thong and nothing else?' Maeve suggested. 'That's what I'd wear. You are one lucky girl! I know women who'd pay to go out with Kevin Mills.'

Dee pretended to consider this. 'I'm a bit broke right now, what with all the legal bills and paying the mortgage on my own. How much were you thinking of offering cash-wise?'

'I wasn't talking about me,' Maeve said, throwing a balled-up paper bag at Dee. 'I'm blissfully happy with Karl. But I have had my girlish daydreams about that delectable photographer . . .'

'There was nothing girlish about them, I'll bet,' Dee joked. 'Unless you mean "girlish" in a "Girlish Vixens In Leather Get Their Men" sort of way.'

'That's *exactly* what I meant,' Maeve agreed, with a salacious smirk. 'It's the idea of going out with a photographer, you see. Normally, you have the bother of wondering where you're going to get your sexy photos developed because Boots aren't going to do it. But with a photographer, he has his own darkroom . . .'

Dee threw the paper missile back at her friend. 'We're only going out for a drink, not re-enacting this month's colour spread in *Hustler*.'

'Shame.' Maeve grinned. 'So, what *are* you going to wear?'

Dee wore the russet velvet trouser suit she'd bought ages before and had never had the confidence to wear until now. She'd worn it around her bedroom, naturally, figuring out what would look nice underneath as she flounced about, gazing at herself critically in the mirror. But she'd always balked at wearing it outside in case the velvet fabric highlighted every lump and bump unmercifully. Until now.

Kevin had known her for years, he'd seen her at her fattest and her thinnest. Regular aerobics sessions meant she was more toned than she had been for years, but she wasn't thin by any means, as the bathroom scales testified. And he'd *still* asked her out.

He knew what she looked like and obviously liked what he saw, spare tyre or no spare tyre. So there was no point in desperately trying to gild the lily before their date. All of which made things much more relaxed, Dee thought cheerfully as she closed the top button of her black fitted shirt for the third time. It kept popping open.

She didn't really need any lipstick at all, she realised

as she pouted in front of the mirror. Her mouth had been permanently stretched into a grin since this morning. But she slicked on some glossy russet lipstick and, with a squirt of Obsession, was ready.

She was about to leave the house, when she made a quick detour into the kitchen. Just in case, she thought, as she filled the sink with suds and washed up three days' breakfast dishes.

Meeting Kevin in the pub right beside the office might not have been such a good idea, Dee reflected as she walked into Magee's at five past eight to find at least a quarter of the *Sentinel* staff propping up the bar inside the door. She waved weakly at a couple of reporters who'd spotted her. Yes, definitely a mistake. So much for having a quiet drink together.

With a fixed grin on her face, Dee wove her way through the throng, eyes peeled for Kevin's dark head. She couldn't miss him, he was so tall. Too tall for her, really. Still, having a crick in your neck would be a small price to pay for dating him. Then again, he mightn't be dating material. Just because he *looked* nice didn't mean diddly squat. He could be a lazy, possessive, bad-tempered pig with a mother from hell and the sensitivity of an armadillo who'd wait just until he got his feet under the table before he started criticising her clothes, her make-up . . .

'Dee! Over here.'

Kevin stood at the long bar at the back of the pub, surrounded by the remaining three-quarters of her colleagues from the newsroom. Talk about getting stuck in an embarrassing situation.

There was no way they'd be able to slip out of the pub together without everyone demanding to know if they were going on a date. Or, worse still, without people laying bets as to how long it would take them to end up in bed together. The staff of the *Sentinel* weren't great on respecting other people's privacy, especially fellow hacks who might be having a fling.

Dee wasn't ready for the jokes to start, not just yet. Few things ruined a relationship quicker than having the chief news sub running a book on how long it would last and laying fifty to one that the guy would get bored before the girl did, which was what had happened to one ill-fated couple dumb enough to make their liaison obvious. Blast, blast, blast!

We can say we're doing an assignment together, she thought, improvising wildly as she approached the bar. She gave everyone what she hoped was a laid-back grin, determined not so much as to look in Kevin's direction in case she let the cat out of the bag.

He, however, didn't appear to have any plans to cover up their date. He pulled her into the small group of reporters, slid one long arm around her waist and bent down to whisper in her ear, his lips brushing against her skin as he did so.

'I *was* going to kiss you but I thought I'd better check first, in case you didn't want your colleagues to see you going out with me?'

Dee nearly choked.

'I was going to suggest saying we were going on an assignment together in case you didn't want people to know you'd asked me out,' she whispered back.

He gave her waist a squeeze. 'You think I don't want to let people know?' he said. 'I want to order drinks for the entire bar to let everyone know you've finally agreed to go out with me. It's taken you so long to say yes, I want to celebrate. Or would you prefer we kept it a secret?'

Dee's eyes sparkled up at him. Not only was he pleased to see her, he wanted to tell everyone about it into the bargain. 'No.'

Slowly and deliberately, Kevin Mills kissed her full on the mouth, leaving nobody in any doubt as to why they were meeting that evening.

'Whoa!' howled Gerry Deegan. 'Barman, get the hose out – we've got another pair who need to be cooled down!'

Once the good-humoured ribbing had died down, Dee didn't know when she'd enjoyed an evening so much.

She and Kevin stayed in Magee's for another hour, chatting to the other journalists and gossiping about the stories they were working on. Eventually, she found herself leaning against Kevin, her back touching his stomach and his arms loosely around her waist as he propped himself against the bar. It felt comfortable and right, somehow. Every few minutes, he bent down and spoke to her, in a low voice not meant to be heard by anyone else. Dee couldn't resist a small, self-satisfied smile when she saw one of the barmaids staring at her with undisguised envy. Tough bananas, Dee thought triumphantly, he's mine.

It was after nine when they decided to go.

'Are you hungry?' Kevin asked, stifling a yawn.

'Starving,' Dee said. She took in the dark circles under his eyes and the way his face was pale under the five o'clock shadow. 'You're exhausted, aren't you?'

He nodded wearily. 'I was up till three last night on a stake out. If I hadn't been meeting you tonight, I'd have been in bed an hour ago.'

She put her arms around his waist, marvelling at how she felt able to do something so intimate so easily. 'Why don't you come back to my place? We'll have a quick pizza in front of the telly and then you can go home to bed.'

Kevin's relieved grin lit up his face. 'That sounds marvellous. Sitting in front of the TV is all I'm capable of tonight,' he admitted. 'I know I should be bringing you to an exotic restaurant or a club for our first date, especially when you're wearing such a wonderful outfit and look so good.' He fingered the lapel of her velvet jacket. 'But I'm bushed.'

'We can do the exotic restaurant thing another time,' Dee said.

'Tomorrow,' he promised.

Nobody whooped embarassingly as they left, although Dee wouldn't have minded if anyone had. She felt confident now, happy to be with Kevin and, amazingly, sure that he was equally happy with her.

After they'd eaten the takeaway pizza, they curled up together on Dee's settee and watched half of a science fiction movie before she noticed that Kevin had fallen asleep.

She smiled as she watched him, amazed at the almost girlishly long black lashes that fanned his cheeks. They were the only feminine thing about him. Without being even the slightest bit macho or aggressive, Kevin Mills was very male.

It was funny, she thought, gently stroking his short dark hair. If she'd been here with Daryl, they wouldn't have got past the movie's credits before he'd have had her underwear off. Which had been fun once, of course, but ultimately boring.

Spending the evening with Kevin had been very enjoyable and entertaining, yet he hadn't even attempted to grope her. Nor had he taken her invitation to eat a pizza in her house as carte blanche to go to bed with her. The most sensual thing he'd done all evening was wipe some mozzarella cheese from her lips. Yet that tender gesture had, strangely, been more erotic than a million French kisses from Daryl.

Just the way Kevin's long fingers had touched her lips had sent little quivers of excitement rippling through her body. Dee knew that when she did end up making love with Kevin, it would be an experience she'd never forget.

She didn't want to rush into it, though. This was special; *he* was special. She had no intention of jumping into bed with him at the first opportunity and ruining their chance of a future.

'Sleepyhead,' she whispered softly in his ear. 'I think you should go home.' She kissed him on the cheek and then untangled herself so she could go into the kitchen and boil the kettle to make coffee.

'Sorry,' Kevin said, wandering in after her and rubbing his eyes. 'I'm a great guest. Feed me and I pass out.'

Smudge, who had already decided that she loved and adored Kevin and had rubbed herself against him with blissful abandon earlier, followed him besottedly.

Dee went back to making extra strong coffee. 'Don't worry. You can't expect to stay up half the night working and then be the life and soul of the party the following day. Sugar?'

'Yes, honey,' he joked. 'Two. Can I bring you out to dinner tomorrow night to make up for passing out on you?'

Dee pretended to think about it. 'I'll have to check my diary. I think the Sheik is bringing me to Paris for the night. Or was it Cannes . . . Yes, I'd love to go to dinner with you tomorrow night,' she said with a smile and handed him a mug of very strong instant coffee.

When he'd left, she tidied up the kitchen, stuffed the giant pizza box in the bin and headed upstairs, unable to wipe the smile off her face. Smudge had got there before her and was, unusually, curled up on the bed.

Dee threw herself down on the duvet and rubbed her cat's ears until Smudge purred orgasmically.

'Isn't he wonderful?' she said.

Smudge purred louder.

'We can share him,' Dee offered.

Curled up in bed, she thought of Kevin. The way he'd wrapped his arms around her in the pub, laughed at her jokes and chatted companionably. He was lovely, she thought. Handsome, kind, fun. And sexy, that was for sure. Suddenly she remembered what Maeve had said about photographers and sexy photographs and laughed out loud, dislodging Smudge from her position at the end of the bed. Now *there* was a thought.

The newsroom was practically empty when Dee waltzed in early the following morning, determined to catch up on all her work before going out to dinner with Kevin.

She had to write up an interview with a rather eccentric fashion designer, finish her *Dear Annie* column and make dozens of phone calls, all before half-six when Kevin was picking her up from work. She couldn't wait!

'Where have you been?' screeched Tanya Vernon, appearing like the Wicked Witch of the West as soon as Dee dumped her briefcase on her desk.

She shrank back at the ferocious look in Tanya's eyes. Dressed in head-to-toe black with a large jet crucifix dangling at her slender throat, Tanya looked positively malevolent and was clearly very angry with someone. Dee gulped, aware that she was going to be the stunt double for that someone and take the brunt of Tanya's anger. 'I was ringing your mobile phone for *hours* last night!' Tanya hissed. 'Where were you? Don't you ever turn it on, you stupid fat cow? You don't give a damn about this paper or this department, do you?'

For a moment, the only thing Dee was aware of was the pulsing of her own heart, a frantic, rabbit-caught-in-the-headlights sensation. Then, as Tanya started yelling about a hot story they'd missed because she hadn't been able to send anyone to do the interview, Dee realised that the few occupants of the newsroom had stopped what they were doing and were staring.

All eyes were upon them, nobody saying a word, like people on a jeep safari watching a carnivorous lioness rip the throat out of a bewildered animal she'd managed to scare out of the herd.

'Chantal *never* gives interviews! She was here on a flying visit and we had an exclusive last night if only I could have reached you, but I couldn't!' raged the other woman, eyes black pinpoints.

Helplessly, Dee glanced around, desperate for someone to come to her aid, looking for someone to save her.

Suddenly it hit her: nobody was going to save her from Tanya. Oh, Isabel would have done or Maeve. They'd stand up to Ms Vernon all right. They wouldn't let her ride roughshod all over Dee. They knew she couldn't bear confrontation and could never strike back when someone was screaming at her. Especially an irate editorial director.

But they weren't here. Dee was on her own now.

'I'm . . . I'm sorry,' she stammered. 'I was out . . . off duty,' she said feebly.

'That's not good enough,' shrieked Tanya, going in for the kill. 'You either work here or you don't, Dee, and from the way you're behaving, you soon won't. There are plenty of hard-working people who'd be perfect for your job. People with the hunger to do it properly.'

Dee felt her bottom lip wobble. She couldn't be going to cry, not now. It'd look so weak, so cowardly, like an admission of guilt. She *had* been off duty the night before. She was entitled to have her mobile phone turned off. It wasn't as if she worked in news any more where you needed to be permanently available for work. The women's department was hardly a hotbed of breaking news stories.

It did occur to Dee to wonder why, if Tanya was that desperate to get the interview, she hadn't asked someone else? But one look at the editorial director's furious face told Dee it would be a mistake to say anything. Except sorry.

'I'm sorry,' she said again.

Tanya looked down her nose at Dee, grey eyes glacial. 'Sorry's not good enough,' she snarled, before turning on her heel and marching off.

'Jesus,' breathed Anna, one of the freelance reporters who'd seen everything. 'What a bitch. Are you OK, Dee?'

Dee couldn't trust herself to speak. She nodded blindly, hoping she wouldn't cry until everyone had stopped looking at her, and quickly went into Isabel's partitioned office, sank on to the chair and stared at her hands. They were shaking like leaves in a force-ten gale.

She was shaking. That had been one of the most horrific moments of her life. Being publicly screamed at by someone as razor-tongued as Tanya was a terrible experience.

'Morning, Anna.' Dee heard Isabel's warm, friendly tones ring out across the office and felt panic-stricken. She couldn't face her. Just one kind word, one mention that an enraged Isabel planned to confront Tanya and make her apologise for screaming at the staff, and Dee would cry for sure. She had to get out of here.

She bolted out of Isabel's office, cannoning into the women's editor as she did so.

'Dee, what's wrong?' asked Isabel after one look at her deputy's stricken face.

'Can't talk,' she said hoarsely, scooping her handbag off her own desk and running for the door.

She ran out of the office, out of the car park and found herself standing on the street, traffic zooming past her. Dee looked around blindly, wondering why she'd left, why she hadn't hidden in the ladies' and told Isabel the whole horrible story? But she'd had to get away from the office and, if she was honest with herself, Dee knew she couldn't bear to tell Isabel what had happened. She looked up to Isabel, respected her. How could Isabel respect *her* after this?

Dee walked up the street to a small café, ordered a cappuccino with a double helping of sprinkled chocolate and drank it slowly, her mind turning over the morning's events. How she hated Tanya Vernon! No, hated wasn't bad enough on its own: loathed, detested, despised *and* hated. If only she knew why Tanya despised her so much. That was the baffling thing.

Tanya had so much: incredible beauty, a size ten body and long, long legs that made Dee look like one of the seven dwarves by comparison. So why did she hate short, overweight Dee O'Reilly so much? It was a mystery.

After a comfortingly chocolatey second cappuccino,

she phoned Kevin and told him what had happened.

'That bitch!' he spat, venom in every syllable. 'I'll fucking kill her.'

Despite her misery, Dee was thrilled by his reaction. Gary would have told her she was over-reacting. Daryl would have dragged her off to bed to cheer her up. Kevin Mills, on the other hand, knew exactly what to say. And he knew what Dee should do as well.

'I've been working with your news team a lot recently and I keep hearing people say that Vernon is hiding something,' he said thoughtfully, once he'd raged against Tanya for a few moments. 'Nobody had even heard of her until earlier this year and then she appears, saying she's worked in newspapers all over the world.'

'She has?' asked Dee, astonished. 'That's more than I've ever heard about her.'

'Australia, apparently. According to Chris Schriber, she was something in a Sydney newspaper group. The question is: *what*? Hardly a reporter. She's too much of a bimbo to be one and as her management skills are zero, she's obviously only just been given an executive position.'

Dee grinned inanely. It was nice when your boyfriend described a woman you envied as a 'bimbo'. Tanya's endless legs and supermodel cheekbones obviously didn't cut any ice with him. She eyed the café's chocolate éclairs speculatively.

'Don't get upset by her, Dee,' Kevin was saying. 'Get even. You were an investigative reporter for years. Investigate her. Find out where she came from, what she did, and then you might figure out what her problem is. It'll also give you ammunition for the next time she decides to tear you apart in public.' His voice became softer. 'I'd love to go in and tell her that if she says one word to you ever again, she'll have me to contend with. But I can't.'

'I know. I've got to do it myself,' Dee said, without much conviction.

'You do,' Kevin pointed out gently. 'But not today. You're too vulnerable, too upset. I'll cheer you up tonight, I promise. I'll buy you the best dinner in Dublin and then you'll be able for that bitch tomorrow. Oh, hold on for a minute, will you, Dee?'

She could hear another, muffled voice speaking to Kevin.

'I've got to go,' he said rapidly. 'I'll phone you before lunch, OK?'

'OK. 'Bye.'

Pushing thoughts of her unfinished column out of her mind, Dee wandered aimlessly up the street, peering into shop windows. In a tiny boutique, she tried on a slinky silk sweater, a caramel V-neck style that was very slimming. Even though she knew she shouldn't even *think* of buying it as she had enough bills as it was, Dee dug out her credit card and bought the sweater. Then she saw a fake amber necklace that would look lovely with it, so she bought that too. Who needed therapy, she thought, when they could shop?

In the boutique next door, she was riffling through a rack of discount blouses when her mobile phone rang. It was Isabel wondering if she had written her agony column yet. She obviously hadn't heard about the row because she asked if Dee was feeling all right.

'You looked so pale, I wasn't sure if you were sick or something,' she said, sounding concerned.

'I'm not sick,' Dee said reluctantly. Just sick in the head. 'I had to go out for half an hour. I'll be back in a few minutes and I'll finish the column then.'

She had to go back. There was no point hiding any more. Unless she gave in her notice over the phone, she was going to have to face Tanya Vernon again and again, every single day. That was the reality of the situation. And she couldn't resign, although perhaps that was what Tanya wanted.

There are plenty of people who'd be perfect for your job . . . she had said. And Dee had a pretty good idea who she was talking about: her own friends. Tanya wanted to create a mini-empire around herself, made up of sycophantic pals who were undoubtedly as talentless as she was.

Women who had degrees in bossing people around and savaging their self-confidence, but were completely incapable of actually *writing* an article.

Then it hit her: if Tanya had been so desperate for the scoop with Chantal, why hadn't she done it herself?

After all, in an emergency, any newspaper editor worth their salt should be able to do a reporter's job. Dee knew that plenty of editors had started as sub-editors and therefore designed pages, wrote headlines but rarely wrote articles. But Tanya wasn't a sub-editor; she'd said so one day when one of the subs was sick and the head of production needed a stand-in. So her background – if she had any journalistic background at all – had to be in reporting. Which made it doubly strange that she hadn't interviewed the actress herself. Unless she wasn't a reporter, either?

There were three categories of journalist in the newspaper business: sub, reporter or photographer. If Tanya wasn't any of the above, what was she? Apart from a monumental pain.

Kevin was right. Tanya Vernon had to be hiding something. And Dee was determined to find out what.

Dear Annie,

I've had my ups and downs recently but I truly thought things were working out for me at last. I've got a lovely new man in my life who seems to be everything a girl could want and my job is going pretty well, but one of my bosses keeps picking on me.

I know I'm not imagining it. She really seems to hate me. No matter what I do, it's not right. She gives me all the horrible assignments to do, criticises my work and makes me re-do things I've worked really hard on. The last straw came today when she humiliated me in front of my colleagues over something that wasn't my fault at all. What was worse, I let her do it. I didn't say anything and actually apologised, even though I wasn't in the wrong. Please help.

Desperate

Dear Desperate,

You know what I'm going to say, don't you? This woman is a bully and she'll never stop bullying you unless you do something about it. Not somebody else – you. There are occasions in life when you have to ask for help but from what you've told me, this isn't one of them. This woman will continue to bully you because you let her do so. She'll only stop if you stand up to her . . .

Dee sighed. It was true. Unless she took action, Tanya would *never* stop. Even her own alter ego could see it: it was now or never.

She walked back to the *Sentinel* office, dumped her shopping in her car and marched up the stairs to the newsroom. Tanya wasn't in the conference room, which suited Dee perfectly. What she had to say she wanted to say in front of an audience. Dee took a deep breath and pushed open the newsroom door.

The editorial director wasn't difficult to spot. Tall and striking in her black outfit, Tanya was bent over one of the subs' desks, arguing about something if her body language was anything to go by.

Dee walked up to her and spoke loudly, not caring if she was interrupting. 'Tanya, I want to talk to you. Now.'

Disdain on her perfect features, Tanya looked up briefly. 'I'm busy.' She bent back to the screen.

'I said, I want to talk to you now,' Dee said in a firmer voice.

This time, Tanya stood up straight. 'How dare you interrupt me . . .'

Calmly, Dee pulled herself up to her full five foot three and stared coldly at the other woman.

'Shut up, you stupid bitch,' she said, her voice icy. 'Don't *ever* talk to me like that again. This is a news-room, not the fishmarket.'

Tanya stared back, amazed. 'Listen . . .'

'No,' said Dee loudly, so that everyone could hear. '*You* listen. You are a talentless, bullying bitch and if you were that desperate to do the story, you should have gone and interviewed Chantal yourself. But you couldn't because,' she paused, aware that you could have heard a pin drop in the deathly quiet of the newsroom, '*you* couldn't write an article to save your life and you're too stupid to do an interview. You haven't written a single piece since you came here, and that's because you *don't know how to.*'

Tanya's face was a picture of outrage but Dee didn't hesitate, afraid that if she did the editorial director

526

would shout and it would turn into a screaming match.

'We all know that your only skill is kissing ass,' Dee added coldly. 'That and desperately hoping that some executive will become so besotted with you he promotes you above your abilities – which wouldn't be much of a promotion. But that hasn't worked here, has it? Because there's nobody desperate enough to want to sleep with you, so all you're left with is screaming at people who have some writing ability. If you're going to screw your way to the top, Tanya, it helps to have some shred of talent to fall back on when your knees give in!'

Somebody sniggered loudly but Dee didn't stop. She was beginning to enjoy this. Tanya was open-mouthed with anger and shock, her eyes startled.

Dee looked down her nose at the other woman like she was a piece of dog dirt on her shoe. 'Nobody in this office will take your crap any longer, Tanya, especially not me. If you try any more of your bullying, I'll get the union behind me so you're blacklisted and not one single journalist will work for you again. Got it?'

Dee didn't even know if that was possible or not but it sounded good and was having the desired effect on Tanya who was now white-faced with temper, her Slavic cheekbones practically vibrating with temper.

'Who do you think you are?' she shrieked.

Dee summoned every reserve to give Tanya such a look of disdain that the other woman actually recoiled. 'Somebody you'd better have respect for or you'll be sorry. Very sorry,' Dee said in a voice low with menace.

She flicked back a curl, turned away and went to her desk, a grin the size of the Golden Gate Bridge appearing on her face. She'd done it, she'd actually done it!

Behind her, Tanya spluttered. 'D-did you hear that?'

'I think that's game, set and match to Ms O'Reilly,'

said a cool, amused voice which Dee recognised as Chris Schriber's. 'Or don't you like it when the tables are turned, Tanya?'

It was as if the spell was broken and the awe-struck audience breathed again.

'Well done!' said Maeve, rushing up and giving Dee a huge hug.

The subsequent round of applause sent Tanya rushing from the room.

People crowded around Dee, several colleagues clapped her on the back, Jackie kissed her and the subs queued up to shake her hand.

'Tanya deserved that,' said Anna, who'd witnessed the earlier performance. 'I couldn't believe all the things she said to you this morning.'

'What happened earlier?' demanded Isabel. 'Dee, did she attack you?'

'Attack?' cried Anna in disbelief. 'Attack wasn't the word for it. She almost fired Dee because there was nobody to interview some bloody actress last night. She screamed the office down.'

'Is that true?' asked Maeve. 'Oh, Dee, how awful . . .'

'Not so awful after all,' Isabel pointed out proudly, as she grabbed Dee's hand and squeezed it tightly. 'Whatever she said forced you to deal with Tanya, once and for all. I know saying that every cloud has a silver lining is a bit of a cliché, but in this case it's true.'

Dee grinned infectiously. 'I agree.'

'You do realise that Tanya will *really* have it in for you now, Dee?' Maeve cautioned.

'Yes, but I'm working on it.'

When everyone had gone back to their desks, Isabel made tea and brought it back into her cubbyhole for Dee and herself.

'This has been going on for some time, I suppose,' she said. 'I wish you'd told me Tanya was being so vile to you and so hurtful, Dee. I'd have stopped her.'

'I know.' Dee patted Isabel's hand gratefully. 'I know you would have. But I couldn't tell you,' she admitted. 'It was so embarrassing not being able to stand up to her, like being the fat girl in the schoolyard all over again. I felt powerless, useless. And,' she stirred her tea, 'Tanya seemed to sense that. She always commented on my figure, constantly said I was fat.'

Isabel's huge blue eyes were as fierce as Dee had ever seen them.

'Don't listen to a word that woman says. You're one of the sexiest, most vibrant women I know. You can light up a room with your presence. Something Tanya hasn't a hope in hell of doing.'

'Unless she wears a dress made out of Christmas tree lights,' quipped Dee happily. 'It's funny, I can joke about it now. Confronting the lion in its den really is the only way to deal with something like this,' she added thoughtfully. 'I should have done it ages ago.'

'You've done it now, that's all that matters. And I'm so proud of you. I know you hate confrontations or fights.'

'I *used to*,' Dee said. 'I almost enjoyed that. Towards the end, anyway. Because I was winning, I suppose. In the beginning, I was terrified.'

'What I don't understand,' Isabel said, 'is why Tanya's so venomous towards you. I just hope you didn't listen to a word she said earlier, Dee. You work so hard at your job and I certainly appreciate you. I'm going to talk to Malley about this. The editor should be aware of what's going on.'

'She's probably listening to Tanya's sob story right now,' Dee said cynically.

'Probably,' agreed Isabel. 'But she's going to hear my version too. Maeve's right. Tanya will have it in for you now.'

Dee gave a secret little smile. 'Don't worry, Isabel. I'm not finished with Tanya yet, not by a long shot. If she thinks she can mess up my career, one I've fought hard for, she's got another think coming, I promise.'

None of the big Sydney papers had ever heard of Tanya Vernon. Neither had the TV news stations. By the time she'd contacted every news organisation in the city, Dee was no longer surprised. It had taken her three days to cover them all, what with the time difference and the difficulty of locating the correct person to talk to in each organisation.

Kevin had helped, of course. An old friend who worked as a photographer in Melbourne had been making his own discreet enquiries.

'Tom spent two years in Sydney freelancing before he got this job,' Kevin explained. 'He still knows a few journos there.'

Whoever Tom knew, they came up trumps. On day four, Dee opened her e-mail to find a message from him.

Discovered your pal worked as a weather girl about four years ago in one of the small New South Wales stations for a couple of months. A paper ran pictures of her from a soft-porn mag, something she did when she first arrived in Australia. It caused quite a scandal because she'd made a big deal about being this holy, Catholic Irish girl. That was part of her trademark, the cute but holy thing.

Dee was stunned at the notion of the hard-nosed, malicious Tanya managing to pull off any combination of cute and holy.

It really worked. She was quite good at it. My friend says she could have made it in the big stations. But she left after that and nobody's heard of her since. She never worked in any of the papers here. This might be useful to you.

The paper that printed the pics said her real name was Concepta Gorman and she was from a village near Athlone, which they said was a few miles outside Dublin.

When you're in a country as big as Australia, Athlone does seem like it's only a few miles outside Dublin! I've got a bad photocopy of the article. Will I fax or snail-mail it? Only it's such bad quality it might not fax very well. The pictures are hot!

Dee felt a faint glimmer of pity for Tanya. Or Concepta. It must have been dreadful to find something you were good at – and Dee could imagine Tanya being very good at TV, she had just the right looks for a faintly insincere, sexy smile – and then have it all ripped away from you because of something you'd done in the past. None of us is perfect, Dee thought. Everybody has a skeleton in the cupboard. What a pity Tanya's had turned out to be soft porn pictures.

Then she realised what she was doing – feeling sorry for the woman who'd systematically made her life a misery for the past six months.

'*Snail-mail it,*' she typed on to the computer.

'*Thanks a million, Tom, I owe you.*'

A couple of phone calls later, and with the help of an Athlone-based reporter she knew from her time as a news reporter, Dee had tracked Concepta Gorman down to a small secondary school in the Midlands. Three school yearbooks from around about the period Tanya would have been there were being posted up to her. If the pictures of Concepta Gorman were obviously of a young Tanya Vernon, then Dee had hit paydirt and could find out for sure whether Tanya had any journalistic experience or not.

'You wanted me?' asked Dee sweetly, standing outside the conference room where her nemesis sat at one end of the massive table, surrounded by newspapers, A-4 pads and pens.

It was a week after their confrontation and so far, Tanya had studiously avoided Dee, not even speaking to her at editorial conferences.

Today Dee had arrived back after lunch with Kevin to find a note from Tanya stuck to her computer screen: 'See me in the conference room when you get in'.

No 'please' or 'thank you', she noticed without surprise. Tanya had never been much of a one for the simple courtesies.

'Yes.' Tanya spoke with barely disguised dislike.

'Come in.'

Dee went in and sat down, purely because Tanya hadn't asked her to. Sitting back in a leisurely manner, she put her notebook on the table, crossed her legs calmly and adjusted her suede wraparound skirt carefully, to hide the fact that she was actually as nervous as hell.

Confronting Tanya in front of the entire office when her adrenaline was as high as an Olympic athlete's had been one thing; confronting her on a wet Tuesday afternoon with nobody around to back Dee up if things got nasty, was another scenario entirely.

'I've an assignment for you,' Tanya said.

Dee raised her eyebrows questioningly but said nothing.

'There's a new fish canning factory ship just about to be launched in Donegal. The biggest in the world. We want you to join it for twenty-four hours of the maiden voyage.'

'*We?*' asked Dee sceptically.

'The editor suggested it. She asked me to tell you,' Tanya replied, making it perfectly plain that she detested having to pass on as much as the time of day to Dee O'Reilly.

'Why me?' Dee asked. 'It's hardly women's pages stuff.'

'Malley thought you'd be able to write a good colour piece, something atmospheric.'

'Oh.' Dee sat up straight and widened her eyes innocently. 'You mean, the editor likes the way I write and thinks I'd make a good job of this?' she asked pointedly.

'Yes,' snarled Tanya. 'You go tomorrow.'

'Tomorrow!' said Dee in shock.

Tanya gave an evil little smile, having finally scored a point in the battle of wits. 'Tomorrow. At seven. Several other journalists are going.'

'Bitch!' hissed Dee to Maeve a few minutes later as they stood in the kitchen making coffee. 'She must have known about this for days but only told me now. How am I expected to finish all my work and still be ready for seven in the morning?'

'I told you she'd be out for your blood,' Maeve said. 'You're lucky she mentioned the trip to you at all. If she was as clever as she thinks she is, she'd have pretended you knew all about it and couldn't be bothered, which would go down like a ton of bricks with Malley.'

'True,' Dee muttered. 'Anything for me?' she called, seeing the post girl walk by with a trolley of afternoon post.

'Just one.' She handed Dee a parcel with an Athlone postmark.

'If this is what I think it is, I'm in a better mood already,' crowed Dee, ripping open the envelope.

'The year books,' said Maeve, who knew the whole story.

They found Tanya in the earliest year book – 'Making her at least three years older than she pretends to be,' Maeve said.

Dee couldn't say anything at all. She was speechless. The pictures were generally all pretty unflattering, the way year-book pictures are. Most of the people pictured probably wouldn't recognise themselves twelve years on. But Tanya Vernon, or rather Concepta Gorman, was even more unrecognisable than most.

Her eyes were half hidden by a deeply unflattering shaggy perm and the heavy rock 'n' roll moll eyeliner didn't do her any favours. But what was most startling was Tanya's size.

She was huge, a vast moon face staring at the camera, fat cheeks obscuring the cheekbones everyone now admired, and several chins hiding the modern Tanya's delicately pointed chin. The photo stopped at shoulder level but it was enough to show off enormous shoulders squeezed into a brown jumper, a colour that did nothing for her sallow skin.

'It can't be the same woman,' said Maeve, peering at the picture close up.

'It is,' Dee said in amazement. She'd recognise Tanya anywhere: those hard, cold eyes and that slightly surly expression on the full lips. Several extra stones couldn't hide Tanya from Dee. She was used to looking at a heavy woman in the mirror and wondering what she'd look like about three stone lighter.

'She must have lost a hell of a lot of weight,' Maeve commented. 'Maybe that's why she hates you so much,

Dee? Because you're gorgeous and voluptuous and she wasn't.'

'That's too much analysis to waste on bloody Tanya Vernon,' Dee said briskly. 'You could spend half your salary trying to work out why she's such a bitch and it'd still be a waste of time and money. There are some people for whom in-depth personal analysis is wasted – people like her. She's a cow. End of story.'

Maeve laughed. 'So who wants to be the one to cover the psychoanalytical convention in Galway next month, then? You sound caring and interested enough.'

'I *am* interested in therapy,' protested Dee. 'But there comes a time when it's pointless trying to work out what motivates someone to do something horrible. It's far better to stop thinking about the other person at all and work on developing your own coping mechanisms to deal with them.'

'Sorry, Dr O'Reilly, my mistake. I think you should *join in* the psychoanalysts' convention.'

'I might need a few days intense psychoanalysis after the weekend,' Dee pointed out. 'Millie and Dan are having their baby christened on Saturday. And guess who'll be there?'

'Lovable Gary?' Maeve said sourly.

'Yeah. I'm not looking forward to it,' she admitted. 'I haven't seen him for so long, it's going to be very strange . . .'

'It won't be strange at all. Just garotte the pig if he comes near you. Is Kevin going with you?'

'I haven't asked him,' Dee confessed. 'It's not really fair to bring him along as a "look, I've-got-a-boyfriend" prop. I tried that with Daryl at Millie's dinner party and it was nearly a disaster. No,' she added thoughtfully, 'I've got to do this on my own.'

'I'll go with you,' offered Maeve. 'I'm not working on Saturday.'

Dee grinned. 'Knowing how you feel about my ex-fiancé, we'd spend the night in a cell somewhere while I tried to convince the police you didn't really mean to stab him with a pastry fork!'

Isabel touched the velvety petals of the pale pink roses and smiled. They brightened up her desk, and her face, she admitted happily. Trust Jack to know that she'd be utterly miserable that morning, faced with four days without him. She read the card again, written in Jack's elegant scrawl.

Darling Isabel, just a note to tell you I love you and that I'll be home on Sunday night. I miss you so much even though it's only been a few hours since I saw you. All my love . . .

Brussels felt like a million miles away. But he'd phone several times a day, he'd promised.

'I want to hear your voice all the time,' he'd said the night before.

And she wanted to hear his.

Isabel glanced at her watch. Nearly half-twelve. He'd be there now, on his way to a meeting probably.

'What a trip! I thought it'd never end.' She looked up abruptly to see Dee appear beside her, looking decidedly the worse for wear. Her curls were tied back severely in a scrunchie, the only make-up she wore was the smudged remainder of the previous day's mascara and her eyes were red-rimmed.

'How was the canning ship?' Isabel asked, not expecting a thrilled response from the exhausted look on Dee's face.

'Not my finest hour,' she said, stifling a yawn. 'You'll

never believe what happened. Tanya told me to be there at seven for the flight to Donegal and when I got there, they'd gone! The woman who'd organised the whole thing told me they'd faxed Tanya yesterday evening to say the trip was starting an hour earlier. The cow never told me!'

'Ouch,' said Isabel. 'What did you do?'

'Panicked for about ten minutes,' Dee admitted. 'Then,' she grinned mischievously, 'I hired a helicopter to fly me there! I had to. They wanted the story and there was no other way I'd be in Donegal for the maiden voyage otherwise. And it was one of the editor's ideas, after all.'

'You did what?' Isabel gasped. 'Tanya will go out of her mind.'

The thought of Tanya Vernon's apoplectic expression when she discovered what had happened struck both of them at the same time and they burst out laughing.

'She'll have a spasm!' roared Dee.

'So long as I can be here to see it,' chuckled Isabel, wiping her eyes. 'Are you sure you'll be able for her when she gets angry?' she asked in a more serious tone.

Dee nodded confidently.

'Come on then, I'll buy you lunch,' Isabel said fondly. 'You look like you need some pampering and building up before you face Ms Vernon.'

'Thanks, that sounds wonderful,' said Dee. 'I'm starved.' She glanced at the huge bouquet on Isabel's desk and smiled.

'Jack?' she mouthed.

Isabel beamed at her.

'Tell me all about it over lunch,' Dee said, collecting her handbag.

Isabel didn't quite tell her everything – she didn't

want to blab that he was leaving Elizabeth; not until he'd actually done it. Then, she promised herself, Dee would be the first to know. Dee had been so kind to her since she'd found out about Jack. She'd covered for Isabel so she could go for long leisurely lunches with him and had been a shoulder to lean on when Isabel needed to talk to someone about how hard it was loving someone who was married. So she told Dee about the proposed trip to Paris and her new Ben De Lisi dress, but not about their plans for the future.

'*New* designer clothes instead of second-hand ones,' Isabel joked. 'Imagine it. I'll be turning into Elizabeth Carter soon, right down to a Gucci G-string to go with my Ben De Lisi dress.'

Dee, who'd been quite animated during the meal, suddenly became subdued. She didn't finish her ricotta cake, pushing the half-empty plate away from her.

'Isabel, there's something I have to tell you,' she said hesitantly.

'What?' She sat up, startled. 'What is it? Has someone at work said something to you about Jack and me?'

Dee shook her head slowly. 'No. I don't know whether this is good or bad news . . .'

'Tell me?' urged Isabel.

'Kevin's best friend is a photographer too. This morning he told Kevin about this great scoop he'd got last night in a nightclub in the city. Pictures of Elizabeth Carter with this young bloke. She was wrapped around him all night, apparently.'

Isabel was stunned. Elizabeth with another man? It was unbelievable.

Dee wasn't finished. 'This snapper followed them back to a hotel nearby. They booked a room, went in and left together this morning, still in the same clothes.

Kevin says they're great photographs, apparently. She was obviously strung out on something in the nightclub. This photographer has seen her with scores of other guys before, but he's never bothered to take photos until now.' Dee paused.

'He took snaps this time because the guy she was with is that TV presenter from the young people's programme. His name is Mannix Delaney,' she continued. 'You know, the good-looking, squeaky clean guy? I didn't know whether to tell you or not. I thought maybe Elizabeth knew about you and Jack and this was her way of getting back at him. And . . .' Dee grabbed Isabel's arm and squeezed it comfortingly. 'Well, you know the way guys go back to their wives when they think *they*'re being cheated on,' she said gently. 'I was afraid this would ruin things for you both. I know you love him so much. I'm sorry, Isabel.'

She sat silently for a moment, digesting the information. Elizabeth with another man. Elizabeth with lots of other men. Elizabeth with a twenty-something youth TV presenter who'd made a career out of being a favourite with both teens and their mothers. Robin adored him, never missed his programme. He was very good-looking after all, in a floppy-haired, arty way.

'Isabel, are you feeling all right?' Dee asked anxiously. 'I didn't mean to upset you but I thought I'd better let you know.'

Suddenly, Isabel laughed, a joyous sound that cut through Magee's like an alarm. She threw back her head and laughed, with Dee clutching her arm, shocked.

'Are you all right?' she demanded, frantically.

Isabel stopped laughing. 'I am absolutely wonderful! Happy. Delirious. That's the best news I've had in years.'

'It is?' Dee asked.

'It is. You see,' she leaned forward conspiratorially, 'I didn't tell you that Jack is planning to leave Elizabeth but he's worried about her. How upset she could be by the news . . .'

'But if you're being given lots of lurve by the hunky Mannix Delaney, who could be worried?' supplied Dee, immediately getting the point.

'Exactly!'

'This calls for a celebration!'

'I've been celebrating ever since Jack told me he wanted to be with me,' Isabel said, eyes shining. 'This puts the icing on the cake. Elizabeth has her problems,' she explained delicately, 'but he felt responsible for her and hated the idea of hurting her. If she's been having affairs herself, she can hardly complain, can she? She'll probably jump at the idea of a divorce. It'll leave her free to pursue Mannix.'

'My only fear was that Jack would get a shock, hearing about her relationship,' Dee said. 'I don't know which paper the photographer will sell the pictures to but they're bound to run it soon, and I kept thinking the scandal could push the Carters back together.'

Isabel shook her head confidently. 'Their marriage is over. Jack would never go back to her, I know that for a fact.'

Still high from the bottle of champagne – 'cheapie stuff, I'm too broke to buy good champagne' – Dee had insisted on buying to celebrate, they finally wandered back towards the office at half-three, giggling and whispering happily.

'No, we're not hiring a helicopter to go back,' Isabel teased. 'I know you only travel in style, Dee, but really, you must be prepared to walk occasionally.'

'Please, please, let me have a helicopter?' begged Dee, before dissolving into giggles. 'Just because you fly all over the country with our dear and glorious boss in one, doesn't mean the rest of us can't . . .'

Tanya Vernon, who met them at the door to the newsroom, wasn't giggling. Far from it. Her face was furious, the perfectly arched eyebrows drawn down in an angry line.

'I want to talk to you,' she hissed at Dee.

Before Dee could say a word, Isabel drew herself up haughtily and stared at Tanya. 'Don't speak to my deputy like that,' she said in a clipped voice.

You'd never think she'd finished half a bottle of champagne just minutes before, Dee thought, full of admiration for Isabel's instant poise and calm.

'You've been attempting to bully Dee for months now, Tanya, and I've had enough of it.'

Isabel swept into the newsroom with Dee and Tanya following her.

'You have no idea what's happened,' snapped Tanya, taken aback by Isabel's attack.

Dee decided it was time to speak up for herself. Isabel was so good and so loyal, but the only thing Tanya understood was being stood up to in person.

'She knows exactly what happened,' Dee said loudly.

Tanya whirled around, gimlet eyes fixed angrily on her.

'Does she?' she snarled.

'Yes. So does the editor, in fact. You see, Tanya, when I discovered that you'd purposely misled me about the time the trip to Donegal started, I decided to get some evidence to back me up.' Dee was pleased to see Tanya's eyes widen in astonishment. 'So I got a copy of the fax sent to you on Tuesday, confirming the earlier departure time, and I've given that, a report of exactly what happened, and a copy of the helicopter bill to Malley. She can decide whether I made the right decision in hiring a helicopter. But as she was keen to get the story done, and as she'll see that you deliberately tried to mislead me into missing the trip, she's unlikely to take your side in this.'

'How dare you try and go behind my back?' Tanya blustered.

'I dared because I won't take any more of your bullying, Tanya. You should have remembered that,' Dee said, her voice strong and confident. 'And if that makes you wonder if you want to continue working here,' she whispered in a voice only the other woman could hear, 'I believe they're looking for a weather girl in a TV station in New South Wales, although they want one without glamour photography credentials, I believe – *Concepta*.'

Seeing the look of sheer horror on Tanya's face made the hours spent checking into her background well worthwhile.

'What did you say to her at the end?' asked Isabel, watching in amazement as Tanya ran from the room.

'I'll tell you the whole story later,' Dee replied quietly.

CHAPTER TWENTY-THREE

The phone line from Brussels was very poor. 'I'm in a bad signal area,' Jack said, his voice crackly with interference. 'Can you hear me?'

'Just about,' Isabel replied, pressing her mobile phone even closer to her ear so she could hear better. 'Can you speak up?'

'I'm already shouting. We're in heavy traffic, maybe that's the problem.'

Isabel grinned. She was in very heavy traffic herself. Usually, driving home in rush hour sent her insane, stuck behind a line of cars, all moving at three miles an hour. But tonight she didn't care. Tonight she was blissfully happy.

Elizabeth Carter was having an affair, a madly passionate fling with a handsome youngster, which would surely make it much easier for Jack to walk away from the marriage without too much guilt. Of course, the scandal of seeing his wife's face plastered all over the papers would be dreadful, but Isabel was convinced that Jack had enough influence to kill the story stone dead. There was always a trade-off to be made in the world of media moguls.

She wondered if he knew yet? She'd tell him, but couldn't over their mobiles, especially if Jack was in the back of a chauffeur-driven car in Brussels yelling his head off because they had a bad connection.

'I miss you,' Isabel roared cheerfully. 'Did you hear that?'

'Yes, I miss you too. But, Isabel, something's happened . . .' He stopped for a moment. His voice sounded funny, she thought, and not just because there was interference on the line.

'Are you all right, Jack?' she asked, not minding that a woman with a walking stick was moving faster than her line of traffic.

'No. No, I'm not,' he said slowly. 'I've had some terrible news. Terrible. I'm devastated.'

Isabel practically hit the car in front in shock. She slammed on the brakes and wondered if she'd heard him correctly. He was devastated, he felt terrible.

'Isabel, I can't talk about it over the phone . . .' He hesitated. 'I know we were to go out on Monday night but I won't be able to. I can't explain now, I'll need to see you in person, to explain properly,' he added ominously.

Isabel listened mutely, her brain processing what Jack had said. Then it struck her: he'd heard about Elizabeth's affair and was devastated by the news. He hadn't said he was shocked or angry at the thought that his wife's affair would soon be breakfast-time reading for the nation.

No, he was devastated. Which meant he loved Elizabeth and couldn't bear to think of her with another man. *He loved Elizabeth*. Why else would he be so shocked by the news? And he wanted to see Isabel in person to explain that he was going back to his wife.

'Isabel, I'd better go,' he said. 'This line is hopeless. I can't hear anything so I hope you can hear me. I'll phone later when I get to my hotel.'

She drove shakily into a pub car park at the side of the road, unable to think about driving further. Her whole body was quivering. She was a wreck.

Isabel leant her head against the steering wheel and closed her eyes. Pain washed over her, a grief so bad she felt as if she'd die from it, yet she couldn't cry. This wasn't misery – it was like death. She loved Jack, and he loved his wife. Those were the simple facts. Dee, wise, clever Dee, had been right. What was it she'd said earlier? Men went back to their wives when they realised *they*'d been cheated upon. How right she was. And how stupid, naive and gullible Isabel had been.

She slammed her hand against the wheel in sudden anger. How stupid could she be? Another bloody man had made a fool out of her. Only this time she loved him desperately. And in vain. Or so it seemed.

Dee felt elated as she drove out to Millie and Dan's house. She'd done it! She'd finally told bloody Tanya Vernon that she wasn't taking any more bullying. Judging from the horrified look on her face as she'd backed out of the newsroom at the speed of light, Dee would never have any trouble with her again.

It *was* a bit mean, she conceded, to have snooped around in Tanya's past for ammunition to defeat her. But it had been worth it, she thought gleefully.

When Millie opened the door, Dee was glad she'd gone to the bother of bringing a giant bottle of perfumed body lotion for her along with a big box of chocolates. Millie looked exhausted, her eyes red-rimmed with tiredness. But she was in great spirits, hugging Dee delightedly.

'Thank you for my presents!' she whispered. 'We're

keeping quiet because Tara's asleep.'

'When I visited you in hospital, I realised you had enough baby clothes to keep sextuplets in babygrows for a year, and nothing nice at all for the poor woman who'd done all the work,' Dee said, hugging her warmly. 'Tara has enough presents. You deserve some.'

Over mugs of tea, Millie was remarkably keen to discuss things other than her adorable but sleepless three-week-old baby girl.

'I have been eating, breathing, sleeping – well, not sleeping, actually – nothing but babies ever since I got pregnant and it's nice to talk about something else,' Millie said, adjusting the strap of her maternity bra. 'I love her to pieces but there *is* more to life than Tara.'

'She's so lovely, though,' Dee said, cooing into the crib at the dozing baby. She stroked one tiny hand and admired Tara's pink, round face and downy red hair.

'When she's asleep, she's wonderful. When she's awake, you wonder why Oasis haven't been on the phone asking her to do a backing track on one of their albums,' Millie said. 'She has the most amazing lungs and comes alive at around three in the morning, unfortunately. I swear I'm giving up breast feeding soon. She is so demanding.'

'Can't Dan feed her with a bottle you've made up earlier?' Dee asked.

'He could, but she refuses to have any truck with anything except real boobs,' Millie groaned. 'Unless it's attached to me, Tara won't suck it. She's like her father in that respect,' she said as an afterthought.

Dee laughed as quietly as she could.

They talked in low voices for an hour before Millie got round to Gary.

'I knew we'd end up talking about him,' Dee remarked.

'Well, he *is* going to be Tara's godfather and you're her godmother,' Millie pointed out. 'So you'll be seeing quite a lot of each other on Saturday.'

'I know. I promise I won't bare my fangs across the church at him.'

Millie snorted. 'It's not *you* I'm worried about, Dee. You know how to behave. It's him. I can tell you,' she said, lowering her voice even more, 'if Dan hadn't been so terribly keen to have Gary as Tara's godfather, there's no way I'd want him to be. After the way he treated you, he's hardly the right role model for my child.'

Dee smiled at her affectionately. 'Thank you,' she said. 'Does this mean I am a good one?'

'Absolutely. The thing is, I'm not afraid Gary will act his usual arrogant self on Saturday, I'm afraid he'll be the opposite.'

Surprised, Dee asked why.

Millie rolled her eyes. 'He spent at least two hours on the phone to me the other night, quizzing me about what you were up to and who you were seeing. He's a changed man: in his own mind, anyway.'

'What do you mean, changed?' Dee asked curiously.

'Deconstructed. Or is it reconstructed?' Millie asked. 'I can't remember. Anyway, he misses you like mad, he's lonely in London and wants to come home. And he's even realised that there is no such thing as a Laundry Fairy.'

'I see,' Dee muttered without rancour. 'He's coming home, he's sick of doing his own washing and he hopes that dopey Dee will let him back into her life with access to her Hotpoint.'

'I don't think it's that simple,' Millie said thoughtfully. 'I know he spent three months living with Adrian and Natasha, who is, as you know, a minimalist freak

547

with a tidiness phobia. I think Gary finally discovered what a wonderfully carefree life he had with you.'

'That's hardly flattering, now is it?' Dee asked. 'A few months with a sister-in-law who insists he pick up his dirty laundry and now he's longing to come home to me?'

'But he also says he misses you like crazy and that he was a fool to leave you,' Millie added quietly. 'That he'd be back like a shot if you'd have him.'

Dee stared at her for a moment, listening to the sound of Tara's breathing. 'Dan put you up to this, didn't he?' she said finally.

Millie looked shamefaced. 'Sort of. I did feel a teeny bit sorry for Gary when he rang. I think he really regrets how he treated you and the things he said about your size. And I hate to think of you on your own . . .'

'I'm *not* on my own,' Dee said proudly.

'Is Daryl back?'

'No, I couldn't cope with any more Daryl. The bed would disintegrate. There's a new man in my life. He's a photographer.'

'Why didn't you tell me before this?' demanded Millie so loudly that Tara whimpered in her sleep.

'I haven't seen you since you'd just had the baby,' Dee whispered.

'Are you bringing him to the christening so we can meet him?'

Dee laughed. 'A minute ago you were trying to set me up with my ex-fiancé. Now you want to meet my new boyfriend.'

Millie grinned. 'I've done my bit,' she said. 'Gary's on his own. So, is this photographer coming with you on Saturday?'

'No, I'm not bringing Kevin . . .'

'Kevin! What a lovely name!' cooed Millie.

'. . . to the christening. Tell me,' Dee said, changing the subject, 'has Mumsy Redmond been round once a day and twice on Sundays to see if you're treating the first grandchild properly?'

Millie groaned. 'Don't talk to me about her. That woman is a menace! I thought Dr Spock was someone from *Star Trek* until she started bombarding me with books on the right way to raise a baby.'

'I bet she's none too thrilled that I'm going to be Tara's godmother?'

'Livid doesn't describe it,' Millie said with a smile. 'So I do hope you're going to wear something spectacularly sexy and unconventional just to irritate her? Who knows? Maybe she might go home in a sulk if you do.'

Dee's eyes glinted wickedly. 'I have the perfect outfit in mind. A gownless evening strap . . .'

Millie laughed quietly and Dee pretended to look astonished. 'I meant it,' she joked. 'I suppose I'd better make more tea?'

Although she never did it as a rule, as soon as she got home Isabel went straight to the cupboard where she kept the drinks and poured herself a stiff gin and tonic. She downed it quickly and poured another to drink while she made dinner.

Both girls were upstairs studying for their Christmas exams, Robin with a lot less application than her sister, Isabel knew.

Naomi had now settled into her school brilliantly and worked very hard at her homework. Robin, on the other hand, spent more time drawing up prettily coloured study timetables than she actually spent studying.

But, Isabel thought, hating herself for such an

unmotherly feeling, she was glad they were in their bedrooms this evening and couldn't witness her standing hollow-eyed in front of the cooker, staring into space as she stirred milk into the dried pasta mix.

She'd forced herself to think about the future of her relationship with Jack as she'd driven home. He'd want to keep on seeing her, of course, she'd suffer without him permanently in her life, and he'd always go home to Elizabeth. The eternal triangle. Isabel couldn't face a lifetime of that.

The affair had to end, she decided, feeling a heaviness in her heart that she knew wouldn't go away for a very long time. The affair was over. She wouldn't see him again. Couldn't. She must have been mad having an affair with a married man, and her boss into the bargain. So she was destined to see him for years and years. They couldn't even melt discreetly out of each other's lives. He'd be the boss of the *Sentinel* for a long time.

A tear dropped on to the cooker. Isabel felt as if her heart would truly break. She took a slug of her drink and tried, desperately, to feel strong. She could do it, she knew. She had to get angry with Jack. If she stayed sad and thought of how much she loved him, she'd crumble. Taking deep breaths, she remembered all the things he'd said to her, the loving things he'd said when, all along, he'd really loved Elizabeth. That was it; that would make her angry.

How could he, *how could he*? The bastard, she hated him.

Well, she thought, defiance and pain battling for supremacy inside her, she wasn't giving up her job for anyone. Women who had affairs at work were nearly always the ones who left the office when the relationship soured. Isabel couldn't take that risk. She certainly wouldn't get another job as good as this one and she had fought too hard for it to merely pack her bags and leave.

Her daughters needed a stable environment and a mother with a bank account in the black. She'd put up with seeing Jack Carter snub her for the rest of her life for their sakes.

Isabel blinked back the tears and finished her drink, before mixing a third one. The shrill ringing of the phone made her jump. For once, she got to it before Robin.

'Yes,' she said hoarsely.

'Isabel.' Jack sounded better this time, not so upset. The bastard. 'Hello.'

'Hello,' she said, her voice breaking.

It was his turn to ask, 'Are you OK?'

'No,' she said, 'not since you told me you were devastated about the news.' She dragged the phone into the kitchen so the girls wouldn't hear her. 'You see, Jack, I thought you really loved me, so when I find out that you're "devastated" because Elizabeth is having an affair, then I can finally see the truth. You don't love me after all, I'm just your bit on the side, your piece of fluff. At least you have some vestiges of decency left – you want to see me in person to explain why you're leaving me. Well, don't bother.' Her voice rose hysterically.

'Isabel,' he said, 'you don't understand . . .'

'No. *You* don't understand: we're over. Our fling, our cheap, tawdry affair, is over. Call it what you will, it's finished, Jack. So don't ring me again. I don't want to talk to you. I hate you for making me love me and then doing this to me. I hate you for that. Goodbye. I hope I never see you again!'

She slammed down the phone, dumped it on the kitchen floor and burst into tears.

It rang again, shrill and insistent. Isabel stared at it but refused to pick up the receiver.

Inside, she wanted to. Desperately. She wanted to hear Jack's voice telling her he was crazy about her and that it had all been a big misunderstanding, that he loved her, not Elizabeth.

But she couldn't allow herself to do that. Picking up the phone would be another huge mistake. She'd made her choice – now she had to live with it. To live her life without Jack.

She'd only known him such a short time, four months, but already he was a vital part of her life. She'd felt as if she'd found that perfect person, the one she wanted to spend the rest of her days with. And now it was over. The phone stopped ringing. A minute later it started again, the shrill sound drilling into her skull.

Isabel picked up the phone and pressed the button to cut Jack off. Then she laid the receiver on the ground. If she left it off the hook for a few hours, he'd get the message. Better still, she'd disconnect it. In the hall, she pulled the connection out, stuck the phone on the hall table and went back into the kitchen.

She roughly dried her tears with a piece of kitchen roll, poured herself another drink and returned to the cooker, where the pasta mix was now a congealed mess. Like her life, she thought bleakly.

Saturday morning dawned bright and sunny for late-December. Perfect, thought Dee, who'd planned to wear a clinging V-necked black body under her velvet trouser suit if it wasn't pouring from the heavens. Rain ruined velvet, so her other option had been a navy pinstripe coatdress Isabel had insisted she buy. Classy and elegant though it was – a lot like Isabel, Dee thought – the coatdress didn't have the immediate 'wow' impact of the richly coloured velvet. And Dee wanted people at the christening to say 'wow' when they saw her. Especially Gary and his insufferable mother.

Not that Mrs Margaret Redmond would say 'wow' exactly, Dee thought with an evil little grin as she sprayed a blast of Contradiction perfume into the heaving valley of her cleavage revealed by the daring black top. Her one-time future mother-in-law would more than likely mutter, 'Thank God my Gary didn't marry that trollop!' But he couldn't fail to be impressed by her rig-out, she thought.

With the tortoiseshell sunglasses that went so well with her rippling curls and subtle make-up that had taken ages to apply, Dee looked a million dollars.

'Hello, Gary,' she practised in front of the bathroom mirror, pitching her voice low and sexy, and making sure she bent forward, to give him a tantalising glimpse of fake-tanned bosom.

An hour later, she got the chance to do it for real. She was standing just inside the church door talking to Millie's mum when Gary appeared beside her. For someone reputedly pining away with misery, he looked pretty good. He wore a Prince of Wales check suit she'd never seen before with his favourite yellow tie. His wavy hair was collar-length and neatly brushed back, and he radiated health and good spirits. He was obviously still playing soccer, Dee thought, noticing that he was as lean as ever.

He briefly kissed Millie's mother in greeting and turned to Dee.

'Hello, Dee,' he said softly. For a moment it looked as

if he was going to kiss her too, but he apparently thought better of it.

'Hello, Gary,' she said coolly.

Millie's mother, who knew the whole, sordid story thanks to regular bulletins from her daughter, drifted discreetly away.

Gary's expressive eyes roamed over Dee's figure, taking in the more toned curves and the glamorous outfit she wore with such verve and confidence.

'You look great, really great,' he said admiringly.

'I know,' she replied, tossing back her hair. 'You look pretty good yourself,' she added. 'Still playing soccer?'

'Yeah.'

'I've got your old sports bag in my house.' She emphasised the word 'my'. 'You left it behind.'

He shrugged. 'It's ancient, throw it out.'

Dee was about to ask if that was what he did with everything that had passed its sell-by date: throw it out. But she restrained herself. She didn't want to start a battle over the font. Baptismal candles weren't there to be hurled at your ex.

Millie arrived with Tara, who was wearing yards of antique lace and screaming at the top of her voice.

'I hope you've got earplugs with you,' Millie groaned. 'You look fabulous, Dee. As *always*,' she added, with a glare at Gary.

'Hello, Millie,' he said, without rising to the bait.

She ignored him. 'We're about to begin,' she addressed Dee. 'Are you ready?'

Grafton Street was packed. What seemed like the entire population of Dublin thronged the pedestrianised street, pushing and shoving as they did their Christmas shopping.

Isabel stopped counting the number of times she'd been elbowed in the ribs and tried to feel grateful for the fact that it wasn't raining, so at least there was no chance of being poked in the eye by an army of umbrellas.

Robin was leading the way, shoving through the crowd expertly. Naomi and Isabel followed her black, PVC-clad back into Next, where another million women congregated, grabbing at hangers and cute bits of jewellery like there was no tomorrow.

'I'm tired, Mum,' said Naomi, leaning against the stairs as Robin disappeared in search of the perfect present for Susie, with the enthusiasm of Indiana Jones looking for the Lost Ark.

'Me too.' Isabel put an arm around Naomi and leant wearily next to her. 'An hour and a half of this is enough for anybody. I just want to sit down.'

She didn't add that she wanted to sit down on her own in a darkened room and sob her eyes out, because she felt more alone than ever before in her entire life. Life without Jack stretched out in front of her like a barren expanse, with nothing to see, nothing to believe in, nothing to love.

She'd got through Friday on autopilot, barely functioning. She'd hung up on Jack twice when he rang the office. He couldn't get through to her at home as the phone was still disconnected – a fact which hadn't pleased phone-a-holic Robin.

'Nuisance calls,' Isabel had said blandly when her daughter demanded to know why the phone jack had been pulled from the socket. 'Use my mobile if you must make a call but turn it off immediately afterwards.'

She couldn't bear the thought of having to talk to

Jack. She was so afraid she'd weaken and tell him she loved him, that she didn't care if he stayed with Elizabeth, so long as she could still see him sometimes. Which would be emotional suicide, she knew.

She might as well go back to David if she wanted that much pain in her life, Isabel thought in one of her rare, clear-headed moments.

Now she was spending Saturday trawling through the shops on a shopping trip she'd been promising the girls for ages. Isabel had planned to keep an eye out for a Christmas present for Jack, something special. She was always useless at keeping surprises and just days before he'd joked that he wouldn't be home from Brussels five minutes before she'd have spilled the beans on his present. What a difference a few days can make, she thought sadly.

On Thursday at lunchtime she'd been the happiest woman in the world: now, she was the most miserable. Although, naturally, she was pretending to be jolly for the girls' sake. It wasn't fair that they should have a bad day simply because she'd messed up her love life so spectacularly. They were her first priority, not her broken heart.

Naomi wilted beside her, her small frame resting tiredly against her mother's.

Isabel gave her a hug.

'C'mon, let's find Robin and get a cup of hot chocolate somewhere,' she said brightly. 'We'll need our energy for one last batch of shopping when I buy your Christmas present. And then you've got to decide which film you want to see!'

Dee had always loved buffets. That way, you could pick the most delicious dishes and leave all the boring stuff like celery and curried rice. Yeuch! Who'd want to eat curried rice?

She sailed past bowls of lettuce, celery, cucumber and tomato before stopping at the egg mayonnaise and fat, glistening spirals of pasta drenched in olive oil. That was more like it.

She had just lifted a generous ladle of egg from its bowl when Gary materialised beside her with an empty plate. Immediately determined not to look like she was still a big eater, Dee capsized the ladle until only two puny slices of mayonnaise-covered egg remained on it. Then, she delicately transferred them to her plate. Five pasta spirals joined the egg before Dee dumped a forestful of iceberg lettuce on top, with a few lumps of celery for good measure.

Bypassing the bread rolls steadfastly – she was *so hungry* – Dee finally turned round.

'Hello again,' she said, smiling icily at Gary. 'Are you following me?'

'No,' he said evenly. 'I wanted to talk to you and you left the church so quickly I didn't have a chance to.'

'What did you expect?' Dee asked tartly. 'That we'd drive to the hotel together, holding hands and giggling about how wonderful the old days were? I don't think so.' She wheeled around and headed for a table beside a picture window overlooking Dublin Bay.

Gary followed once he'd filled up his plate. *He'd* got a ton of pasta salad, Dee thought enviously, as she munched a bit of lettuce. It was very difficult playing Ms Sophisticate. Eating, drinking and enjoying yourself were out for a start.

Gary dug his fork into some coleslaw. Dee drooled. She'd eaten all her pasta and was still hungry. This was hell.

'Wine, madam?' asked a waiter.

'Lovely,' Dee said thankfully, grabbing a glass of white wine. She needed it, considering she wasn't eating.

'How've you been?' Gary asked.

'Wonderful,' she said brightly.

'I mean, *really*, how've you been?' he repeated.

Dee gave him a hard stare. 'I've had a relationship with an incredibly sexy Texan, whom you might remember.' She ignored the muscle flickering in Gary's jaw. 'And now I'm seeing someone else.'

'Anyone I know?' he asked tensely.

'No.' She beamed at him. 'How about you? Is London stuffed to the gills with skinny, classy women who dress correctly, don't drink and never wear too much make-up?'

At least he had the grace to look ashamed, she thought triumphantly.

'I wanted to apologise, Dee,' Gary said, his expressive eyes sombre. 'I said some terrible things to you, I shouldn't have. I had no right to . . .'

'No, you bloody didn't,' she snapped.

'I'm apologising now,' he pointed out.

'How nice for you,' she said pointedly. 'But it's a bit late and I wouldn't bother getting Dan and Millie involved any more. It's a waste of time.'

As if on some secret cue, Dan appeared, cradling his daughter in his arms, a photographer in tow. 'We're doing spur-of-the-moment pictures,' he said, crouching down between Dee and Gary and holding Tara at an angle for the photographer.

Dee posed. The flash went off and Dan straightened up.

'How are you two getting on?' he asked tentatively.

'Great,' said Gary, tickling Tara's tummy and making her giggle.

Dee kissed her goddaughter tenderly before Dan loped off to the next table.

'I love kids,' Gary said, surprising her. 'We'd have had wonderful kids, you know.'

Dee stared at him, imagining how voluptuous she'd look if she were pregnant. She remembered all the awful things he'd said to her about being fat, about how he'd have loved to have bought her sexy little dresses but hadn't been able to because of her size.

Kevin Mills didn't mind her size: he loved the way she looked, fancied her rotten – both for her body and her mind. And she didn't feel the need to sink six vodkas when she was with him, simply so she didn't feel like heap of the week when they went out. He gave her confidence, didn't take it away.

'Don't you want kids?' Gary said longingly.

'Of course. But can you imagine the trauma of being seen in public with me while I was pregnant, Gary?' Dee demanded. 'You found it hard enough to be seen with me normally. If I was pregnant, you'd have to have a special trailer made to tow behind the car so I'd fit in it. Imagine the shame.'

'That's not fair,' he protested. 'I only said you could lose a few pounds and that you were hung up about your weight. You look stunning *now*.'

'That,' said Dee calmly, 'is because I feel happy, confident, and have nobody telling me I'm a big, fat lump, day in, day out. It took me a while to get my confidence back, Gary, after you'd knocked me down like a rag doll. But,' she leant forward and poked him firmly in the chest as she enunciated each word, 'I did it. And if you think you can rewrite history and forget all that, then you're wrong.'

'Dee, come on . . .'

Dee wasn't listening. She was thinking of Kevin. They were going skiing in January and she couldn't wait. He was so wonderful, so funny, kind and . . . well, he liked *her*. Not who he wanted her to be, but *her*.

That was what she wanted, a man who liked her for who and what she was. Not one who couldn't say two words to her without reminding her why she was well shot of him.

'Hello, Mother,' said Gary.

Dee's eyes widened. Margaret Redmond stood in front of her, sturdy in a floral two-piece with a rather mad purple hat jammed on to the tight perm that had, unless Dee was imagining it, been treated to a faintly blonde rinse.

'Deirdre. Long time no see. How are you? Still working for that newspaper?' Margaret said primly.

'Yes,' Dee answered shortly. 'And you?'

'I'm doing very well since I have lovely Tara, my first grandchild,' Margaret said happily, her face alight with pride.

'Tara's beautiful,' Dee said fondly.

'I was surprised to see you were her godmother,' Margaret said, the shrewish expression returning to her face.

'Why?' Dee asked, resisting the impulse to say something very rude. It would be fun but Margaret simply wasn't worth upsetting herself over, Dee realised with stunning clarity.

'Well, it's not as if you're going out with Gary now, you're not one of the family . . .'

Margaret looked down her nose at Dee, gaze directed at her cleavage.

'*Mother!*' hissed Gary.

'It's all right,' Dee said, watching Margaret's shocked

expression with delight. Gary had never, ever spoken to his mother like that before. No wonder she was shocked. 'Your mother can say what she wants. She always did anyway.'

Margaret's mean eyes grew smaller.

'I never did like you, Deirdre,' she hissed.

'*Mother, stop that!*' shouted Gary, so loudly that everyone in the room turned to look at them. 'How dare you speak to Dee like that?'

'Gary, how *could* you?' shrieked Margaret, stomping off in high dudgeon.

Dee watched her go with amusement. Once, Gary's mother had had the power to drive her to despair. But not any more.

'I'm sorry about that,' he apologised.

Dee looked at him thoughtfully. Even that, even telling his horrible mother to shut up, hadn't made any difference. Gary was history. She still cared for him: she always would, she supposed. You couldn't spend four years of your life with someone and then consign them to limbo because they weren't around any more. But as for being *in love* with him . . .

'That was sweet, Gary,' she said. 'Very, very satisfying and sweet. But it was also about six months too late. Six months and four years.' She leant forward and kissed him on the cheek, a sisterly kiss, which seemed appropriate.

She looked into his earnest face and sighed. Poor Gary. He really had thought that he'd trundle up to her at the christening, apologise, tell her she looked beautiful, and then everything would be forgotten. They'd be back to square one again: Gary 'n' Dee, like egg 'n' chips. Only even more boring and predictable.

'Dee . . .' he began anxiously.

She didn't let him finish. That was the last thing she wanted: to humiliate him when he was doing his best, poor love.

'Gary, it was nice of you to try again,' she said, her voice sympathetic, 'but you must realise it's over between us. I'm happy now.' She patted his shoulder. 'I do hope you find somebody special, I'm sure you will. Take care.'

With that, she rose elegantly from the table and walked across the room, conscious that more eyes than Gary's were focused upon her. Tough, she thought happily. She had a date tonight, a date with a handsome photographer who was cooking her dinner: mussels, despite all the scrubbing they entailed, and chicken Kiev. She wouldn't have to lift a finger. Except, perhaps to unbutton Kevin's shirt . . .

Being in love made you promise ludicrous things, Isabel thought, as she laid the dining-room table for dinner. Why else would she invite her parents for dinner on a Saturday night when she *knew* she was going to be spending the entire day in town with the girls and would, therefore, be exhausted? But then, the dinner invitation had been pre-break up, when she'd felt invigorated and full of zest. It wasn't her parents' fault that she now had all the vigour of a dead halibut.

'Mum, Granny and Grandad are here!' yelled Naomi from the hall.

'Mum, the pork steaks are burning!' yelled Robin from the kitchen.

Isabel ran to the pork steaks. In the few minutes it had taken her to organise the table, the pork had turned from soft and succulent into the sort of things art students could quite possibly draw with. Robin, mashing potatoes

industriously and watching TV at the same time, hadn't noticed until it was nearly too late.

Isabel gazed at the smouldering mess. She didn't care. Everything she'd eaten for the past two days had tasted like charcoal anyway.

'Mum?' Naomi stood beside her, hopping from foot to foot in a way she hadn't since she was at least nine.

'What is it, love?' Isabel asked tiredly, trying to remember what she had in the freezer that her mother would actually eat.

'A man came in with Granny and Grandad. He says his name's Jack and he wants to see you.'

Isabel gasped. Jack was here! At the same time as her mother?

She rushed to the hall. Standing in a formal little threesome were her parents and Jack. Making even her stately mother appear small by comparison, Jack looked wonderful in an elegant Italian suit.

'Isabel,' he said, his strong face lighting up at the sight of her.

'Isabel?' said her mother reprovingly, clad in her lavender twinset and tweeds. 'Aren't you going to introduce us?'

'Er . . . yes,' she stuttered. 'Mother and Father, this is Jack Carter. Jack, these are my parents, Pamela and Harry Mulhearn.'

All three shook hands formally, as if they were at a royal garden party instead of standing awkwardly in Isabel's tiny hall.

'Nice to meet you,' Pamela said warmly.

Isabel's eyes locked with Jack's. He looked exhausted, she realised with a sense of shock. Very pale and tired. He was overdoing it, she thought worriedly. As usual.

'We'll go on in,' Pamela announced.

Isabel followed her mother into the kitchen.

'I know it's strange, Mother, I'll explain later. Jack is . . .'

'Your lover?' Pamela supplied helpfully.

Isabel stared.

'You think I didn't know?' her mother asked, raising one eyebrow. 'Goodness, Isabel, what sort of fool do you take me for? I knew there was a man in your life and assumed that when you'd sorted it all out, you'd tell me. He seems very charming,' she added. 'So sort it out.' She fluttered her hands, as if shooing chickens. 'Robin tells me you've been like a zombie for the past two days. I presume he's the reason.'

'Robin said what?' asked Isabel anxiously. She was sure she'd managed to hide her misery from the girls, or at least had thought she had . . .

Her mother's eyebrow lifted another couple of milli-metres. 'Robin isn't stupid, either, Isabel. She knew something was wrong and came to the same conclusion as I did – man trouble.'

Isabel's jaw dropped. 'Robin knew?'

'Since the day he dropped you home in his car. A Jaguar, I believe. She's nearly sixteen, Isabel, not six. Of course she knew.' Pamela paused. 'A Jaguar suits him, actually. Such a nice car.' She sniffed the charcoal-scented air with distaste. 'I hope he likes omelettes – assuming you have eggs?'

Isabel grinned, hugged her mother, and returned to the hall.

Jack stood there silently.

'You're home a day early,' she said, immediately wondering why she'd said something so obvious. 'I thought you had an important meeting?'

'I did. This was more important,' he said quietly.

'You're more important than any meeting.' He moved towards her.

Isabel took a step back towards the kitchen. What did he want? she asked herself. If he came any closer, she wouldn't be able to control herself. She'd let all her good intentions fly out of the window and then she'd cling to him and never let him go. And she couldn't do that. She'd promised herself she'd never see him like this again. He was gone from her life forever. She closed her eyes at the thought.

'Isabel.' His voice was like a silken caress. 'I had to come home, to make everything right. When you wouldn't answer my calls, I couldn't understand it at first. I was so upset on Thursday, I couldn't see what had happened.'

Isabel, who'd been staring at his broad shoulders longingly, stood up ramrod straight. 'Upset, were you?' she asked, feeling the pain in her heart like a JCB crushing through every tender part. 'I wonder why? No, don't tell me. I know.'

'But you don't.' He stood so close to her she could smell his aftershave and the scent of his skin. The scent she'd dreamed of for the past two nights, imagining his body wrapped protectively around hers, holding her close and telling her he'd never let her go.

'Isabel, did you believe I loved you? Did you believe I would leave Elizabeth for you?'

'Yes.' Her words were just a whisper. She wanted to scream at him to leave her, to go away. But she couldn't. She wanted to be with him just a few moments longer, even if then he left forever.

'How could you think I'd lie to you about anything?' he asked softly. 'When I spoke to you on the phone on Thursday, I'd just heard that the man who started me off in business had died. William James . . . I owe him so much. He had a stroke. It was very sudden. We hadn't spoken for months because we'd both been so busy, and then he was gone.' There was a catch in Jack's voice. 'I was devastated. Life can be so cruel.'

Isabel gazed up at him, suddenly comprehending what he was saying, why he'd sounded so upset when she'd spoken to him on the phone that terrible evening.

'You thought I was upset about Elizabeth?' He laughed hoarsely. 'I didn't even know about that at the time. It was only the next day, after I'd spent the night trying to phone you here and on your mobile, that I found out about her. It was a shock, I'll admit it, and it meant I had to spend an hour on the phone getting the story quashed, but it was hardly devastating news. Did you think I could just abandon you?' he asked seriously. 'Did you think I was lying when I told you I loved you and wanted to be with you?'

'Oh, Jack.' She fell into his arms, clinging to him with all her strength. He held her tightly to him, arms clutching her body hard against his. 'Isabel, I've never experienced anything like these past couple of days. I couldn't understand what had happened, why you wouldn't talk to me. You hung up on me twice and I went crazy when your phone just rang and rang. I thought something awful had happened, until I found out about Elizabeth and it all fell into place.'

Her face buried in his shoulder, Isabel explained: 'I thought you'd heard about her and Mannix Delaney and that's why you were so upset.' She was almost unable to believe how wonderful it felt to be in his arms again. 'I love you! And was so upset. I thought you loved Elizabeth, I thought . . .'

'I understand.' He held her away from him so he

could gaze into her eyes. His were tender, full of love. 'My darling, it's you I love.'

'I know, I'm sorry I ever doubted you,' she said, half-laughing, half-crying.

'There's only one problem,' said Jack.

Isabel looked at him lovingly. 'We can sort it out, whatever it is,' she said happily.

He grinned and indicated the suit carrier at his feet. 'Can I stay for good?' he asked. 'I know it's short notice and everything, but I thought we should stop procrastinating and do something definite. Do you think the girls will mind my moving in?'

Isabel put her head to one side briefly and considered. 'Well, remember the way you told me over our first lunch that you didn't know much about teenage girls?'

'Yes,' he said, pulling her even closer to him.

'You're about to get a crash course . . .'

Now you can buy any of these other bestselling Headline books from your bookshop or *direct from the publisher*.

FREE P&P AND UK DELIVERY
(Overseas and Ireland £3.50 per book)

Olivia's Luck	Catherine Alliott	£5.99
Backpack	Emily Barr	£5.99
Girlfriend 44	Mark Barrowcliffe	£5.99
Seven-Week Itch	Victoria Corby	£5.99
Two Kinds of Wonderful	Isla Dewar	£6.99
Fly-Fishing	Sarah Harvey	£5.99
Bad Heir Day	Wendy Holden	£5.99
Good at Games	Jill Mansell	£5.99
Sisteria	Sue Margolis	£5.99
For Better, For Worse	Carole Matthews	£5.99
Something For the Weekend		
	Pauline McLynn	£5.99
Far From Over	Sheila O'Flanagan	£5.99

TO ORDER SIMPLY CALL THIS NUMBER

01235 400 414

or e-mail orders@bookpoint.co.uk

Prices and availability subject to change without notice.